Prince Guénaël is caught in the midst of a scandal not of his own making. To protect the family name, *ius auction*, an archaic practice that transfers responsibility for a minor to a protector, has been called. The winning bidder not only wins Gen, but the control over his vast properties.

Prince Lairgnen, Chosen counselor to Anwyll, king of Kizerain, is sent to Merifael in the hopes of discovering the truth and putting a stop to the auction.

What neither man knows is that the Goddess has plans of her own.

An Auction of Roses
Copyright © 2021 Jo Tannah
ISBN: 978-1-4874-3037-5
Cover art by Martine Jardin

Published by eXtasy Books Inc or
Devine Destinies, an imprint of eXtasy Books Inc

Look for us online at:
www.eXtasybooks.com or www.devinedestinies.com

An Auction of Roses
Season to Love 1

By

Jo Tannah

AUTHOR'S NOTE

The Great Passage refers to the crossing between time and space to escape a war-ravaged mother world. To protect their people, the king and Consort of the time had destroyed the gateway created by the sprite, forever making that world unreachable. It was a desperate but necessary act, for otherwise, no one would have survived the systemic massacre of people and magical creatures considered strange by members of the tyrannical ruling race under guise of an emerging religious group. This is the world of Kizerain, where the Druids of lore settled in safety and peace.

CHAPTER ONE

"Tell me a story. Please, Gen?"

Gen smiled down at his younger sister, Laoghaire. At only six years, she already promised an intelligence that might surpass his. He loved her. Other than his father, she was his whole family and was his champion.

"And what story do you want to hear, this time?" He reached to tuck a curl behind her ear.

"How King Anwyll chose Consort Pedr." Laoghaire's response was immediate.

Gen couldn't help but chuckle. Laoghaire could be so predictable. "But you've heard that story so many times."

"It's my favorite," she said as she snuggled down into her pillow. "Please, Gen?"

"Oh, all right." Gen sat on the bed, tucking his right leg under his left thigh, and pulled the blanket up Laoghaire's chin.

"Don't leave out any details," Laoghaire instructed in her youthful stern voice.

Gen shook his head, but his smile was as broad as Laoghaire's. He looked up at the ceiling as the unforgettable memories surfaced. "So. Where do I begin?"

"I know where, I know where. You were caught behind a crowd and had to look over the heads and shoulders of those in front of you," Laoghaire said, practically bouncing in the bed. "Good thing Maccus was there and saved you a place up front."

Gen side-eyed Laoghaire. "Are you going to let me tell you

the story, or are you?"

"No. You are. Go ahead. I'm all ears." Laoghaire's eyes widened with a look of anticipation.

Gen gave her a mock glare, which was met by a toothy smile. Once more, he shook his head. Ever since Laoghaire had first heard him narrate how their prince—now King Anwyll—had selected his Chosen Consort on Yula four months earlier, she had demanded he tell the story before going to sleep.

"Okay, so there I was, up on my toes, trying to see where Father was when I heard someone call out my name . . ."

"Gen! Over here," a voice called out over the crowd.

Faces turned in Gen's direction, looking at him, and he was about to turn away in embarrassment when he spotted his best friend. Maccus Cambon was gesturing excitedly. A grin broke over Gen's lips, and he moved to join Maccus. No one said anything when he shouldered his way over to his friend, but many moved out of his way so he could pass. Gen excused himself through the maze of bodies until he reached Maccus.

"Thank you," Gen said, even as a giggle escaped his lips.

"Be quiet," Maccus said with a broad grin.

Gen nodded his thanks before looking in front of him once more. He found himself standing just two rows from the center of the courtyard. Ahead of him, with his back toward him, stood his father, Martin.

Martin was a priest of the Goddess of fertility, Sheela. He had been granted the esteemed assignment to guide the prince and his potential Consort within the sacred grove so they could confirm their choosing. It was a task usually performed by a higher-level priest, but the one who had been assigned bowed out at the last minute. Gen didn't know how, but in spite of his lower ranking, Martin had been asked to step in and perform the ceremony instead.

Dressed in the yellow robes of a cleric, Martin stood just beyond the edge of a wooden floor, inlaid with the image of the tree of life, in the center of the room. Gen bit his lip when Martin looked over his shoulder, his stern gaze searching the crowd until they settled on him. Gen flushed under the look and bowed his head in embarrassment. The chatter around him dwindled to whispers and then there was silence.

"The gods are upon us," Martin intoned, his voice echoing throughout the courtyard. "Tonight, after over twenty-five years, we celebrate Yula once more. As with every generation, we give our thanks to the old king and welcome a new one. Let us never forget that without the king's service and sacrifice, our people would have faced annihilation."

Gen listened intently to his father's recounting of the tale of the Great Passage. It told of their ancestors' bravery. How the royal family, aided by the sprite, had crossed through time and space in search of a safe haven for their people.

As his father's continued narrating the tale, Gen looked above the canopy of the sacred ancient oak tree. There he clearly saw how the three moons began to align. A sense of anticipation rose around him. Time came to a standstill, and the hush in the courtyard deepened.

The sprite, who had been excitedly flitting and singing among the branches before his father's tale began, had settled. Their lights, although dimmed, continued to pulse. With every pulsation, their tiny bodies seemed to grow bigger and change in color. Where previously they'd been bright points of white light, they now seemed to glow a softer gold. Gen's smile broadened.

The shift in color meant the confirmation was close. They were soon to have a Consort for their king. Gen wondered who it could be, but then, as his father's voice began to rise, his tale about to conclude, Gen noticed a man approach from the far side of the courtyard. Gen gasped at the sight of the silver-haired man dressed in white robes trimmed with gold. He had only been five or six when he'd been introduced to the prince, but no one could mistake who he was – Anwyll, the prince and heir to the throne of Kizerain.

Someone gasped out loud, and Gen turned to peer to his right. A man standing beside a man Gen recognized as Llewellyn, one of his cousins, looked confused. The man took one step back, as though he *wanted to run, but then he froze mid-flight, his gaze locked on the prince.*

"Do you think he's the prince's Chosen?" Maccus whispered in his ear.

Gen quickly touched his friend's arm and motioned for him to be quiet. While the prince and the unknown man stared at each other, murmurs began to rise around him as more and more spectators began to take notice. As suddenly as the rumble of whispers rose, they hushed, and silence descended over the crowd until it was only Martin's voice that could be heard.

Gen turned to see Prince Anwyll move forward and stop right at the edge of the tree of life, continuing to hold the man's gaze with his. The man took another hesitant step back, but once more stopped, as though some invisible force were preventing him from moving further away. Seconds ticked, and Gen felt a compulsion to act. He stepped forward and stood beside his father, ignoring startled comments coming from the crowd. Gen turned to look at his father, and his heart gladdened at the understanding way Martin looked at him.

"Is that the Chosen Consort, Father?" Gen asked in a low voice, so only his father could hear.

"Yes, my son. It is indeed," Martin said with a satisfied smile.

"Do you know who he is?"

"We'll find out soon enough. Now be still, I have yet to finish the tale." With his mouth set in a determined line, Martin resumed his story.

Gen, too caught up in the moment, didn't pay attention to his father's words. Something was happening between prince and the stranger, and he was about to watch everything unfold. At that moment, Gen understood that he was going to witness history. Gen moved when, as one, the crowd began moving to create a circle around Prince Anwyll and his potential Chosen Consort.

The Chosen threw a quick glance around him before turning to look back at Prince Anwyll. More seconds passed before both men made a move. They began to circle each other, Prince Anwyll within the boundary of the floor, and the Chosen Consort an inch outside of it until they once again stopped. It seemed as if they were following *instructions from someone only they could hear.*

It was the sprite. Gen didn't know how he knew, but he noticed a difference in their pulsating lights when he looked up. They were faster and seemed to be glowing brighter.

Gen looked away from the magical creatures and turned back to observe the ancient ceremony of Choosing. Prince Anwyll had moved closer toward his Chosen, but Gen saw something else in his eyes. It was as though he was asking forgiveness from his Chosen.

The Chosen Consort continued to look around him until he stopped to stare somewhere on Gen's right. Gen craned his neck to see who it was and then gasped when he recognized the older man standing beside Prince Llewellyn.

Gen's heart stuttered – the dark-haired man was Llewellyn's older brother. Ever since he could remember, he'd always been in awe of Prince Lairgnen. He could still remember when he'd first seen him. Gen had only been eight or nine. He'd been immediately drawn to him but had been too shy to go up and speak with him. It had been hard to turn his back at the time, but he'd never forgotten. He was sixteen when his mother told him how Prince Lairgnen had upset a few career diplomats. King Eljin had named him Finance Minister – the youngest to have ever been appointed.

Maccus gasped softly beside him, and Gen reluctantly turned away from Prince Lairgnen and back to the center of the grove. He was just in time to see the Chosen Consort look over his shoulder toward Prince Anwyll, who had stopped moving. Unhurriedly, as though in slow motion, Prince Anwyll extended his hand with his palm up toward his Chosen.

Gen thought his heart would break at the pleading look in his prince's eyes. He finally understood what the look meant. The prince was hoping that his Chosen would take his hand. The Chosen paused and appeared to be considering the offer, looking intently at the proffered hand, a myriad of emotions flitting over his face. Gen could feel his own heart pound hard inside his chest in anticipation.

Should the Chosen Consort refuse the prince's hand, it would not stop Anwyll from becoming king, but he wouldn't last long. It would be a short-lived rule, for no king could stand alone and hold *the minds and hearts of his people without a Consort to ground him. Like everyone else, Gen knew that all kings needed someone of a scientific mind to help them through their time of rule until the next king took his place.*

Throwing one last, pleading look in Prince Llewellyn's direction, the Chosen turned back once more and faced Prince Anwyll. Gen knew gladness when the man breathed out and took a step forward. It was a start, but he was still just outside the edge of the floor.

Gen turned toward Prince Anwyll and saw the despair rise in his eyes. Murmurs once more rose in volume as everyone began to see the unwillingness in the Chosen. But then something changed. The sprite above them began to glow brighter. The Chosen looked up at them and placed one foot inside the circle, followed by another . . . and another. As he walked toward the waiting Prince Anwyll, a happy, beaming smile of relief bloomed over the prince's face. Gen wanted to shout for joy. The ceremony was successful. He looked toward his father and saw the same joy on his face. Martin didn't stop talking, but he turned and met Gen's gaze. As one, they watched the Chosen Consort hold Prince Anwyll's hand in his, a look of shock on his face. Gen laughed nervously under his breath.

Prince Anwyll's eyes were shimmering with unshed tears as his Chosen Consort brought the hand he held around to rest against his lower back. The Chosen reached out for the prince's other hand and raised the arm to go around his neck, pulling him in closer until their faces were only an inch apart. Gen didn't notice that his father had ceased speaking.

Suddenly, the sprite rose in the air, the flutter of their wings reverberating around them. For a long second, there was absolute silence, then Gen heard their voices. It began softly, gradually increasing in volume until it was the only thing Gen could hear.

Anwyll . . . Pedr . . .

"Pedr," Laoghaire said in a dreamy voice. Her eyes were closed, and she was almost asleep.

"Yes. Pedr Gardner. Our king's Chosen Consort," Gen

murmured.

He leaned forward and placed a kiss on Laoghaire's cheek. She breathed a tired sigh and then lay still in sleep, a smile lingering on her lips.

Gen waited until Laoghaire's breathing evened out before leaving her side. He was still thinking about what he'd had the privilege of witnessing as he walked to his bedroom. His father had been so proud. Martin was a priest, but having been chosen over the rest of the *clerus* was an unexpected but extraordinary honor. Gen wasn't blind to his father's goal to be recognized among the highly exclusive fraternity.

He blinked away the sudden tears that blurred his vision as he remembered the way Anwyll and Pedr had stood in the middle of the sacred grove, staring at each other. There was no mistaking their love. Gen wished he would meet someone who would look at him that way. Someone who would marry him because they loved him for being himself. Not because he was the son of a priest or that he was nobility and highly eligible for the name and fortune his late mother had bestowed on him.

A face came to mind, but Gen shook his head against the image. He had no hope to be with the man of his dreams. For one thing, he was too young. He was only twenty, much too young for such an experienced man of the world. Also, he wanted to marry for love. Gen sighed as he closed the door and made ready for bed. The man probably didn't even know he existed. Gen could only dream.

His communicator started to beep. He took it out of his pocket and looked at the screen, only to see it was Maccus calling. "Maccus, it's late. Why are you calling?"

CHAPTER TWO

Three hours later, Gen found himself in the one place his father had forbidden him to step into.

"Why did you bring me here, Maccus? I told you I never wanted to even come near this area. You lied to me when you said you were taking me to the festival. I was looking forward to it, too." Betrayal had been the last emotion he thought he'd ever feel with his friend.

Gen looked around in trepidation, quickly spotting more than one recognizable face milling in the crowd. If his father found out, he was going to be in so much trouble. Many were sons of nobility and rich merchants, and their attendance at the soiree thrown by a known procurer proved that he shouldn't be caught with this group. He could barely hear himself think. The combined volume of laughter and loud music playing made logical thinking impossible. Even if he'd wanted to come here—not that he did—so far, he knew he didn't like this place. It wasn't a place he'd fantasized about going.

The place reeked of alcohol, the pungent odor making his head spin, and he hadn't even been there very long. This manor was owned by Devos Cricirus, a well-known merchant whose financial success was highly suspicious. Gen had heard his father speak of Cricirus in scathing tones. If Gen was to believe the rumors, and he did, procurement was not a reputable business. Most of the time, it involved illegal activities.

"Stop worrying, Gen. Nothing bad's going to happen. Just relax and enjoy." Maccus' words brought him back to the present.

"I'm not going to relax, Maccus," Gen said through clenched teeth. "If someone sees me here and tells my father, I'll get into so much trouble. Not only that . . . Word will reach the king, and Goddess knows how that's going to come down. No. I need to get out of here before somebody recognizes me."

"No one here's going to recognize you." Maccus smiled sweetly at him. "And even if anyone did, they're not going to say anything. They wouldn't dare. You're a prince, and your father's a priest. Nobody would dare go against him. Now come on, let's get inside. We're missing out on all the fun."

Maccus took hold of Gen's upper arm to pull him deeper into the manor, but Gen twisted away.

"No, Maccus. It is especially because I am a member of the royal family that I need to get out of this place. Secondly, what part of *I don't want to go in there* don't you understand?" He glared at Maccus before turning on his heel to go out where they came from.

Maccus cursed behind him, but Gen didn't look back.

"Gen, come on! Don't be an idiot."

Gen bit back a rejoinder but stopped and turned around to stare at Maccus in disbelief.

"Who are you calling an idiot? Me? Because I don't want to get involved in this sort of gathering? I already told you that I didn't want to come here, and you completely ignored me. You lied to me, Maccus, don't you understand that? You're unbelievable."

He shook his head, not waiting for what Maccus had to say. He turned around and exited the house in a hurry. Thankfully, the front door was only a few steps away. As he rushed down the stairs, a public transporter stopped in the driveway. When three young men whom Gen didn't recognize exited the transport, he waved and called out. The transporter blinked blue, and he hurried over so he could catch a ride home. Thankfully, the newcomers didn't look at him as they ascended the stairs, and no one else was around to compete for the ride.

From behind him, Maccus shouted out his name, but Gen didn't bother looking over his shoulder. An automated voice greeted him with good tidings and asked him his destination. As he gave it his address, a loud banging on the window made him jerk back in surprise, only to frown when he saw it was Maccus.

"Should I stop to allow the gentleman in, young sir?" The disembodied voice asked in formal tones.

"No. Don't. Lock the doors and take me to my address as quickly as possible."

"As you wish, young sir."

Maccus continued to run alongside the transport, yelling out Gen's name and pounding his fist on the window. He flinched in his seat but chose to ignore what was going on outside. That was not the Maccus he had come to consider as a friend.

Gen had known Maccus for over three years, but tonight, he could sense a desperation in his friend's behavior that had been shocking to witness. He breathed a sigh of relief when the transporter sped away and Maccus was left behind.

He glanced at the timepiece on his wrist and saw it was still early enough to beat his father home. Gen leaned back and closed his eyes. Going out without telling his father had not been the best decision. If his father found out about where he'd been, he would be furious.

Two days later, Gen's world exploded. The sharp slap across his cheek momentarily blinded him. He raised a hand to his cheek, incredulous that his father could react so violently.

"Father, please. I didn't do anything wrong. I left as soon I

learned whose house it was. I swear I didn't even go inside."
He tried to reason everything out when his vision cleared
again.

"Be silent. Your actions have cast shame upon our family
name." Spittle flew from Martin's lips as he spoke.

Gen lowered his head as words failed him. He wanted to
say that the name his father was speaking of didn't even belong to him. It belonged to Gen, to Laoghaire, and his mother,
Frigga. It had been Frigga who had been the princess. Her late
father, Maik Toullec, had been second cousins to the former
king, Eljin. It had been he who had insisted that Martin take
Frigga's name when they'd been married. As Frigga was the
only surviving child of the royal line of Toullec, it was not
only tradition, but also a logical choice. But Martin had refused, and to this day, carried the name of Leafbow.

"Your mother would turn in her grave if she'd been alive.
What would she have thought of having a disgrace for a son?"
Martin paced the floor of the study.

"Father, I did nothing wrong. I told you. As soon as I found
out where Maccus had taken me, I left," Gen emphasized.
Something itched at the corner of his lip, and when he flicked
the tip of his tongue on it, he grimaced at the sharp sting.

"Not soon enough." Martin stopped his pacing and turned
to glare at him. "Your Aunt Marina saw you."

Gen dragged his hand over his face. His father didn't need
to explain further. Marina wasn't technically related to him.
But because she had been a good friend to his mother when
she'd been alive, he regarded her as his honorary aunt. Of
course, that didn't stop her from talking about his downfall.
She was a true gossip and had only gotten worse after Frigga
had died. From what Gen understood, it had been Marina's
fear and respect for Frigga that had controlled her wagging
tongue.

"I can speak to Aunt Marina. She'll listen to me."

Martin pointed a finger at him. "You. Are. Forbidden. You do not talk to her." He emphasized each word with a stabbing motion. "As it is, she's moved to the south and won't be coming back anytime soon. Stupid woman, selling everything she owned." Martin shook his head.

Gen stilled at the words. "But why? I'm telling you, Father, I can talk to her. She's the only one who can refute her own gossips. She can spread the word that I am innocent of what you think I am guilty of. All this is a misunderstanding. An overreaction."

"Well, it's too late." Martin shrugged and sat down on his favorite chair.

"Too late?" Gen felt so confused.

So what if he had been seen exiting that house by one person? Just his Aunt Marina. That didn't mean anything. Why was his father blowing things out of proportion? He studied his father's face, but Martin didn't raise his head to meet his gaze.

A cold shard of fear traveled down Gen's spine. "Father? What did you do?"

"Do? It is not I who has done something, boy. It's you. You've forced my hand." Martin looked Gen up and down before picking up a pen and turning his face away. "I should have this done a long time ago."

"What are you saying?" Gen openly stared at his father in bewilderment.

"I have to call for an auction." Martin picked up a pen and started to write.

"Wh-wh-what auction? You can't sell off the estate. This belongs to the Toullecs, Mother's family, and I am her only heir." Gen began to feel lightheaded as his breathing became rapid and uneven.

Martin looked up and glared. "No longer. You forfeited that right when you cast shame on the Toullec name."

Gen gaped, his mouth opening and closing until he finally got the words out. "I have not!"

"Tell that to the people who will be talking about your scandalous behavior. By this time tomorrow, our reputation would have been shredded. Did you even think about your sister and her chances for a respectable life? Did you think about my position as a cleric? Of course not. You never think. After the auction, once you're married, your spouse, whoever he or she may be, will place you under their direct supervision."

Gen's lungs hurt. He couldn't breathe from the shock of what he was hearing. He felt as if he was traversing a tunnel where he had no hope of getting out, with the walls closing in all around him.

A sharp slap across his cheek snapped him out of his panic.

"You always were a weak child. I can't believe you're my son. What a disappointment." Martin sneered and walked away.

Gen hadn't even realized his father had stood up, much less come near him. The pain on his cheek told him that he hadn't imagined things. Tears coursed down his cheeks as he looked at his father's back.

"Father, I'm twenty years old. I'll be turning twenty-one in a few weeks. I have the right to refuse this auction. I'm of legal age to contest your decision. Also, I'm not ready for marriage." Gen's voice quaked as he fought back his tears.

"Oh, do shut up, you pathetic little mouse. I'm your father. I can do whatever I want. If I want to marry you off, I can. It wouldn't matter whether you agree or not. How, you ask? Because of what you have done. I have called for the rite of *ius auction*. Two weeks from now would be too long, but I have guests living far from here, and there's the required number of days for a public announcement. The first step that will clear our name is to follow the required processes."

Gen shook his head emphatically, letting out an uncontrollable whimper of despair. "No, you can't do that. That practice has not been invoked in centuries."

"I can and I will. No one may have called it, but it doesn't mean it isn't applicable to your situation. Your actions have ruined our family name. Your mother's royal name. Now get out of my sight." Martin waved a dismissive hand before turning his back on him.

Gen wanted to say something to convince his father to call off the auction. Yet he knew he had no choice but to go or risk bearing the brunt of his father's wrath. As he walked back to his room, his mind was a jumble of conflicting thoughts.

Would King Anwyll even allow this *ius auction* his father was talking about? There had to be a reason why Martin was so adamant in marrying him off. Gen stopped in his tracks as the answer dawned on him. Terror filled him, spurring him to run the rest of the way until he reached his room. He flung the door open with so much force, it bounced against the wall in a resounding thud. It bounced back rapidly, barely missing his face, but he grabbed its edge and slammed it just as fast in a thundering crash.

Gen fought to breathe, forcing himself to calm down and think. The minutes passed slowly, and he was still panting for breath when common sense won over his panic, and the answer once again came to light.

Quickly, he walked over to his desk, set before a window overlooking the back gardens, and sat on the chair. For a long moment, he could only stare at his tablet, trying to figure out how to go about fighting against his father. Finally, when logic and reason took over, he opened the tablet and did some research.

The first thing he needed to do was find out what this *ius auction* was really all about. He had heard of it but didn't know how it worked. One thing he knew was that he didn't like its implications. When his search garnered several results, he started to read the first articles. The more he read, the more he became frightened until horror descended over him. Once more, he could feel the panic rising inside him.

An *ius auction* was a last resort taken by a parent or legal guardian. It was considered a form of sacrifice or payment for an affront or an unfulfilled task that could not be repaid by monetary means. Bidders of equal or higher status were expected to compete for the honor of the auctioned minor—in this case, Gen. In exchange, protection and responsibility would be turned over to the winning bidder.

Another entry spoke of cases where inheritance was involved. It stated the minor in question would forfeit their rights as heir in favor of a surviving parent or parents until such time as the *ius auction* was completed. Upon completion, the winning bidder would wed the minor, and as their spouse, would take over all responsibilities of the minor.

There were two options for the spouse with regard to the control over the property. The spouse could give back the control over the property if one or both parents were still living, or the spouse could retain control whether both parents were alive or dead.

Sudden insight hit Gen as he read the last part. Everything began to make sense. His father was likely using this made-up scandal to gain control of the money and properties Gen was to inherit once he turned twenty-one in a few weeks. Although a priest, technically, Martin was not a member of the respected *equites*. He was not a member of the royal family or the noble-blooded gentry, who generally were the only ones recruited for the position.

Martin's family were commoners, *plebs*, but they had been wealthy. Gen, through his mother, was an *equite*. As the children of a princess of royal blood, he and Laoghaire were closely related to the royals. Because he was the eldest child, everything—name, status, titles, wealth, position—would go to him. Unfortunately, Frigga had died before Gen's eighteenth birthday. Being young and naïve, he had readily turned over the management of the estates to Martin.

With Gen out of the way, Martin would have the wealth and privileges that came with Frigga's name, except for the royal title. Martin could be guaranteed his place in the *clerus*.

Gen was being sacrificed, and he didn't know how to stop it. As he thought about his predicament, he knew he had no one to turn to other than the one person who barely even knew him. The only person on Kizerain who had both political and religious authority to stop his father from selling him to the highest bidder. King Anwyll.

CHAPTER THREE

Lairgnen passed through the cool corridors leading to the great double paneled doors. He had news to deliver, and there was only one place the person he was looking for would be found at all times of the day — the royal gardens.

Before Pedr became King Anwyll's Chosen Consort, he had been a gardener and had run one of the more successful private conservatories on the planet. Before his marriage, nothing much could be said about the grounds surrounding the palace on Kizerain, except that it had been planted with ornamentals. There was no denying those had been quite colorful and a bit formal, just not useful.

Pedr had grown more than just ornamentals. He had also been quite popular for vintage herbs and medicinal plants. In fact, his gift to King Eljin on his abdication had been a pot of winter roses.

Historically, that plant had been the symbol of the royal family in the mother world but had failed to thrive on Kizerain for unknown reasons. After one thousand years, many, including renowned horticulturists, had thought the winter rose to be no more than a myth. Pedr, however, had made use of his scientific talent and successfully encouraged the millennia-old seed stored in his family's seed vault to sprout. Since then, winter roses had thrived in the capital. They had even spread beyond the sacred grove where it had first been transplanted from the pot. Soon there would be enough seeds to spread across the planet. For the clerics, it had been a clear sign that Pedr and Anwyll would lead the way to a prosperous and peaceful future.

Unfortunately, there was the corresponding scrutiny with the rise to royal status, and Pedr had found he could no longer go about the capital or the Common Grounds in anonymity. From the time he accepted his position as the king's Chosen Consort, several warriors followed him around and watched his every move.

Since Pedr was not the type to gripe about his curtailed freedom, Anwyll had contacted Lairgnen and his brother, Llewellyn, and expressed his worries over Pedr's difficulties. He had feared his Chosen was being pushed and pulled in every direction and only pretending to be unaffected. Anwyll had been convinced, and rightly so, that his new husband was actually miserable. Their bond made it possible for them to share their feelings. Such was the gift of the Heart Call.

After much discussion on how to help Pedr adjust to his new position, Llewellyn had suggested that Anwyll have his gardens translocated to the capital. The three of them had briefly considered the possibility before the royal nuptials, but nothing had been done. Said transfer had been successfully accomplished three months earlier, and that was where Pedr could be found ever since — at least when he was not sitting with Anwyll at the throne room in his capacity as Consort.

The new location of Pedr's gardens had been placed directly below that of Anwyll's offices. Even at his busiest, all Anwyll needed to do was look out the window to easily spot his beloved husband. Pedr, of course, ever the logical man, had merely rolled his eyes and thanked Anwyll for his thoughtfulness. Later, upon inspection, he'd claimed that the spot was perfect for his plants' health and growth.

Lairgnen couldn't help admiring the flowers. There were so many of them, one had to squint to find a leaf among the rainbow of colors. He stopped and sniffed the air with familiar scents, but he could never remember the names of the plants. The orange trumpet-like flowers drew him to bend down and take in the heady, intoxicating blend of sweet honey and citrus scent. The fruity fragrance flooded his senses and made him feel relaxed and happy.

Before meeting Pedr, he had never considered himself a lover of flora. He had thought he was too scientifically-minded, but that was all in the past. He straightened once more and followed the familiar path leading to Pedr's breeding workrooms. The hut was located just at the edge of the gardens and was where Pedr could be usually found, tinkering with vintage seeds or crossbreeding. Although Lairgnen didn't know the science behind it, he knew it was where the winter roses had regained their life.

He lengthened his stride, needing to share his news with his friend.

At the door, he stopped to check if the red light over it was lit. Seeing that it was, he knocked and waited for Pedr to open it. A shadow moved on his periphery, making him tense and grip on the handle of his stunner. When the man came into view, he saluted, and Lairgnen recognized the warrior as one of Pedr's personal detail. Lairgnen returned the salute and relaxed. He knocked on the door once more and waited. Seconds later, the door opened to a frowning Pedr, who quickly smiled at Lairgnen.

"Lair, what are you doing here? I thought you were joining us for dinner tonight."

"I am going to join you for dinner, but I came here for a different reason, which is why I'm early. I wanted to talk to you about some news I've just received."

Pedr raised a questioning brow. "Should I be worried?"

"No. In fact, it's good news," Lairgnen said, shaking his head.

"Hold on, let me shut down everything in here, and then

you can tell me all about it." Pedr grinned broadly and pointed a finger over Lairgnen's shoulder. "Anwyll's waving at us from his offices."

Lairgnen turned around and looked up. Just as Pedr said, Anwyll was leaning over a window, waving at them. Lairgnen waved back, chuckling over Anwyll's exuberance.

"Come up to my office. I need to talk to both of you," Anwyll called down, gesturing with his hand for them to join him. "Lairgnen, whatever you have to say to Pedr, you can say it up here."

"All right, we'll be right up." Pedr laughed and turned back to Lairgnen. "His Majesty awaits us. Let me close up, then we can go."

"I'll wait out here," Lairgnen said and watched as Pedr went back to his hut.

Anwyll had gone through a lot of changes since he'd met his Chosen. In the past, he had been quiet and worked too hard. Now he laughed freely and took breaks more often. Such was the result of his bond with Pedr, who was not merely the love of his life. As Chosen Consort of the king, Pedr acted as Anwyll's anchor, thus preventing his magic from turning destructive. It was not a life Lairgnen wanted or wished on anyone.

The Heart Call, or the *Pull* as many called it, was something not exclusive to the kings and queens of Kizerain, but it was only they who had to go through the ordeal of the Search. When successful, they mostly lived long and happy lives.

Lairgnen wouldn't mind finding someone to love and be loved by unconditionally, and he dreamed of finding such one day. The sound of a door closing him brought him out of his thoughts, and he turned in time to see Pedr lock the door and walk toward him.

"You came to tell me something," Pedr said as they walked toward the castle. "What is it?"

"Would you rather I tell you now, or should I wait until we join Anwyll?"

"I have a suspicion my husband knows what you're going to say."

"I'm not sure what he knows. What I do know is that I got this missive not ten minutes before I got here, and no one else has seen it yet."

"Tell me, then. What is this news you're so excited to tell me?"

"Remember I told you about a month ago about this piece of land being offered to me? In Merifael? Well, the agent just sent me a message telling me that the owner had accepted my offer."

Pedr's brows furrowed. "You mean that vineyard you wanted to buy?"

"Yes, that one. It's close to Llewellyn's estate there, but I've long coveted it. The old lord who owned it left a lot of unpaid debts. His heirs thought to sell a part of their lands to pay them off." Lairgnen nodded. "I told the agent I was still interested, but that before I close the sale, I wanted someone to look at it first."

Pedr nodded in understanding. "Ahh . . . So, you want me to accompany you and take a look at the vineyard?"

"Yes, that is, if it's all right with you, and Anwyll, of course. He's quite protective of you."

"What has that got to do with my going with you?" Pedr's frown deepened.

Immediately, Lairgnen regretted his wrong choice of words. "You misunderstand me. I'm not saying that he won't let you go. I'm saying that I would have to submit a complete itinerary of your schedule of activities to him and discuss your warrior detail with Llewellyn. As the king's Consort, preparations for a short trip can be brutal for those who have to arrange it. Me." Lairgnen pointed to himself. "I was just wondering if you could help me convince him that you're safe with me."

"Why wouldn't I be safe with you?"

Lairgnen shrugged. "I'm not known for my skill with the sword, but I am a good shot with the stunner."

Pedr shrugged. "You're not a soldier, Lair. You're the Finance Minister. But that settles it. We'll take Llewellyn with us." He patted Lairgnen gently on the back. "Don't worry, I'll take care of Anwyll."

When they entered the king's office a few minutes later, they found Anwyll sitting at his desk, scowling at a letter he held in his hand. A lock fell over his forehead, and he brushed it away with an impatient hand. His hair had once been silver but had turned golden after he'd taken on the mantle of king. The frown disappeared as soon as he looked up and saw them.

"Good, you're both here. I need to speak to you two about this." Anwyll stood up, waving the letter in the air.

"What is it?" Pedr asked as he took the letter from Anwyll.

"My blasted cousin's widower has made an ass out of himself, and someone needs to knock some sense into him. If no one does, I'm going to have to do it myself. That may mean a personal appearance so I can strip him of his priestly status, his position as a member of the royal family, and my cousin's name." Anwyll started to pace.

"Aren't you being a little overdramatic, love? Please calm down and allow me to read this." Pedr sat on the chair Anwyll had vacated.

Lairgnen raised his brows. "Who are we talking about now?"

"Martin." Anwyll rolled his eyes but didn't stop his pacing.

"Cousin Frigga's husband? That priest?"

"The same. Yes. He presided over the Choosing."

"The over officious one," Pedr commented without taking

his focus off the letter.

"Ah." Lairgnen nodded his understanding.

The man cousin Frigga had been married to was an ass, a known social climber who'd used his family's money to buy him entry into the *clerus*. Lairgnen didn't really want to waste a minute thinking about the man. When Frigga had married him, it had caused quite the stir. Her father, Prince Maik, had allowed the union, but under certain caveats. Though a priest, Martin was not of noble or royal blood, so he had to adhere to certain protocols or not be allowed to marry into the family.

Two years before, Frigga had come to the capital to ask permission from then King Eljin for a divorce. Unfortunately, Frigga died en route before it could be granted.

Lairgnen walked over to a table laden with a delicious array of cakes, candied fruits, and a carafe filled with iced juice. He poured himself a glass.

"For Goddess' sake. What is he thinking?" Pedr exclaimed.

Lairgnen hastily lowered the glass he was drinking and turned around to see what had aggravated Pedr.

Pedr looked up, his eyes wide with shock. "Is this for real? Legal even?"

"Now who's being overdramatic?" Anwyll finally stopping his pacing and raised a brow at Pedr.

"Why? What's happened? What's Martin done?" Lairgnen looked from Anwyll to Pedr.

Pedr waived the letter in the air. "This priest, is he your cousin or uncle? According to this letter, he has put up his son for auction. The highest bidder gets to marry him."

CHAPTER FOUR

By the time Lairgnen got home, it was close to midnight. The discussion about the auction had gone on the rest of the afternoon and extended beyond dinner.

The letter Anwyll had received had been written by Frigga's son, Prince Guénaël of Toullec. It was a plea to the king to help him out of what he claimed was an inescapable situation. He had ended his message with a code of urgency only known to those within the royal family. Upon seeing it, Anwyll's anger had been understandable. As king, he made the decision to put a stop to the auction. Pedr, however, had surprised everyone by telling him he should allow the auction to proceed.

"Where is this coming from, Pedr?" Anwyll asked, looking just as surprised as Lairgnen felt.

"I believe that if you put a stop to it, we will never learn why this cousin of yours — "

"We're not related." Anwyll quickly interrupted, his eyes narrowing.

Pedr merely smiled and patted his hand. "We'll never find out why this Martin is bringing up an antiquated and highly immoral practice. Which, by all rights and purpose, should have been declared illegal on Kizerain centuries ago. I'm not saying we will allow the auction. That can never happen. What I am suggesting is, let this Martin think you're not opposed to it. Or that you don't know anything about it."

"I already know why he's doing this," Lairgnen said.

"We all do. It's the prestige that comes with the title." Pedr's mouth twisted into a grimace.

"Not only that." Lairgnen shifted on his seat. "Martin would want to take full control of Frigga's money and properties — which he thinks should have gone to him and not to Guénaël."

Pedr raised a finger and nodded. "That, and something else."

Lairgnen frowned. Pedr was incredibly astute and intelligent. From his expression, he had caught something that Lairgnen and Anwyll had missed.

"What are you thinking, Pedr?" Anwyll leaned forward in his chair.

"Earlier, when you told me about your cousin Frigga, you mentioned that Father Eljin had received a request from her asking him to grant her a divorce from this man, but that she'd died before he could take action. Yes?"

Lairgnen and Anwyll looked at each other before turning back to Pedr. They both nodded but didn't say anything.

"How did she die?"

Pedr's question surprised Lairgnen. He blinked and turned to Anwyll again, who met his gaze with a frown.

"The transporter she was in crashed, I think," Anwyll said.

Lairgnen shrugged. He'd had no idea how Frigga had died.

"I'm not talking about the crash itself," Pedr clarified. "Transporters are equipped with the best technology. There have only been a handful of incidents through the decades they've been around. What I'm asking is, do you know the specifics of how Frigga died?"

Anwyll frowned and appeared to think about the question but soon shook his head. "I must admit, I have no idea. Father never told me, and I don't remember ever asking."

"I know someone who may know," Lairgnen offered. "Uncle Fiacre."

"All right, we'll need to talk to Uncle Fiacre. Though I think that can wait until tomorrow. It's getting late, and I'm exhausted." Anwyll chewed on his lip. "However, you raise a very good question there, Pedr. It never occurred to me to question Frigga's death, and now I'm curious. In the meantime, I think it best to send Lairgnen over to Merifael."

"About that . . ." Pedr began, but Anwyll reached over and squeezed his hand. A look of disappointment fell over his face.

"I'm sorry, Pedr, but I can't let you go. Not this time. Don't be disappointed, but I think Llewellyn should take your place." Anwyll turned back to Lairgnen. "Lair, I think you'll have to make do without my husband's expertise this once. Use your cover of needing an expert to inspect the vineyard you're hoping to buy. Get in touch with Guénaël, ask him to help you out. I'm quite sure Martin will not object to a member of the royal family around his son. While you're distracting Martin, we'll let Llewellyn do the background investigations on Martin's activities. I know for a fact that Guénaël is a well-educated young man and is quite acquainted with running vineyards, given that he owns several. Father has talked to him a time or two and mentioned he thought Guénaël to be quite intelligent and logical. Not someone prone to dramatics."

"How old is he?" Lairgnen furrowed his brows.

"If I remember it correctly, he should be turning twenty-one in two weeks. Which makes me highly suspicious about Martin's real motives. Should the *ius auction* push through, it would negate Guénaël's position as heir. Now that boy may be young in years, but I know for a fact Frigga raised and educated him the same way Uncle Maik did her, so I suspect he's more than qualified. More than Martin, I'm sure." Anwyll paused. "Lair, I need you to get to know Guénaël, find out everything you can from him. We need to learn more than what he's already written. I have a feeling his father made this scandal up, especially after what Pedr said. It reminded me that royal properties and names always go to the son, not the spouse. If Martin is thinking of getting rid of his son so he can get his hands on the money and properties, he has another think coming. This is why you and Llewellyn need to be there."

"I'll call Llewellyn, tell him to come back as soon as he can or to meet up with me in Merifael," Lairgnen said, nodding in agreement.

"Good. That's settled, then." But from Anwyll's expression, he was far from satisfied with the decision.

Lairgnen was lying in bed, still thinking about the conversation. It took him a moment to realize the beeping sound from an incoming call had been going on for some time. He answered as soon as he saw it was Llewellyn.

"I'm sorry, I didn't get your message until now," Llewellyn said. "I thought you were having dinner with Anwyll and Pedr."

"Yes, about that. Anwyll has an assignment for us."

Lairgnen proceeded to brief Llewellyn on the events of the day. By the time he was done, Llewellyn was cursing.

"That bastard. What the hell is Martin up to? I agree with Pedr. There's something more to this, and most likely, it's connected to Frigga's death."

"Anwyll said that you and I should go, and use my trip as a cover."

"I agree. I'll meet you at my estate in two days' time. Your room is waiting for you, so all you need to do is get there."

"Thank you, I appreciate it. What do you think? After I buy the property, we'll be sharing borders." Lairgnen smiled.

"I look forward to it." Llewellyn chuckled, but then his tone turned serious. "This is incredible. The thought that

Frigga might have possibly been killed by that impostor is making me so angry right now." He growled, something he habitually did when frustration got the better of him. "Other than the auction, have you learned anything about her son? What's his name again?"

"Guénaël."

Llewellyn snorted. "Poor boy. All right. We'll take care of this. I'll see you in two days."

The connection ended, leaving Lairgnen to his thoughts.

He turned onto his back, staring at the ceiling as he planned how to spend time with Guénaël without his father's interference. There was a reason why many looked at the *clerus* with suspicion. Although their fraternity had persisted, it wasn't a secret that their forebears had to leave the mother world because of them. If they had not betrayed the old king and his daughter — the first of the magical queens — their people would not have had to suffer. Then again, without their betrayal, their forebears would not have traveled to Kizerain, freed from the religious constraints and bigotry that had ruled the population of that time.

Anwyll, as the magical king and spiritual leader, was a just man. And with Pedr beside him, he had a Chosen who could ground him to reality and logic. Theirs was a perfectly balanced pairing of magic and science that Lairgnen could only dream of ever experiencing. Closing his eyes didn't stop his mind from going over the plan of investigation over and over.

Two questions kept tumbling through his mind. One, how were they to prove Frigga's death had not been accidental? And two, how were they going to stop the auction from happening?

The next day, Lairgnen arrived in Merifael. The small quaint town was located at the base of a massive rock column rising almost two hundred meters high. According to legend, the natural formation was the site selected by Queen Adelgunde, third queen of Kizerain, to build a fortress. She had the structure built at the top of the rock and decorated its sides with frescoes of the Great Passage.

History never stated why, but although the construction had been completed, Adelgunde never stepped foot on it. The city of Merifael had risen around the fortress over several hundred years. Adelgunde's children and other families had begun setting up vineyards from grape seedlings that scientists and horticulturists had coaxed into growing on Kizerain. It just so happened that the land at the base of the fortress was rich in silt, clay, and sand — three requirements that made the loamy soil highly fertile. The meadowlands were also rich in nutrients and organic matter. The combined soil elements made grape propagation easy and productive and generated the best wines on Kizerain.

When Llewellyn first brought him here, Lairgnen knew immediately he wanted a share of the fertile lands. Admittedly, although he was good at keeping Kizerain's economy flourishing, he didn't know a thing about raising the grapes. He would need to find someone who knew how that end worked. Hopefully, this trip would gain him some insight and connect with a potential manager.

Before leaving the capital, Lairgnen sent word to his agent, Felix Uthman, about his arrival in Merifael but cautioned him to keep his presence quiet. As Finance Minister, he invariably became the crown's representative. Should people hear of his appearance in the southern continent, those seeking political or royal connections and favors would come in droves. He wanted to avoid that.

At Llewellyn's estate, Lairgnen was greeted by a butler and upper servant only to find out they weren't expecting Llewellyn until that evening. He was shown his usual room, which was situated right beside that of Llewellyn's. Rather than wait around for his brother, he decided to give his agent a call. The agent answered quickly enough for Lairgnen to suspect the man had been waiting all the while.

Half an hour later, Lairgnen sat in the back patio of the tea house, where he and Uthman had agreed to meet. However, when Uthman showed up, he wasn't alone. Lairgnen kept his opinion to himself, clenched his jaw, and pasted on a polite smile as he was introduced to Uthman's wife. Leonie seemed like a soft-spoken woman in her forties. She excused herself after the introductions to go inside the tea house.

"I apologize, Your Highness," Uthman said, rubbing the back of his neck. "My wife knows the owner here, and she wanted to spend some time with her friend."

"No need to apologize," Lairgnen reassured politely as he sipped his tea. He was never one to call out someone's faux pas, but he felt Uthman should have known better. It wasn't as if he hadn't insisted on his anonymity.

"Thank you, my lord. She's a prudent woman and won't speak of your presence here," Uthman said, visibly relaxing.

"I'd appreciate it." Deep inside, he hoped Uthman was telling the truth.

"You said you wanted to talk to me about something. I hope you didn't change your mind about buying the property?"

"No, I'm still very much interested. As I said, I wanted to go and look it over first before I make a final decision. I was thinking of taking a cousin of mine over. Do you think you can make arrangements with the manager there?"

"I'm sure it can be arranged. When do you want to go?" Uthman took out his communicator. "I can give them a call right now."

"I was hoping tomorrow afternoon, if possible."

Uthman nodded and began to type on his communicator. "Do you mind if I ask who you're taking with you? The property manager will need the names, so once you get there, you can get in without any problems."

"It'll be me, my security detail, and my cousin, Guénaël."

Uthman nodded as he continued to enter the information. "And this Guénaël's last name is?"

"He doesn't have one. As I said, he's a cousin."

Uthman looked up. "Guénaël? As in Priest Martin's son, Prince Guénaël of Toullec?"

Lairgnen gave a reluctant nod. "Yes, do you know of him?"

Uthman blinked several times before shifting in his chair. He looked uncomfortable and hesitant. Suspecting that Uthman might know something about the *ius auction*, Lairgnen waited patiently for Uthman to speak.

"Your Highness, do you mind if I ask you something personal?"

"You may, but it doesn't mean you're going to get an answer," Lairgnen cautioned.

Uthman bit on his lower lip. "I understand, but I'll ask it anyway if you don't mind."

Lairgnen studied Uthman. There was no doubt the man knew something that he didn't, so he motioned for the man to continue. "Go ahead. Ask."

"I don't know the exact details, but there's talk about town that Prince Guénaël is involved in a rather unfortunate scandal. Unjustly so, if I may add."

Lairgnen gave Uthman a steady gaze. "What kind of scandal?"

Uthman smoothed his palm over his thinning hair. "As I said, I am not all too familiar with the details, but I do know someone who is."

"Why so cryptic, Uthman. Who is this individual?"

"My wife. Leonie," Uthman said. "She knows the woman who saw the prince at the merchant's house that night. The woman who is the source of spreading the rumors."

Lairgnen arrived at Llewellyn's manor later than he'd planned, only to discover Llewellyn had arrived earlier than expected. Lairgnen immediately sought him out and shared the new information he'd obtained as soon as they were alone in the study.

"So according to this Leonie, her friend saw Guénaël exit this place, owned by some known procurer, a merchant, and Guénaël's reputation is instantly ruined." Llewellyn summarized what Lairgnen had narrated to him.

"Not his. The family's."

"For exiting a house. Alone."

"Yes." Lairgnen nodded. Even to him, the narrative sounded ridiculous and far-fetched.

"And he's getting auctioned for that one simple act."

"Yes."

"Who is this merchant? Did Uthman say?"

"Yes, one Devos Cricirus. A procurer of souls."

"Goddess. No wonder Martin reacted to the rumors. I've been trying to pin Cricirus on his activities, but he's a slimy bastard and has all his documents in place, so we can't touch him. At least for now." Llewellyn took a sip from his wine. "Uncle Fiacre called me on my way here. He said that Martin invoking the right to sacrifice his son through *ius auction* is within his rights, and no one can stop him. According to my sources, it's slated for next week. Somehow, Martin managed to find someone to approve an earlier date."

Lairgnen sat up. "What? But that's insane. That's only one week from Guénaël's birthday."

"That was my reaction. I've talked to Anwyll, and he grudgingly confirmed what Uncle said. After you left, Anwyll consulted with the clerics in the capital, and they told him the same thing. Martin can't be stopped. Even though the practice is archaic and has not been invoked for hundreds of years —

because it is not entirely ethical — it is still technically legal."

"Meaning, no one thought to proclaim the practice unjust and immoral. Pedr was right. Anwyll should do something about it." Lairgnen ran his fingers through his hair. The whole situation had quickly turned complicated.

"I agree, but he can only do so for future auctions. It won't put a stop to Martin now. It's been . . . hmm . . . forgotten, I think, is the term we're looking for." Llewellyn's face twisted at the irony of the situation.

"Goddess." Lairgnen rubbed his hand over his face. "The whole thing's a mess."

"What I said." Llewellyn raised his glass in a toast.

"What next? What do we do?" Lairgnen squinted up at Llewellyn.

Llewellyn shook his head and grimaced. "Uncle Fiacre said that the only one who can stop the auction is the parent or legal guardian, and knowing Martin, he won't. Anwyll can as well, but Martin can contest his interference on the grounds of parental rights. Legally, all Anwyll can do, as head of the family, is to take Guénaël under his protection and declare guardianship over a minor."

"For how long?"

"Indefinitely. Or until Anwyll or his successor lifts the protection. Or Guénaël gets married, and his spouse takes responsibility for him. It's all very complicated, and I think Martin was counting on that."

"It would mean Guénaël will have to live with the scandal of the auction looming over his head for his entire life."

"Yes."

"Goddess. That would be unbearable. What can we do for now?"

"Uncle said that Anwyll expects us to do whatever we can to put a stop to the auction. That maybe we can talk to Martin and hopefully change his mind."

Lairgnen's jaw dropped. "Is Anwyll insane? Does he not know Martin?"

Llewellyn shrugged. "It's worth a try."

Lairgnen thought over what his next move would be, tapping the tip of his fingers on the glass he was holding. With every tap, he counted it out. It made finding a solution clearer and faster.

"I'm going to the Toullec manor tomorrow," Lairgnen said after a while. "I had your butler call earlier. To inform them that the king's Chosen Counselor, Finance Minister, Prince Lairgnen, would like to visit with his cousin, Prince Guénaël of the Royal House of Toullec, tomorrow afternoon. That way, Martin won't be able to make excuses or stop me from seeing Guénaël."

Llewellyn smirked. "Pushing the royal titles, aren't you, brother?"

"Well, Martin's always coveted our titles, might as well show him what we royalty can do." Lairgnen shrugged. He met Llewellyn's gaze and flashed him a grin before taking a sip of his drink.

"That's an obnoxious move, but he'll be so jealous." Llewellyn grinned broadly.

Lairgnen raised his glass in a silent salute, just like Llewellyn had earlier.

"Fortunately, Martin isn't in town. He's gone off to some village to perform a marriage," Llewellyn said.

Lairgnen frowned at his brother. "Anyone we know?"

"Some minor nobleman's daughter and a warrior's son. I have their names somewhere in my notes, but I forget where they are," Llewellyn said, shrugging.

"I'm glad Martin's not around." Lairgnen didn't bother to question how Llewellyn had managed to get that piece of information. "I guess that's good news. We'll have time to get to the bottom of this."

"Not much, but I hope we can do it. What about Guénaël? Will he be there to meet you?"

"I don't know yet. He'll have to be. It wouldn't be proper to ignore a higher-ranking prince's request. Plus, he was the one who sent Anwyll that letter asking for help. He'll do what he needs to do."

"Of course he will. If he doesn't, he loses his chance to plead his case to the king's Chosen Counselor. You." Llewellyn set down his glass and picked up a paper and pen. "Now, let's take everything we know so far and send an update over to Anwyll. He's personally invested in this situation, and Pedr called earlier to make sure he gets an update as often as we can manage. Translate that to hourly updates."

Lairgnen let out a sigh. "You really like your job, don't you?"

"I love it. That's why I am the king's Chosen Protector and Minister of Security, not you. You're just here as my cover." Llewellyn grinned.

Lairgnen rolled his eyes. "I'll try my best to be a good, boring cover, brother. Let's get to work."

CHAPTER FIVE

Gen looked up at the sound of a knock on the front door. When a second knock sounded and Horst, the old butler, still hadn't come to answer it, he hurried over to open it himself. His father and Laoghaire had left two days before, and Gen had been told he was not allowed to set foot outside of the manor house, even to inspect the vines, and that he was expecting a visitor. When Gen asked for the name of the visitor, Martin hadn't provided him with one. It surprised Gen that his father would instruct him to make sure an anonymous guest be welcomed. Martin had worn a smug expression, which Gen hadn't been able to interpret. Was the mysterious guest the one knocking on the door?

Martin would have chastised him for acting like a commoner by answering the door. But as he was away on some business and wouldn't be back for another day or two, Gen thought he could get away with it. He didn't want Horst to get in trouble and be fired from his job. It was ridiculous that simple actions like opening a door — in Martin's reasoning — could potentially cause more humiliation for his family. Even though Martin was his father, Gen thought he was reaching too much.

Just as he opened the door, an inexplicable sense of longing caught him by surprise. Before he had the chance to examine his feelings, he caught sight of three expensive-looking transporters hovering on the driveway. The longing increased in intensity when he laid eyes on three imposing-looking men standing on the stoop before him. The one who had his back to Gen looked oddly familiar. He was dressed more elegantly, with no visor, and continued to ignore him. He appeared to be studying the sprawling landscape fronting the manor. Gen examined the man's profile thoughtfully before turning to the other two, who were standing closer.

They were built like warriors, wearing black leather uniforms that enhanced their tall and muscled bodies. The lowered visors mirrored Gen's reflection, making it difficult to see their faces. Gen frowned. As soon as he did so, they raised the visors. The expressionless faces made Gen take a step back. Strangely, both men managed to lift their brows simultaneously, as though they'd been practicing the move for some time.

"May I help you?" Gen asked, looking from one man to the next.

"His Highness, Prince Lairgnen, would like to speak to His Highness, Prince Guénaël," said one of the men facing him.

Gen paid him no attention, for right at that moment, the third man turned around. Their gazes met, and his ears started to ring. Gen's jaw dropped as his stomach cramped painfully while his heart began to pound hard inside his chest. He could hear it thundering in his ears. Suddenly, he longed to kiss the man. He had to know what those lips tasted like against his own.

The two of them stared at each other for a long second before the man's identity registered. Standing before him was none other than Prince Lairgnen, the man of his dreams, who had a smile curling on his lips. Gen thought he would lose his balance. Goddess, the prince was stunning.

"Hello, you must be Guénaël. You look just like your grandfather, Maik," Prince Lairgnen said.

That and the well-mannered way the prince spoke made Gen feel suddenly hot and self-conscious. He'd never heard the prince speak before, and now he was reacting to the voice in the most inexplicable but pleasurable way. When he didn't respond immediately, the prince's smile was replaced with a look of confusion.

"I apologize for the inconvenience, but I thought I was expected." A slight furrow formed between Prince Lairgnen's brows, but he kept on smiling.

Quickly recovering, Gen bowed his head in respect. What would the prince be doing standing on the front steps of his home?

"Prince Lairgnen, Your Highness, I must apologize. I didn't know you were coming, or I would have . . . Please come inside." Gen stepped aside to make way for them to enter the house.

The two warriors didn't say anything. They just turned their backs and stood guard on either side of the front doors.

Lairgnen walked through the door, and when he passed Gen, their gazes met once more. Gen's cheeks heated in mortification, and he hurriedly closed the door.

"Thank you. Uhm . . . Mother used to say that, about my resemblance to Grandfather, I mean. Please, call me Gen. Guénaël's too formal. Ah . . . uhm . . .Father told me that he was expecting a guest today, but he didn't mention your name. I sincerely apologize for the lack of welcome." Gen wanted to kick himself. Why was he suddenly stuttering? He knew why, but he was better than this and suddenly wished he were more mature or sophisticated so he could mask his attraction to the prince.

Prince Lairgnen smiled gently and appeared to study Gen's face. It only made Gen more self-conscious than ever. Still, the prince looking at him like he actually existed felt strangely satisfying.

"Hmm . . . I think the error is on me, Gen," Lairgnen said. "I had someone call on ahead yesterday, and they assured my brother's butler that they'd spoken to yours. Also, I would have thought you would have expected someone from the capital to come here." He lowered his voice. "You did send that letter to the king, Gen."

Gen raised his brows in surprise and took a step back. He quickly looked around to see if any servants were lurking about. What did Lairgnen have to do with the letter he'd written? Had the king sent him to Merifael to help him out? Much as he wanted to, he couldn't show his excitement. His father's servants had ears and eyes everywhere.

"Oh, that. Yes. Uhm . . . Horst must have forgotten about telling me you were coming. Again, I must apologize on his behalf. He's getting on in years, and I'd assumed . . . but that's neither here nor there. Can I offer you a drink, or perhaps something to eat?" *Please, please, please don't say yes.*

The bright smile Lairgnen flashed back at him didn't reflect the glimmer of suspicion in his eyes. Gen hoped the prince had read his mind.

"No, no, there's no need. I've already eaten. Unless you haven't?"

"I've eaten as well." Gen shook his head, silently thanking the Goddess that Lairgnen was an astute man. "Sir, what can I do for you? As I said, Father didn't advise me on your arrival. He's not here at the moment. He's away on business."

"I told you, I'm here because of you," Lairgnen said gently.

Gen shivered at the way Lairgnen was affecting him and suddenly feared he was dreaming all of this—that Lairgnen was here to help him.

"My father doesn't know I wrote to the king?" Gen whispered.

"And he still doesn't know. I told my brother's butler not to inform your father that I was coming," Lairgnen whispered back and smiled brilliantly. "If this Horst forgot to tell you, I'm sure your father doesn't know I'm here, either."

"You really came to help me?" Gen didn't know how to

react. He was going to be saved . . . By Prince Lairgnen, of all people.

"Yes. I did. Now, when your mother was alive, Frigga used to boast of the talent you showed in administering the farms."

"She did?" Gen blinked in surprise. Lairgnen was a strange man. He seemed to jump from one topic to the next. "I didn't know she'd done that. She was forever pushing me to do better."

"Well, she learned everything she knew from Uncle Maik, and he was a hard man. In any case, I'm here to ask you out."

Gen's heart stopped. "Out?"

"Yes. Out. We have a lot to discuss about your situation, and I also need you to come with me. I require your knowledge of vineyards."

"Oh. All right," Gen said, feeling mysteriously disappointed about Lairgnen's explanation. For a minute there, he'd hoped for something else. He shook off his foolishness and focused on the task at hand.

"Where are we going exactly?"

"Well, I've been offered this property adjacent to yours, and I want to buy it. It's beautiful, and the manor house has drawn me from the moment I first saw it five years ago. That was when my brother first bought his land here. The only problem is, I know nothing about grapes or vineyards. They come with the estate property, and I thought, why not ask for help from my cousin."

"Cousin? Oh, you mean me?" Gen pointed to himself.

"Yes, you," Lairgnen chuckled. "You may be younger and a relative several times removed, but we're still family. What do you think? Are you up to helping me avoid a big mistake? I have my transporter with me, and the warriors, of course, so I can fly us over. That would give us enough time to talk along the way in privacy. No one needs to know what we're going to talk about."

Gen didn't need to think twice. This was his only opportunity to get the help he needed, and he wasn't about to let this time go to waste. "Can you give me a few minutes so I can change my clothes?"

"Of course, take your time. I'll let my agent know that we're going to be a few minutes late."

Gen started to turn but then remembered his father's guest.

"What about my father's guest? He'll be mad if he finds out I was not here to greet them."

"What time are they coming? Did Martin say?"

Gen shrugged. "I don't know. Father just told me to expect them at any time."

"Then it won't be your fault if you're not here to greet them. But just in case you do and Martin overreacts, you can inform him that I came for you and requested your presence." Lairgnen's one raised brow and small smile took on a different meaning.

Gen gave a slow nod as understanding came to him. His father would not dare go against the prince, especially of Lairgnen's rank and status as Chosen Counselor.

"Give me a few minutes, and I'll be right back."

Gen hurried to his room and quickly changed into clothes similar to those Lairgnen was wearing. As for the prince, thank the Goddess, he lacked pompousness, but then Gen really shouldn't be surprised. From what he'd observed at the Yula celebration the year before, the higher-ranked royals were quite laid back. He thought it was because they didn't have to prove anything to anyone, while those in the lower rungs — like his father — had to fight for their positions.

Gen fisted his hands in frustration. He still hadn't found a way out of the auction. Would Lairgnen succeed in putting a stop to it? Even though he hoped that he could, Gen doubted it. It wasn't that he didn't trust the king's intervention or Lairgnen's skills in negotiating. Martin liked to listen to only one man. Martin.

What worried Gen was how Martin would react should he learn that Lairgnen was here. Worse, how would he respond to Lairgnen's snubbing him? He was likely to let out his frustration on Gen. Not physically. Martin dared not hit him. But he could do worse things—although, what could be worse than getting auctioned off?

As for the mysterious guest that Martin had told him to watch out for? He couldn't believe his father would keep the identity from him. It was typical of Martin to place him in a difficult position.

Tears blurred Gen's vision, but he swiped them with the back of his hand. He had to forget about his situation and focus on Lairgnen being actually there and ready to help him out. Of course, going out with the prince was a bonus. Truth was, he looked forward to it. He hadn't been allowed out since the auction had been announced. Time spent with Lairgnen should also diminish his attraction to the older prince. At least, Gen hoped it would. Didn't they say close proximity with someone would reveal the good and the bad of that person? Maybe Lairgnen was pretentious and obnoxious when he didn't have to put on his public persona. Gen shrugged dismissively, not really caring to dwell on matters he knew nothing about.

One thing he did know and was considered an expert on was running a vineyard. Inspecting the vines was something he genuinely enjoyed, and not having to think about his predicament would be a reprieve.

Gen ran back through the corridors leading away from his bedroom, anxious not to keep Lairgnen waiting. When he reached the doorway to the hall where he'd left Lairgnen, he slid to a stop. Lairgnen looked up and frowned.

"You shouldn't have run, Gen. I would have waited for you no matter how long you took," Lairgnen said. "But come, let's not keep my agent waiting. He's a nervous sort of fellow."

"I didn't want to inconvenience you, sir," Gen said, lowering his head as embarrassment swept over him.

"Oh come, come, Gen. Call me Lairgnen." He raised a finger when Gen opened his mouth to argue. "No. I insist. We're cousins, Gen. It wouldn't be right to call me *sir*. Makes me feel old."

"Well, you are much older than I am, sir . . . uhm . . . Lairgnen."

"I am not!"

"At least twenty years," Gen couldn't help teasing.

"Most definitely not twenty." Lairgnen huffed. He looked to think it over before shrugging. "Well, maybe at the most . . . ten years, I'm thinking."

"You don't look your age," Gen mused.

"And you're too young looking to be almost twenty-one."

At the mention of his age, Gen hung down his head. Lairgnen stepped up in front of him.

"I sense your trouble, cousin," he said in that low, gentle voice of his, which continued to wreak havoc on Gen's heart. It truly was an alluring sound and one he would never forget after they parted ways.

Gen shook his head. "It's nothing, sir."

"And we're back to sir. Hmm . . . I think it's time we leave. The walls have ears, as they say. Let's get you in my transporter. We can talk there without fear of anyone eavesdropping."

"I don't want to talk about it," Gen said in a soft voice.

"Get inside the transporter now, Guénaël, and yes, you are going to talk." Lairgnen's voice lowered, making him sound very serious.

Gen looked up and met the intense gaze. For a moment, he fought the urge to turn away, but he quickly shook off his nervousness and led the way to the front door. He didn't look to see if Lairgnen followed behind. He entered the transporter where a warrior stood, holding the door open, and quickly strapped himself in.

To his surprise, Lairgnen motioned for the driver to get out, took his place in the driver's seat, and strapped himself in. He'd expected the driver would pilot the transporter, and the two warriors would join them, but none were on board. He was alone with the prince.

He didn't know what to think about sitting so close to the prince. But his senses were already in overdrive, and the prince's proximity drove them to hyperdrive. Was he overreacting? Maybe, but when all outside noise was canceled as the doors clicked to a definitive close, he knew he was in trouble.

Chapter Six

"**W**hy don't you come up front and sit here? There's no sense sitting at the back when I'm all alone up here." Lairgnen didn't look up as Gen transferred to the chair beside his even though he really wanted to. Instead, he pretended to look over the control panel.

He didn't want Gen to see how ruffled he'd been earlier. Still was, to be honest. Instead, he focused on powering up the transporter. His body, though, was reacting to everything about the young man sitting beside him. Now that they were alone in the transporter's confined space, he was becoming more than hyper-aware, and he didn't know what to do about it.

The young man was everything he'd ever dreamed of in a lover. For one thing, they were about the same height, Gen being an inch or so taller. Thoughts of that particular advantage made his crotch tighten between his legs. Thank the Goddess for sparing him from embarrassing himself.

He shifted in his seat as his back continued to tingle. The sensation had started at the top of his scalp earlier while still inside the house. It had quickly spread to the base of his spine. Now, sitting next to Gen, the goosebumps on his forearms refused to calm down, so he opened and clenched his hand several times until he felt the muscles relax. It didn't do anything for the tingling, which continued to thrum through his body.

Lairgnen breathed in deep and let it out slowly. He turned on his seat so he could speak to Gen, face to face.

"Talk to me," he said.

"What do you want me to say?" Gen sounded as though he'd given up and for some reason.

That only managed to irritate Lairgnen. Hadn't Gen been listening to him? He was here to take care of him, and by the Goddess, he was not going to fail.

"Look, Gen," Lairgnen said a little too impatiently. "You were the one who wrote to Anwyll. As king, there is only so much he can do to intercede on your behalf. However, for him to make things happen, he needs to know everything, every angle, every bit of information. He told me to come here to Merifael and help any way I can. On the day I arrive, I hear of a scandal involving you, which, by the way, you never mentioned in your letter." He glanced at Gen only to mutter an expletive when he saw a tear fall down one side of his face. Now he'd hurt the boy's feelings. He went for a different approach and softened his voice.

"Gen, it's never a good sign when gossip becomes regarded as fact. People are talking about you, and their version is, to be honest, quite disturbing. But I want to hear your side of the story. I want to know everything. Who you were with, and what you were doing there. Why were you conveniently in the wrong place at the wrong time? Because, believe me, Gen, that was a pretty convenient way of entrapping you. Finally, who started the gossip?" Lairgnen paused. Well, everyone he'd talked to knew that last part, but he was still curious if Gen was aware of it or not.

"Everything I wrote about is true. My father has called for a sacrifice, and I must pay for my sins. At least, that's his way of seeing things."

Lairgnen frowned at the resignation in Gen's voice. It didn't sound like the defiant Gen who had written the letter.

"Exactly what sort of sin did you commit, Gen?"

Gen didn't respond at once, but Lairgnen was a patient man. He had a feeling the boy — no, the young man, had a lot to say but had never been given a chance.

He pulled on the levers, directing the transporter to slowly rise. A quick check of the console showed that his driver had already dialed in the coordinates. All he had to do was sit, relax, and allow the transporter to take them to their destination while he waited for Gen to speak. His patience paid off.

Gen shifted in his seat and faced him. "It all started when my friend, Maccus, invited me to a music festival, or so I thought at that time. Instead, he had gone behind my back and had the transporter take us some other place," Gen began.

Lairgnen listened as Gen told how his friend had coerced him into going to a party at a house owned by a man everyone knew had ties to a procurement syndicate. When Devos Cricirus' name came up, Lairgnen didn't react.

By the time Gen was done talking, tears were freely coursing down his cheeks. Lairgnen didn't miss the anger in Gen's voice. That was a consolation. At least it didn't look or sound as though Gen had lost his will to fight back. Lairgnen knew he would need more time with Gen to find out everything, but so far, his tale corresponded to what Uthman's wife had told him.

"So your father called for an auction because of one woman's tale?" Lairgnen asked.

"Yes. I also know he never bothered to confirm anything. I told him I never even went past the entryway of that house, but he wouldn't listen to me. He said all that mattered was that people were talking about me."

"What about this Maccus? Who is he to you? Do you know if he has any ulterior motives in taking you there? Is he your lover?"

Lairgnen had to ask even though the thought of Gen having a lover didn't sit comfortably with him. Which, even to his own mind, was an understatement. He really wanted to do what he couldn't even think about, for the mental image would probably reflect on his face, and he didn't want to scare Gen away.

"No." Gen shook his head emphatically. "I've stopped talking to Maccus. One lie is enough for me to realize he hadn't really been a friend to begin with. Also, he's never defended his actions to our mutual friends when they confronted him about what he'd done. I'm just now realizing . . . He had been very insistent I go into that house. It's as though he was afraid of failing. Like he needed me there, but I don't know why. As for an intimate relationship with him?" He shook his head once more. "Never. I've never been with anyone. I thought of him as a friend, nothing more. I'm not even attracted to him. I mean, physically."

Lairgnen's brow raised a fraction at the unexpected revelation. He cleared his throat, not so much as to stop himself from saying the wrong thing, but to cover his surprise.

"Can you think of a reason why he did it?" Lairgnen asked as diplomatically as he could. He didn't want to make Gen feel even more insecure about his bad decisions than he already did.

"I think I already know why. I spoke to Ian Ó Ceallaigh — he's a mutual friend we share classes with — and we both came to the same conclusion. Maccus has long wanted to be a part of an influential circle. He's not from a very rich family, but we've all heard him say that he'd always coveted material wealth. He never hid his jealousy, either. I've known about that for a while, but I'd ignored it. I couldn't relate to his struggles, and he was fun to hang around with. Maybe that was my failure. I admit I was naïve."

"What you're saying is, he basically wanted to use your name and influence, maybe your status, to climb the social ladder. And you feel guilty that you allowed him to do it."

"Yes." Gen looked out the window. "I don't know how to stop the auction."

"You can't. No one can." Lairgnen hated saying the words, but he wasn't one to sugarcoat the truth.

Gen's shoulders slumped. "I know. I'm getting desperate, Lairgnen. Sometimes I wish . . ."

"What?" Lairgnen prodded.

"I wish I could just take my sister and get away from here. Disappear from Merifael."

Lairgnen froze and examined Gen's face. He needed to see his expression so he could determine what the man was feeling. "Are you thinking about harming yourself?"

Gen grimaced. "Goddess, no. I literally just want to disappear, so I don't have to go through that auction. Spare Laoghaire any pain."

Lairgnen looked out of the window. The speed of the transporter caused the scenery to whip by. "I know you don't want to hear this, but there's a huge chance you may have to go through with it."

Gen bent his head but didn't respond. Lairgnen wanted to say something else that would reassure him, but words failed him. The sense of failure made him angry at himself. There must be something he could do to help his cousin. At the sound of a sniffle, he glanced at Gen and saw tears flowing down his cheeks. Lairgnen knew Gen was grieving for his future and didn't blame him for the tears. The quiet crying gripped at Lairgnen's heart. He wanted to give Gen a hug, but a beeping sound distracted him. He looked down to check the console.

"Come on, wipe your tears away. We're almost at the property. Let's focus on the task at hand and forget about the auction for now."

Once more, Gen didn't respond, but he did nod and wiped at his face with the palm of his hand. Lairgnen swallowed a curse, reached into his pocket, and handed over a handkerchief. Gen took it from him, still silent as he dried his face.

Neither of them spoke as the transporter lowered itself in the middle of what appeared to be a freshly tilled field. When they finally landed, Gen looked around curiously before turning back to him, his face dry and cleared of tears.

"This is the Bolton vineyard," Gen said as he stepped out of the vehicle. "Is this the one you're thinking of buying?"

"It is, yes. Have I made a mistake?"

"Oh, no. Other than the Bolton's not affording to upgrade their machines, you've made a good choice. This has one of the best sources of fresh water in the area, and the soil's fertile." Gen turned and pointed. "On the other side of that hill is the Thréinfhir vineyards, which has the rights to the major waterway system. It's got three rivers feeding your tributary, and most ends up in the natural catch basin just a mile from where we're standing. That means you'll be controlling the water resources that feed the land beyond this one and Toullec's." Gen grinned broadly. "Do I have to pay for rights to the waterway?"

Lairgnen was pleasantly surprised and smiled back. "You seem more than familiar with this property, Gen." He crossed his arms over his chest, refraining from answering Gen's question. He didn't want to remind Gen that there was a high possibility he would not be in charge of the running of the Toullec properties. That was unless Anwyll barred the auction itself and claimed responsibility for Gen. The latter was not an impossibility, just very difficult to achieve.

Gen massaged the back of his neck. "I'm sorry, I should have told you I was. It's just that I wasn't paying attention when we were flying overhead. But yes, I used to come here a lot with my mother when she visited Bolton's eldest daughter, Reginia. They were childhood friends. Reginia died five years ago."

"Oh, that's sad to hear."

"I remember Mother was devastated. I haven't been here

since the funeral." Gen sounded wistful.

"Well, we have the afternoon to inspect the property. My agent sent in his inspectors a few weeks ago and gave their go signal, but I wanted someone objective to tell me the truth."

"Are you buying it for the vineyard or for the manor?"

Lairgnen laughed out. He couldn't help admiring Gen's intuition. For a young man, he was quite perceptive.

"Both. Well, let me clarify. You're right in assuming I bought this place for the manor house. In fact, I have every intention of making this my summer home. I don't mind the winters, but summers in the capital are horrible. It's too wet and too hot. But I digress. What I really wanted to say is that the manor comes with the vineyard, and I would need someone to take over the operations and manage this place for me."

"That's fantastic. We'll be . . ." Gen's voice drifted off, and he quickly turned away. "Come on, I know where to start."

"All right. Lead the way." Lairgnen didn't miss the way Gen had stopped himself from saying they would be neighbors, but he was glad that Gen at least appeared to be enthusiastic.

Lairgnen couldn't relate to love for the soil and plants, but he understood those who did. It was the same with him and numbers. He smiled at the thought of Pedr's confused expression every time he had to sit with Anwyll and listen to his briefing on economic affairs for the royal couple.

They spent the next two hours inspecting the vineyard. Anwyll had been right. Gen knew what he was doing. He checked the soil and the canals. He even checked the condition of the leaves, trunks, and side canes of randomly chosen vines. It was early spring yet, and Lairgnen found himself laughing with Gen as he valiantly tried to explain, in the best way that he could, how the vines needed to be pruned. And the best methods used to gain the largest yield of sweet, tasty grapes from mature plants. All the while, Gen struggled to use layman's terms. When Gen started talking about budding stages, the information completely went over Lairgnen's head. He begged to be spared, but he couldn't help feeling pleased.

It was apparent Gen's knowledge came from years of Frigga's training, but he didn't look as though he had been forced to know the facts. Gen was having too much fun, and Lairgnen found himself in serious trouble. Until he'd met Pedr the previous year, he'd never considered the subject of plants and agriculture interesting. He still didn't know anything about it. But now he knew two men who did. Was the Goddess trying to tell him something?

"All right, stop," Lairgnen said, waving a hand in front of him.

Gen clamped his mouth shut and looked away. Lairgnen couldn't help chuckling again at the comical expression the man was trying to hide. Poor Gen looked to be caught between frustration and hilarity.

Lairgnen had enough. He had to stop Gen from giving him more information than he could manage to remember.

"Forget my obvious ignorance. Just tell me what you think. Is the vineyard still viable?"

"Oh, it's more than that." Gen looked relieved to hear Lairgnen's question. "You're sitting on a treasure here. These are mature plants, yes, but there are also large tracts of healthy, young vines. The water sources are deep and clean. Plus, the soil is volcanic, which drains quite well. The more the tannin and minerals, the more the flavors intensify. With the right equipment, you're going to be producing a top tier wine that would be hard to compete with."

Lairgnen squinted, making the younger man chortle in obvious amusement. But his mind was already running a mile a minute, because Gen had just tapped into his favorite topic.

"You're saying all that's good for grapes?"

"Yes. Volcanic soil has more tannin and minerals than regular soil. The combination should give the grapes the most intense flavors, and the better the flavors, the better the wines. The rest is economics. Once you put the wines out there and people get a taste, they're going to be wanting for more."

"Now we're talking. That's just the kind of language I understand. Not tannins." Lairgnen shook his head and looked at the lush, green vines around him. He'll have to ask what tannins was again, but he'd do that later. He was already proving how unknowledgeable he was, and that wouldn't do at all. He was a prince, after all. He looked back at Gen to find him chuckling. "All right, you can stop laughing. You can tell me all about tannins later, and I promise to pay close attention even if I don't understand chemistry." Lairgnen breathed through his nose. Once he'd settled Gen's affairs, he was going to enjoy winemaking. "I guess it's time to check on the house."

Gen grasped on to his suggestion like a lifeline. "Yes, let's. The last time I was here was just before my mother died. I remember how beautiful the gardens had been."

They walked toward the manor in no hurry. Occasionally, Gen would stop to examine leaves or branches before moving on ahead. The breeze rose around them, and Lairgnen heard the soft, tinkling sounds. He stopped to listen, but when the breeze dropped, so did the sound. Something bright on the ground caught his attention, and he crouched down to examine it. It was but one of the hundreds of tiny yellow flowers blooming beneath the vines. Just as he was about to reach out to touch one, the breeze kicked back up. The flower heads shook, and the bell-like tinkling started up again.

"What are these lovely beauties?" Lairgnen asked. He'd never seen their like before and wondered if Pedr would know what they were. He'd been to Pedr's gardens enough times to know he'd never seen them there.

"They're pretty, aren't they? You should see them when they're in a field. Once I stepped into a meadow, and the air was filled with their symphony."

"It must have been incredible." Lairgnen studied the flower structure, noting the delicate petals that seemed too fragile to hold the stone-hard center that appeared to be dotted with micro holes on them. He frowned when he expected to hear the sound as he moved the flower head but heard nothing.

"Try blowing at its center," Gen said.

Lairgnen did as suggested and was delighted when he heard the whistling sound.

"The sound is created when air passes through the holes. People around here call them bell tulips, but they only appear during the spring season. They say that when the vineyards were first put into place, these grew alongside them. I think that somehow the tiny bulbs stowed away with the soil the seedlings were packed in during the Great Passage. I've checked, and I've not seen any of their kind on Kizerain, native or otherwise. They seem to be endemic to this area."

"They must be, for I've never seen their kind before outside of Merifael. I wonder if they're hybrids. I'll take some samples up to the capital and show them to Pedr." Putting his words to action, Lairgnen took hold of a bunch of bell tulips and pulled gently until they uprooted. After carefully checking that the roots were undamaged, he tore off some leaves from a broad-leafed weed and wrapped them around the roots. Satisfied the tulips would survive the trip back to the capital, he stood up and grinned.

Gen pointed at the bundle Lairgnen was holding. "You seem to know what you're doing. The king's Chosen was a gardener, right?"

"He still is. Pedr taught me how to transplant without killing the plant. I sometimes go to his gardens just to relax, but he's the type who doesn't like to see idle men around and puts me to work. It's a calming activity."

Lairgnen was still examining plants he'd picked when he heard Gen exclaim in the distance. Looking up, he saw Gen crouching on the ground. He appeared to be picking fruits off a low growing, jagged-edged wide-leafed plant. He stood up and walked over to where Lairgnen still stood. In his hand were tiny red fruits, which he offered up to Lairgnen.

"These are wild strawberries. I remember eating these when I was a child." Gen said, laughing when Lairgnen hesitated. "They're safe to eat."

"Are you sure?" Lairgnen looked at the tiny fruit skeptically. He'd never seen strawberries that small before.

"Yes, I'm sure. Go on, open your mouth," Gen said.

Lairgnen hesitated, but he did open his mouth. Gen popped one red berry into his mouth. The action sent tingles of desire down his spine, so he closed his mouth quickly and chewed on the berry. When the sweet, clean tartness burst in his mouth, he realized he'd never tasted anything so good or fresh before.

"Well, what do you think?" Gen grinned.

Lairgnen couldn't help but smile back. "I think these far surpass those served in the capital."

Gen crouched down and harvested more of the fruit, which he dropped into Lairgnen's palms.

"I've only ever been once to the capital," Gen said.

Lairgnen glanced at him and saw the pensive look on his face before it disappeared under a smile. It dawned on him that Gen had a penchant for smiling when he wanted to hide his true emotions.

"I remember now. You were at Yula last year."

Gen nodded as he wiped his hands together. "Yes. That was the first and only time I'd been there. Well, that which I can remember. I think my mother took me there right after I was born and maybe after, but I'm not sure."

"You'll have more chances to go," Lairgnen said, instantly regretting the words at the crestfallen expression on Gen's face. "I'm sorry, Gen. I shouldn't have said that."

"It's all right. There's no use of dreams when someone else will control my life."

"We don't know if that's going to happen."

"If you say so." Gen's shoulders drooped as he turned and moved ahead.

Lairgnen stared after him, angry at himself. He walked faster to catch up with Gen, who didn't speak again until they neared the manor house.

"If you should end up buying this land, I'd ask that you protect the spring tulips and wild berries. Also, if I remember correctly, there are blueberries and raspberries up ahead. Unfortunately, many here consider them weeds and would not hesitate to uproot them. I remember how Bolton's daughter loved them so much he ordered they weren't to be cleared for any reason. Even if it meant delaying the expansion of the vineyard."

"That's a promise I can easily give and mean to hold. I love berries and wouldn't dream of killing them." And Lairgnen meant it. For some reason, the thought of making Gen sad or disappointed didn't sit well in his mind.

The thankful smile that formed on Gen's lips made Lairgnen's heart jump.

"Thank you," Gen said in a soft voice.

They continued on to the manor in silence. Lairgnen stopped, momentarily stunned by the color explosion from hundreds of blooming flowers, plus the overwhelming fragrance of their combined scents in the air. He gaped at the wonder he was soon to own. Gen stepped into view beside him.

"Well, is it as you remember it to be?" Lairgnen said,

glancing at Gen.

Gen nodded as he looked around. "It is, only it's bigger. Shouldn't it be smaller? It's just as beautiful, too." Gen flashed him a smile. "You're going to love it here."

Something punched Lairgnen in the chest, and for a split second, the breath knocked out of his lungs. He didn't know how to process the weird feeling. After a moment, he breathed easier, but the ache lingered. He massaged his chest with one hand tipping his head toward the house.

"Come, let's get inside," Lairgnen said.

"I don't think you need me to inspect the place," Gen said as he walked beside him.

"True. Then again, you're quite observant, so you may see something I won't."

"I doubt that, but I'd love to go inside again. It's been a while."

The two of them were greeted by a servant who showed them in. To Lairgnen's relief, Uthman's inspectors were already there. The three men met him in the foyer and gave him their all clear. After thanking them, Lairgnen and Gen walked through the empty hallways. The manor might be structurally sound, but the previous owner's furnishing and paintings had all been removed. All that was left were the pale imprints left on the walls.

"I remember the paintings that used to hang these walls. They were beautiful. Pity they're all gone now," Gen murmured as he touched the walls.

"It's likely they've been sold off to cover for the debts. They can be replaced," Lairgnen said.

"I guess they were, but I would imagine not too easily. Those were works of a master artist, and there's only a few out there who could afford them," Gen said.

Lairgnen didn't respond as he stood looking up at the domed ceiling. Someone had once painted a mural there, but it was too faded, and he doubted it could be restored. Gen moved on ahead, looking thoughtful as he trailed his fingers along the blank walls. Lairgnen followed at a short distance, and when Gen turned a corner, Lairgnen lost sight of him. A strange impulse made him want to run after him. The need only increased until it became almost unbearable, and he could hardly see ahead of him. He shook his head, trying to clear the fog that had descended over him.

"Lair? Come out here, you need to see this," Gen called out excitedly.

Lairgnen followed the sound of Gen's voice, walking faster until he finally caught up with him in a large room. It appeared to be a spacious solarium, only it was more than a regular garden. What drew the eye was the glass-domed ceiling set upon towering walls of windows. It was so high Lairgnen's neck began to ache as he continued to look up.

"Look at this. This is incredible," Gen said, looking up at the ceiling with undisguised pleasure on his face.

Lairgnen stopped walking and looked around him. Gen was right. Whoever had designed and chosen the plants growing in it had managed to create an indoor oasis. There were fully mature trees with thick canopies stretching out and above, casting shadows everywhere. In front of him, Gen stood under the lush foliage of what appeared to be giant ferns. They were a species he recognized as having been native on the mother world, and its spores had survived their migration. The species had thrived on Kizerain and now grew everywhere.

Stunning as the discovery of the solarium was, it wasn't the greenery that truly caught Lairgnen's attention—and heartstrings. The unguarded look of pleasure and happiness on Gen's face outshone nature's wonder. The misery Lairgnen had gotten used to seeing on Gen all day was no longer there. He was breathtaking to look at. Shaken at his unexpected reactions to Gen, Lairgnen recognized this as a decisive moment for him.

He would do everything and anything to help Gen. How he was going to do it still evaded him, but nothing, no one, was going to stop him. Not even the king.

CHAPTER SEVEN

Gen turned to see if Lairgnen had joined him, only to freeze when he locked gazes with the older man. Lairgnen was looking at him intently, and Gen didn't know how to react. His cheeks burned, but neither could he think to look away. He didn't want to look away. He'd crushed on Lairgnen since he'd first seen him, and after spending a few hours with him, he thought his heart would break at the thought of never seeing him again.

Lairgnen shifted his gaze and moved toward a copse of miniature fruit trees. Suddenly feeling embarrassed, Gen turned away to check the entrance to see if someone else had joined them. Seeing there was no one there, he breathed a sigh of relief. He knew what he'd seen in Lairgnen's eyes. He hadn't made a mistake. And he definitely couldn't deny the sudden lust shooting down to his cock.

Gen shot another glance at Lairgnen only to see the prince had turned the other way and seemed to be closely examining the bark of one of the taller, mature trees. A trumpeting call made him look up and gasp out loud. Distinctive yellow and green bands on widespread wings identified a skyhawk hovering above, just beneath the dome. For a moment, he could only stare and wonder how it could have gotten inside. Then he noticed that several panes were missing.

The distraction gave him the chance to think about his reactions around Lairgnen. Discovering that he'd been crushing on the prince was something he hadn't wanted to complicate his life. Yet that look Lairgnen had given him made him rethink his position. Had he made a mistake and misinterpreted things? He probably had, because the thought of Lairgnen being attracted to him didn't make sense. In all likelihood, Lairgnen had someone special waiting for him in the capital.

Gen's heart plummeted at the thought, and bitterness swelled inside him. Why was it he was never going to get the chance to have a happy relationship with someone of his own choosing? Was the Goddess so spiteful that she had turned her back on him? Would he ever find happiness at all? He swiped at the swell of angry tears that pooled in his eyes.

"Hey, what's going on? Why are you crying?"

Gen jerked in surprise at the sound of Lairgnen's voice so close. He hadn't even heard the man's footsteps.

"It's nothing," Gen said, not turning around. He swiped his face with the palm of his hands before dragging them down his trousers. Pasting on a fake smile, he turned around to face Lairgnen. "Come on, you can check this room out when you have more time. I have to show you the other parts of the house. When I was here last, about two years ago, they had a kennel of sorts. The old lord was a collector of exotic animals."

Although he didn't say anything, Lairgnen's expression clearly showed he didn't believe him. To Gen's horror, a wayward tear fell down one cheek. Before he could wipe it dry, Lairgnen had already reached out and done it for him.

"You do realize," Lairgnen said in a low voice, "I can take you away from here any time, don't you?"

"I can't leave my sister with him," Gen whispered and shook his head. "I just can't risk it."

"What if I told you that I can make you and your sister disappear from Merifael? Your father wouldn't know where you went."

Gen thought over Lairgnen's tempting offer but then changed his mind.

"Thank you, and I know you're going to think I'm naïve, but I think the best way is to address this head-on. Also, I can't risk Laoghaire. She's got a gentle soul. If I run, she wouldn't understand, and I can't tell her the truth, either." Gen shook his head again. "I'm not making sense, am I?"

"No, you're not, but I know what you're trying to say," Lairgnen's tone was serious, but he was smiling.

Surprisingly, Gen didn't feel the weight of a reprimand. Then Lairgnen bumped his shoulder, and just like that, his world righted.

"Come on, let's tour the rest of the house," Lairgnen grabbed Gen's hand and pulled him out of the solarium. "I'm pretty sure this place has a lot more secrets to reveal."

Gen's mood lightened considerably as he followed Lairgnen back to the hallway. Together, they discovered more rooms. On the second floor, they found the master suites. Lairgnen was commenting on how he would have to hire workmen to slap fresh paint on the walls and fix leaking pipes when Gen spied on something that didn't look right. Lairgnen was still rambling on, but Gen ignored him. One part of the wall next to the armoire had a thin, vertical crack over it. Worried that the wall might be crumbling, he carefully ran his fingers over it only to realized it was deeper than he'd first imagined. However, when he leaned on the wall, he jumped in surprise when it moved under his hand. Using the tips of his fingers, he gave it a tentative push, and the panel opened further inward, revealing a dark space.

"Gen? Are you all right?" Lairgnen said from behind him.

Gen looked over his shoulder and gestured for Lairgnen. "I'm okay. I was just surprised. Take a look at this."

Lairgnen hurried to his side. "What is it?"

"Check it out. It looks like a door," Gen said.

"A secret door?" Lairgnen frowned as he bent to examine the space.

"Yes, but it's kind of too short and narrow," Gen said, dropping his hand down to his side.

"Interesting," Lairgnen said. He pressed his hands against the panel, and it gave way some more with a creak. Another push, and it opened all the way. The top of the opening only reached to his waist, but it was wide enough to enter.

They looked inside the small space and discovered a short, narrow passageway.

"Where do you think it leads to?" Gen said.

"Let's go inside and find out."

With Lairgnen leading the way, they crawled through the door. He stopped at the end of the short passageway. "I see a room, it's small, but I think we can both fit. Hold on."

Once Lairgnen had moved through the opening, Gen crawled over and took hold of his proffered hand. Once inside, he saw that although there was barely enough room for both of them side by side, the ceiling was high enough for them to stand without stooping. Gen's gaze followed to where Lairgnen pointed.

"Looks like another opening. Follow me," Lairgnen said.

They walked through another narrow passageway. They found another door at the end of it, which opened easily when Lairgnen twisted the knob.

"Oh, wow," Lairgnen said at the doorway.

"What is it?" Gen asked, craning his neck, but he couldn't see inside the room over Lairgnen's shoulders.

"Come and see for yourself."

Gen's curiosity grew tenfold as Lairgnen stepped further into the room. When he finally saw what had surprised Lairgnen, Gen's jaw dropped.

The inches-deep dust made everything look gray and old, but there was no mistaking that whoever had built this room had done it to keep its existence a secret. That meant the next generation of owners had never known about it.

Up against the four walls were floor-to-ceiling open shelves stacked with what appeared to be packages wrapped in brown paper. Three closed chests had more of the same packages placed on top of them, and the floor was littered with even more. Some looked like they had been carefully laid out, while others looked to have fallen on their sides.

"Is this a secret storeroom or something?" Gen asked. His nose itched from the dust. His fingers itched as well, but that was only because he was holding himself back from wanting to touch each item.

"Only one way to find out," Lairgnen said, moving to grab one of the packages nearest him.

Gen reached out and held him back. "Wait. Before you touch anything, have you signed any papers to officially buy this place yet?"

The look of surprise that flashed over Lairgnen's face was immediately replaced by a grin.

"Oh, I'd completely forgotten." Lairgnen looked back at the room with a wistful expression on his face.

Gen giggled. "You really want to find out what's in those packages, don't you?"

"Of course I'm curious. They may just be old documents. This manor is over five hundred years old and in prime condition in spite of it, and nothing in the papers I'd been shown mentioned this secret room. I'm dying to open them!"

Gen laughed out only to have it cut short by a sudden fit of coughing. It felt as though he'd swallowed a mouthful of dust. He smiled gratefully when Lairgnen lightly slapped his back. When his coughing subsided, he was still laughing.

"Let's get out of here," Lairgnen suggested.

Outside the manor, Lairgnen instructed one of his men waiting for them by the transporter to advise Uthman to meet him at his brother's house in an hour. Once they were settled inside the transport, Gen couldn't help feeling sad that he wouldn't find out what secrets that room kept.

"Let's go over to my brother Llewellyn's estate. I can introduce you to him."

Gen frowned. "Wait, you're not taking me home?"

"Oh, I only assumed . . ." Lairgnen smiled. "Of course, if you don't want to come, I can take you back. I just thought that with your father not being around, or your sister, you'd want to join us for dinner."

Gen couldn't stop grinning even if he wanted to. He'd honestly thought . . . He didn't know what he thought, but he nodded eagerly at the invitation. "Thank you, sir."

"I thought I told you to drop the sir?" Lairgnen's brow went up a notch.

"Thank you, Lairgnen."

"If you prefer, you can call me sir or whatever lordly title I hold whenever we're in public, but please, call me Lair when we're alone. You did so earlier."

Lairgnen's megawatt smile made Gen's heart take a tumble, and he couldn't help smiling back.

"Oh, and you're coming back with me here tomorrow," Lairgnen added. "We can hide and open those packages in private, and you can document the whole thing."

"What about my father's guest? What if he comes back?"

"Unless that guest is Anwyll, I don't think your father can stop me from insisting you help me out in my time of need." Lairgnen winked conspiratorially.

"And opening packages is a time in need?" Gen frowned.

"Opening secret and Goddess knows how old packages. There's a huge difference. In any case, I can always say I ordered you to assist me."

"I like the way you think, Lair." Gen smiled but quickly turned away to look outside the window when Lairgnen flashed his megawatt smile again. It made his insides melt like butter and was just as delicious and satisfying.

The Bolton property was older than Toullec's by a century. Not as large or as technologically precise as Toullec's, but it was just as beautiful. With the right manager, it could be just as productive. He was glad Lairgnen was going to be his neighbor — that way, he would have someone to talk to.

At least, he hoped whoever bid on him would be kind enough to allow him to visit with his cousins.

At the thought of the auction, whatever happiness he'd felt that afternoon faded. At least his cousins were on his side. Gen watched the speeding view below him, lost in thought. What if Martin succeeded? What would happen to Laoghaire then? Would he even get to see her again? Or be allowed to?

"We're almost at Llewellyn's place."

Lairgnen's voice brought Gen back to the present, and he pasted on a smile before turning back to face the front. He might lose his freedom soon, so he saw no reason why he shouldn't take advantage of Lairgnen's invitation. Also, Lairgnen had mentioned introducing him to Llewellyn. Who didn't want to know about the handsome Chosen Protector? He'd never actually spoken to him, so this was his chance to get to know the man. That was something he looked forward to as well.

CHAPTER EIGHT

"That was an interesting turn of events."

Lairgnen set his mouth into a grim line and forced himself to focus on pouring himself a drink and not on responding to his brother's statement. He'd always known Llewellyn was a perceptive man. Dangerously so.

"He's an intelligent kid," Llewellyn continued.

"He's not a kid." The moment the words left his lips, he knew he'd fallen into Llewellyn's trap and cursed under his breath.

"And that's the crux of it, isn't it, Lair?"

Lairgnen could feel Llewellyn's gaze on his back but chose to ignore it. He turned and walked toward a chair opposite where Llewellyn was sitting. Damn, his brother was too astute for his own good.

"I don't know what you mean," Lairgnen said as he took his seat, but he knew he was hopelessly failing in trying to sound noncommittal.

After dinner was over, Gen had begged off staying much longer. Lairgnen had fought his instinctive need to not let Gen go and had arranged for Gen to be flown back to his home. He understood that even with Martin away, Gen continued to fear his father's wrath. Lairgnen wished he had the power to take Gen away from the man. He didn't like the thought of Gen being afraid of what Martin's response would be simply because he'd been unable to refuse Lairgnen's request. Once he'd seen Gen off on his transporter with two of his personal warriors to keep him safe, he and Llewellyn had retired to the study.

Llewellyn let out a low whistle. "We came here to help him out, not romance him, brother."

"I wasn't romancing him." Lair shifted under what he knew was intense scrutiny, but he persisted in his determination not to meet Llewellyn's gaze. For his younger brother to rebuke him made him uncomfortable, but he hadn't been able to help himself with Gen. Goddess help him, he'd tried.

"You may not have been aware of it, but you were. He's just your type—the hair, the build, the brain. Guénaël's surprisingly intelligent and mature for his age. Oh, I know you, brother."

"So what if he's my type? What about it?" Lairgnen clenched his jaw belligerently and frowned at Llewellyn.

"The boy's already infatuated with you. It was quite obvious, even though he successfully hid it. You, on the other hand . . ." Llewellyn wagged a finger at him. "You were not quite as discreet."

"I was doing nothing of the sort." Lairgnen raised a brow and glared at his brother.

Llewellyn tilted his head and raised a skeptical brow. "From the way you're looking at me, I'd say you're acting defensive. Why is that, do you think? Maybe you're unaware of doing so, but you were definitely placing your claim on him, and he was letting you."

Lairgnen shot Llewellyn a withering glance, but that didn't deter his brother from speaking his mind, not that anything would stop Llewellyn from doing exactly that. He was like a *canes* with a bone.

"Look," Llewellyn continued in a tight voice. "What I'm saying is that Gen, for some unknown reason, is looking at you as his savior." He tilted his head to the side and narrowed an eye. "Did you kiss him?"

"Of course I didn't." Lairgnen swatted the air in front of

him. "Why are you asking all these questions?"

"Did you show him or promise him anything other than helping him out with his problem?" Llewellyn went on, obviously choosing to ignore Lairgnen's denials.

"No. I was frank and honest with him the entire time. I didn't show him anything other than kindness and understanding." When Lairgnen raised his glass, his hand trembled, and he immediately lowered it, hoping Llewellyn didn't see his reaction.

"And maybe that's all it took?" Llewellyn said in a kind voice.

Lairgnen looked up to see Llewellyn's gaze locked on his traitorous hand. He hastily took a drink and sent Llewellyn a challenging look.

Llewellyn shrugged it off. "Don't take me wrong, Lair, but the way I see it, Gen has already formed an attachment to you."

Maybe it was the way Llewellyn was speaking that had Lairgnen thinking he should no longer keep lying to himself. He took another sip from his drink, this time taking a bigger gulp for courage, only to grimace as the heat stuck to his throat.

"How could that have happened?" Lairgnen finally wheezed out after regaining his breath. To his relief, his brother didn't tease him.

"Because you were the one there?" Llewellyn shrugged, but his face betrayed his concern.

When Lairgnen didn't respond, Llewellyn pursed his lips and shook his head. He looked so much like their Uncle Fiacre at that moment that Lairgnen fought the urge to squirm.

"But you don't mind that, do you, Lair?" Llewellyn said in a soft voice.

Lairgnen flinched. "What do you mean?"

Llewellyn stared at him for a long time before drawing in

a harsh breath. "Goddess, Lair. What have you done? This is not just about Gen's behavior around you. You've gone and gotten yourself attached to him as well, haven't you?"

Lairgnen couldn't respond. He could only stare at the amber liquid in his glass and pray Llewellyn didn't see through him completely.

"Lair? Look at me."

Words failed Lairgnen, and he refused to look up. Fear gripped at him—fear of the unknown. He didn't know what was happening to him, but he couldn't acknowledge the truth, either, whatever that truth might be. He squeezed his eyes closed and dragged his hand over his face. He didn't know what was going on or why it affected him so profoundly.

Llewellyn let out an expletive. "You don't have to say anything. I saw how you acted toward him at dinner. I heard how you were speaking to him. Damn it, Lair. This is going to complicate things."

"How was I speaking or acting?" Lairgnen barely managed to get the words out. His throat felt tight, and his breathing labored.

"Lair." Llewellyn snapped. "You're not exactly known for your patience. Quite the opposite, in fact. And yet tonight, you were the epitome of it. Damn it, Lair. You even served him his stew."

Lairgnen couldn't deny that last part. He didn't understand it himself. All he knew was that once Gen sat beside him at dinner, something pushed him to make sure he only got the best servings. The need to take care of Gen had been impossible to ignore. He couldn't tell Llewellyn that he didn't want the servants to serve Gen. That it should only be he who had that privilege. Goddess, what was happening to him?

"I don't know what going on, Llew." Slowly, Lairgnen raised his gaze to meet his brother's. "I . . . it . . . I don't know how to describe it. There was just this . . . this . . . connection. I felt it the second I met him. No, I felt it before I set eyes on him. I couldn't see him, I'd never met him, but I felt him approach the front door. I could see him in my mind reaching out and opening that door. I tried not thinking about it, but it just got stronger and stronger the more we were together today."

Llewellyn sat up, and his gaze intensified. "Tell me more. What else were you feeling? Describe it to me."

"I . . ." Lair ran his fingers through his hair again. "It's powerful, and I . . . it was difficult to breathe. I'm thinking about him now, and it's making me anxious he's not here or that I can't see or feel him. I didn't know what was happening, but it felt like something was gripping my soul and drawing me to him. Pulling at me, like there was this string tied around me and I couldn't resist it. I can't even think of resisting it." Lairgnen shook his head. "I'm sorry, but that's the only way I can't explain how I feel."

Llewellyn fell against the back of his chair in a soft thump. He blinked slowly and chewed on the inside of his lip as he continued to stare thoughtfully. For a long moment, he simply sat there, tilting his head from side to side, his gaze never leaving Lairgnen.

"What are you thinking?" Lairgnen said when he could no longer stand his brother's silence and intent scrutiny.

Llewellyn turned away and carefully set his tumbler on the delicate table beside his chair. "How do you feel right now since he's no longer near you? Has it gotten better, or is the feeling worse?"

Lairgnen lowered his head, unable to stand Llewellyn's intense scrutiny. It felt as though his brother were trying to see something inside him that he wasn't ready to reveal even to himself.

Lairgnen shrugged. "Sad. Lonely. It was hard saying

goodbye, Llew. I'm missing him already. I want him by my side now. At all times."

"Are you aware that you've been rubbing your chest for some time now, Lair?"

Lairgnen blinked in surprise. "What?"

Llewellyn simply pointed. Lairgnen frowned and looked down, jerking in surprise when he saw that indeed he was absently massaging the ache away with the tips of his fingers.

Only then did he acknowledge the dull, incessant numbness at the center of his chest. "There's this ache, here," Lairgnen murmured, pointing at his chest. For the first time since he'd been a young boy, he felt like crying. He was missing Gen so hard, and once that thought entered his head, his eyes started filling with tears. "All I can think of right now is he's not here with me. I don't understand what's happening to me, Llew."

The last was a plea for help. Lairgnen felt so confused, and that never happened. That was just the way it was . . . until that moment.

"I'm beginning to think I do," Llewellyn said. He stood, picked up an ornate bell sitting on a carved console, and rang it twice.

Lairgnen stood on trembling legs. "What are you doing?"

Almost immediately, there came a knock followed by the door opening, and a man entered. It was one of the two warriors stationed outside the room.

"Your Highness?"

"Inform the staff to have our things readied. Tell the men my brother and I are leaving immediately for the capital. Call the Toullec residence and have them inform Prince Guénaël that Prince Lairgnen and I had been called back by the king. Advise them that we will be returning by the end of the week."

The warrior bowed his head and clicked his heels together

without saying a word. After he left the room, Lairgnen faced Llewellyn.

"What are you doing? Why are you doing this?"

"I need to take you out of here and back to the capital, Lair. Anwyll will need to talk to you, and so will Uncle Eljin and Uncle Fiacre."

"Why? I can't leave Gen here to face Martin on his own. He needs me here." The dull pain in his chest intensified. "You can't make me go. No." Lairgnen shook his head vigorously.

Llewellyn walked over and took hold of his shoulders. He shook him until he had no choice but to meet Llewellyn's gaze.

"Lair, listen to me. I can make you go, and you will come with me whether you want to or not. I cannot risk leaving you here alone with Gen. We cannot afford to complicate things even more for him. Think about Gen, Lair. If you stake your claim on him when there's still that auction taking place, you can ruin any chances of getting him from under Martin's control. Think about it. We need the king's support in this. We need Anwyll to make a stand."

An irrational sense of panic rose inside him. The thought of being unable to protect Gen almost made him gag. He felt sick to his stomach.

"No. You will not separate me from him, Llew. I won't allow it." Lairgnen didn't know where the words came from. He could hear them coming out of his mouth, but surely he wasn't speaking them. What was going on? The terror grew, and he began to tremble. His vision narrowed. Why was Llewellyn suddenly standing so very far away?

"Lair? Lair, listen to me. I just need to take you back to the capital. That's all. Once we get there, everything will be all right."

"No."

Lairgnen raised his hand to ward Llewellyn off. Not

looking where he was going, he took several steps backward. The back of his knees slammed against the edge of something hard, and his legs crumpled under him. All of a sudden, he found himself lying on the floor, blinking up at Llewellyn's concerned face.

"Lair." Llewellyn knelt on the floor and began running his hands over Lairgnen's arms and legs. "Did you hit your head? You fell pretty hard."

"What's wrong with me, Llew? Why am I feeling this way? Why am I panicking? I never panic."

"I'm not exactly sure, but I have my suspicions. And don't be scared. We'll get to the bottom of this. I promise. You're my big brother, and I'll never let anything bad happen to you. You must trust me."

"What are you talking about? Please. Tell me."

Llewellyn's face sobered. He sat back on his heels and let out a resigned breath. "I think what you're going through is similar to what Anwyll experienced when he found Pedr. I think you're experiencing a Heart Call."

CHAPTER NINE

The nightbird that lived in the powo tree had been singing for several minutes, but unlike other nights, its sweet song failed to lull Gen to sleep. The events of the day had confused him. He still didn't know how to interpret his feelings for Lairgnen or what he was going to do about the auction. But that wasn't what he was confused about. No.

Dinner with Lairgnen and his brother had been an incredible experience. The food had been simple fare, but it had all looked and tasted better than anything he'd ever had before. He'd sat beside Lairgnen while Llewellyn had sat opposite them. The best part of the night, though, was that Lairgnen had served him.

Even now, thinking about that, he didn't know why Lairgnen treated him as though he were a spouse or a betrothed. As though he had a right to it. To add more to his confusion, Gen hadn't objected. It never once occurred to him to deny the service, for everything Lairgnen had done had actually felt right.

Gen couldn't remember what they'd talked about. Well, mostly. He'd been too self-conscious with Lairgnen sitting so close that their thighs touched whenever he or Lairgnen moved so much as an inch. That had felt right as well. Lacking, but right all the same. Why was he feeling that way? It made no sense whatsoever.

The more he thought about the events of the day, the more he began to feel uneasy and uncertain about his future. Once the transporter dropped him at his doorstep, he'd gone straight to his bedroom, ignoring all the servants along the way. It was late, and they were still up. If that didn't clue him in that they were watching his every move and reporting to his father, he would be stupid.

Gen didn't trust any of the servants, not since he'd learned the hard way that they held no form of loyalty to him or his sister. The Toullec retainers had all been fired and replaced by the present ones the day after the cremation ceremony. None of them had any form of connection to their family.

Martin was his father, but he was not of the aristocracy. He was a *pleb*, and therefore could not be granted a title other than what he was, a priest. Gen, through Frigga, was of royal blood, and had been raised and educated for that role. At Martin's insistence, Laoghaire bore the name of Leafbow, and although of royal blood, could not be given the title of princess or inherit any property belonging to the Toullecs. Once, long ago, he'd learned from his mother that Martin had wanted Frigga to carry his name, but her father, Prince Maik, had put a stop to that. On the prince's death, Gen had been named heir after Frigga.

Gen began to tremble. He was so afraid and worried about what was wrong with his father, and it frightened him so much he felt powerless.

Would his family's legacy end with him? Would Martin destroy whatever was left of the Toullec branch of the royal family? With Lairgnen and Llewellyn there to help him out, he hoped they could stop whatever Martin was planning to do. Not just about the auction, but possibly his time spent with Laoghaire as well. Thinking about his sister increased his worry, since he didn't know where Martin had taken her.

A sudden tugging at his heart turned his fear into desperation. The Pull became stronger and stronger, gaining strength as each second passed until his heart started to physically hurt. It was almost like he'd lost something with no hope of ever getting it back. He massaged his chest, gasping at the agony of inexplicable feelings of separation. The pain continued to deepen until something broke inside him, filling him with misery and despair. Unable to comprehend what was happening to him, he screamed in distress.

Lost in the pain of loss and separation, he barely noticed the door to his bedroom slam open. He tried to fight off the arms that closed around him, but whoever held him proved to be stronger than him. Blinded by tears, he helplessly sobbed into the thin chest his face was pressed upon. A gentle crooning registered in his ears, and soon, he began to feel oddly comforted. He held on to whoever it was holding him, gripping at the wrists. The tears flowed freely for a long time but eventually subsided.

When Gen finally gained enough composure to lean back and see who was holding him, he was surprised that it was Horst. The old butler gazed at him with gentle cloudy blue eyes.

"Are you all right now, young sir?" Horst said, palming the back of Gen's head.

Still unable to find his voice, Gen could only nod.

"Did you have a nightmare?"

"No," Gen said, shaking his head.

"Did you hurt yourself?"

Once more, Gen shook his head. "No, it wasn't anything like that."

"Can you tell me what it was, then? I have never been more frightened in my life. I thought you'd hurt yourself, or someone did."

"I can't understand what it was I was feeling." Gen purposely kept his response vague. There was no reason to trust Horst, even if he was the one who had come in his time of need.

"Can you describe it?"

Gen sniffled as he explained what he could. "The last time I felt like that was when Mother died, but this was worse. Way worse."

Horst pursed his lips and patted Gen's hand. "Well, no one has died, thank the Goddess."

"That's good." Gen turned away. It felt good getting comforted and talking to Horst, but he didn't understand why the man had come.

His expression must have hinted his thoughts, for Horst stood up easily before straightening his back and bowing his head respectfully.

"If there's nothing else I can do for you, young sir, I think I will go back to my room now and get some sleep." Horst turned and moved to exit the room.

Gen stopped him. "Why did you come, Horst?"

Horst turned to face him. "I will always come, young sir. Always. All you need do is call for me." A gentle smile formed on his thin lips.

Gen suddenly realized what he had been missing. Gone was the stooped, shuffling old man he had gotten used to over the years, only to be replaced by a tall, lean man whose easy gait betrayed his health and apparent strength.

"If that will be all?" Horst turned to leave.

But Gen stopped him again. "You've been deceiving us all this time, haven't you, Horst?"

The small smile that curled on Horst's lips broadened to a grin. It transformed his face to that of someone younger than he'd let on previously. He tilted his head to the side before giving Gen another small bow.

"All the better to see and hear things, young sir. Good night." With a final bow, Horst left the room, quietly closing the door behind him.

Gen stared at the closed door, realizing Horst had been his mother's butler. The man had visibly aged after her death, but apparently, that had been a ruse. Glad to discover he had at least one loyal ally by his side, he stood from the bed and walked toward the door.

Slowly, so as not to make any noise, he opened it and peered out. Horst was walking away briskly from his line of sight, his movements sure and alert. Gen stared after him for a long moment before finally closing the door.

He sank into the bed once more and stared up at the ceiling. The pain he'd felt earlier had completely disappeared. There was, however, a lingering ache. He didn't know how else to explain it.

And what was that with Horst?

The day had turned out to be truly confusing, and the rush of conflicting emotions didn't help him any. In fact, he was utterly exhausted. His lids began to droop. Outside, the bird started singing again, but unlike earlier, he felt the bird's lullaby take effect. He sank deeper into the bed and wearily pulled the blankets over his chin, allowing sleep to overtake him.

His last thought just before everything went dark was an image of Lairgnen's face. Only it wasn't Lairgnen smiling. In fact, he looked to be in pain, with tears in his eyes. The vision made Gen's heart ache, and he wished he could comfort his prince.

We'll be all right, Lair. Everything will be all right once we're together again.

CHAPTER TEN

"**W**ell. This complicates things, doesn't it?"

Lairgnen braved Anwyll's wrath by glaring at Pedr, but the only response he received was amused smiles from both royals. Biting back a retort, he shifted in his seat and studied the dark amber at the bottom of his glass. He was really getting tired of that particular proclamation.

He and Llewellyn had reached the capital in the early hours of the morning. The trip from Merifael had taken them over two hours, and as soon as they'd reached their rooms, they'd immediately asked for a meeting with Anwyll. Unfortunately, they'd had to wait until after the midday meal of the following day, as Anwyll could not get out of a previous appointment.

It was now the middle of the afternoon. Llewellyn had wasted no time explaining the situation, after which Anwyll had called for his father, Eljin, and their uncle, Fiacre, to join them. It took another half an hour of waiting until the two men arrived, and Llewellyn had to narrate the story all over again. Before Llewellyn could finish his tale, however, Eljin raised his hand.

"It's the Call. There's no doubt about it," Eljin said and peered at Lairgnen. "This complicates things, doesn't it?"

There it was again, but Lairgnen resisted rolling his eyes. "Yes. So I've been told." He kept his tone as respectful as possible.

His Uncle Eljin was, after all, the former king of Kizerain, and Lairgnen couldn't risk hurting him, even with words. It was not just because of his deep respect for the man. He also truly loved him as an uncle. He and Fiacre had been fathers to both him and Llewellyn when they'd lost their parents at a young age.

Eljin had been a brave king, continuing to rule Kizerain without his Chosen there to balance out his magical powers. Lairgnen had no idea how Eljin had stayed sane, but he'd managed to remain strong until Anwyll's time had come.

The time since his abdication had been good for Eljin. He no longer bore the golden mantle of power, so his eyes and hair had reverted to the more normal non-magical colors of blue and white. The stress and wear on his face had faded to relaxation, but the wrinkles remained deep. It was now months after stepping down, and Eljin had recovered enough of his energy, even gained some weight, and looked healthy, happy, and peaceful, at last.

"I'm not surprised why this is happening to you, Lair. But I'm curious as to why you are?" Eljin asked.

Lairgnen squirmed under Eljin's penetrating gaze. The man might have been weakened from losing his Chosen, but he'd never lost his astuteness. With or without his crown, Eljin was, and would always be, a king. So yes, Lairgnen was scared of his uncle.

"I never thought it would happen to me."

"And why is that?" Uncle Fiacre spoke up. "You're a direct descendant of magical kings. We all are." He looked at all present and shrugged.

"I think what Lair's having a problem with is that Gen is young. Like, really young," Llewellyn said in a hushed tone.

Lairgnen's head snapped up. "He is not a child. He's of legal age and will reach maturity in less than two weeks."

Llewellyn threw back his head and howled out in laughter. To Lairgnen's embarrassment, the others laughed along with him. He felt his cheeks burning, and that only made Llewellyn laugh even harder. Horrified, Lairgnen bent his head to hide his face. After the laughter subsided, it was Uncle Eljin who spoke up.

"Above all, the Call cannot and should not be ignored. As it takes precedence, I think you have the answer on how to stop this blasted auction."

Lairgnen sat up at that bit of information. "Are you saying that if I claim Gen as my Chosen, Martin can no longer hold the auction?"

"Of course." Fiacre shrugged as if he thought everyone knew what he did. "As a priest, Martin should know when not to cross the Goddess and her plans. For members of the royal family, the Call for a Chosen is not only a gift from her, but it is also her will. There is always a reason why people are meant to be together. No one can fake a Call without facing the wrath of the Goddess."

"Or the sprite will get you," Llewellyn warned.

"Yes, they will." Anwyll nodded, and everyone fell silent.

Sprite were the Goddess' little warriors, after all. They not only assisted the kings on all things spiritual and magical, but they were also their closest allies. They had been the only magical creatures who had placed themselves between their ancestors and the invaders that had driven their people across dimensions. Despite many of their members perishing, they remained loyal.

One thousand years before, during the Great Passage, the sprite, along with their loyal guardsmen, the giants, had sacrificed their lives to assure the success of their task. The giants made sure no invaders came through their axes and shields as the sprite used the last of their magical energy and life force to open the interdimensional portal to Kizerain, an alien world they all now considered home. With the Goddess' blessing, the handful of sprite and the strongest of the giants who had survived the tasks they'd sworn to do joined the journey. So yes, sprite were known to show their displeasure on those who faked the Call, and giants were loyal to the sprite.

"How do we do this?" Lairgnen said, looking at the men around him.

"Anwyll declares Gen as your Chosen. That's it." Fiacre said. "Even Eljin could do it."

"I can and I will. I don't think Martin would be unwise enough to go against us. Or the Goddess, for that matter. It would be foolish of him," Eljin said, looking like he was enjoying himself.

"None of us really know Martin." Lairgnen twisted his mouth. "I have to admit that I never liked the man, so I'd always avoided him whenever we were in the same area."

"And maybe that's where our fault lies," Anwyll said thoughtfully. "I, too, never liked him. Frigga once said to me that we never really gave him a chance. What if we'd given him a chance and truly embraced him?"

"If we had, he'd have used us all," Fiacre grumbled as he shifted in his chair. "Among us here, I think I was the only one who attempted to accept the priest. I remember one time he came to my home and lorded it over the servants. I'd never spoken ill to any of them, or mistreated them. So when I heard how condescending he'd behaved around them, I asked Frigga to intercede. I tell you, it was the most uncomfortable two days I ever spent at home. Goddess, I found myself apologizing to the servants. It's a good thing they understood, but that was the last time Frigga brought him over. Poor girl, I'd never seen her so embarrassed."

"I don't understand what she ever saw in him. He's so different from those Frigga used to go out with," Llewellyn said.

"That may have been the draw," Pedr said. "Opposites attract. At least, that's what I've heard some people say."

"I wonder what it was that made Frigga see through him?"

Lairgnen wondered.

Fiacre cleared his throat, drawing Lairgnen attention. "Frigga came to me, not two months before her accident. She told me that she intended to divorce Martin."

"Did she say why?" Anwyll asked.

"No." Fiacre shook his head. "I tried to find out, but she wouldn't have it. She was adamant I not learn why. Said she would talk only to Eljin, for he was the only one who had the power to dissolve her marriage. But she did make me promise her something, and now that I'm thinking about it . . ." Fiacre met Lairgnen's gaze. "She told me that we should protect her children should anything happen to her."

"She actually said those words?" Lairgnen leaned his forearms on his knees to gaze directly at Fiacre. "She said *we*. Meaning us?"

Fiacre's eyes widened. "Yes," he said, nodding as though he'd had a sudden epiphany. "She said *we*. Not *I*, or Anwyll or Eljin. Goddess, I remember it clearly now. She said *we*. Goddess, why didn't I realize this sooner?"

"Did she write anything and send it to you? Or to any of us?"

"No." Fiacre stabbed a finger at Lairgnen. "As soon as I heard Guénaël had sent that letter, I directed my staff to search for anything that might have come from Frigga."

Llewellyn stood and started pacing. After a moment, he stopped and leaned on the console set against the wall. He frowned down into his drink. "Uncle, how did Frigga die?"

Fiacre swallowed his drink before he answered. "She was on her way here, actually. She'd sent me a message saying she had something important to tell me. An hour later, I heard that her transport had some kind of malfunction and crashed on the side of a mountain, not but a few miles from here."

Everyone started speaking at once, throwing out theories and possibilities. Lairgnen stayed silent. He was getting impatient, and maybe all this talk about Frigga's death had everything to do with Gen, but it did nothing to help the situation. Time was running out, and his gut told him that if they didn't act soon, Martin would make his move, and then there would be nothing anyone could do. His frown deepened, and he clenched his fingers around the glass he was holding.

He was missing Gen so much, and he feared that the longer he was away, the more Martin would take advantage of their absence. His stomach cramped, and he clenched his fists. His fears were growing by the minute.

"Lair? You seem anxious," Eljin said in a gentle tone. "What is it?"

The conversation died down, and everyone's gazes were trained on him. How could he explain what he was feeling or thinking?

"One of the things I missed most about not having Cressida by my side was our connection with each other," Eljin said. "She didn't need to be physically present, she only needed to be somewhere, and I knew she was all right. As she lay dying, I felt our connection fade, and it was the most terrifying thing I ever experienced. When she died, our connection held only for an instant before it was finally totally gone. I will forever mourn my Chosen. She was my other half. My soul. Such is the way of the Call."

Lairgnen raised his eyes and met Eljin's.

"If you're sensing Gen right now, focus on that feeling and try to touch it with your soul," Eljin said.

"How?" Lairgnen's voice broke.

"Focus on the feeling," Eljin instructed. "Find it. Use your senses. Reach out to him. Focus."

Lairgnen closed his eyes and tried to do what Eljin suggested.

"Think of Gen," Eljin whispered.

Sweat beaded on his temples as he struggled to find the

cause of the pull. To his surprise, he felt a spark grow inside him and turned toward the source. An invisible string pulled on him, and he followed where it led. Suddenly, he could see Gen standing in front of him. He wasn't doing anything, just standing there, staring at him. No. Not at Lairgnen. At himself. He was standing in front of a mirror staring at his reflection, his shirt only half-buttoned.

Lairgnen watched Gen shiver as though he were cold. He was dressed in what appeared to be simple traveling clothes. There was something off with the style of clothing. At first, Lairgnen could not put his finger on it, but as he continued to study the simple embroidery, he realized they were not for travel. They were clothes of a *pleb*, not the royal garb that Gen should wear.

Gen raised his hands to finish buttoning his shirt, and Lairgnen noticed how his fingers trembled. Gen sniffled, and that was when Lairgnen saw the tears falling freely. He shifted his attention to the window behind Gen and saw that the day was losing its brightness outside.

Lairgnen's eyes snapped open and met Eljin's gaze.

"We've underestimated Martin. The *ius auction*. It's happening today."

CHAPTER ELEVEN

Gen couldn't stop shivering. His bedroom wasn't cold. In fact, it was quite warm. He'd tried adjusting the temperature earlier, but no matter what he did, he still felt cold.

Not a day had passed since he'd spent time with the prince, and already his situation had turned dire. Martin had arrived before dawn, while Gen had still been sleeping. When he had walked into the breakfast room, Martin was halfway through with his meal. He felt the impact of how Martin had looked at him and coldly announce that the auction was to be that evening.

Gen had tried to remain calm and even managed to finish his breakfast without once choking. However, once Martin left the breakfast room, he'd tried calling Prince Llewellyn's manor, only to be told that he and Lairgnen had left the night before. Gen had left a message with the butler to have Lairgnen call him back but had yet to hear from him. The hope he'd nourished, that somehow Lairgnen would find a way to help him, had gradually turned to resignation as the day went on. He'd tried calling his friends, but not one of them had returned his call. He was all alone, and time was fast running out.

His dread grew as evening approached. He was going to lose not only his name and position but also his mother's name and family's legacy. He still didn't know what Martin's intentions were, but he knew it was not for the love of the family name.

Gen glanced at the mirror to his right. His reflection was

evidence of how miserable he felt. He wore the clothes his father claimed he'd had made for him — a pair of cream-colored linen bracaes topped with a simply designed linen shirt. His father explained the lack of embroidery around the collar and hem as another sacrifice, though Gen could not see how.

He felt trapped in a world that no longer made any sense. Gen clenched his eyes shut until they began to throb from the pressure. He wanted to shout out his misery, but where would that get him? Waves of horror and panic swept through him. Gen drew in a harsh breath and started shaking uncontrollably as the world around him whirled.

How was he to escape this scandal? This embarrassment?

Martin had declared it had been Gen's actions that had caused all of this, but Gen knew it had been his father's call for an *ius auction* that had caused a bigger disgrace.

The door opened, and Martin walked in. Bitter bile rose in Gen's throat at the excitement on his father's face when he motioned for Gen to follow him. Gen stayed silent as they walked toward the ballroom, where the auction was going to be held.

"The guests have arrived. Get a hold of yourself, Guénaël. You're going to ruin your chance of a good bidder." Martin grabbed his hand and pulled him along the corridor. "Try to remember we are doing this to save our family name. And for the Goddess' sake, smile. You don't want to cause more ruin to our name."

Name. Name. Was that all Martin cared about? It wasn't even his name. Was he thinking of adopting it? He had been requested to do so, but had refused on the day of his marriage to Frigga. Was his father that much of a hypocrite?

Despite his tumbling thoughts and feelings, Gen remained quiet. What was the use? His father would only tell him to shut up, and he would still be bought by the highest bidder. What would happen to Laoghaire? Gen still didn't know where Martin had sent her. She probably didn't know what was going on.

They stopped in front of the closed doors of the ballroom, and there was no mistaking the sounds of excited voices on the other side. The heavy wooden doors were not thick enough to muffle the sounds. Gen didn't know who his father had invited to bid for him, but from the raucous laughter and discernible lewd words, it didn't sound as though they were genteel folk. His throat tightened, and his breathing turned erratic as he grew more and more confused.

Was Lairgnen going to be there? He hoped not. He didn't want him to witness his downfall. The tears threatened to fall again, but he swallowed them away. He would meet his bidders eye-to-eye and not look away. The feeling of impending doom increased, but like his tears, he swallowed that away, too.

"Stay here," Martin said. "I will introduce you to our guests, explain to them once more the reason behind this auction, and then call for you. That's when you come in. You will enter at that moment."

Why wouldn't the bidders already know why he was being auctioned off? Nothing made sense, but Gen gritted his teeth and gave a brief nod. Martin gave him one last warning glare before opening the door and stepping inside. At once, the voices inside lowered to a hush until there was silence.

Gen could still hear his father's voice despite being on the other side of the closed door. The more Martin spoke, the more horrified Gen became. He cringed at how Martin narrated the scandal, much of which he embellished, making it sound more immoral than it actually was. Embarrassment turned to a simmering rage when Martin made much of how his dead wife would have turned over in her grave had she lived to see what her son had done. Martin seemed to emphasize that Gen was Frigga's son, not his.

All of a sudden, Gen didn't want to go through with the auction. His father's call for a sacrifice be damned. Gen was a Toullec, a royal blood. He was a cousin to the king, albeit a far off one, but still, he was a status higher than his father. But before he could turn and make a run for it, the doors flung open, and he gasped in horror at the people staring at him.

He stood frozen in the doorway when everyone began to murmur amongst themselves. His vision blurred, making it impossible for him to recognize anyone. One thing was apparent, none of the men and women who were in attendance were noble or royal. It was a direct violation of the requirements for an *ius auction.*

Suddenly, a voice rose from the back of the crowd. "A hundred gold pieces!"

"Two hundred!"

"Three hundred fifty!"

Gen stood rooted to the floor, his mouth agape as the bids were called out. He didn't know whether to feel even more insulted at how low the bids were or appalled when he caught sight and recognized one or two of the bidders.

None of those standing in front of him were from the *equites* or even an *eques* family. They were all *pleb*s, commoners, and not even middle class. He recognized the owner of a bar in a disreputable part of town Maccus had taken him to the year before. Another was a waiter in a tea house. What was going on? If Martin was thinking of salvaging his mother's family's name, this was not the way to go about it. Gen turned when his father let out a curse.

Martin marched out of the ballroom, grabbed him by his wrist, and pulled him inside. Gen stumbled over his feet but found his balance and defiantly faced the crowd.

"Come now, sirs and madams! Surely my son is worth more than three hundred fifty gold pieces? Do I hear a thousand?"

Aghast, Gen turned slowly to look at his father. In that instant, he realized Martin had never loved him. It confirmed what he had figured out three days past that his father was using him to gain money and solid control of his mother's property and name. He was a shameless man who used his position as a priest for his own gain.

To Gen's disgust, a woman who looked to be in her forties approached him and began palming his chest, checking out his muscles, even going so far as to squeeze on his pecs. He took a step back, but then an old man pushed the woman aside and began feeling him up as well. When one of the hands reached down the waistband of his bracae, Gen shoved their hands away, which only made the woman cackle. The rest of the bidders began to laugh crudely as well.

"One thousand gold pieces." said another voice directly behind him.

Gen jerked around. He hadn't felt or heard the man approach. Bile rose in his throat when recognition hit him. It was none other than Devos Cricirus, the same man his father had scorned for his unethical business practices. Gen turned to run, but his father reached out and grabbed him by his upper arm.

The woman yelled at Cricirus. "He's mine." She turned to Martin and made another bid. "One thousand five hundred gold pieces!"

Cricirus threw back his head and laughed. "A mere pittance? Two thousand."

Another voice rose in the crowd. "Three thousand."

The woman turned and pointed at the third voice. "You pig. You're so hungry for young flesh. I tell you he's mine."

Gen's panic grew as the man and woman continued to yell at each other. He took another step backward to remove himself, but Martin tightened his grip on his arm.

"Don't even think of running away," Martin said in a low

growl. "You embarrass me further than you already have, and mark my words, I will sell you to the lowest bidder."

Tears freely rolled down Gen's cheeks. All his will lost to the shock that his own father would treat him this way. That Martin would stoop so low and willingly place ruin upon Gen's reputation. All for the sake of gaining money and property. He thanked the Goddess that Laoghaire was away, spared from the humiliation of witnessing him being auctioned.

Something tugged at his heart, and hope broke through his despair. The invisible lifeline blurred his vision, but he looked around, searching wildly for the source. He turned left to right, scanning over the crowd. A voice called out from somewhere in the back of the ballroom — a voice he'd come to think of as his savior.

And he found his voice. "Lair!"

CHAPTER TWELVE

Lairgnen had never been so furious in his life. Even he was surprised at the depths of his feelings, for he had never felt like this. Ever.

His heart nearly broke in half when he caught sight of Gen's tears, and it almost brought him to his knees. It was clear to him that Gen was in a state of panic, and he couldn't fault him. He had arrived just in time to see a man and a woman go up and grope Gen like he was an animal being bought for sport or cattle. At that moment, he felt he was capable of killing someone. He hadn't realized he'd pulled out his pulse shooter until a grip on his arm held him back.

"Control your temper, Lair. You'll only cause more embarrassment for Guénaël if you make a scene," Llewellyn whispered harshly in his ear.

Llewellyn's voice was too low to be heard by anyone else, but Lairgnen heard him clearly, and at that moment, he hated his brother.

"It's Gen. His name's Gen," Lairgnen said through gritted teeth, but he stayed where he was.

"I said, calm down, Lair. You need to calm down for Gen. Remember, he can feel your emotions." Llewellyn's grip on his arm tightened.

The words registered, and Lairgnen started to nod, but then Gen called out from across the room.

"Lair!"

Waves of desperation and need swept over Lairgnen, and something alien surged up within him. It knew no logic. He moved, driven to run and protect Gen from the predators in the room. Llewellyn's tight grip remained on his arm, and he stepped in front of him, using his much taller and heavier body to prevent him from moving.

As Llewellyn had reminded him, Lairgnen now knew Gen could feel him, yet at that moment, his only thought was that he must get Gen away from these people, from being shackled to one of these sadistic, opportunistic predators in the room. He needed to keep Gen safe from their questionable intentions. With Llewellyn holding him back, Lairgnen did the next best thing. It surprised even him. He opened his mouth and made a bid.

"One million pieces of gold!"

A collective intake of breath and a sudden hush descended over the room as curious faces looked over their shoulders. As there were only the two of them standing at the back, shocked gazes settled on Lairgnen and Llewellyn.

"Sold!" Martin shouted the word and followed it with a loud guffaw, sounding excited at the amount of money bid.

It was the last straw. Lairgnen didn't care if he was going to cause a scene. He jerked away from Llewellyn's hold and managed to side-step him, then shouldered his way through the pack of gawking bidders. At first, no one moved to give him room, but Lairgnen pushed his way through. When he was blocked again, he lost patience and drew his stunner. The reaction was immediate, and the people stepped out of the way. They were still moving too slowly for Lairgnen's patience, but a few more steps brought him to Gen, with Martin standing in front of him. The man and woman who had felt Gen up had stopped yelling at each other and turned in his direction.

Lairgnen holstered his stunner as his gaze locked in on Gen, who stood unmoving, blinking rapidly and gaping at him in obvious shock. His heart broke when Gen started to visibly tremble, his face wet with the free fall of tears. Lairgnen ground his teeth, and his hands clenched into tight fists.

He tore his gaze from Gen and focused on Martin as he continued, moving forward, completely ignoring the crowd. Somewhere from behind, he heard Llewellyn's clear voice letting out a curse, but he didn't even turn to see if Anwyll, Pedr, or their warriors had made an appearance. He didn't pay attention to anything except what was in front of him. He was too angry and determined to punish those who had dared to hurt his Gen.

Martin stepped in front of him, as though to bar him from reaching Gen.

Lairgnen rested his hand on the hilt of his weapon once more . . . just in case. "I believe I've won the bid," he growled through clenched teeth.

"I . . . I didn't know you were going to be in attendance, Your Highness," Martin said, paling under Lairgnen's glare.

"You must have missed sending us an invitation, my dear Martin," Anwyll voice came from behind.

Martin jerked as though struck by lightning. He blanched when he looked over Lairgnen's shoulder. The murmurs had quieted, and a feeling of expectation hung heavily over the room.

Footsteps neared, and Lairgnen stepped to the side to give way to his king, but his gaze never left Martin. Beside Anwyll, Pedr stood glaring at Martin as well. Llewellyn stepped out from behind Martin, the sound of a sword leaving its scabbard hissing menacingly. Martin gulped, obviously taken aback at the august presence of the men before him. He had probably never been in the attendance of such royal personages in his life. Lairgnen smiled spitefully.

"Lair?" a soft voice called from behind Lairgnen.

Lairgnen tore his gaze away from Martin and glanced over his shoulder, spotting Gen. His anger melted away, immediately replaced by an overwhelming need to hold and protect Gen. He didn't even think. He opened his arms and pulled Gen into his embrace. A trembling Gen slammed himself into Lairgnen's chest and began to sob.

"It's all right, Gen, it's all right. I'm here, now," Lairgnen murmured into Gen's hair.

Gen cried into Lairgnen's shirt, repeating his name over and over again. Lairgnen took several steps backward while pulling Gen closer. His back hit something solid, and he realized he'd backed against a set of heavy doors. He stayed there, murmuring comforting words, rubbing his hand on Gen's back until the crying subsided. Gen continued to tremble, which was most likely from shock, but he seemed to be calming.

Lairgnen looked up and searched for Llewellyn, who met his gaze wide-eyed. Around them, the crowd began to murmur amongst themselves once again. Someone protested that their presence was unfair.

"We need to take Gen out of here. Now," Lairgnen said to Llewellyn in a tight voice.

Before Llewellyn could respond, Anwyll spoke up.

"I agree with Prince Lairgnen." Anwyll turned to Llewellyn. "Prince Llewellyn, I think it best we take the Chosen Finance Minister and his betrothed, Prince Guénaël of Toullec, back to your estate. As for the priest Martin Leafbow, I expect his presence in the capital three months from now, and not before. Not later, either."

Llewellyn bowed his head respectfully to Anwyll, who continued to stare at Martin. For those familiar with the king, like Lairgnen was, his polite expression was, in fact, a look of distaste. Anwyll was gifted that way, and it was a gift that made Lairgnen proud of his king.

"Come, my Chosen. It's time for us to leave." Anwyll was not just speaking to Pedr. He included both Llewellyn and

Lairgnen as well. Anwyll raised his arm waited until Pedr placed his hand on it before giving Lairgnen a brief nod.

Lairgnen acknowledged Anwyll with a nod of his own and didn't waste any time tucking Gen closer to his side. Anwyll and Pedr led the way, and with no one moving to block their path, they walked through the crowd. With twelve warriors dressed in royal regalia standing off to the sides, none of Martin's guests dared prevent their leaving.

But then Anwyll stopped. Lairgnen stopped as well, wondering what was going on.

Anwyll started to slowly gaze at the crowd around him, his expression inscrutable. He raised a brow and lifted his chin a notch before he took one step to the side. Pedr's countenance turned grim, and he lowered his arm to his side. A humming sound began, one Lairgnen was quite familiar with, for it always heralded magic. Anwyll's form started to glow with a soft, golden light, turning brighter and brighter until, one by one, the guests bowed their heads. Even Lairgnen lowered his head. Gen gasped and did the same thing.

"But what about my payment?" Martin asked, his voice sounding loud in the now silent room.

Lairgnen's head snapped up just in time for him to see Anwyll whirl around and point a finger toward Martin. No one dared move, not even Lairgnen. He'd never witnessed the wrath of a king before, but he was ready to see it firsthand. Especially as that king was Anwyll, a man who never showed anger. Lairgnen was annoyed enough to wish Martin obliterated in front of witnesses. To his frustration, Llewellyn stepped between Anwyll and Martin.

"It would be best, priest, if you awaited your king's decision." Llewellyn snarled the words. "As for now, the sacrifice has been made. The auction was a success. Your son is now under the protection of Prince Lairgnen, the king's Chosen Counselor, which means the crown's as well. Good day."

Martin clenched his jaw and bowed his head, but he didn't say anything.

"Kneel, and apologize to your king!" Llewellyn didn't rein in his anger.

Martin's jaw worked. Silently, he bent a knee, yet Anwyll didn't lower his arm. The silence stretched until it became unbearable.

"Do I need to make your mouth work for you, priest?" Llewellyn leaned forward, hissing in Martin's face.

"I ask that the Goddess forgive my trespasses upon you, my king," Martin intoned. "May she continue to bless you and your family."

"My family, priest?" Anwyll's voice dripped with scorn.

Lairgnen closed his eyes. He couldn't believe Martin had botched up even the simplest of blessings.

Probably realizing his mistake, Martin knelt on both his knees and placed his hands together in prayer.

"I'm sorry, I'm sorry. May she continue to bless you and the people of Kizerain." Martin's words came out in a rush, but they were still understandable.

Anwyll walked toward Martin, his finger still pointed at the man. "You have disappointed me, Martin Leafbow, in more ways than you can imagine. Not only that, but you have also insulted my people. As punishment, I will see you in six months, not before, not after."

Anwyll looked up and faced the crowd, who now wore expressions of terror. Some were openly weeping, while others were shaking where they knelt. They were witnessing the king's justice firsthand, and even Lairgnen had to admit he was terrified. But Anwyll was not done. He began to walk amongst the crowd of witnesses, his magical light bright and golden. The hum of magic continued to thrum throughout the room.

"Hear my words. From this day onward, Martin Leafbow,

priest, once husband to Frigga, Princess of the Royal House of Toullec, has rescinded his rights as a member of the said house. He is stripped of all the rights and privileges the Toullecs had afforded him upon his marriage. My cousin, Guénaël, previously a Prince of the Royal House of Toullec, shall henceforth be known as my adoptive brother and a Prince of the Royal House of Kizerain until such time he is married to my Chosen Counselor, Prince Lairgnen of the Royal House of Kizerain. Furthermore, all properties belonging to Prince Guénaël before the *ius auction* shall be reverted once more under the protection of the crown until such time as the wedding. Whereafter these shall be gifted to both Prince Lairgnen and Prince Guénaël. Such is my judgment. Such is my will."

The golden light dimmed, and the humming ceased. Anwyll lowered his arm, turned, and walked out of the ballroom. Pedr following close behind.

"Come, Gen, let's go. You're safe. You're with me now," Lairgnen murmured into Gen's ear.

Gen nodded but stayed quiet. They continued their way out of the manor, following Anwyll's lead while the warriors flanked their sides. Finally, they were strapped inside the transporter.

"My estate is nearest," Lairgnen said when he saw the flight plan on the control panel. "I suggest we go there instead of Llewellyn's. Gen needs rest, and being enclosed in this transporter for an hour is not good for him."

Llewellyn opened his mouth as though to argue, but Lairgnen shook his head. Anwyll merely closed his eyes. Llewellyn let out an exasperated sigh and directed the driver to change the coordinates.

Despite having the travel time cut in half, it was the longest fifteen minutes of Lairgnen's life. He'd had his staff close the deal with Uthman that same afternoon Gen had given his approval. His people had not wasted time in starting the cleanup and refurbishing. Thankfully, there was not much to do, as the manor had been well maintained by the caretakers. He didn't expect the redecorating and renovations to be completed, as that would be impossible. He only hoped there were enough rooms for all of them to sleep in.

Once they reached the house, they were met by the staff. Lairgnen had decided to rehire the former employees, as he found it only logical and fair. That the misfortune of the original owners should never affect the loyal servants had been ingrained in his psyche by Fiacre since he'd been a boy, and Lairgnen found that to be logical.

They were led to the salon, and after seeing to it that his guests were served refreshments, he excused Gen and himself. With a soft word of encouragement, he led Gen up to his bedroom. There were other rooms already furnished, and he could have taken Gen to one of them, but he needed to have Gen on his bed.

"Why don't you get some rest, Gen. You can come down when you're ready," Lairgnen said as he sat Gen on the bed.

Gen nodded but didn't say a word. He lay on his side and closed his eyes. Lairgnen sat there, caressing Gen's head for a long time, simply watching him. When Gen's breathing even out in sleep, Lairgnen stood and breathed a sigh of relief. At least he had Gen in his house, where no one would dare disturb him. With one last look, Lairgnen quietly closed the door and descended the stairs.

A few minutes later, he joined his cousins in the salon. At his entrance, they all stopped speaking, but he ignored them and went directly towards the bar to pour himself a drink.

"How is he?" Pedr asked.

"Still in a state of shock," Lairgnen said. He sipped at his drink and went to sit with the others. "He fell asleep as soon as I put him to bed."

"Poor boy," Pedr said. "How old is he again?"

"Twenty," Lairgnen said. "Twenty-one in two weeks."

"He seemed to trust you, cousin," Anwyll said.

"We spent some time together when I asked him to check these vineyards for me. We talked quite a bit."

"By the Goddess, Lair. You do realize what you just did, right? When you bid and won the auction?" Llewellyn exclaimed.

Lairgnen peered at his brother. "I think I do. But go ahead. Tell me, brother. What did I do exactly?"

"Oh, please, yes. Allow me to tell you exactly what your bid did." Llewellyn took a deep breath, opened his mouth, then closed it. He opened it again but still said nothing. Finally, he turned to Anwyll. "I don't know how to say it. Without, you know, sounding like an ass."

"Llewellyn seems to be in a state of shock as well." Anwyll's mouth curled into a grin. "What he's trying to say, Lairgnen, is that by winning the bid for Gen, tradition dictates that you have to marry him. In case you're wondering why I said what I said earlier. About you two marrying."

"At least he's of age," Pedr said.

Llewellyn stared at Pedr. "Are you seriously suggesting Lairgnen should actually marry that kid?"

"Technically, he's two weeks away from his twenty-first birthday." Lairgnen sighed tiredly. He slumped in his chair and stared up at the ceiling. "So, although he's definitely young, he's far from being a child. He's also quite mature for his age."

"You're thinking of actually marrying him?" Llewellyn stood and stared down at him.

"He's another part of me, so yes, I am." Lairgnen looked up and met Llewellyn's gaze. "Heart Call or not, I won the bid, Llew, and Anwyll basically ordered me to marry him. That means we're already technically and legally bound to each other. Betrothed, I think, is the word I'm looking for. In fact, if memory serves me correctly, Uncle Fiacre mentioned that the winner owns the auctioned person. Which means, right now, as we speak, I own Gen. Ownership's tighter than a regular marriage contract, I believe."

"Are you mad?" Llewellyn's mouth gaped wide. He pointed at Lairgnen but looked toward Anwyll. "Tell him he's mad."

"Maybe I am. Maybe I'm not." Lairgnen took another sip of his drink. "What I am certain of is even without the Heart Call or Anwyll's intervention, tradition demands I marry him. The important thing to remember is that I promised, by bidding for him, to protect him and his name." Lairgnen shrugged and took another drink. "I can do that. It won't be a great difficulty."

"He's also quite the handsome young man, if I may add," Anwyll said.

"That's beside the point," Pedr said, sending a warning look at Anwyll.

"Other than the obvious, do you even want to marry him, Lair?" Llewellyn asked.

"He doesn't have to marry me."

At the sound of Gen's voice, Lairgnen jumped to his feet.

CHAPTER THIRTEEN

"You don't have to marry me, sir," Gen repeated from the doorway. "I wouldn't want to force you into doing anything more for me than you've already done."

"What are you talking about?" Lairgnen said, shaking his head. "We *are* getting married. And yes, before you ask, I do want to marry you. Come here, sit with us."

Gen didn't like seeing the grim line of Lairgnen's lips directed at him. To cover his embarrassment, he turned toward the king.

"Your Majesty," he began but was stopped from saying anything else by Anwyll raising a hand.

"We're all cousins, here, Guénaël. Call me Anwyll, please." With the same raised hand, he gestured to the others in the room. "You already know Llewellyn."

Llewellyn waved at him, but his mouth was set tight.

"And this is my husband, Pedr."

Gen nodded shyly at Pedr. "Yes, I was at your Choosing last year at Yula."

"Yes, of course. I thought you looked familiar," Anwyll said. "You were there with Martin."

Lairgnen set the glass he was holding on a table and walked closer. "You're not forcing me into anything, Gen. And I thought I told you to call me by my name. Now come. Sit with us. We have much to discuss."

Gen nodded, took Lairgnen's proffered hand, and followed him to the sofa. Lairgnen waved him to sit, and to his surprise—and relief—Lairgnen sat beside him.

Lairgnen reached for the glass he'd set on the table and offered it to Gen. "Here, take this."

"I don't drink," Gen said.

Lairgnen sat back and took a sip from the glass. The move brushed their thighs together. Gen froze and pretended to ignore the press of Lairgnen's hard flesh, but then he looked up to find Anwyll staring at him. His eyes glowed a pale gold, proof of his ever-present magic. A sense of peace and calm washed over him. Knowing it was Anwyll responsible for his changing mood, he didn't resist it.

"Now that you're up, I think we can discuss what we're going to do next," Anwyll said.

Pedr held up his hand and stood. "Don't start just yet. Let me go talk to the butler to ask him to prepare us some food and get it served here. This is going to be a long night."

"I'm sorry. That's my job. Let me go and talk to the staff," Lairgnen said, moving to stand, but Pedr waved him back down.

"No. You stay with Gen. You're just as exhausted as he is," Pedr insisted.

"I'll go with you," Llewellyn said, taking to his feet. "I'm very hungry."

After they left, Anwyll turned back to him. "Tell me how all this started, Guénaël. I've read the reports, and I've heard what Llewellyn and Lairgnen reported about their findings. But I want to hear from you. I want to know what your version of events is and what you think led your father to call for your auction."

Gen didn't immediately respond. He didn't know why he suddenly felt anxious. Wordlessly, he reached out for Lairgnen with his hand, thankful he immediately took hold of it. He turned his head and met Lairgnen's reassuring gaze.

"It's all right. You can trust that everyone here won't think badly of you, not that you did anything wrong," Lairgnen said in a low voice.

Gen didn't know if it was the way Lairgnen was looking at him or the warm grip of his hand, but he quickly found the courage to speak. He looked at Anwyll and began his narration. Once he started, he couldn't stop himself. He didn't even pause when Llewellyn and Pedr came back.

Fresh tears fell down his cheeks, and he would have brushed them with his sleeves, but Lairgnen beat him to it. He handed Gen a handkerchief, just like he'd done before. The piece of cloth took him by surprise, for who went around with a handkerchief every day? It was such an innocuous piece of fabric — something he'd seen used by his mother but never by a man other than Lairgnen. Conscious of the men waiting for him to continue, he wiped his tears and continued.

When he reached the end of his tale, he felt curiously freed. These men had listened without interrupting once. None of them said or did anything that ridiculed him. He sighed and quietly reached for Lairgnen's hand once more.

Gen watched as Lairgnen opened his hand palm up then laid his on top of it, measuring the two together. Lairgnen's fingers topped his by half a knuckle, and Gen thought that strange, as he was taller than Lairgnen. He bent a little closer to examine the lines on Lairgnen's palm.

"Before we even talk about your eventual marriage," Pedr began and then stopped.

When Pedr continued to remain silent, Gen looked up from playing with Lairgnen's hand. Pedr raised a brow at him. Belatedly, Gen realized he was not giving him his full attention.

"I'm sorry, Pedr. Please go on."

"We need to know, do you have a lover?"

Heat flooded Gen's face, and he couldn't look at any of them. "No." He shook his head, gripping Lairgnen's hand tighter.

Pedr turned to Lairgnen. "How about you, Lair? Anyone

we don't know about, waiting for you out there, thinking you're marrying them anytime, sometime, or soon?"

"No. I have no one." Lairgnen's response held no hesitation.

Relief flooded over Gen. He didn't know how he would have reacted if Lairgnen had said he had a lover. Lairgnen turned, and their gazes met. Immediately, Gen was lost in the blue depth of his eyes.

Llewellyn huffed. "I could've answered that."

"It's best to clarify sensitive topics before diving into marriage contracts and other arrangements," Anwyll said.

The words caught Gen's attention. Reluctantly, he looked away from Lairgnen and raised a hand. "Uhm, I do have a question before we proceed." He looked at each of the individual faces of the men around him.

"What is it, Gen?" Lairgnen said.

"What about my sister? Laoghaire?"

"What about her?" It was Llewellyn who asked.

"Father took her with him four days ago. I don't know where she is or how she is. He wouldn't tell me when I asked."

"I'll have my men find her and bring her here," Llewellyn said. "I take it you don't want her with Martin?"

"Before Mother died, she was very specific about Laoghaire and me. She left all the properties in my name and turned Laoghaire's care over to me. I am her guardian, not my father."

"She left nothing to Martin?" Anwyll furrowed his brows and leaned forward.

"No. She didn't." Gen looked at Lairgnen. "I told you this before. Father had taken over the administration of her properties right after she died. At the time, I didn't understand what was going on, and I was grieving. All I know is it shouldn't have happened, especially as Mother had taught me so well. I tried to regain control, but Father was quite adamant against it. He made so many excuses with regards to the money and properties, though he gave over Laoghaire's upbringing and education to me easily enough."

"What Gen's saying is correct." Anwyll nodded and leaned back in his seat. "Martin, not being a royal or an *equite*, has no right to the property owned by a member of the royal family. All royal residences are owned by the family, and I, as king, have absolute control over them. Frigga's property is different. That one is owned by her direct family, the Toullecs. By all rights, everything here should belong Gen. It is one of the lands granted them at the time of the Great Passage. Seven men and women, in addition to the king of the time, were gifted the lands by the people as reward for helping bring them to safety. However, it also means that no one other than direct descendants of those lines can own the land. As Gen's the last male of the Toullec line, he, not Laoghaire, is the only one who should have absolute control over it. Today, however, I took over the properties and will hold custody over them until Lairgnen and Gen marry. Then I will gift it back over to them."

"Then what you're saying is that Father was lying about the property?"

"What exactly did he tell you, Gen?" Anwyll asked.

"He told me that the winning bidder would have absolute control of the property in my name, as my protector. But I'm confused. The people he invited were *plebs* . . . all of them."

"I think Martin intended for the winner to hand him control of the Toullec lands," Pedr said.

"He'll learn soon enough that what he did was the real scandal here," Llewellyn said. "Goddess. What a rat bastard. Sorry, Gen." He looked at Anwyll, a wicked grin spreading over his face. "I really enjoyed watching Martin's face when you were doing your justice earlier."

"I always strive to make sure I continue to entertain you as much as possible, cousin." Anwyll grinned just as broadly and wickedly.

"All right, let's talk about the wedding." Pedr rubbed his palms together. "When's that going to be?"

"Tradition states a week after the auction," Anwyll said.

"But you told Martin to see you in six months?" Lairgnen frowned, looking confused.

"He doesn't need to be there to witness his son's wedding, Lair. He can stew until then. When the time comes, he'll be handed his just due." Anwyll turned to face Gen fully.

The look on Anwyll's face made Gen tighten his hold on Lairgnen's hand, but what Anwyll said next startled Gen to speechlessness.

"That will be my wedding gift to you, cousin."

Pedr chuckled and sidled closer to Anwyll. "I didn't know you had a vindictive streak in you, Anwyll?"

A glint of gold flashed, and Anwyll's amused expression turned grim. "I didn't know it myself until Martin cast humiliation on our family. Public shaming and abuse for the sake of status and money? Those things are simply never done, especially coming from a priest."

Gen wanted to say something, but words escaped him. When Lairgnen pulled him into his arms, he went willingly. If he hadn't been afraid of Anwyll before, he was now. Thank the Goddess, the king was on his side, and he had Lairgnen to protect him and Laoghaire.

CHAPTER FOURTEEN

Lairgnen and Gen were quietly married under the canopy of the blessed oak tree in the palace courtyard two weeks after the auction, the day after Gen's twenty-first birthday. They were surrounded by Eljin, Fiacre, Pedr, and Llewellyn. Much to everyone's surprise, Anwyll officiated the marriage himself.

The biggest surprise was the appearance of the sprite. When Lairgnen and Gen were led into the sacred grove, the magical creatures came in droves, flitting from one branch to the next, singing and glittering in joyous abandon.

Lairgnen . . . Guénaël

The sprite flew above Gen and Lair, twinkling their joy and chanting their names, just as they had done at Anwyll and Pedr's Chosen ceremony. It was a clear sign of their approval and the Goddess' blessing. The look of pure joy on Gen's face as he looked up at the sprite would be embedded forever in Lairgnen's heart and mind.

Lairgnen hoped their appearance would put a stop to the gossip surrounding his marriage to a much younger man.

Gen said his vows in a clear voice, but the red in his cheeks betrayed his nervousness. When it was Lairgnen's turn to say his vows, he did so with no hesitance. He had always been good at hiding his feelings and sent silent thanks to the Goddess for giving him the confidence to conceal his own nervousness.

The days leading to the ceremony had been trying. To the

public, Lairgnen had acted the caring fiancé to the young Prince Guénaël. In private, he wasn't as controlled. Many times he had locked the door to his office so he could hide in peace.

The scandal of the auction had only gained momentum, especially after the announcement of Lairgnen's winning bid and Anwyll's adoption of Gen. The report of their marriage taking place only added fuel to the fire. Lairgnen was not known for philandering ways, not like Llewellyn, so the news of his nuptials had taken everyone by surprise. Everybody talked about the subject at some point, like a few courtiers and ministers who had appeared to forget that they were attending meetings with him to discuss Kizerain's financial matters.

To complicate matters, back in Merifael, Martin had released a public statement congratulating Lairgnen and Gen on their upcoming marriage. He went so far as to petition a thanksgiving mass for Lairgnen's taking pity on his son. Thankfully, word had reached the capital, and Anwyll put an immediate block on the petition.

Things soon quieted after that, especially as Anwyll had ordered Martin to remove himself from the Toullec manor. When Lairgnen had read the missive directing Martin to leave, he had wanted to go back to Merifael and confront Martin personally, but Llewellyn had stopped him.

Lairgnen had never before felt so unstable and illogical.

The wedding reception was a bit on the extravagant side for Lairgnen's taste, but Pedr had insisted. He said the royal family needed to show the whole of Kizerain that the union between the two royal houses was blessed not only by the Goddess but by the king as well. Two hundred guests had been invited to the reception, and all were in attendance. The palace bloomed with wedding flowers that had been carefully chosen by Pedr himself.

As for Gen, Lairgnen had no idea how he was doing. Outwardly, he looked happy enough. He even managed to get Pedr to allow him to assist him in the gardens. However, there were times when Lairgnen caught glimpses of despair in his eyes, and that bothered him a lot.

His one regret was the lack of time they had spent together prior to the ceremony. Because of the wedding preparations taking over everyone's time and him working overtime to clear his schedule, he had not had the opportunity to talk to Gen other than when they joined the others for dinner. And even then, Gen stuck to small talk or said nothing at all. He'd seen Gen look at him and then look away when he realized Lairgnen had seen him.

Lairgnen was at a loss. Separation or divorce was not an option for them, not that he hoped for either option. They were of royal blood and were fated to each other. Also, the auction had permanently sealed Gen's destiny to him as the winning bidder.

Finally, after spending the required time with their guests, Pedr told them to go on their way for their honeymoon. Before Lairgnen could follow Gen outside, though, Fiacre quietly took him to one side and offered his estate in the south.

"The distance from the capital should ease Gen's anxiety and hopefully put a stop to the gossip about the hasty marriage," Fiacre said in a serious tone.

"Thank you, Uncle, I really appreciate it. I hope our honeymoon will give us a better chance to get to know each other. How long can we stay?"

"I would suggest a month, or even two would be appropriate. Though extending your honeymoon to three months is also acceptable."

Lairgnen shook his head. "No, three months is too long. I can't leave the ministry alone for that amount of time without someone trying to mess with the numbers and causing chaos for our economy. A month, two at most, it is, and again, my thanks, Uncle."

Fiacre thumped Lairgnen's back. "Anytime, nephew. Your cousin Venex and his wife will be there to welcome you, but they won't be staying long. They are expecting their third child, and Sila is close to her time."

"Congratulations, Uncle. How many grandchildren does that make?"

"Twelve."

Fiacre said it with such seriousness that Lairgnen had to stop himself from laughing. Of Fiacre's nine children, only four had gotten married. There would be more grandchildren to come in the future to keep the old man busy. He only hoped that he and Gen would be as happy as his uncle and the king were.

The one thing that kept Lairgnen's hopes up was that now they were officially married, Gen didn't avoid him or shy away from his touch. In fact, he would reach out for Lairgnen's hand and stand closer whenever others were about to give their salutations. Lairgnen didn't know if Gen's behavior was influenced by the Heart Call or not. Personally, Lairgnen knew his feelings for Gen had gotten deeper in the past two weeks, and he'd missed him when they weren't together.

"Where exactly are we headed?"

Gen's question pulled Lairgnen back to the present. Gen was looking out the window of the transporter and craning his neck to see the view. Lairgnen glanced out to see miles of forested land. They had reached the south three hours before, and he recognized where they were.

"To the Trennet Coast. The Black Coral Cove, to be specific. Uncle Fiacre's Chosen, Uncle Fiedrico, bought the property as a gift on their thirtieth wedding celebration."

"Are we meeting Uncle Fiedrico there?" Gen shifted in his

seat to face him.

"No. Unfortunately, he died seven years ago. He was much older than Uncle Fiacre by a good fifteen years."

"Oh, that's so sad. I had no idea. Were they happy together?"

"Yes, as far as I saw, they were. Very. We will meet their second son, Venex. He's currently staying there with his wife, Sila."

"Oh. So we'll be staying with them?"

"Hmm, let's just say, we will, and we won't. You'll see," Lairgnen smiled.

"I'm excited," Gen said. And he looked it. He was sitting at the edge of his seat, and his eyes were wide. "I've never seen or been to the sea before."

"Well then, this trip makes it even more special, doesn't it?"

They smiled at each other for a moment before Gen looked away and cleared his throat. "Lair? Can I ask you something?"

"Of course. What is it? Is something troubling you?"

Gen looked down, and his hands were clenched into fists. "Well, it's just that . . . I'm so embarrassed."

Lairgnen had to smile. Gen was such an innocent while he was so much older. What had the Goddess been thinking?

"You should never feel embarrassed around me, Gen. Now, speak up. What's troubling you?"

"I'm . . . our . . . Goddess. How do I ask you? All right. Here goes. I was wondering about our wedding night."

"What about it?"

"I don't want to hurt your feelings, and I know we're expected to consummate our marriage, but I'm not ready. I like you too much. And you already know I've been attracted to you for the longest time. And then, of course, there's the Call. But as much as I want to sleep with you, I think logically, I . . .

we should get to know each other first. Before, you know, we have sex." The words came out in such a rush that by the end of his speech, Gen was breathing hard.

Lairgnen chuckled. "I knew there was a reason the Goddess put us together. I think you are not only intelligent, but you are also very logical. The two don't necessarily go hand in hand."

"You mean you're all right about us not sleeping together?" Gen looked surprised.

"Sleeping and having sex are two very different things, Gen. Surely you know that? But to answer your question, no. I don't mind not having sex right away. However, I don't think we can get away with not sleeping in the same room. And to be honest, I don't think I can stand another day without being near you. It's been a miserable two weeks for me. Also, servants gossip, and your father has a very long ear."

Gen seemed to think over Lairgnen's words, and the longer he did, the more Lairgnen got nervous.

"So, what you're saying is that we stay in the same room?" Gen waited until Lairgnen nodded. "We can do that. It will give our getting to know each other a different perspective."

Lairgnen frowned. "How is that?"

"Well, you may do things in your sleep that I may not be comfortable with, and so could I." Gen crossed one leg over his knee. Gone was the nervousness. Instead, he looked quite confident.

Lairgnen wondered where Gen was going with the conversation. "Like what?"

"Farting, for one," Gen said with a shrug.

Gen said it so innocently it caught Lairgnen unprepared. He began to cough when his saliva went down the wrong pipe. He couldn't help himself and started laughing so hard his eyes started tearing.

"Oh Goddess, that's . . . You surprise me, Gen. Of all the

things to mention." Lairgnen wiped at his tears.

"Well, I remember when my nurse used to sleep in my room whenever I was sick, and she would fart all night long," Gen said with a straight face.

Lairgnen didn't know if he was telling the truth or making a joke, which triggered another laughing fit.

"Stop. I can't deal with the visuals. You're a riot, you know that?" Lairgnen said when he finally regained his breath.

"Well, I am right." Gen flashed a mischievous grin.

"Yes, you are. Goddess, Gen. I can promise you that I don't fart in my sleep."

Gen raised his eyebrows and leaned back against the backrest.

"How can you say that? You wouldn't know what you did in your sleep. Now I'm scared. What if I fart?"

"Can we drop the farting issue, please?" Lairgnen couldn't stop grinning.

"All right. It's dropped," Gen said, waving his hand dismissively.

Lairgnen put his palms together in mock prayer. "Thank you."

Lairgnen shook his head, picked up his tablet, and opened the file his assistant had sent him to review. It didn't take long before he lost himself to different budget proposals.

"Lair?"

Gen's voice pulled Lairgnen from his reading, and he looked up at his new husband.

"Yes, Gen?"

"What's going to happen to us?"

Lairgnen closed the file and set aside the tablet. He'd been expecting the question, but now that Gen was asking it, he was hesitant to respond. He knew what he was going to say, but he wasn't sure how Gen would react. They'd known each other a little over three weeks, and he knew neither of them was the type to make presumptions.

"If you mean our future, what about it?"

"I . . ." Gen shrugged, repeating the same question. "What do you think is going to happen to us?"

"How do you mean?" Lairgnen studied Gen's face. He read curiosity and confusion, but thankfully, there was no fear.

"As a couple," Gen said, shrugging again.

"Ah . . . Well, I don't really know. Does anyone have an absolute idea of what their future will bring them? However, I think we're on the right track. You were right earlier when you said we need to get to know each other better before taking our relationship to the next level. Become friends first and take it from there."

"Eventually, though."

The way Gen was looking at him made Lairgnen think that all Gen sought from him was reassurance.

"One thing we both should never forget, which works in our favor, is that we're fated. You're my Chosen, and I am yours. We can't keep fighting this connection we have with each other. The Goddess won't permit that. But I think that it sets us off in the right direction, and the promise of a happier life."

"The Goddess will never lead us astray." Gen smiled down at his hands. He was quoting one of several reassurances the Goddess had promised their people a millennia ago.

"No, she won't. That was a promise she has kept. We have that in our favor, and it's best to trust in her. So I think, eventually, we'll be okay."

"Yes, we'll be okay." Gen nodded as though trying to convince himself.

"It's just difficult for us right now because of the obvious reasons. But really, Gen, what are you afraid of?" Lairgnen tilted his head to the side as he continued to study Gen's face.

"Not afraid. More like anxious. My father will not settle for what has happened. I think he has finally realized he is no longer in control of the money and properties. Knowing him as I do, he's not going to take this lying down. We still don't know his motives, but after Anwyll stripped him of his money and prestige, he's bound to do something drastic."

Lairgnen drew in a breath. Gen might be young, but he was an astute young man, and that pleased him.

"Right now, the most he can do is cause more drama. But that's only going to affect his name, not yours. But you're right. It's best we be prepared." Even as he spoke, he could see Gen was still troubled. "What are you really worried about, Gen? Surely you don't think I'm going to hurt you, do you?"

Gen shook his head. "No. I may be young and innocent about sex, but I trust you. Plus, the Pull is hard to ignore, so I'm not that anxious, but I am afraid for Laoghaire. I still don't know what's going on with her."

Lairgnen shifted in his seat to hide his erection. Gen talking about their eventual sex life had made the blood rush down to his groin.

"Llewellyn's on it, Gen. He's promised to keep in touch and give us daily updates."

"Yes, I know. I still worry, though." Gen's smile eased the furrow between his brows, but it was apparent he was putting up a brave front.

"That's only normal. Now, my turn. I have a question," Lairgnen said.

"What is it?" Gen's brows rose slightly.

"What do you want to do after our honeymoon period is over? Where do you want to live?"

Gen looked taken aback, but he chuckled. "With you, of course. I want to live with you. Living apart never crossed my mind."

A surge of happiness swept through Lairgnen when he heard Gen's words. He couldn't help the grin from breaking over his face.

"Mine, either. Strange, isn't it — that I can't bear being apart from you?"

"It is, but at the same time, it isn't." Gen nodded, directing a soft smile at Lairgnen. "I thought my life was over when I couldn't feel you nearby when they started bidding on me. I didn't know what was going on or why you'd left me. You don't know how it felt. Then my heart leapt when I first realized you were somewhere nearby. It was an exhilarating feeling. And then you were there, and I wasn't alone anymore."

"Believe me when I tell you, I felt worse, especially when Llewellyn didn't want me to call you. I admit I panicked there for a minute. If Martin had found out we were going to crash the auction, we don't know what he would have done."

"No. What you did was right. I realized that early on. But going back to what we were talking about, I don't want to be away from you. Ever. Your work, do you need to be based at the capital?"

Lairgnen was glad Gen was asking these questions. They needed to be raised, and the previous weeks had made it impossible for them to have a moment to discuss any of it.

"Not all year round, but most times. Why? Do you want to go back to Merifael? Live there?"

"Well, that's where my properties are." Gen stopped speaking, bent his head, stared at his hands, and slowly clenched them into fists. After a while, he shook his head as though he were clearing his thoughts. Then he looked up with a tentative smile. "It's strange that I can say that freely now."

"I was wondering about what to do with my estate." Lairgnen made a face.

"Well, about that . . ." Gen licked his lips. "I was thinking . . . Right now, I don't feel safe in my home. Not while my father's still in Merifael, or his servants and men are all over the place. Plus, I've always loved the Bolton estate. What if we made that our home base?"

There was an eagerness in Gen's voice that surprised Lairgnen, and he didn't hesitate to go along with the suggestion.

"That sounds like a plan. But I have another question. What do you intend to do with your studies? You left in the middle of the year because of what happened. Do you want to go back?"

"Not right now, no." Gen shook his head, emphatically. "I'm hoping to go back sometime. Maybe once we find Laoghaire, or after about a year. I would like to get to know you better."

"Do you want to go to the capital in the meantime?"

That seemed to gain Gen's interest, for he sat up, and his brows rose in curiosity. "You have a university there?"

"Not at the capital, no. This may surprise you, but the Royal Kizerain University is located in the Common Grounds. That way, those who want to study can. No matter their social status. The administrators look at the overall grades of the applicants, not their names or wealth. For example, if the applicant displays magical abilities, regardless of their level, the mages take them into their conclaves where they are given training."

"Did you go there?"

"I did, yes. I studied economics, just so you know. So did Llewellyn. It was only the king who didn't go there. That's because his silver hair and eyes were a great distraction, and he chose not to go after his mother died. He did take advantage of the education, thanks to an agreement he had with the university deans."

"He must have been lonely growing up." Gen smiled ruefully. "I know how that feels."

"Llewellyn and I tried our best to keep him entertained. We

were orphans, and King Eljin, with the help of Uncle Fiacre, took us in after our parents died."

"I'm so sorry, I didn't know that. I didn't even ask about them when they didn't appear at the wedding."

Lairgnen waved off his concern. "Don't be. Llew was just a baby, and I was a year old, so neither of us remember our parents. For both of us, King Eljin is our father, and Anwyll is our brother."

"How did they die?"

"What they enjoyed doing the most. Paragliding. They were confident in their skills and didn't tell anyone what they were going to do. Both their bodies were found at the bottom of the mountain. Their gliders had malfunctioned, so death was instantaneous."

Gen's eyes widened. "Oh . . . wow. Now I really don't know what to say."

Lairgnen smiled and shook his head. "I'm not going to lie. Both of our fathers were quite the irresponsible princes who loved to party. I don't remember them at all, no fleeting memory, no early bonding. One of my nannies said it was because they never visited the nursery. King Eljin saved us."

"I supposed it won't be considered bad if I said that you and Llewellyn were lucky?" Gen's face contorted between a grimace and a wince.

Lairgnen shook his head. "Let's just say that I wouldn't be a Minister of Finance if my upbringing had been left up to my parents."

He and Llewellyn had indeed been very lucky to be raised by a king who had treated them as his own children. Because of Eljin, Lairgnen would always remain a loyal cousin and minister to Anwyll—his younger brother, for all intents and purposes.

Gen let out a long sigh. "There's always one in every family, isn't there."

"What you said," Lairgnen said. "Now, if you would excuse me. I need to finish reading this file and send off my notes within the hour. I promise you, this is the last thing I want to do, but it came up at the last minute, and I didn't get the chance to address it before the wedding."

"Go ahead. I was just going to say I wanted to take in the view." Gen peered out the window, his eyes getting bigger from whatever it was he saw. "Stunning. Oh, is that the sea out there? Right over the edge of the forest?"

"I'm glad you like what you see. Just wait until we get down there and see it firsthand." Lairgnen chuckled, happy to see Gen's exuberance as he continued to talk about his observations.

Lairgnen didn't mind the chatter. He actually liked listening to this Gen, who was happy and excited. Carefree. Lust shot through him. He tore his gaze off his temptation, and reluctantly picked up his reading material.

Goddess help him. How long could he last?

CHAPTER FIFTEEN

Gen had never been to the southern hemisphere, and when he first set his eyes on Fiacre's estate on the Trennet Coast, he thought he had died and gone to heaven.

The golden beaches had drawn his eye while they were flying in, and when he finally got to walk on the sand, he couldn't believe how such a place could exist in the world. The surface of the sea sparkled as it reflected the light from the sun, almost blinding him with its brightness. Lairgnen had laughed at him before handing over a pair of dark opticals to protect his eyes. Even with the sunglasses, the scene didn't disappoint.

Venex, Fiacre's son, had personally welcomed them when they'd first arrived at the manor. He'd apologized that his wife, Sila, could not meet them as she was feeling weighed down by the impending birth of their third child. Lairgnen had graciously excused her absence, and as he and Venex talked about the affairs of the world, Gen had investigated his surroundings.

Black Corral Cove, as the estate was called, was located in a peninsula to the west of the southern hemisphere. When he'd first set eyes on the manor where he and Lairgnen were going to stay, he had been astounded. It was just as large as the main house and just as grandiose.

Their first night together was hilarious when Gen found himself struggling to keep away from Lairgnen. Although he was too shy to sleep in the same bed with him, he found it next to impossible to stay away. The dilemma was quickly resolved with Lairgnen pulling him close to his side. Of course, that only led to more problems.

Gen shifted uncomfortably as he tried to hide his erection. But every move he made only ended up making him more aware of Lairgnen's lean body next to his.

"Stop wriggling around," Lairgnen said.

Gen froze. He didn't know where to lay his head, and he was getting a crick on his neck. Slowly, he shifted until he was more comfortable, but it still didn't help.

"Place your head on my shoulder if you must, but please, Gen, stop moving," Lairgnen groaned.

Gen closed his eyes and concentrated on sleeping but found himself longing to kiss Lairgnen. He had to know what it would be like to have his lips against another man's. He trailed a hand down Lairgnen's chest. Maybe if he kept his eyes closed long enough, he could achieve sleep and hopefully dream of something nice — like kissing Lairgnen. The sudden intrusion of the mental vision made him jerk before he could stop himself.

"Are you all right?" There was just a hint of exasperation in Lairgnen's voice.

Gen looked up at him. "Everything's fine." He tried to move away, but that only resulted in getting pulled back to his original position.

Lairgnen stared down at him with the relentless intensity he was becoming familiar with. His brows rose in a silent query as he tried to interpret what Lairgnen was thinking. Lairgnen placed a hand on Gen's face, making his heart pound as he was forced to rest his hands against Lairgnen's chest.

They stared at each other for a long moment, Lairgnen's gaze burning into Gen's. The pull between them rose to almost unbearable levels, causing him to close his eyes. And then he felt Lairgnen's lips brush against his, sending ripples of heat throughout his body.

His mouth opened, and Lairgnen's tongue delved into it. At the same time, fingers thrust into his hair as the kiss turned hungrier. Gen's body felt like it was on fire. He pulled on Lairgnen's body, wanting to get closer than they already were. Lairgnen eased to lie over Gen, making his body tremble as he felt, for the first time in his life, another man's body against his own. The intimacy fanned the heat between them that felt like it was going to engulf him. He fought for breath, but he didn't want to turn away from the kiss. Lairgnen's hands dropped down to his arm, and he suddenly ended the kiss.

Gen fought through the haze of desire, confused over what had happened. Lairgnen pushed himself up until he looked down at him with blue eyes that had turned almost black. He recognized it for what it was, for it reflected his own emotions.

"If I didn't stop, I would have gone further than you'd have been ready for," Lairgnen said.

Fighting against his rising self-consciousness, Gen bit on his lip but didn't look away from Lairgnen. "That was my first kiss."

Lairgnen didn't react, but his hand trailed down Gen's cheek. When he continued to say nothing, whatever insecurities Gen felt earlier dissipated.

"I was moving around so much because I wanted to kiss you, and I didn't know how to do it."

"I know," Lairgnen said. "You were shouting out your emotions. It was very hard not to listen."

"You felt what I was thinking about?"

"Yes."

Gen blinked, perplexed at the strangeness of the Pull. Something in his chest seemed to flicker, and he suddenly felt an apprehension, a hesitation, and a sense of guilt. At first, he didn't know where it was coming from, for he didn't feel any of those things. Then he cast a wary glance at Lairgnen and saw those emotions reflected in his eyes. Tentatively, he reached out with his senses as he tenderly caressed Lairgnen's face.

"Remember when I was telling you earlier about when I started to realize you had come to save me from the bidders?" He paused, waiting until Lairgnen nodded. "No one has ever made me feel the way you make me feel. From the first moment I set eyes on you, you were the only one for me. That was when I was six or seven. And now, whenever you touch me, it's like my whole being is complete."

"Not making love to you is going to be the most difficult thing I ever endured, but I made a promise."

"I never said anything about not kissing," Gen said in a rush.

Lairgnen's eyes widened, but then he broke out into laughter. "That's true. We never said anything about not kissing."

"Also, I never said we couldn't touch each other or do other things . . ." Gen's voice faded as sudden embarrassment swept through him.

"No, we never said that either," Lairgnen said in a low, husky voice.

Shivers of desire swept down Gen's spine. "You're doing it again."

"One thing at a time," Lairgnen said. He rolled onto his back and drew Gen next to him. "As much as I want to do more, I'm exhausted. Now, let's go to sleep."

Gen nodded and lay his head once more on Lairgnen's chest. He felt more confident and relaxed, so he closed his eyes and drifted off to sleep.

The next day, Lairgnen took him to the village. Gen thought it didn't look much different from Merifael, and for some reason, that kind of disappointed him.

"Villages around the world share a lot of commonalities,"

Lairgnen said. "They have small populations and are mostly either agricultural or livestock focused. Here in the south, it's mostly agriculture."

"I see that, and now that I have firsthand experience with how hot it is down here, I understand why the *bakare* are raised in the north."

They walked further toward the outskirts, which gave Gen a chance to check out the fields. Hunkering down, he dug his fingers into the soil and examined it.

"What are you doing?"

"Looking to see if the soil is viable for grapes," Gen said. He rubbed the soil between his fingers and took a whiff.

"And?"

"It's sandy enough, but there's too much clay in it." He looked up and saw how the plains they were standing on were surrounded by hills.

"Meaning?"

"There's not enough drainage. The vines can grow, but if there's too much rain, they can drown. See those hills surrounding us? This area can become a catch basin of sorts and turn this whole area into a temporary lake. I noticed that the trees near here are looking thin. They're not like that for lack of water. In fact, it's the opposite."

Lairgnen blinked in surprise and started to slowly turn. "You're right."

"Maybe there are other areas that can be viable, just not here. Pity." Gen stood up and dusted his hands off.

By the end of the week, Gen had gotten used to having Lairgnen sleeping right next to him. One night, he had to go to bed alone because Anwyll had requested a video call with Lairgnen. Try as he might, he couldn't relax enough to sleep. Frustration and discomfort made him seek out Lairgnen. He found him in the study, sitting on the sofa, staring at a monitor where Anwyll's disembodied voice could be heard. Lairgnen looked up and raised his brow in a silent question.

Gen closed the door as softly as he could and proceeded to walk over to his side. Anwyll paused whatever he was doing and smiled at Gen from his side of the monitor. After giving Anwyll a sleepy wave, Gen quietly lay down beside Lairgnen on the sofa. Lairgnen helped him settle and even covered him with a blanket hung over the back of the sofa. He ignored whatever Lairgnen and Anwyll were talking about and promptly fell asleep.

By the second week, Gen still had not gotten tired of the view or swimming in the sea. He met some youths visiting the area and spent time with them, lying around sunbathing or hunting down five-eyed orange starfish to grill. He had first tasted the grilled meat sold by a vendor who'd set up on the shore. At Lairgnen's encouragement to try it out, Gen discovered he liked the delicacy. The search for the burrowing marine animal at low tide was just part of the fun.

One night, Gen had come back to the manor with a bucket full of the fish. Much to his amusement, the butler had looked at his cargo in horror, but his teasing brought out a smile from the normally expressionless face. That night, they shared a feast with the household staff.

For Gen, the evening was something he would remember forever. The smell of the sea and the fat fish cooking over the coals were some of his best memories. He couldn't remember ever having so much fun, even when he had gone out with his so-called friends in the past.

Lairgnen had been a surprise as well. He'd shed his princely bearing, interacting and laughing with the servants with ease. There was also much drinking, which Gen refused to take part in.

Later, as he lay with his head on Lairgnen's shoulder, he

realized he had never been so happy before. Lairgnen slept peacefully beside him with his mouth slightly ajar. He carefully raised himself, and instantly, Lairgnen's eyes flew open.

"I'm sorry I disturbed you," Gen said, suddenly feeling guilty for waking Lairgnen.

"What time is it?" Lairgnen asked sleepily.

"About two in the morning."

"Oh." Lairgnen searched the room before closing his eyes once more. "What's wrong?"

"Nothing," Gen said.

Lairgnen huffed and pulled Gen back into his arms.

Gen didn't resist. He relaxed and closed his eyes, wanting to kiss Lairgnen but not knowing if he should. Lairgnen suddenly moved onto his side, lifted Gen's chin, and kissed him. The brief touch sent a wave of heat through him, dissolving his earlier hesitance. His body yearned for Lairgnen's in a way he knew he wouldn't be able to resist for much longer.

Lairgnen pulled away to gaze at him. He seemed to be searching for something, but Gen didn't know what. His hand cupped the back of Gen's neck and drew him closer for another kiss. Gen melted against him, his body reacting in ways he was unfamiliar with as their tongues touched and teased. The kiss grew deeper and more urgent, drawing an involuntary moan from Gen as he held on to Lairgnen. A groan escaped Lairgnen as he nibbled at Gen's lips and his hands caressed down the length of Gen's back. When Gen thought he couldn't stand the heat any longer, Lairgnen drew back once more. From his expression, it was obvious Lairgnen had halted their kiss for Gen's sake, knowing he wasn't ready to take that next step.

"The next time you want me to kiss you, just tell me, all right?"

The smile on Lairgnen's lips warmed Gen's heart, and he realized something. Never had anyone been so kind, understanding, or patient with him before.

"I love you."

Lairgnen froze, and the hand he'd brought up to comb through Gen's hair, as was his wont, stopped halfway down Gen's head.

"Why do you say that?"

"Because I do." Gen took a deep breath.

"I don't know what I ever did to deserve you," Lairgnen whispered. "I love you, too. I have for the longest time. Since I met you, in fact."

"I know, *amaer*," Gen said.

Lairgnen's shock at the endearment was something Gen never dreamed of seeing, and he was glad he'd said the word. *Amaer*. Beloved.

Lairgnen's mood shifted. Through their bond, tentative as it was, Gen felt the joy grow inside of Lair. Suddenly, everything was all right, and Gen knew he would never be happier.

"Let's go to sleep," he said and leaned over to kiss Lairgnen on his lips. "I was thinking. Can we kiss before we go to sleep?"

"Why then? Why can't we kiss any time we want?"

"Because then I get to relax after we kiss."

"All right."

Gen kissed Lairgnen's lips one last time before settling on his side and closing his eyes. It was nice to be married. He dreamed of kisses and loving.

By the third week, Gen thought he was going to go stir crazy. He received a call from a friend about a property he'd always wanted to buy but hadn't had the chance to say anything to Lairgnen. He searched for Lairgnen and found him in the office.

"Can we get out of here? Please?"

Lairgnen took one look at him and shook his head. "I was

wondering when you'd start begging."

"I'm not begging," Gen huffed, but Lairgnen's laughter was too contagious, and he had to laugh at himself. "All right, I am. So, can we?"

"Of course, I was going to ask if you wanted to go with me to the village, but I must tell you in advance that I can't be with you the whole time. I'm meeting with the local *adept* there."

"I see," Gen nodded, but he didn't really, and he was also a little disappointed. He'd looked forward to spending the day with Lairgnen and instead had stepped his foot into it. "I can stay here if you're busy."

Lairgnen gazed at him for a long moment and then took his hand. "Look, I know that face too well by now, and I can see your disappointment. If you're wondering why I'm working when I should be by your side getting to know you, the answer is simple. I was thinking of buying property in this area."

Gen was taken aback. That was the last thing in his mind when he'd sought Lairgnen out.

"Why?"

Lairgnen shrugged. "I like to invest in land, and I saw how you've fallen in love with the place. I thought it would be nice to have a house here so that whenever we want to visit the sea, we can fly over at a moment's notice without having to ask Uncle Fiacre to put up with us. It's really that simple."

Gen looked around and took in the beautiful scenery. Loving it as he already did, he knew he didn't want to buy land here. He had his heart set on something else, and if he didn't act soon, he would lose his chance of achieving a lifelong dream.

"What is it, Gen?" Lairgnen asked, cupping Gen's face in his hand.

Gen closed his eyes briefly. "The idea of having a house

here is really tempting, but I think that it would be a waste of money."

Lairgnen's brows rose. "Why do you say that?"

Gen watched Lairgnen's face for signs of disapproval, but he could only sense curiosity. "Well, if you think about it, Uncle Fiacre only comes to visit, and that's even rare. Venex and Sila are only here because Sila is pregnant and didn't like the cold at the capital. But their older children stayed behind."

"What are you getting at?" Lairgnen crossed his arms in front of him and gave Gen his full attention.

"Uncle Fiacre's family rarely uses this place and basically leaves the running of the property in the hands of managers. The ones who are actually enjoying the place are their many visitors and the staff. That takes a lot of money to maintain."

"If you're worried about money, don't be." Lairgnen shrugged.

"No, Lair, you're not getting my point," Gen said, shaking his head vigorously.

"Then what is your point?"

"Uncle Fiacre won't be forced to put up with us because he never comes here. When was the last time he was here, did you ask him? Or Venex?"

Lairgnen frowned. "I never asked."

"Well, I asked the butler, and he told me that the last time Uncle Fiacre was here was before his Consort's death. That's over fifteen years ago."

Lairgnen dropped his arms to his sides and took a step back, just staring at him. After a moment, he started to pace, then stopped and looked up. "So what you're saying is, we shouldn't invest here," Lairgnen finally said.

"Shouldn't isn't the right word. We don't *need* to," Gen said. "However, if you really want to invest, I heard from a friend of mine that the neighboring property to the Bolton's, no, sorry, ours, has just gone up for sale."

Lairgnen gestured with his hand. "Go on, I'm listening."

"Felimid Mac Thréinfhir died two years ago, and since then, his father, Prince Ráibhilin, has let the property go to waste. He lost interest in running the place. He died in his sleep three weeks ago, just before we got married."

"And now the property's for sale," Lairgnen said, nodding his head.

"Felimid was a year younger than me, but he hardly ever went out because he was very sickly. Ráibhilin was the last of his line, and he's survived by his wife, Princess Mealla, who has always been vocal about her distaste for Merifael."

"She can't wait to unload the property," Lairgnen said.

"Yes," Gen said, glad that Lairgnen had caught on. "When Mother was still alive, she told me that my grandfather had always wanted the Thréinfhir land because it lay smack between Toullec and Bolton lands. If we succeed in buying it, we won't have to deal with border taxes. Also, the Thréinfhir have these magnificent forests. They grow oak by the acre, and they used to be the main suppliers of oak barrels. Their cellars can store up to ten thousand barrels per cellar, and they have ten of those. Before we had our own cellars, Mother used to rent one or two from the Thréinfhir."

"What about laboratories?"

"The same. Before Felimid died, Thréinfhir was at the top of the ranks in winemaking, so their laboratories were well equipped. But not anymore."

"Who holds that position now?"

"When Mother was alive, it was us." Gen couldn't quite contain his pride at that announcement.

"But no longer?"

"No. No one is." Gen grinned. "Now that I've regained control, I aim to get Toullec Vineyards back to top. With the Thréinfhir property, I can do that in less than a year."

"You want to regain what your father carelessly threw

away." Lairgnen nodded and his brows furrowed as he appeared to think over Gen's proposal.

"You've read my mind," Gen said.

"So you weren't just playing on the sand," Lairgnen said, a speculative gleam in his eyes.

Gen scoffed. "No. While you were working and leaving me alone, I was reading and learning."

"And biding your time." Lairgnen nodded appreciatively.

"I learned from the best." Gen grinned broadly.

A slow, satisfied smile broke over Lairgnen's face. "You are a Toullec, through and through."

"Thank you," Gen said, swelling with pride. He had managed to please Lairgnen, a feat he'd never thought to accomplish.

"Now," Lairgnen said, rubbing his palms together. "Do we go to the village, or make a bid for the Thréinfhir vineyards?"

Gin raised a finger. "Here's the thing. I think Mealla feels cornered, because, and this is according to my source, the bank is about to foreclose on the property at the end of the month. That leaves us ten days to negotiate with her."

"Is it a direct buyer kind of deal, or can we send in my agent, Uthman, and have him handle the negotiations?"

Gen shook his head. "I'm not sure. My source didn't go that deep."

Lairgnen leaned against the side of his desk and stared into space. After a while, he began tapping his pinky finger against the side of the desk. In the short time they'd been together, Gen learned to recognize some of Lairgnen's habits. The tapping usually happened when he was in deep thought.

Finally, Lairgnen's eyes refocused on him. "What do you think about cutting our honeymoon short and going back to Merifael?"

A slow, broad grin spread over Gen's face. "You've read my mind again, *amaer*."

CHAPTER SIXTEEN

Lairgnen couldn't help how proud he felt watching Gen run up the stairs. His young husband had once more proven he had a head for business. Frigga had trained her son well in the ways of business and property management. If he had one regret, it was that she could not see just how well she'd succeeded. For all her sweet personality and angelic beauty, she had inherited the Toullec intelligence and toughness.

He still remembered how Prince Maik used to boast about Frigga's talent and beauty. That was, until she married the priest, Martin. Then Maik had stopped going to the capital entirely. The next thing Lairgnen had heard was that Maik had died in his sleep.

As he looked back at everything that had happened to Gen's family since Maik's death, he began to suspect he was missing some vital information. There were too many questions and too few answers. Most important was how a powerful royal house like Toullec had fallen into the hands of a *pleb* turned priest. There was undoubtedly much more to the scandal that had resulted in the deplorable *ius auction*, and Lairgnen was determined to find out everything he could.

Turning his thoughts back to the present, he wondered about the land that Gen wanted to buy and what it could represent. He shook his head as he walked into the library, where he had set up a temporary office. He picked up the tablet he'd left there earlier and began searching for more information.

"Lair, I've got everything ready. When do you want to leave?"

Lairgnen looked up from his tablet to find Gen had entered the room without him realizing it. With a start, he looked out the window and saw the afternoon sun high in the sky. And his stomach let him know he was hungry.

"How about after lunch?" he said, setting aside his tablet and getting to his feet.

"Our meal is being laid out in the dining room as we speak." Gen smiled.

Lairgnen smiled in return and joined him at the doorway. "You've gotten to know me so well these past three weeks." Then, because he couldn't help himself, he leaned up and placed a kiss on Gen's mouth.

"A little bit, yes," Gen said after kissing him back. "Not as much as I want to, but I don't think it's possible to accomplish that in a lifetime. We learn something new each day, and that allows us to grow."

"Such wise words from such a young man," Lairgnen said.

Gen let out a long sigh. "I wish you'd stopped referring to me as a young man."

Lairgnen frowned. Was that disappointment in his voice? "All right, I'll stop. From now on, I'll just call you by your name."

Gen nodded. "Thank you, that would be much better. I know I'm young, and you're *eons* older than I am, but I'm not that young or naïve. Not anymore, at least."

"Eons?"

Gen laughed. "Well, admittedly, you're not that old, but fifteen years is still fifteen years."

"Why, you little brat, I'm not that old. I'm only nine years older than you." Lairgnen was happy Gen had become so much more confident and relaxed around him.

"My friend got back to me and said that from what she knows, Maella is still in Merifael, but she doesn't know what kind of sale Maella's thinking about. What she is certain of is that Maella wants to unload as fast as she can to beat the bank."

Lairgnen chewed on his food thoughtfully. "Then I think it's a direct buyer she's looking for. She's got her pride and wants to have as much control over her affairs as she can. Were you able to get a number so we can call her directly?"

Gen nodded, his eyes twinkling. "I can do better than that. I got the number, and I've already called Maella."

"You did what?"

"She knows who I am. And remember, we're neighbors, so she knew Mother as well. Maella asked that we go directly to her so we could discuss options."

"You continue to astound me, Gen. Good work," Lairgnen said, and he meant it.

"My only problem would be that she's very familiar with who I am and may use that to her advantage."

"Did you tell her you're my husband?"

Gen scoffed. "Who doesn't know we're married is the better question. But yes, she does know you. I didn't tell her you were coming with me, though."

"What are you planning to say to her?"

"I'm still thinking about it, and from what I remember of her, she was quite the proud lady. She never let anybody forget that she was of noble lineage."

"Maybe that's the reason why she's doing all this in a rush . . . to save face?" Lairgnen was quite familiar with how families who'd retained their names but lost their fortunes behaved.

"Most definitely. That would mean she's going to ask for a lot of money for the land. Maybe too much?"

"Hmm, let me call my contact at the bank it's tied to." Lairgnen was just about to do that but stopped when Gen held up his hand.

"If you do, they'll know something's going on, and we may

have a bidding war instead."

"Don't worry, I can be discreet."

"Okay. I trust you," Gen said.

Lairgnen didn't know how to respond to that, so he kept his silence. But his heart did somersaults. Once they finished their meal, they didn't waste any more time in Black Corral Cove.

They were settling into their transporter when Lairgnen belatedly remembered he hadn't called to advise his host about their change of plans.

Thankfully, all Venex did was laugh, as though he knew the extended honeymoon was not going to last as long as had been planned. "I don't blame Gen. I'm beginning to climb the walls myself. There's nothing much to do here other than seeing the sights and strolling around the beach. Sila can't even manage either of those activities anymore. Just last night, she told me she couldn't wait to get back to civilization after our child is born. I'll see you at the capital in a few months."

With nothing else holding them back, Lairgnen and Gen eagerly left for Merifael.

It was a twelve-hour flight that soon found Gen sleeping with his head resting on Lairgnen's shoulder. The position should have been uncomfortable, but Lairgnen only felt reassured that he was giving comfort to his husband. The Call had become stronger over the weeks, and Lairgnen didn't know how much longer he could hold out. Maybe it was time for another late-night discussion.

He was still mulling over how he would make his move when his communicator rang. Relieved with the momentary reprieve from his lustful thoughts, he hurriedly picked up the call.

"Lair, I heard you've ended your honeymoon early. I hope everything's all right?" Llewellyn's voice came through laced with worry.

"There's nothing to worry about. Gen wants to buy the property adjacent to ours, and we wanted to talk to the owner before anyone else could make an offer."

"Goddess, you married a miniature you," Llewellyn said. "You two are truly matched."

"I already told you Gen's got a brilliant mind, but you're right. We're more compatible than even I initially thought." He looked down with a smile and ran his hand down Gen's shoulder to his elbow. "What's the real reason you're calling, Llew?"

"I managed to track Laoghaire's whereabouts, and she's now under Anwyll's protection."

Lairgnen's hand froze mid-caress. "Where did you find her?"

"I hope Gen's sleeping?"

"How did you know he's asleep? And what's that got to do with Laoghaire's whereabouts?"

"Because you're whispering. So, is he sleeping? Because if he is, I urge you not to make a sound when I tell you where she's been all this time."

"Will you stop being melodramatic and just tell me where she was?"

Llewellyn snorted. "With the Sisterhood of Gallizenae."

For a moment there, Lairgnen thought Llewellyn had spoken wrong. "Are you sure? Why would—"

"Lower your voice," Llewellyn cut in sharply.

Lairgnen bit out a low expletive, glancing down at Gen as he did so. He didn't want him to hear this news about Laoghaire.

"Why would Martin send her there of all places?"

"None of the nine knew why. But they did confirm that it had been Martin who had brought her there. He left them money for her upkeep."

"How is she?" Lairgnen asked, attempting to focus on Laoghaire and not the subject of the poor nuns.

"She's amazingly pretty and quite the chatterbox, but otherwise, the nine were quite relieved we got her out of the monastery. One of them said she was a distraction none of them needed."

"You're saying they willingly surrendered her over to you?" Lairgnen smiled stiffly, trying his best not to lose it, but his resolve broke, and he started to laugh. He struggled to keep himself quiet, but he couldn't get away from the image of how the poor nuns could have suffered in Laoghaire's presence.

"Don't laugh," Llewellyn said, but his voice shook with mirth. "I left them a considerable amount of money to recompense them for their time of great difficulty, which, of course, was more than welcomed. They claimed they couldn't hear themselves pray because the little brat kept interrupting them by asking all sorts of questions. Before we left, they added that under no circumstances would they accept Laoghaire back into the monastery unless it involved a situation that would potentially harm her."

Lairgnen drew in a deep breath, but his lips kept breaking out into a grin. "Did she tell you anything that may tell us about Martin's motives?"

"No, but dear Laoghaire told me that she may have caused a storm because the nine couldn't focus on their prayers. The little brat's version was that she tried to help in the prayers but kept confusing words. She may have accidentally prayed for rain clouds instead and caused a deluge. Goddess, she's adorable, but I think she may have worn out those poor women."

Lairgnen's control broke. His shoulders shook as he tried desperately not to startle Gen from his sleep. The Sisterhood of Gallizenae was composed of nine women, usually virgins, who were well known for their healing gifts and their ability to control the weather. They were highly revered by farmers and fisherfolk, who asked for their assistance in times of need.

"What's important is that she's safe and under Anwyll's protection. Gen will be relieved," Lairgnen said when he finally regained control over his hilarity. "This is good news, Llew, but it leads us to another question. Why did Martin go to such lengths as to send Laoghaire away? It couldn't have been because he was concerned over how the auction could have affected her."

Llewellyn scoffed. "Not likely. Martin's proving more and more to be a thorn on our side."

Lairgnen sobered and absently combed his fingers through Gen's hair. He'd found that whenever he did that, Gen would fall into a relaxed sleep. In his case, though, it helped him focus and remain calm.

"How long before you reach Merifael?" Llewellyn asked.

"Not for another six hours. It'll be late by then, so we'll have to play catch up in the morning."

"I'm still at the capital, so I won't be able to see you until the day after. Tell Gen not to worry about Laoghaire. Anwyll's fallen in love with her and has instructed his aides to get her tutors and dresses befitting a princess. Apparently, her clothes were beneath his good taste. I had no idea our king was so well informed about fashion for little girls."

Lairgnen chuckled. "I think you're talking about Uncle Fiacre, not Anwyll. All right, I'll see you the day after tomorrow."

"Before you go, I need you to speak to Gen. Tell him that Anwyll has decided Laoghaire should stay in the capital until such time as we get to the bottom of Martin's plans. I'll send you the details after I get all of them. She's going to be a spoilt little princess, that Laoghaire. Pedr's already gone and made preparations for a separate wing assigned to her."

Lairgnen had to laugh. Pedr and Anwyll might say they were not yet ready to have children, but if what Llewellyn was saying was true, their actions were telling of their real feelings.

"No need to worry, I'll tell him. I was just going to suggest it, and I think Gen will understand."

After Llewellyn ended the call, Lairgnen found himself contemplating the changes in his life. With their honeymoon over, he and Gen would be living openly as a married couple. His villa at the capital had been good enough when he was living alone, but he'd known it wouldn't be sufficient after he married.

The day after they'd arrived at Black Corral Cove, Lairgnen had made arrangements with his agent to rent out the small house and search for a more appropriate dwelling. He'd received word the week before that his agent had been successful in his hunt and just the day before had given his approval on the purchase. However, the new house needed repairs and wouldn't be habitable for another month or so. It also required new furnishings, and he wondered how compatible his and Gen's taste in decoration would be.

Their trip back to Merifael had come at a good time. Work at Bolton manor had been completed, and Uthman had taken it upon himself to forward documents for registration of a new name. Lairgnen thought about his options but had yet to decide on one.

Gen continued to sleep through the rest of the flight, leaving Lairgnen plenty of time to make plans.

CHAPTER SEVENTEEN

For the first time since his mother's death, Gen felt happy and free. To be so had been the furthest thing in his mind. The Goddess was truly kind, and he sent a silent prayer of gratitude.

His age and the scandal of his auction had made him a target to be taken advantage of. With Lairgnen's protection, and indirectly, the king's, he was now at a point in life where his own actions would direct his future. He had two options. Either take charge and act responsibly, or throw away his future by becoming complacent. He knew exactly which direction he was going to take.

He couldn't stop thinking about the *ius auction*. It was an outdated practice that needed to be stopped. It stripped the victim of their basic rights and dehumanized them, possibly to a degree that could cause irreversible damage to their psyche. He was lucky it had been Lairgnen who had outbid everyone. He couldn't even begin to imagine how his life would have turned out had it been anyone other than his husband.

It was still hard to believe that he was actually bonded, but he was grateful. Only three months before, marriage had been the farthest thing from his mind, much less being bonded. Now he was locked in a situation he never would have considered as an option. Although he was happy and comfortable with how it turned out. Thank the Goddess for her intervention.

Another thought to consider was the idea of having children. Gen smiled to himself. The thought of mini versions of himself and Lairgnen didn't repulse him. In fact, he couldn't wait to meet them once they were born. His thoughts sobered when memories of what he'd endured during the *ius auction* rose its ugly head. That was the moment when Gen determined precisely what he wanted to do . . . and become.

"You want to study law, become a *brehen*? But what about the vineyards? I know nothing about how to care for grapes or manufacture wines. I'm a financier, not a viticulturist." Lairgnen sat back in his chair behind the desk and stared up at Gen.

Gen grinned at him from where he stood in front of the desk with his arms behind his back. Despite his position, he didn't feel like a schoolboy. He felt ready to take charge of his life. After he'd finally determined what he wanted to do, he had immediately come down from their bedroom and asked to talk to Lairgnen about his plans.

"Winemaking is in my blood, so you don't have to worry about that part. I know the ins and outs of the industry, from managing to manufacturing all the way down to marketing. I also want you to know that before I came to talk to you, I made a few calls and reached out to my mother's former managers and chemists. After she died, my father fired them without out consulting with me. In any case, I talked to them, and they have all agreed to come back. Once I assured them that my father was no longer in the picture, they started packing their bags. They're waiting for me to send them funds so they can get to Merifael at the soonest time possible."

Lairgnen leaned forward and rested his elbows on his desk. "You don't need my permission to send them money, Gen. What's mine is yours. But back to what we were talking about earlier. Why are you not taking a subject that could help you run the vineyard? Why law?"

Gen bowed his head. "I thought about that, and I realized

I wouldn't learn anything that I didn't already know. My family, as well as the Thréinfhirs and Boltons, were the ones who wrote the books on the science and art of viticulture on Kizerain. It was they who discovered that the old ways could not be applied here and experimented on different techniques to achieve the best results. Studying law wouldn't directly have anything to do with viticulture, but it would ensure that our children, and their children's children, will never have to suffer the way I did."

"King Anwyll is already working on outlawing *ius auction*," Lairgnen said.

Gen met his gaze and took a deep breath to calm himself. There was a peculiar dark look to Lairgnen's eyes that always made his heart race and his skin tingle.

"I know he is." He sighed. "But what I'm talking about are the other archaic practices that are equally dehumanizing. I can't enjoy my freedom when others might go through the pain and embarrassment from being sold like they were nothing. The men and women who touched me as if I were nothing more than an animal was the most terrifying and degrading moment of my life. I've thanked the Goddess countless times for sending you to me, Lair, and I can't . . . I refuse to allow the possibility of our children having to go through that. Or to be threatened by similar practices. I just can't."

"You're talking about children," Lairgnen said. "Our children."

Gen felt his cheeks burn, but he bravely met Lairgnen's gaze. "I know we haven't consummated our marriage yet, but I know that eventually, we will. I can't resist you for much longer, as you well know."

A smile tugged on Lairgnen's lips, and his expression softened. "So, the thought of having children with me, you're all right with that?"

"Yes, I look forward to it. I even started praying to the

Goddess to grant us a visit from the Sheelan Sisterhood."

"What makes you think they will grant us a child when they haven't even approached Anwyll and Pedr?"

"I can only hope, Lair. Why are you asking? Do you not want to have children?"

"Rest easy, Gen. I do want children. It's just that we've never discussed it before, and you took me by surprise by bringing it up."

Gen nodded. "So, can I go to university and take up law?"

Lairgnen shook his head, and Gen felt his heart drop. He had hoped to gain permission. He braced himself to hear whatever excuse was forthcoming when Lairgnen got up and stood in front of him.

Lairgnen placed one hand on his shoulder while the other lifted his chin to meet his gaze. "You didn't have to ask mine or anyone's permission, Gen. I am thankful, however, that you came to me and explained the reasons behind your decision."

Gen searched Lairgnen's face and saw only amusement and a curious light in his eyes that he thought was pride.

"You mean it? That I didn't have to get your permission?"

"Yes, I mean it." Lairgnen dropped his hands and placed them inside his pockets. "Gen, when you married me, you immediately gained maturity, and that means you have full control over all your properties, including Laoghaire's upbringing. I thought you already knew that."

"I . . . It didn't occur to me," Gen said, suddenly self-conscious. Once again, he had shown his naïveté.

"There's another thing that I should mention, and I hope you pay close attention." When Gen nodded, Lairgnen grinned. "May I remind you that now we're married, what's mine is yours, but not the other way around."

Gen frowned. "Why? Isn't that unfair to you?"

"While we were in the Trennet Coast, I dug deeper into the

laws surrounding *ius auction* and have confirmed my findings with the cleric council. As the winning bidder, I became your protector, and by extension Laoghaire's, as well as your properties. I agree, it is a disgusting practice, but you have to know how it came about. Its history, and most of our people's history, is centered around clan wars, deaths, rape, property theft, and so on." He paused and shook his head. "The elders declared that through *ius auction*, the innocent should not be punished. Because they were innocents in the first place, it meant they could not protect themselves or what they owned. However, those who were stronger and capable could ensure families and their properties were safe from unscrupulous land grabbers."

"But what about those who abused their roles, what about them?"

"I read up on it and discovered their violations were punishable by death. As far as I know, that has not been changed either."

Something in the way Lairgnen chose his words raised Gen's suspicions. "What are you saying?"

"That Martin, because of his mishandling and abuse of the right to *ius auction*, can be sentenced to death by the king."

Gen's heart dropped at the unexpected detail. "How is he to die then, should he be found guilty?"

"First, his family line is to be stricken from the annals of history, and their name shall never be used again. Family, by definition, reaches down to the farthest blood relative. Second is the question of how he is to be put to death. The king only has one option listed under the violations."

"And what is that?"

"Decapitation."

"I don't think . . . I don't think it should come to that." Gen gave an involuntary shiver.

"I understand, and personally, I don't think it's the right

choice. However, we can't deny that Martin chose a particularly archaic practice so he could grab Toullec lands from the royal family. What he did, should it be proven, can be seen as treasonous and unholy." Lairgnen shook his head. "Martin didn't think too far with this one. His only concern was his greed."

Gen felt as though the weight of the world sat on his shoulders. With a sudden need for comfort and stability, he walked toward Lairgnen, who opened his arms and welcomed him.

"Why did Mother have to marry him?" Gen wrapped his arms around Lairgnen's back and buried his face into his neck.

"That, Gen, is the question that I keep going back to. Frigga made a particularly bad mistake, but if they hadn't met, you wouldn't be here, and I wouldn't be bonded to you."

"You always come up with something positive to say," He stayed snuggled to Lairgnen and breathed in his scent, thinking about what to say next. When it came, he leaned back and met Lairgnen's gaze. "Can I ask you to do something for me? Please don't tell anyone."

"Of course, Gen, anything. What is it?"

"Who can we go to for a test to see if I am Martin's son?"

"You mean . . ."

"I was talking to Laoghaire last night before you came in, and she said that I was a Toullec while she was obviously Father's daughter."

"You think there's a possibility Martin's not your father at all?" Lairgnen's brows furrowed.

Gen nodded. "I thought about what she said all night, and at that time, I felt sorry for myself. But then this morning, I got to thinking. I've always wondered why Father disliked me so much. With Laoghaire, he was so different, even loving. He would listen to her even when she prattled on endlessly. With me, all I had to do was be in the same room, and he would go off in a mood."

Lairgnen sighed. "Gen, if we do go and get that test, and the results show you are not his son, it could mean an immediate death sentence for Martin."

"I know that, and I don't like the thought of it, but it would explain a lot of things for me. I also want to know why my mother died when she did. I was away at school at that time and only learned of her death several days after. I barely made it to her funeral. Lair, I need answers. I need to know."

Gen searched Lairgnen's face, silently begging him to understand where he was coming from. After a long minute, Lairgnen gravely nodded.

"I'll make an appointment for next week," Lairgnen said.

"Thank you," Gen said before brushing his lips against Lairgnen's.

CHAPTER EIGHTEEN

"Stop fidgeting." Lairgnen didn't have to look at Gen to see how excited he was. The chair they shared squeaked and shook from his movements. Instead, he focused his attention on the scenery below them.

They were flying above the Thréinfhir property, which he and Gen had just closed the deal on. The early morning mists had been burned off the ground by the sun, and Lairgnen could clearly see the three rivers that Gen had told him about. No wonder Gen and his mother had coveted the Thréinfhir lands. It was prime property. The rivers were not big enough for commercial use, but they provided easy transportation between the Toullec, Bolton, and Thréinfhir properties.

Upon their arrival at the manor, Princess Maella hadn't wasted time on small talk. After exchanging greetings, she led Lairgnen and Gen to the morning room, where two of her *brehens* were waiting for them. Documents for transfer of property had already been drawn out and ready for their signatures. Lairgnen had read over the contract, pleasantly surprised when Gen pointed out the same points of discussion that he had found. It was a simple sale contract, and once the price was agreed upon, seals were pressed. Maella excused herself, simply stating her transporter was ready to take her back to the capital. One hour later, Lairgnen and Gen had the papers and keys to the property.

"I'm just nervous, Lair. And excited. And scared. What if someone had approached Maella and made her an offer she couldn't refuse?"

"No one did."

"You sound so calm and unaffected. Why can't I be like you?" Gen threw up his hands and slumped back into his seat.

"You have to be of a certain age." Lairgnen smirked when Gen rolled his eyes.

"You mean old?"

"Brat," Lairgnen teased. "Is the property that important to you?"

"I can still remember Mother getting frustrated whenever we passed by its borders. She had dreams. So yes, it is that important to me."

"Then we did well." Lairgnen smiled and waggled his brow. "Maella not only had documents drawn out ready for us to sign, but she also lowered the buying price so we wouldn't get a chance to change our minds. As you said back in Trennet Coast, she was in a hurry. Also, you have to remember that the Thréinfhirs are royals, so no one can just come in and offer to buy their property. The worst-case scenario was if the bank had pulled the property, all they could have done is to inform the king and allow him to purchase it from them. Should he refuse, they would have to go through the hierarchy of royals. With over twenty thousand members, that can take years."

"I didn't know they had to do that," Gen said, understanding lighting up his eyes. "See? That's why I need to take up law. Why didn't I know about that particular detail? Why didn't Maella?"

"All right, you've made your point." Lairgnen chuckled.

He ran the tip of his finger down Gen's cheek and followed the path with a kiss. Gen turned slightly, so the kiss landed on his lips and lasted more than a mere second. Lairgnen sighed and breathed in Gen's scent. It was becoming more and more impossible to hold himself back. Thankfully, Gen seemed to have lost most of his shyness and no longer looked nervous whenever they were this close together. Little steps, Lairgnen told himself, not for the first time.

"Do you have to get back to work soon?" Gen asked after a while. He relaxed more and laid his head on Lairgnen's shoulder, clasping his hand.

"No. Technically, we're still on our honeymoon." Lairgnen turned his head to kiss the top of Gen's head. "Why?"

"Oh. Okay. So, what's next on our agenda?"

"We have the whole day free. Again, why? What do you want to do?" Lairgnen could sense the eagerness Gen couldn't quite hide.

"Can we go to Farholde?" Gen straightened and faced him.

"We can do whatever you want." Lairgnen nodded slowly, sensing Gen wanted to do something specific, and he was curious about what that would be. It would give him a chance to get to know Gen better.

"Then, can we go to the fair?"

"What's that about?" Lairgnen didn't want to reveal he'd never been to a local fair before and didn't know what to expect.

"It's a local artisan fair where everyone gets to display their art and crafts," Gen explained. He laughed when Lairgnen scrunched his face in doubt. "I promise you're going to have fun."

"Sounds . . . interesting," Lairgnen said with care. He wasn't really interested in art but was willing to give it a try if only to please Gen.

"There's this stall I go to every year. I'm friends with the daughter of the family that drafts homebrewed beer. She's the one who tipped me on the Thréinfhir property. I was thinking of introducing the two of you, because she's very important to me." Gen grinned from ear to ear, obviously eager to go to the fair.

Lairgnen blinked his surprise. This was the first time Gen had mentioned someone important to him other than Laoghaire. "How important?"

Gen leaned forward and kissed him on the lips. "Nothing to worry about. We're only friends, promise. You'll see why later when you meet her."

Lairgnen cleared his throat. He was more affected by Gen's freely given kiss than he let on.

"You don't drink wine, but you drink beer?" Lairgnen said instead.

Gen looked and acted so innocent, and he'd always refused a drink whenever he was offered one. That he actually drank beer was something quite unexpected.

"I drink her beer. She brews non-alcoholic as well as alcoholic. Plus, she developed this grading system, where you can choose just how strong you want your drink to be. I taste wine, but I'm not so keen on drinking because it gives me a headache. Please don't tell anybody I told you that."

Lairgnen's interest grew despite finding the thought of a viticulturist who didn't drink wine amusing. "All right, I won't say a word. Where is this fair you're talking about?"

"At Farholde. It's not far, only about fifteen minutes by transporter to the south of Merifael. They hold the fair in the middle of the week each week. It's early yet, so there won't be much of a crowd. That happens in the middle of the day when the food merchants start dishing out their delicacies."

The mention of food made Lairgnen lean forward to tap on his driver's shoulder. They had gotten up early to meet with Princess Maella, but that had been over four hours earlier, and he was getting hungry again.

"Take us to Farholde," he instructed.

The driver nodded and typed in the coordinates on the control panel.

"You won't regret it, promise." Gen grinned ear to ear. His

eyes sparkled and gleamed with excitement, making him look even more handsome than he already was.

Lairgnen leaned back and smiled, willing his erection to stay down. "We're not scheduled to get back to the capital until next week. We can do whatever we want until then. What other things do you want to do?"

Whatever excitement Gen had was quickly replaced with the nervousness from earlier. Only this time, Lairgnen felt it was because of something darker. Gen closed his eyes tightly and bent his head, clearly trying to hold onto his composure. Whatever was causing Gen's pain gave rise to a driving need to protect him at all costs. Lairgnen reached out with his senses to get a feel of what Gen was thinking about. But all he could see were corridors filled with dark shadows mixed with a sense of hopelessness and despair.

"I was thinking about going back to Toullec manor to get all my things," Gen said in a soft voice.

Lairgnen nodded in understanding. He reached out to engage the privacy button so the driver wouldn't hear their conversation. He hadn't misinterpreted Gen's reluctance to the house that he now seemed to dread.

"That's been done and taken care of weeks ago." Lairgnen gave his driver a side glance. He didn't doubt the privacy mode worked perfectly well, but he couldn't help checking to see how the driver reacted to it being closed. "While we were in the south, Anwyll gave instructions to have the house cleared of Martin's belongings, while yours were taken to my home in the capital."

"Oh, I didn't know that." Gen looked away and bit on his lip.

Lairgnen reached out a hand and lightly tapped Gen's wrist. "What is it? Talk to me. No one can hear us." He tilted his head toward the driver.

Gen shook his head and took Lairgnen's hand in his.

Lairgnen looked down at their clasped hands.

"I didn't want to say anything to you before," Gen said. "To be honest, I wasn't too keen about going back there."

"Anwyll suggested you might feel that way, so I kept quiet and waited until you were ready to talk about it." He slanted his head to the side, trying to read Gen's body language. He could see doubt and a hint of fear in the way Gen bowed his head. Lairgnen turned his hand so he could hold Gen's in his.

Gen shook his head but kept it down. "I can't think about that house as home, not anymore. Not since Mother died."

Lairgnen sighed and, not for the first time, wished Gen hadn't had to go through what he did. He wanted to kick himself for not getting to the auction earlier, but logic prevailed, like it always did.

"You know, it's perfectly normal for you to feel that way. As for the house, it is the Toullec royal family seat, and you are the last of the male line. Should you have no children, Laoghaire's husband would have to take up your name so their children will become your heirs. Like it or not, you're going to have to go back."

"I know, but right now, I can't think about it. I just can't." Gen flexed his fingers, curling and uncurling them.

"What do you want to do with the house?" Lairgnen asked, keeping his voice soft.

Gen took a deep breath and turned his head until his gaze met Lairgnen's.

"I want to close it up, leave a caretaker to maintain the property." Gen shrugged. "I don't know, maybe Laoghaire may want to stay in it in the future. What I do know is that I can't go back there. Or raise our children there. In any case, we'll be in the capital for most of the time until we have a new king or queen. When the time comes, we can stay at Bolton manor or Thréinfhir." Gen shrugged. "It doesn't matter."

"Your house is so much bigger and grander than the

Bolton's — "

Gen held up his hand to stop him from continuing. "It is, but then, it doesn't have that domed solarium, and we still have to check out the contents of that hidden room by the master's suite." Gen grinned. "I know what I want to do for the rest of the week."

"The room?" Lairgnen flashed a grin of his own. He hadn't forgotten about the mysterious hidden room and was just as excited as Gen about discovering the contents.

"The room," Gen gave a swift nod. "Let me call ahead, so my friend knows we're meeting her."

Lairgnen smiled, seeing Gen's gloom had lifted.

A beeping noise distracted him, and for a moment, he was confused where it was coming from until he saw the driver waving to get his attention. He released the privacy mode and met the driver's gaze when he turned to look over his shoulder.

"We're approaching Farholde, Your Highness," the driver announced before Lairgnen could say anything.

They landed in a clearing where other transporters were parked, hovering over the grass. Lairgnen looked around curiously and felt a bit apprehensive and out of his element. Unlike the Trennet Coast or Merifael, Farholde was basically a village. All around him were trees, fields . . . and cattle? He puzzled over the curious animals and blinked at the oddity of their form.

The cattle, as that was what Lairgnen assumed them to be, had a rigid neck with a large bear-like head, two dark compound eyes, and wide, slitted nostrils. They had short, stubby ears that flicked every which way as though the beast were listening to the noise around them. What really caught his attention were the two sets of dainty-looking wings on their backs, which glinted in a wonderful prism of colors wherever the sun hit them. Their bodies were covered with long, silky gray hair that hung close to the ground.

Gen stepped up beside him, and their shoulders brushed. Lairgnen reacted on instinct and took a step closer to Gen.

"Have you never seen a *bakare* before?" Gen asked.

"No, never. Well, only in pictures. They look incredible." He'd seen the hybrid in pictures before, but seeing the real live beasts sent shivers of nervousness down his spine. "I never imagined them to be so big."

"Those are calves," Gen said. "The mature beasts have to be separated from the young ones as they can get too aggressive. When the scientists bred the original animals with the indigenous ones here, they never considered it would be impossible to breed out the aggression."

"Their wings look so delicate," Lairgnen said, taking a step forward.

"Don't be deceived by the fairy-like appearance. It's strong enough to carry an adult *bakare's* weight, plus more should they choose to carry something off. Their claws are powerful and can eviscerate their prey in seconds."

"How do they even shear off the hair if they're that dangerous?"

"Well, they're aggressive only to those they're not familiar with," Gen shrugged. "They're actually quite docile once they imprint on you. Or, in the case of this herd, their shepherd. Also, they demand to get sheared during the summer months. I've watched shearing competitions where the *bakare* rushed to take their turns under the scissors."

"They're like pets, then."

"Well, if you're their shepherd, I guess you can consider them to be that. Once the calves gain maturity and can defend themselves from the older ones, they manage to live alongside the others without trouble. They love their shepherd to the extent they will sacrifice their lives to protect him or her."

"Yes, I heard that shepherds are particularly considered

untouchable, but I never imagined how. Now that I see the *bakare* for real, I'm not surprised. They really are quite beautiful, aren't they?"

"They are cute, in a huge kind of way," Gen said hesitantly, but he didn't seem convinced saying it.

"They must weigh at least two or three tons each."

"I've seen bigger, but they're mostly used for breeding rather than work."

Lairgnen's stomach chose that moment to growl. "All right, enough of the beasts, I'm getting hungry, and I'm beginning to smell all sorts of delicious scents coming from behind us." He rubbed his palms together and looked eagerly toward the entrance of the fair.

Gen's laughter rang out across the clearing, the sound of which made Lairgnen pause and stare at his husband's retreating back. The carefree sound was a far cry from Gen's usual, which in hindsight, sounded restrained. It left Lairgnen wondering just how controlling a personality Martin was. A fresh surge of anger rushed through him, and he let out a sigh of frustration as he quickened his steps to catch up with Gen.

They left the parking area and strolled across the clearing toward the fair entrance, followed closely by four of Lairgnen's warrior detail. Soon they arrived at a colorful booth and paid the entrance fee. The farmers and artisans had set their stalls off to the sides, creating an aisle down the middle. Many were vendors hawking their wares, bidding for attention from wandering customers. It was all so quaint and interesting, and Lairgnen soon found his mouth watering as the delicious scents wafted to his nose.

Other stalls had mimes and mummers, some wearing intricately carved masks. People grouped to watch as the performers prattled out scripted lines littered with colorful jokes that had Lairgnen choking back surprised amusement. The raunchy tale was more imaginative than he'd been prepared for.

At another site were gasps of surprise and admiration as groups of acrobats sailed high up in the air from trampolines. Lairgnen motioned to his warriors to keep close. He had no doubt that hiding amongst the crowd were thieves and pick-pockets.

They meandered through the stalls and stopped whenever something caught their eyes. Lairgnen soon found that Gen had a talent for haggling prices. There were times when Lairgnen thought he was bidding too low on an item and wanted to stop him, only to be surprised when the merchant or artist would laugh out loud and compliment Gen.

The sun was high by the time Gen tugged at Lairgnen's sleeve and pointed him to a stall at the very back of the fair.

The first thing Lairgnen noticed as they approached was its size. It looked much like the other stalls erected in the clearing, but it was about twice as tall as it was wide. Also, it had a look of permanence to it. The materials used didn't look cheap or meant to last only a week. Once there, Gen was greeted excitedly by a pretty, young girl of about seven years.

"Gen, you made it," she said, running into his arms.

He swept her off her feet and swung her around, causing delighted squeals. The numerous thin braids of her long blond hair whipped around Gen's head before they fell back down over her shoulders.

"Hello, young Noirin. Where're your parents?" Gen said as he set her back on the ground.

"Mama's at the back. Fafa won't be back until later. I'll go get her," Noirin said. Without waiting for a reply, she spun around and quickly disappeared to the back of the stall.

"Is this your friend's beer stall you were telling me about?" Lairgnen looked at the many wooden vats that lined the top of the counter. The smell of hops was strong — a heady mix of spice, mint, plus a multitude of different aromas all in one.

The overall effect was deliciously exotic.

"Yes, I'll introduce you to her once she's come out." Gen closed his eyes and sniffed in appreciation. "The headier the aroma, the more intense the alcohol content." He opened his eyes and grinned broadly.

"You sound like you know a lot about beer." Lairgnen looked at him in surprise.

Gen coughed into his fist. "I never told Father, but Caitriona and I used to hang out a lot whenever school was out and experiment on drafting different kinds of beer."

"Caitriona?"

The situation was getting curiouser and curiouser by the minute. Who was this woman that was so influential that she could make Gen drink beer?

"And he got so drunk one time, I had to drag him by his collar, because he fell asleep on a boat, fell over, and nearly drowned," chimed a husky, feminine voice. "You're late, shorty. Lunch is getting cold."

Lairgnen swung around to see who had spoken, gaping at the woman who came out from behind the stall. Her blue gaze studied him from the top of his head down to his feet and back again. Her shining mass of coppery hair was braided much like Noirin's had been, but instead of falling loose over her shoulders, hers was piled up high on her head. It was also adorned with feathers that appeared to have come from the tail of a blue-banded hawk. The leather trousers she wore hugged her curvaceous form like a second skin. She was probably the most beautiful woman Lairgnen had ever set eyes on—also the tallest and biggest. To his surprise, Gen's friend also happened to be one of the rare giants of old.

Caitriona wiped her hands with a white rag, and when she was done, she threw it onto her shoulder. She grinned broadly and threw her arms around Gen, lifting him into a bear hug.

"Cait, come on, we're not kids anymore," Gen protested

between bouts of laughter.

"I thought you up and got married already, squirt. How come you haven't grown an inch since then? You're still short." Caitriona tsked as she lowered Gen onto the ground.

Gen grinned at Caitriona, who placed her hands on her hips as she checked Lairgnen out once more.

"Is this the prince you married?" Caitriona asked, shaking her head. "Why, he's just as short as you are."

"Lair's not short. You're just a giant, Cait," Gen said in a teasing tone.

"Well, he's shorter than you are," Caitriona said.

Gen mock growled and jumped her, but she twisted away and playfully swatted at him with her rag.

Lairgnen couldn't recall having ever met a woman as tall as Caitriona, and *giant* was an understatement. Gen was taller than he was at an inch over six feet, but his head only came up to her stomach. She was clearly over three heads taller than he was.

"I'm just average, Gen, you know that. Admit it, you're short like the rest of those humans," Caitriona said. Without waiting to be introduced, she faced Lairgnen and offered her hand in greeting. "Caitriona Ailín, Master Brewster, at your service, highness."

Lairgnen looked down at the proffered hand before him. He took her hand and watched in consternation as his hand disappeared into her much larger one.

"You're really a giant, aren't you?" Lairgnen said. As soon as the words left his mouth, he closed his eyes and mentally kicked himself.

Caitriona laughed, throwing back her head and slapping her hands over her thighs. "Yes, I really am. Farholde's where my people settled after the Great Passage."

Lairgnen frowned up at Caitriona thoughtfully. Her name rang familiar. "You don't happen to be related to the General

Ailín of history, do you?"

"I am," she said with a tilt of her chin. "In fact, he's a direct ancestor of mine. If I'm not mistaken, he's my great, great . . ." Caitriona's voice faded as she ticked off on her fingers, then shook her head and dropped her hand to her side. "I can't remember how many greats exactly, but yes, we're related."

"Forgive Lair, Cait. He's never actually met a real giant before," Gen said.

Lairgnen slowly turned his head to glare at his husband but gave up the effort when Gen merely raised a knowing brow at him. Fine time for him to develop a spine.

"I also have never been to a country fair or seen a *bakare* herd before. As for our lateness, Gen gave me a brief lecture about them. Then I got curious and looked around the fair before coming over." Lairgnen widened his eyes at Gen in a mock challenge.

"I was just teasing, highness. Now. Have you tasted Brewster beer before?" Caitriona asked in a challenging tone.

Lairgnen chose his words carefully, not wanting to earn her ire. "Only those brewed by men."

Caitriona scoffed and waved a dismissive hand. "Charlatans, the lot of them. The best beers are those that are brewed by women. Why do men have to shoulder their way into everything whenever they smell money in the air? Come. I'll serve you a fresh batch. I cooked it up yesterday, so it should be a perfect accompaniment to our lunch."

Caitriona didn't wait for a response. She turned and went behind the counter. With her standing in the stall, it seemed to shrink in size, but Lairgnen forgot all that when she bent and hefted up a vat as tall as an average man.

Lairgnen sidled close to Gen and leaned in to whisper in his ear. "I hate to sound so ignorant, but is Noirin really her daughter? I mean, she looks human to me."

Gen nodded, but before he could say anything, Caitriona

spoke up.

"We all start out about the same size as you humans do when we're children, highness. After we reach maturity at around nine or eleven years, we begin to grow to our full potential. I'm still young and won't get to my full height until I'm fifty. I've got twenty years of growing left in me." She smirked. "Didn't you know that along with our size, giants have superior hearing as well?"

"No, I didn't know that," Lairgnen said, feeling embarrassed again.

"Nah, of course you didn't. None of you humans dare to ask us anything about giant biology. Then again, not your fault, 'cause we normally don't talk to humans unless they're going to buy something from us or they need us to help them end conflicts they started and couldn't finish. I'm abnormal in the sense that this guy here, this squirt, is one of my best friends. Gen was such a rascal that he had the cheek of befriending a giant's daughter when said giant went to work over at the vineyards for his mother."

"Your father did?" Lairgnen turned to Gen. "He worked for your mother?"

Gen nodded. "Crannog was her trusted oenologist."

"Eno what? I apologize, but I'm not familiar with that word." Lairgnen was so out of his element, he could only scrunch his face with his confusion.

"Oenologist," Gen said again and then spelled the word for clarity.

"Spelling it out won't help your husband understand what it means, Gen," Caitriona said, dipping a huge ladle into the vat. She poured the contents into a mug she had magically fished out from over the counter. "Fafa worked directly with the princess as the wine production supervisor. He also acted as manager for Toullec Vineyards. What he did was proper. Men and women can be oenologists, but when it comes to

162

beer, only women can be Brewsters. A proper Brewster, that is. Not those pretentious men who are only in it for the money."

Understanding dawned on Lairgnen, but secretly, he was laughing at Gen's disconcerted look. The two obviously knew each other quite well. He was glad Gen had a true friend in Caitriona, for she seemed to be the no-nonsense type of woman who could stand on her own ideals.

"You're talking about your father in the past tense," Lairgnen said.

"Fafa died with the princess when they were on their way to the capital to speak with King Eljin. At least, that was what he told me they were going to do." Caitriona handed the filled mug to Lairgnen and began to fill another. "Give this a try, prince. Mind you, it's quite strong, so if you're not used to alcohol, consider yourself fairly warned."

"I'm used to alcohol, thank you," Lairgnen said.

"Lair, Caitriona's beer isn't like the ones you're used to. That's really quite strong," Gen warned as he pointed at the mug.

Lairgnen looked into the mug. The golden brew looked much like what he thought beer to be, except the liquid was clearer and had more bubbles in it. He took a tentative sniff and was awarded a mild, almost sweet aroma. It truly was different from what he was used to, but it also smelled better. Hesitantly, he took a sip and was surprised at the cool, semi-sweet taste. Strangely, it felt like it coated the back of his throat, and whatever thirst he'd felt before was quenched.

"Well? Tell me what you think," Caitriona said in a curious tone.

"I like it, actually. This is really good," Lairgnen said. He took another sip and savored the way the flavors hit his palate. He let it sit a moment longer and found he enjoyed the tingling sensation before it dissipated into a beautiful and aromatic after taste.

"Good. Glad you like it." Caitriona turned to Gen and handed him another mug. "This one's similar to his, but it's non-alcoholic. Not as great tasting, but just as good, if you ask Noirin. Now go on out back. I was cooking up lunch just before you arrived, so go ahead and take a seat while I pour some of these into pitchers."

"Thank you, Cait." Gen took a sip from his mug. "Is Gentry joining us?"

"He said he was coming in later, so we can go ahead and eat without him," Caitriona said.

"This is great, by the way. Delicious as always. Come on, Lair, let's go eat. Caitriona's a great cook." Gen tilted his head in the direction of the back of the stall and led the way.

"Who's Gentry?" Lairgnen asked.

"Oh, sorry. Gentry is Caitriona's husband. He's a shepherd, but he's also Farholde's mayor."

"Does the *bakare* herd we saw earlier belong to him?"

Gen pursed his lips. "I'm not exactly sure. There're quite a few shepherds scattered about Farholde, but I wouldn't be surprised if that particular herd was his. This is his land we're sitting on."

Lairgnen filed away the information as he continued to sip on his beer. The more he drank, the more he realized it was probably the best he'd ever tasted. "Gen, do you think we can buy some of this and take it home with us?"

Gen nodded. "We can talk with Cait while we eat. I'm sure we can come to a good price for a vat or two to take back to the capital."

"I was thinking more like several vats, not just one or two." Lairgnen took another sip of his beer and savored the burst of flavors, finding it sitting light and easy in his stomach.

"That shouldn't be a problem. You're looking at a stall, but the Ailín women have brewed beer since before the Great

Passage, so you can trust she will be able to manage several vats at a moment's notice."

"No worries, squirt. When and where do you want the beer, highness?"

Caitriona placed the two pitchers on the table. They were so big Lairgnen wondered how they were supposed to finish it.

"Can you get them sent up to the capital by next week?" Lairgnen asked, taking his gaze off the pitchers.

"Done. After lunch, we can talk about the details, but right now, I'm worried you're going to keel over and sleep where you're sitting. You're nearly done with that mug, and your stomach's been grumbling since we got introduced." Caitriona raised her voice and called for her daughter.

Noirin came running around the front of the stall and sat beside her mother.

Time passed inconspicuously. Lairgnen, Gen, and Caitriona sat at the picnic table talking about anything and everything around the affairs of Kizerain. His warrior detail looked like they were enjoying themselves as well, sitting at another table Caitriona had pointed them to.

Lairgnen poured himself another mug of the beer, laughing off Gen's warning that the beer was stronger than he thought it was. The more Lairgnen imbibed, the more Gen became agitated. He couldn't understand what was worrying Gen so much. He'd had stronger drinks than beer and never gotten drunk.

"Lair, don't you think you've had enough?" Gen asked in a worried tone.

"No, no, let him be, Gen. He's an adult and can control himself if he wants to," Caitriona said as she sipped from her mug of beer.

"But Cait, he's not used to your beer," Gen said, looking up at Caitriona.

"All right, sweet Gen, I'll stop. But only after I finish this." Lairgnen raised his mug to Gen. His heart felt light and happy. He was pleased he was sitting close to Gen and didn't understand why he was so worried.

"Come on, Lair, enough of the beer," Gen cajoled. "The hour's getting late, and we have to get back. Also, Caitlin still has to sell her beer."

At Gen's coaxing, Lairgnen put down his half-full mug and rose unsteadily to his feet. Noirin started to giggle into her hand while Caitriona openly grinned at him.

"I think I may have over imbibed," Lairgnen said when the world lurched under his feet. He spread out his arms and grinned broadly when he found his balance. "See, Gen? I'm fine."

Caitriona snorted into her mug, but Gen was the one who took his arm and began to lead him away.

"Come on, Lair. Let's get you home to sleep the alcohol away, all right?"

Lairgnen grinned at Caitriona. "I bid you farewell, most lovely lady," he said and bowed.

"Oh, for Goddess sake, Gen, help your husband." Caitriona chuckled.

"I can walk on my own, thank you." Lairgnen pushed Gen's helping hand away, took a step, and immediately lost balance. Thankfully, Gen was there to fall into. "Gen, why is the world spinning?"

"Oh, Lair."

Lairgnen smiled at Gen's soft voice and thought his heart would burst with joy at the sight of the gentle smile directed at him.

"Do you know how much I love you, Gen?" Lairgnen said and leaned forward.

Gen let out a gasp and wrapped his arms around him.

Happy he was finally in his husband's arms, he dropped his mouth over Gen's in a deep kiss.

CHAPTER NINETEEN

Gen lurched forward to catch Lairgnen when he did a quaint little step and began to lose his balance, only to gasp when Lairgnen's mouth dropped a kiss on his shoulder. When Lairgnen started sucking on his jacket, Gen almost panicked. He looked around, caught the eye of one of the warriors, and beckoned him to come and help. Immediately, the warrior stepped forward while the other three stood circled to hide them from curious eyes.

"Looks like someone's over imbibed." Caitriona's expression was serious before it changed, and she started laughing behind her hand.

"You'll have to excuse us, Cait. I'll take Lair back to our house," he whispered so only his friend could hear.

He grimaced when Caitriona continued to laugh, but he couldn't blame her. If it were someone other than his husband, he would be laughing as well. He couldn't believe Lairgnen had gone and gotten himself drunk.

"It's just so funny, Gen. He's so serious and has this air of confidence . . ." Catriona's giggling interrupted whatever else she was going to say.

Beside her, Noirin started to snigger as well.

"Oh, Goddess." Gen grasped one of Lairgnen's arms while the warrior got the other. Between them, and after many false starts, they shouldered their way through the crowd.

Gen encouraged Lairgnen along the way and was thankful he seemed receptive and moved along with them, albeit slowly and with much staggering. Lairgnen drunk was something he'd never thought to witness. He let out a sigh of relief when he caught sight of the exit a few feet away and prodded Lairgnen to move faster. They made it across with no incident and had just managed to walk through the gates when a loud voice rang above the crowd.

"Well, well, what do we have here? Two highborn slumming in a *plebian* fair." The taunting voice was followed by raucous laughter.

Gen made the mistake of looking over his shoulder and let out a curse when he recognized the man who had spoken up.

Devos Cricirus.

What was the merchant doing in Farholde? He flicked his gaze to the sides and immediately realized that Cricirus was not alone. Flanking him on both sides were burly men who looked as though they all needed baths and a good hair and beard trimming. Gen's quickly counted how many there were even as his mouth twisted in distaste.

Cricirus obviously saw Gen's rising concern and grinned, revealing a full set of blackened, broken teeth. A breeze blew upwind, making Gen grimace and turn away in disgust. For all the man displayed his wealth, he was also flaunting his total lack of hygiene.

"Ignore them, Your Highness," the warrior supporting Lairgnen on his other side said in a quiet tone.

"Let's hurry out of here. I don't want to cause a scene. Plus, there's about twelve of them," Gen said. "I'm sorry, I didn't catch your name?"

"Elley, Your Highness. Sion Elley. I'm sure we can handle them, but I'm not too keen on doing that here in the middle of a crowd. We don't know how many supporters he has among them." Elley's eyes shifted from side to side, clearly assessing his surroundings.

"What? Are you pretending not to know who I am, boy? I could have had you in my bed had your precious prince not interfered in your sale." Cricirus' voice was loud enough for everyone to hear. His words were followed with much laughter and jeering from his men.

Gen gritted his teeth, half wishing the transporters were parked closer. Under his arm, Lairgnen let out a grunt and stopped walking. Before Gen could say anything, Lairgnen straightened up and started to turn toward the merchant.

"Come on, Lair, step it up. We need to get out of here," Gen cautioned and signaled to the men to hurry over to their vehicles.

"Your highness, I've got a stimulant that we only use in emergencies. I think this is one of those occasions," Elley whispered in a rush.

"Hurry and give it to him," Gen said, exasperated by the situation. The transporters were still a couple of yards away, and he turned to speak to the warrior closest to him. "Go on ahead and open the doors, please." He back turned to Elley. "Did you give it to him?"

"Yes, Your Highness."

"Your Highness," said another one of the warriors who pointed toward Cricirus and his gang.

Gen shook his head. "It's all right, we're right behind you," Gen insisted. Lairgnen's body sagged under his arm, and he paused so he and Elley could lift Lairgnen a little higher.

"Why, you little bastard. I'll teach you to turn your back on me," Cricirus called out harshly, sounding closer than expected.

Before Gen could think to react, he felt a hand grab hold of his arm and jerk him back. Caught unprepared, the force of the pull loosened his hold on Lairgnen, and he found himself waving his arms about as he fought to maintain his balance.

"Lair," Gen cried out and lurched toward Lairgnen, who had slipped to the ground.

Elley tried his best to keep Lairgnen steady, and the other

three warriors began to run back toward them. Gen saw an arm drop down toward him, and acting on instinct, took a step to the right and dropped low to the ground with his hands over his head. Cricirus laughed louder and looked to his men standing behind him.

"It appears the little rabbit knows how to duck," Cricirus said while the members of his gang sneered their contempt.

Gen signaled to Elley that he was all right. Elley was now crouched beside Lairgnen, who sat on the ground limply with his head bowed. Gen glanced at Elley as he began to move imperceptibly and removed something from his weapons belt.

"What? You actually think four warriors are enough to stop us?" Cricirus chuckled.

Gen wasn't really listening, though. He was caught between wanting to massage his aching arm, check on Lairgnen, respond to the merchant, or pray to the Goddess, hoping that whatever stimulant the warrior had given Lairgnen was going to work soon.

Gen observed Lairgnen's drunken state and thought over the different options he could take. None of what he came up with ended in any scenario that didn't involve a physical confrontation and Lairgnen getting hurt. Reasoning with the merchant was out of the question, for he doubted Cricirus would willingly converse with him. Most likely, it would only end in him throwing insults at Gen.

"Look, Cricirus, we're just going to go to our vehicles so we can leave, that's all," Gen said, choosing to try to placate the merchant, though he doubted it would work.

"Doesn't matter, rabbit. I just want to have a little bit of fun," Cricirus said as he licked his lower lip. "Why don't you come with me for a while? See what you're missing from your husband."

"I hate to disappoint you, Cricirus, but I'm not going

anywhere with you," Gen said in a firm tone. "My husband wouldn't like it, and our warriors won't allow you to come near me."

"And how exactly are they going to stop us? Your prince is drunk, and we've got your warriors outnumbered. Come now, all you need to do is come closer so we can talk, eh?"

Gen opened his mouth to respond when Cricirus gave out a pained yelp and slapped a hand over his shoulder. His eyes went wide as he tried to see what was stuck on his back. As he did so, he began to turn in place. Gen stepped to the side to get nearer Lairgnen. The change of angle allowed him to see what it was that Cricirus had on his back. He winced when he caught sight of a stunner pin there. Its lights were blinking rapidly, indicating that its pointed end had successfully pierced flesh and was now deeply embedded. There was only one way it could be removed, and that was through a master control. Any other way would get quite bloody.

"My husband isn't going anywhere with you," Lairgnen said, casually getting to his feet.

The stimulant must have finally worked. Elley and the other three warriors had drawn their own stunners and had them aimed at Cricirus and his gang. Relieved that the tide had turned in their favor, Gen backed up until he was standing next to Lairgnen.

"Are you all right?" they said simultaneously.

Gen gazed at Lairgnen and smiled. "I am now. You?"

"I could be better," Lairgnen shrugged and then turned to face their assailants once more. "Cricirus, is it? I've heard a lot about you. Thank you for introducing yourself. If you want, you can go ahead and try to take Gen with you, or you and your men can leave. But if you decide to try, then I'll have to change the setting into something a lot more painful and permanent."

Cricirus roared out a challenge, and his men backed him

up with their own screams of rage. When they ran toward them, Lairgnen pointed the control piece in Cricirus' direction and slowly pressed the button with his thumb. Immediately, Cricirus fell to the ground in a loud thud. He lay with his eyes widened in surprise and his mouth working as though he were trying to say something. His men froze in their tracks, staring in horror at their incapacitated leader. With Cricirus down, they didn't seem to know what to do.

"Should anyone think to make a move against us, I would sincerely hope you change your minds," Lairgnen said to the gang. "You have dared attack my husband and me in public, and if you think you can get away with your actions, think again."

One by one, the men slowly raised their hands in the air. Elley signaled to the other warriors, and they moved to rid the gang of their weapons.

After the restraints were placed on Cricirus' men, Lairgnen walked over to stand above a still gaping Cricirus and braced his feet braced over the immobile man. The wind picked up, and strands of hair that had loosened from its ties moved to reveal a stern face with eyes that sparkled with rage. Lairgnen's lips parted, and the words came out hard and strong.

"Before thinking about laying a hand on what is mine, merchant, you should have sought refuge in the farthest lands of Kizerain. Then again, I would have eventually caught up with you. As it is, I am restrained by law from simply ending your life right here and now after making sure you suffer every moment until you take your last breath." Lairgnen paused and glared down at the man. "Do you hear me?" he demanded when Cricirus did not respond.

Cricirus blinked his eyes several times, and Lairgnen moved away. He held out his hand, and Gen took it in his. As they turned to leave, Lairgnen stopped and faced the still stunned merchant.

"I almost forgot. For the past six months, we've been re-ceiving reports of your illegal activities, evading paying your taxes, among other things. Now that you've shown your con-tempt for the law, as of this moment, all your assets and ac-counts, active and inactive, are frozen and untouchable."

"Don't worry, highness. I'll make sure this idiot and his fol-lowers get to enjoy *bakare* pens until they can be transferred to the proper facilities," Caitriona's voice chimed in.

Gen looked toward the gates where a crowd had gathered to watch the commotion.

"Many thanks, Lady Caitriona," Lairgnen said with a slight bow of his head.

Caitriona rolled her eyes. "I'm no lady, so you can drop the title. Let me introduce you to my husband, Gentry." She chucked her thumb over her shoulder.

Gen groaned when a thundering horn blared out a series of rhythmic sounds across the meadow.

A hush fell over the crowd, followed by moans of nervous-ness and fear from men and women alike. Even Gen, who had witnessed the event that was to unfold several times before, could feel the nervous excitement leap in his bones.

"Is Caitriona's husband really that fearsome, Gen?" Lair-gnen whispered.

"He's worse," Gen said and dropped his hands. "I wasn't sure it was his herd earlier, but at least, now you can see how shepherd and *bakare* work together."

When the sound settled, the silence that immediately fol-lowed lasted for only a moment. Then the humming began. It started out almost too low to hear but then grew in volume, and Gen felt the hairs on his arms stand.

"What the hell is that?" Lairgnen asked, pulling Gen closer to his side.

"Wait and see," Gen whispered. He wrapped his arm around Lairgnen's waist and pointed with his other hand toward the herd.

The humming grew more intense, the vibrations making it hard to stand still, for the ground had started to shake. Across the meadow, wings began to flap and twirl while the *bakare* calves raised their heads and rumbled in their throats. Finally, the calves started to rise from the ground. Gen heard Lairgnen gasp when the beasts hovered low over the meadow. The trumpet calls changed in rhythm, and the herd turned and flew into the distance until they disappeared over the hill.

"Goddess, what a sight," Lairgnen said, his voice filled with awe.

"Ah, that's not what you should watch. There's more. Turn around," Gen said.

Lairgnen looked at him curiously until Gen pointed to the right.

"Goddess, is that the mature herd?" Lairgnen said, his eyes widened in surprise.

Gen nodded. "The calves had to be sent out of sight before the older ones came here to land. If I know Gentry, he should be appearing any moment now with the older ones following close behind."

Just as he finished explaining, a giant figure of a man came into view. Above him flew six mature *bakare*, three times the size of the calves, and acting most protectively over their shepherd. The playful way they swooped and butted against Gentry's thighs and shoulders would have killed a human, or at the very least, incapacitated him. But Gentry, being a giant, would only feel bruised if anything. Gen threw a glance at Lairgnen, who openly gaped.

Gentry stood almost twelve feet tall, his bright red hair tied high on his head and glinting in the sun. He had a short cape, which appeared to be made from *bakare* hair, thrown over his shoulders, revealing his naked torso and rippling muscles. He wore a pair of light-colored leather trousers and boots. One hand carried a massive horn while the other held a whip. The muscles on his stomach rippled with every movement he made. Like Caitriona, other than his height and mass, he appeared human-like. When he came into full view of the crowd, he raised a hand, and the *bakare* immediately stopped their antics to hover above him. Everywhere there was silence except for the loud humming of wings.

"My wife tells me you need my assistance, Guénaël, Prince of the Toullecs. How may I be of service?" Gentry's voice rumbled clearly across the clearing.

"If you please, Gentry, I would ask that my husband speak to you in my stead," Gen said formally.

"Of course, Guénaël," Gentry said, folding his hands in front of him.

"This is my husband, Lairgnen, Prince of the Royal House of Kizerain, Chosen Counselor to the king."

Gentry dipped his head briefly but didn't speak.

"Lair, go ahead and speak to him," Gen said, turning to Lairgnen.

"He's a formal kind of fellow, isn't he," Lairgnen commented.

"Yes, Gentry is older, so his ways are more formal compared to us young folk."

"Tell me about it later," Lairgnen said, dropping his arm from Gen's shoulder. He stepped forward and gave Gentry a brief nod.

"Gentry, I request your assistance in your capacity as Lord Mayor of Farholde."

"Speak, Lairgnen, Prince of the Royal Blood. Tell me how I may help you," Gentry said.

Lairgnen went straight to the point and explained the situation. When he was finished, Gentry turned to look at Caitriona, who gave him a bright smile and a thumbs up. The giant's lips curled into an indulgent smile that completely transformed his features into something less fearsome. Gen shook his head at the loving exchange. If Gentry weren't so big and fearsome, he was actually a good-looking guy in a mature sort of way. Like his Lairgnen.

"My *bakare* will have fun guarding their new toys, Prince of the Royal Blood," Gentry said. He signaled to his herd, and there was some peculiar communication between shepherd and *bakare*. Suddenly, the *bakare* wings flapped several times, and the giant beasts made a sudden, downward swoop toward the crowd.

Cries of alarm rang out everywhere. It was soon followed by laughter as the *bakare* found their way to where Cricirus and his men had been grouped together. At the beasts' approach, the men started to struggle in fear only to faint dead away as black claws gripped them by their shoulders and flew off with them.

The whole thing lasted mere seconds, but to Gen, and he also thought Lairgnen, it seemed like hours had passed. Gentry led his herd away, and the crowd dispersed until it was only Caitriona left standing beside them. Gen walked toward his friend and gave her thigh a hug. Caitriona chuckled, but the sound was soothing.

"Thank you, Cait, for being my friend and helping us," Gen said.

"I'll always be your friend, Gen, you know that. Simply because I am bigger and older than you doesn't mean we shouldn't be. Gentry will make sure those men are kept under close watch until the proper authorities come to collect them." Caitriona smiled gently and pried Gen's arms from her thigh. "Now, go with your husband while I go to mine. Let's catch up when you come next time."

Gen nodded. "I'll definitely be back." He turned around to leave only but quickly snapped his fingers when he remembered something. "I forgot to tell you something. Lair bought the Bolton property next to mine, and we've just closed the deal on the Thréinfhir estate."

"You'll be needing an oenologist then," Caitriona said, her grin broadening.

Gen had to laugh. "Yes, I will, especially as I'll be living in the capital most of the year. Also, I'm going to take up law. You're going to have your hands full. Can I count on you once I get everything in order?"

"Anytime, Gen. I'll look forward to taking Fafa's place."

"Thank you," Gen said. He looked over his shoulder when he heard Lairgnen call his name. "I guess I better get going. Lairgnen's going to have to make a report, and he can get impatient until he gets it done."

"He's much like my Gentry, then. All right, go and be with your husband. I still have a lot of beer to sell."

Gen jogged toward where Lairgnen and his men were waiting by their vehicles. Once Gen reached Lairgnen's side, he was pulled up close, and welcome arms engulfed him. Soothing kisses were dropped on his temple, and the arm that still throbbed from where Cricirus had grabbed him was gently massaged.

Gen smiled at the care and concern Lairgnen displayed. He had discovered throughout the weeks since they'd married that Lairgnen didn't speak much about emotions or his feelings. Showing them, however, was a very different thing. As Gen was of the same temperament, he couldn't ask for anything more.

"We should go. I want to spend some time with you alone today," Lairgnen said, dragging the tips of his fingers down Gen's cheek.

Gen felt his face heat up and couldn't stop his grin from broadening, but he turned and stepped into the waiting transporter. Lairgnen joined him seconds later, and they were off. Gen looked down at the scenery below and sent a prayer of thanks to the Goddess. Without her interference, he doubted he could be this happy.

CHAPTER TWENTY

L airgnen closed his eyes and began counting. It was a method he found suited him best whenever he felt stressed. And now was one of those times.

The day had been quite eventful, and although most of the day had been enjoyable, he wanted to forget the incident with Cricirus. He'd made a quick call to report the merchant's capture to Llewellyn, whose only response was that he would send his men to transfer the merchant to official premises. Meaning jail.

The bed dipped beside him, but he didn't open his eyes to see who it was. Almost instantly, his body reacted to Gen's presence, and he didn't stop to think as he rolled onto his side and pull him close. The ache in his chest eased as relief swept over him, and he knew it was all because of Gen. The love he felt for his husband was something he'd never felt before. He'd had relationships in the past, but there had always been that lacking element he hadn't been able to find. Until Gen.

Was this how it was for others who experienced the Call?

"Are you all right, Lair?" Gen asked.

"Just trying to calm down a bit, Gen. But I'm okay. Now that we're home and I know you're safe, I'm feeling much better."

"No aftereffects from the stimulant Elley gave you?"

"The injection site feels a little sore," Lairgnen said and tried to get back to his breathing exercises. But then Gen moved, and to his shock, pressed their lips together.

There was no time to think. Lairgnen twisted his body to

lie on top of Gen, not once letting go of their shared kiss. They'd done a lot of kissing before, but they had mostly been chaste and shy exchanges. Those had been very different from the one they shared now.

Through their shared bond, Lairgnen could feel a rising need similar to his own. He raised his head and gazed down at Gen, who looked dazed. As they both gasped for air, their gazes didn't waver. No, this was a very different circumstance.

Slowly, hesitantly, Lairgnen lowered his head and covered Gen's lips once more. His hand slipped into the collar of Gen's shirt, following its path with his lips. Gen nestled closer, and Lairgnen allowed his tongue to entwine with Gen's as his mouth opened in a silent welcome.

Instantly, his cock hardened and throbbed, and he shifted so Gen wouldn't feel the obvious lust he was trying to hide. Winding his hands in Gen's hair, he leisurely imitated with his tongue what he wanted to do with another part of his body. He imagined long, smooth thrusts once he was inside Gen and just knew that once he started, it wouldn't ever be enough.

He continued to stroke Gen's hair and back, at the same time grinding his hips into the bed to ease his ever-growing desire. Gen moaned when Lairgnen's hand continued its descent down the muscled body he'd longed to join until he finally reached the hard erection beneath Gen's trousers.

Lairgnen rolled Gen onto his side and leveled himself beside him as he continued to run his hands over Gen's cloth-covered groin. Gen was unbelievably responsive to Lairgnen's touch, his hot erection rocking back and forth until Lairgnen couldn't wait anymore. He quickly undid the strings that held Gen's trousers together and slipped his hand under the band. When his hand enfolded Gen's bare cock, it felt hot and hard. He gently stroked up and down until Gen began to thrust within his grasp.

Lairgnen forced himself to pull away from their kiss. He wanted to see if Gen was willing to allow him to take their relationship one step further.

Gen gazed up at him, his eyes clouded with passion and his lips swollen from their kisses.

Lairgnen trailed a finger along Gen's bottom lip and was rewarded with a smile and a nod.

Lairgnen wanted to shout out with joy. Finally, the time had come, but he had to be careful. He was fully aware that it would be Gen's first time, and he didn't want to hurt him in any way.

"Why are you stopping?" Gen murmured. He cuddled closer while his legs parted further. It was an unspoken language that could only mean one thing.

Yet Lairgnen needed to hear the words. "I wanted to make sure you're ready."

"Yes, but did you have to stop?"

Lairgnen gazed deeply into Gen's eyes and saw no sign of fear or trepidation, only desire, and a questioning look easily interpreted as confusion.

"Yes, I had to stop. If I didn't, I could have hurt you. You should know by now how you drive me crazy." Lairgnen chuckled softly.

The corner of Gen's mouth lifted in an almost mischievous smile. Then his fingers worked to undo the ties on Lairgnen's trousers before they dipped inside the band and gripped his hardened cock. Lairgnen's breath froze as Gen's warm hand slid up and down his length. The movement wasn't smooth, and Gen was looking down and biting on his lip as though he were trying to figure out how to do something properly. Lairgnen choked back his laughter and gave Gen a helping hand.

He guided Gen's movements, teaching him how to grip and move without causing too much friction. Gen glanced up and then back down again, continuing to watch his movements as he stroked Lairgnen's shaft.

"Is this all right? Am I doing this properly?" Gen asked and fondled Lairgnen's cock. His eyes were filled with amazement as he continued to pump up and down.

A jolt of surprise rocked through Lairgnen as he tried to process the possibility that Gen might have never even touched himself. Just how restrictive had his upbringing been under Martin's control?

Lairgnen let go of Gen's hand and rolled onto his back so Gen could continue to touch and explore his body. Gen moved, staying on his side, but he didn't stop his stroking or fondling. Lairgnen had the urge to spill his seed as pleasure coursed through his body, but he had waited too long to ease Gen into lovemaking, so he willed himself to persevere. He reached down and pulled his shirt off his torso and threw it over the side of the bed. At the same time, he kicked down his trousers until they were freed. He looked up and pulled on Gen's sleeve.

"May I?" he asked.

Gen nodded but quickly divested himself of his clothes. As soon as he was naked, he went back to what he had been doing, only this time, he lowered his head and licked the slit on Lairgnen's cock. Caught unprepared, Lairgnen almost yelped in surprise, but heat rushed through his body, and he began to tremble.

"I want to kiss it," Gen said.

Lairgnen opened his eyes and nodded. "Go ahead, just be careful. No teeth."

"Promise, no teeth." Gen smiled before dropping kisses up and down Lairgnen's length.

All Lairgnen could do was let out a hiss and bear it. Gen's hot mouth sucked on him, and he almost lost control. He reached down and guided Gen's head, controlling his movements as well as making sure his responding thrusts weren't too fast or too deep. Gen made a choking sound, but before he could help him, Gen managed to correct himself.

"Goddess," Lairgnen groaned and knew he wasn't going to last if he didn't stop Gen. Desperately, he tapped on Gen's shoulder until he looked up.

"My turn," Lairgnen said, twisting away and moving quickly, so he was kneeling over Gen.

He bent his head and reclaimed Gen's mouth, entwining his fingers in his hair. Gen arched into him, but Lairgnen pulled away. Trailing kisses down Gen's torso, he nipped at the skin here and there, causing Gen to jerk in surprise multiple times. Lairgnen smiled when Gen's legs widened more until there was enough room for him to get between them.

Lairgnen used his mouth to caress while his hand moved over Gen's erection. Gen was leaking, which made it easier for him to stroke him up and down. When he looked up, Gen had his eyes closed with his head arched against the pillow. Lairgnen bent his head and swallowed Gen's length until the tip of his cock touched the back of his throat before pulling up again. He did this several times, eliciting groans of desire from Gen before moving on to the next step.

He released Gen's cock and quickly reached out to the nightstand. Opening a drawer, he took out a jar and pumped oil into his hand.

"What's that?"

"It's to protect your skin," Lairgnen said, showing his hand before stroking Gen's cock again.

Gen smiled. "Oh, that feels better."

Lairgnen didn't say anything, but he continued stroking until Gen relaxed further. Slowly, carefully, he used his other hand to slide a finger into Gen's hole. Gen's eyes flew open and met his gaze. They continued to stare at each other as Lairgnen slid his finger all the way inside. Then he slowly pulled it out before sliding it back in. Gen's face transformed from a look of wariness to amazement. When Lairgnen slipped in a second finger and then a third, Gen was panting hard with a look of wonder combined with anticipation, making him reach out to grab Lairgnen's wrist.

"Am I hurting you?" Lairgnen asked.

"Don't you dare stop," Gen growled.

Lairgnen smiled, happy to be pleasing his husband. He continued to make love to Gen with his hand while stroking himself.

"Lair, I need."

The words were said in a whisper, but Lairgnen heard. Weirdly, he felt Gen's need as well. Before he could analyze the feeling, Gen reached out and pulled on Lairgnen's cock making all thoughts disappear.

"Slowly, Gen," Lairgnen cautioned.

"I need," Gen gasped out. "Please."

Lairgnen quickly pulled away and grabbed hold of Gen's hips. He lifted Gen until they were facing each other. Gen blinked, looking surprised at the new position, but Lairgnen shook his head and kissed him. Gen wrapped his arms around Lairgnen's neck, pulling on him, gasping into his mouth. Lairgnen lifted one of Gen's legs and brought it around his waist. The new position pressed their cocks together. Lairgnen grabbed Gen's butt and pulled him closer. Gen moved willingly, groaning into Lairgnen's mouth.

Lairgnen slipped his finger into Gen's entrance, causing Gen to tilt his head back and arch his back. Lairgnen slipped another finger and then a third. Gen's opening was more relaxed, but Lairgnen didn't think he was ready. Soon, he would be, so he continued to kiss Gen while his fingers worked to widen his hole.

Lairgnen's cock felt tight and ready to burst. He ran his hands up and down Gen's back, leading him to lie back once more. Tenderly, he eased Gen on his stomach, kissing his back while pulling on his hips until he was on his knees. The new position would make it easier for Gen to take him. After testing the readiness of Gen's entrance one more time, Lairgnen took his cock and pressed the tip there. Gen froze, and Lairgnen sensed his anxiety.

"Easy, love." He whispered. "Breathe and relax."

He lowered himself over Gen, kissing his shoulders as he slowly, in increments, began to slide into him. His body was so tense that he was unable to slide into him easily. Gen was so tight but also warm and inviting. With every ounce of willpower, he slid further inside, telling himself not to thrust brutally forward. As he inched forward, his hold on Gen tightened.

"Are you all right?"

Gen nodded. "Yes." He breathed out.

Gen's muscles were tense, but those surrounding his hole eased until Lairgnen finally bottomed out. The heat was incredible, and Lairgnen had to stop moving or otherwise lose what was left of his self-control. When Gen finally relaxed, Lairgnen withdrew slowly before easing back in. He moved at a leisurely pace, in and out, allowing Gen to get used to the invasion, stoking the fire inside him. His body was taut, but he continued to force himself to keep calm and pleasure Gen. It was probably the most difficult thing he'd ever done in his life, but he needed to make sure Gen wasn't hurt. He needed Gen to enjoy their lovemaking.

And then Gen began to move with him.

Gen's hips and body arched against his, meeting each thrust. Gen stretched out his arms until his face was buried in the covers, arching his back, so Lairgnen went deeper into him. His moans and enthusiastic responses were the last straw that broke Lairgnen's self-control. Unable to help himself, Lairgnen started thrusting faster and deeper.

Gen's body quivered, and Lairgnen knew he was nearing fulfillment. Lairgnen thrust vigorously as he reached around to fondle Gen's cock, pushing him to the breaking point. Gen's muscles tightened around him, and the force of their joined climax ripped through him. He almost collapsed on top of Gen, but he managed to correct his fall and rolled onto his side. Tiredly, he pulled Gen close to him. Gen's body was still trembling, and his breaths came in pants, but he placed his arm on top of Lairgnen's chest and lay his head on it. Just like they had every night since they'd been married.

As he lay panting, trying to catch his own breath and thinking about how that was the most amazing orgasm he'd ever experienced, something inside him sparked. He couldn't see it as much as he could feel it in his heart and hear it in his head. Alien thoughts and emotions rushed through him, and for a moment, he felt lost, unable to understand what was going on.

Gen began to tremble, and that was when Lairgnen realized they had finally fully bonded. They were now connected as one. He closed his eyes and reached out to the spark and was instantly overwhelmed by Gen's feelings of pride and fulfillment.

Something wet dripped on his chest, and for a moment, Lairgnen was confused. Gen sniffed, and Lairgnen realized he was crying. Concerned, he moved to get up, but Gen pushed him down.

"What's wrong? Did I hurt you?" Lairgnen asked.

Gen shook his head. "A little, but I expected it."

"Then what is it? Why are you crying?"

"I can . . . feel you." Gen's voice broke with his words. "I love you so much."

Anguish and pleasure crashed through Lairgnen in a tangle of confusing emotions.

"I love you, too," Lairgnen said, pulling Gen closer still

until their skin was flush against each other.

At that moment, Lairgnen had an epiphany. Never had he imagined he could love anyone as much as he did Gen. Or that he needed to know he would be loved in return. He was never going to let anything or anyone harm Gen. Neither was he ever going to let him go.

CHAPTER TWENTY-ONE

Gen opened his eyes to the first morning of his new life. Considering he'd been married for over a month, it was strange he would think of this day as the beginning. Outside, the birds sang and squawked their joyous twittering, making Gen smile contentedly. He felt like a new man.

Lairgnen had made love to him two more times the night before. And even though Gen wanted a fourth round, Lairgnen had refused, insisting it would be too much. Gen understood and knew he was acting selfishly. He just couldn't get enough of Lairgnen now that he'd had a taste of what it meant to be fully bonded to him.

He rolled over to his side to get up, only to immediately roll back and groan. It felt like every muscle in his body burned. Some throbbed and stung more than the rest when he tried to move. But after careful evaluation, he found nothing distressing enough to call for a physician. He sighed and closed his eyes. Pleasurable as the night had been spent in Lairgnen's arms, he didn't like having to pay for it this way. There was only one way to get over the soreness, and that was to move carefully. Very carefully.

He spent a few minutes stretching until the tenderness eased to the point where he could move without having to crawl on all fours. Once he was on his feet, however, another set of pain reared its ugly head. He took a deep breath and bravely walked to the bathing room.

The hot water of the shower helped a great deal with easing the muscles, but he winced several times when he soaped his genitals. There was nothing much he could do about it. From his readings, he would most likely feel raw for a few days. Their lovemaking the previous night had been his first time, after all.

As he dressed, he wondered where Lairgnen had gone. Remembering what they'd talked about the night before, he tentatively reached out with his senses. He jerked back in surprise at the instantaneous result.

Lairgnen was somewhere downstairs talking to his brother. Gen couldn't hear what was being discussed, but from how he interpreted Lairgnen's feelings, his husband was a little annoyed at Llewellyn for laughing at him.

In the background, he sensed a note of satisfaction. When he reached out to see what the source was, he shuddered at the image Lairgnen sent to him. It was of him and how he looked when Lairgnen was going down on him—from Lairgnen's point of view. He closed his eyes and let out a soft moan as pleasure rushed through his body.

It was an odd feeling, the connection between him and Lairgnen. Although Lairgnen had explained it to him briefly the night before, he still failed to wrap his mind around it. However, the connection definitely existed, and there was no denying that what he'd thought had been mere attraction to Lairgnen had actually been the Heart Call.

Gen dressed carefully, stepping into his pants without having to lift his legs too high. He was still putting on his socks when the bedroom door opened and Lairgnen walked in, carrying a tray with two steaming cups on it.

"I brought you some powo tea," Lairgnen said as he closed the door. He placed the tray on the mantle over the fireplace and handed one of the cups to him. "Drink up. The physician told me it has healing and muscle relaxing properties."

Gen gazed up at Lairgnen, feeling his face getting hot.

"Don't be embarrassed. It's perfectly normal. I knew it was

your first time and called the physician first thing this morning while you were sleeping," Lairgnen said, taking Gen's hand and placing the cup in it.

"I'm . . . all right." Gen looked down at the cup. The hot liquid was pale yellow in color and smelled like sweet citrus. "You didn't really hurt me last night, you know. Plus, I knew I was going to feel this way after . . . Anyway, yes, thank you for the tea."

Lairgnen pulled a chair and set it in front of where Gen sat on the edge of the bed.

"I called in my report to Llewellyn, but I guess you know that." Lairgnen's mouth twitched, obviously trying not to show his amusement. "I felt your touch, and I presume you caught me thinking about last night. I'm sorry if my thoughts embarrassed you."

"No, not embarrassed. It was strange seeing myself like that, from your point of view. I guess what I'm saying is, no matter what your thoughts were, the fact that I saw myself from your eyes was a little disturbing."

"It's one of the things we need to get adjusted to. I never asked Anwyll about how this could affect us. It never really crossed my mind."

Gen sipped his tea, expecting it to taste as sweet as it smelled, only to grimace at the bitter aftertaste, which also passed through his nose as he breathed out.

"Oh, Goddess, this is vile."

"I know," Lairgnen said. "I tasted it earlier and spat it out. But you need to finish it, then follow it up with the honey tea." Lairgnen pointed at the untouched cup. "Come on, all in one gulp."

Gen twisted his mouth in distaste, clamped his nose with his fingers, and drank the powo tea. It wasn't bitter enough to make him gag, but its foul aftertaste lingered over his tongue and palate. Lairgnen held the other cup to him and took away the empty one. Gen drank down the honey tea and sighed in relief when it washed away the bitterness effectively.

"I hope I don't have to drink that every morning," Gen said.

"You shouldn't," Lairgnen said, but then paused and turned away. "The physician said he would come over should you continue to hurt."

Gen chuckled and resumed putting on his socks and shoes. "What are we doing today?" he asked, needing to change the topic.

Lairgnen turned back around, a look of relief on his face. "Well, I was thinking of taking you downstairs for breakfast first. Then fly over the properties so we can plan out how to manage all of them from the capital."

Gen nodded and stood up. "I forgot to tell you that Cait's also an oenologist and has already agreed to manage for us."

Lairgnen's eyes widened. "She did?" He frowned and looked to be thinking over the new development. "How will she manage to do that if Gentry's over at Farholde?"

"Farholde's only fifteen minutes away, so that shouldn't be an issue. Also, there's the house her father used while he was working with Mother. Cait basically grew up on Toullec land," Gen said as he shrugged into his coat. "Either way, the logistics are favorable."

"All right, I trust you. You are in charge of the properties, because Goddess help us if I should attempt to run it. Anything else we need to talk about?"

"Yes, did you tell Llewellyn where Gentry took Cricirus and his men?"

"Yes, I did. He didn't like it, but then he was laughing, so I don't really know what he's thinking. I guess he knows how *bakare* are with their toys."

"*Bakare* are not meat eaters, Lair. They just really like to play," Gen said.

Their gazes met briefly before they broke out laughing.

"Playing with men like they would a ball can cause physical damage, Gen. We really shouldn't be laughing," Lairgnen said, trying to be serious, but his mouth kept twitching, obviously having a hard time keeping his amusement at bay. "Let's go have breakfast, shall we?"

"You haven't eaten yet?"

Lairgnen shook his head. "I wanted to eat with you," he said, looking embarrassed.

Gen walked up to his husband, placed his arms over his shoulders, and pressed their foreheads together. "We're both so new at this," he murmured.

"Now look who's being the adult," Lairgnen whispered before covering Gen's mouth with his.

Their tongues met and tangled, but there was no fight for dominance. When their lips finally parted, they were both gasping for air, and Gen's stomach growled. They both laughed and turned toward the door.

Two hours later, they were flying high over the Bolton property heading toward Thréinfhir lands. Ahead of them, Gen could see where the three rivers converged.

"I see now why your mother had coveted the Thréinfhir property," Lairgnen commented. He looked out the window of the transporter, then checked the map he held in his hands. After a moment, he frowned. "I think we need to hire a surveyor. There's an inconsistency here that I'm not sure about."

Gen leaned over to see where Lairgnen was pointing on the map and looked at the actual area several times before conceding. Where the three rivers met, the map showed a confluence where a small island should be, but in actuality it was absent.

"Yes, I see what you mean. That's a major discrepancy. Do you think Maella knew about this?" Gen pressed his lips tight as he considered the options. "The survey report is really old, so I don't think her husband even knew about it. We should wait for the surveyor and take it from there."

Lairgnen nodded grimly. "Even if she did know, I have an inkling she doesn't really care, especially as she had no children to inherit the property."

"Then again, I don't think Maella ever got involved in the running of the vineyard. And you're right, she's all alone now and would need the money." Gen let out a frustrated sigh. "It could be that the water encroached on that island and covered it. At the end of the day, it's not going to affect the running of the vineyards or transporting of supplies."

"I agree. Let's get everything resurveyed and see where it leads us," Lairgnen suggested.

"It would have helped if the island were still there, though. I remember Mother saying the lake itself was deep." Gen sighed and shook his head. "Getting it surveyed is going to cost us a lot of money."

"There's no getting around that," Lairgnen said. He leaned forward and tapped on the driver's shoulder. "Take us to that ridge over on the Toullec property. Here are the coordinates."

The rest of the day went without incident, and it was late in the afternoon by the time they returned to the manor. The butler had food laid out in the dining salon, and Gen and Lairgnen ate their fill of the early dinner. When they were done, they retired to the study, where they poured over the maps.

Gen was yawning into his hand when the clock struck midnight, and Lairgnen looked up to check the time. Without saying a word, he began to fold away the maps and straighten his desk. Gen helped him, and they soon headed up the stairs to their bedroom. They took turns in the shower, after which they got into bed. But sleep was far from their minds.

"Is this one of the effects of the Heart Call?" Gen asked as he shifted to his side and leaned his head on his hand so he could look at Lairgnen. "My brain is hyperactive, and yet I know that it's not all me."

Lairgnen nodded. "I agree. It's a little odd, isn't it? I can feel two minds in my head."

"I'm not sleepy yet," Gen said, pressing himself closer and running his palm down Lairgnen's chest.

Lairgnen turned to look at him and opened his mouth to speak but stopped when Gen flashed him a mental image of the two of them kissing, his legs over Lairgnen's shoulders as he thrust deep inside him.

"I don't think we should go that far, Gen. You're still in pain, no matter you never complained," Lairgnen said, but his body said otherwise as he pressed himself closer against Gen's side.

"I know. But can you teach me how to make love to you without it hurting?"

Lairgnen sighed. "I'm really sorry about you hurting. I should have stopped after the first time."

Gen narrowed his eyes. "But you did after the second time. I insisted on a third, which you told me was going to be too much for me. Stop the guilt-trip. I'm fine, and that powo tea is already helping with much of the rawness. Now, are you going to teach me how, or do I have to do it on my own?"

Gen didn't wait for Lairgnen's response. He reached down and cupped him between his legs and gave the engorged flesh there a little squeeze. "So, you don't want me to do something about this? Are you quite sure?"

"Where is all this confidence coming from?" Lairgnen asked, but he was smiling.

Gen had a feeling Lairgnen liked getting squeezed.

"Where else? Ever since last night, I've been getting lessons from you."

Lairgnen frowned. "How?"

"Thanks to our bond, we're kind of connected now." Gen grinned. "I like it."

Lairgnen blinked, obviously thrown off by Gen's change of attitude. "I'm getting to like this new version of you." He pressed against Gen's hand. "Maybe we should have done this weeks ago."

Gen shook his head. "No, I liked waiting. Last night, I was more than ready for us to make love. But, *amaer*, you still haven't answered my question." He squeezed a little harder and relished the fact that the shaft in his hand got hotter and harder. "What do you want to do about this?"

Lairgnen chuckled. "Honestly, I think I'll leave it up to you." He followed his words by thinking of how Gen looked when he had swallowed him down.

"Ah, that again." Gen pulled his hand away.

At Lairgnen's disappointed look, he laughed and began undoing Lairgnen's belt. He slowly pushed the trousers to Lairgnen's ankles and then gave them a shove until they fell over the edge of the bed. He got on his knees and cupped Lairgnen's cock between his hands. It stood to attention, the head leaking a little, and made Gen's mouth water. It was too tempting to resist, and he didn't hesitate to take it into his mouth.

The feel and taste of Lairgnen on his tongue was almost akin to his favorite dessert but without the sweetness. It was something he knew he was going to crave for the rest of his life. The night before, he hadn't known what to do. Now, it came easily. It helped that Lairgnen's thoughts were egging him to continue what he was doing and even guiding him on the amount of pressure to apply. He sucked and licked, enjoying the combination of texture and smell.

Lairgnen's hand gripped the top of his head, urging him to go deeper, and Gen couldn't think to deny him.

"Breathe through your nose," Lairgnen said. His voice was

husky with passion as his hand urged Gen to go deeper.

Down Gen went, opening his mouth wider until he felt the tip of Lairgnen's cock touch the back of his throat.

He smiled around Lairgnen's cock, realizing he had a lot of power over his husband — the power only a lover could have over their partner. He dropped down further but gagged and instantly pulled up until he could regain his breathing. It didn't deter him from his mission. He was going to make Lairgnen come in his mouth. He'd wondered about that the night before and now was his chance.

Lairgnen stiffened under his touch, his breathing growing more ragged and faster by the second. Gen felt his cock jerk slightly in his mouth and knew the end was near.

"Gen," Lairgnen said, sounding desperate. He tapped on Gen's shoulder, and his legs spasmed.

But his responses only made Gen want to keep sucking and licking.

Gen opened his eyes and looked up. Lairgnen's eyes were open and watching him, and they were clouded with passion. His hand stayed on Gen's head, urging him down. Gen felt his own excitement rise, and he reached down to touch himself, slipping his hand beneath the bands of his trousers. He stroked himself for several minutes, never letting go of Lairgnen.

Then he felt the now familiar spark and knew he and Lairgnen were connected once more. His mouth and tongue moved faster, and he knew neither of them could take much more of the exquisite torture. But he didn't pull away. He couldn't. He didn't know how much longer he could continue, but then something snapped, and blissful pleasure crashed upon them. He felt the combined waves of need and lust, pushing them over the edge, catapulting them both into the throes of fulfillment. He couldn't think. He could only feel.

Gen's mouth filled, and all he could do was swallow even as his own hand got wet from his orgasm. He trembled at the overwhelming sensations, his mind filled with the image of himself kneeling over Lairgnen, making love to his husband.

When Gen could finally move away, Lairgnen reached down and captured his head in a firm grip. Slowly, Gen crawled up the length of his husband's body until their lips met. The kiss didn't last long, Lairgnen fell on his back, and Gen followed him down.

"I think we need to take another shower," Gen said.

Lairgnen's chest started to shake until laughter boiled over. Gen couldn't help himself. Here he was, a young husband, and he'd only come to realize his power over Lairgnen.

"You need to promise me something," Gen whispered, trailing his finger down Lairgnen's bare hip.

"What is it?"

"You have to stay strong and healthy, because once I'm no longer as raw as I feel today, I'm making sure you don't get to sleep until we've had at least two rounds."

CHAPTER TWENTY-TWO

Lairgnen closed his eyes and pressed the heels of his hands against the sockets to ease the ache there. Eryn, his secretary, continued to speak, explaining points she'd highlighted, but he couldn't remember exactly what it was she was talking about.

It was his first day back at work, and he had almost immediately lost himself in the intricacies of running the budget for Kizerain. He'd started the day by meeting with his staff, discussing things he may have missed during his honeymoon, as well as making plans for troubleshooting problem areas. Those were tasks he used to enjoy, just not today.

The image of Gen still in bed asleep when he'd left kept making him want to go back and make sure he was all right, that he'd eaten well, was safe. His thoughts made it impossible for him to concentrate. Physically, he was tired. Gen had kept his promise, and thank the Goddess, he'd been able to keep up. So far. He'd have to ask Llewellyn for tips on how to keep fit for Gen.

When Eryn stopped speaking, Lairgnen lowered his hands and gazed at her tiredly.

"What is it? Why did you stop?"

"Should I go on, Your Highness? You look tired and preoccupied. Do you want to continue this tomorrow?" Eryn said.

"Tempting," he muttered but waved his hand dismissively. "Ignore me. Go ahead."

Eryn blinked but didn't say anything. She looked down at

her notes. "Other than the overdrawn accounts, we're almost done."

"Who was in charge of those travel accounts?"

"Lord Traherne, Your Highness."

Lairgnen flipped several pages of the document in front of him. He found the particular page he'd marked earlier and went over the figures again. "Remind me again why Lord Traherne was put in charge?"

"He was assistant to Lord Maellor when he was still Lord Chamberlain under Prince Eljin," Eryn said.

Lairgnen nodded. "I remember now, yes. Ten months ago, Maellor named him to take over the position as Lord Chamberlain after him."

"That's correct. I might add that as of three months ago, there had been no reports that he'd been doing anything wrong. In fact, his record was clean," Eryn said.

"Yes, until three months ago," Lairgnen said, frowning down at the financial report. "Except for that one entry. If someone hadn't made an unsuccessful attempt to erase it, we never would have taken a second look." Lairgnen looked up and met Eryn's gaze again. "This needs further investigation. In the meantime, send a memo to the treasury that all funds are frozen until further notice. And that we are going to conduct an audit beginning first hour tomorrow morning. Notify our auditors of the same, please, Eryn. Oh, try to get a hold of Prince Llewellyn and ask him to come in whenever he's free. We'll need the assistance of the Office of the Protector on standby should things get out of hand."

Eryn nodded her head as she wrote on her notepad. "Prince Llewellyn sent a message earlier. He said he would be dropping by today."

"Did he say at what time?"

"No. I didn't ask. I'm sorry," Eryn said.

"No, that's fine. We both know how my brother's schedule

is, and it's never announced until he's actually here," Lairgnen said. He was exhausted, and his back was beginning to cramp up. "I need a break," he muttered to himself, then shrugged and closed the file.

"Do you want me to get you something to eat or drink?" Eryn looked up from taking notes.

"I'm not hungry, thank you." Lairgnen glanced at the ornate clock sitting on his desk. What he really needed was to be with Gen, but he didn't know how that was going to happen until they both were at home. A knock on the door made him look up and frown at Eryn.

"Why is someone knocking at my door?"

"I'll go see who it is," Eryn said, standing up.

"Unless it's my husband, the king, or my brother, tell whoever it is that I'm not in," Lairgnen quietly instructed.

Eryn didn't make a comment, but her smile spoke volumes. Lairgnen didn't mind her and took up another file while Eryn talked with whoever it was at the door. When she didn't return immediately, Lairgnen started to wonder what was going on and was about to stand up when she reappeared.

"What was that all about?" He kept his face impassive but reached out for Gen, immediately relieved when he received loving reassurance and an image of Gen walking into the university building to inquire about registering.

"The office of the treasury sent you a message," Eryn said, placing a sealed envelope on top of his desk.

Lairgnen pulled back from his connection with Gen and looked down suspiciously at the note. The mark on the wax depicted the seal of the treasury department.

"The wax is still a little warm," Eryn said. "My guess is they know you're back."

"Did the messenger say anything as to what the contents may be?"

Eryn slowly shook her head. "No. I've never seen him

before. He was a young intern, and from the bundle of files he said he still had to deliver, he didn't have the time to read whatever's in there," she said, pointing at the letter.

Lairgnen leaned into the back of his chair and considered his options. "Would they know I'd call for an audit on their department?"

"Maybe, but as you'd issued that directive a few minutes before he got here, it shouldn't be at all possible."

Lairgnen met Eryn's gaze. There was no doubt she was just as suspicious of the ministry's motives as he was. The situation left him one option.

"Call my brother and tell him to come over for a security sweep, please, Eryn. Should anyone ask why, tell them I'm a newlywed and acting paranoid," Lairgnen said. "We'll continue our discussion after he gets here."

"Right away, Your Highness," Eryn said and left the room.

Lairgnen leaned back, closed his eyes, and once more reached out to Gen. A feeling of contentment swept over him when connection snapped into place. Gen's emotions were all over the place, but predominantly, it was happiness over his achievement. Lairgnen pulled up his communicator.

"All I need is your signature on the Guardian Approval Certificate and then I'm registered," Gen said as soon as he picked up the call.

He sounded very excited, and Lairgnen's connection with him gave him a glimpse of Gen's bright smile.

"Congratulations, *amaer*." Lairgnen's smile broadened. "Now, please explain why I'm considered your guardian and why they need my signature?"

Gen scoffed. "Apparently, it's a combination of things. Your position as Minister, and you're more mature than I am. Therefore, you're in a much better position to make decisions than I am. I didn't bother telling them off, so don't worry about it."

Lairgnen kept his emotions under control. Now was not the time to go on a rant about small minds. Instead, he sent soothing thoughts to Gen.

"Come by the office with the documents so you can finish the process by this afternoon."

"All right, but I can't go there just now. I still have some processing to finish before I can get there. Give me about another hour or so?"

"Can't it wait until tomorrow?" He really missed Gen and wanted to see his face. Being needy and clingy were strange emotions, but they were something he knew he could handle . . . eventually.

"I guess, but I just want to get this over with, so all I need to do is submit your GAC tomorrow," Gen said.

Lairgnen tapped his fingers on the desk impatiently. "Go ahead," he finally said, but he had a hard time controlling his emotions and knew he'd slipped up when Gen's touch reacted.

"Don't get mad, Lair," Gen said in a timid tone.

Lairgnen winced. He hadn't meant for Gen to feel his frustrations. "I'm not mad, I'm just . . . I have this desperate need to see you and hold you in my arms." Lairgnen blew air through his nose.

"I miss you, too," Gen said. "Look, I know you're busy, so keep working, distract yourself until I get there. I'll try to finish up within the hour. Is that fair enough for you?"

"All right," Lairgnen said and ended the call.

His thoughts were muddled as he put down the communicator and stared into space. Ever since he'd met Gen, he'd had a hard time controlling his emotions. With their recent physical bonding, it had been much more difficult. Every second of the day, he wanted Gen by his side, which logic told him was not only an impossibility but also a totally insane idea. They were both busy with their own schedules, and Gen was at an age where he needed his personal space. How did Anwyll and Pedr do it? He needed to talk to them both. The sooner the better.

There was a discreet knock on the door before it opened, and Eryn stepped through.

"Your Highness, Prince Llewellyn has arrived," Eryn announced.

Lairgnen nodded, stood up, and straightened his shirt. "Let them in, and please, no calls or visitors until they're done."

"I took the initiative and have informed the outer office of just that, Your Highness. You are to remain undisturbed until further notice. Unless it's your husband or the king."

Lairgnen nodded. Eryn was very good at her job—she deserved a bonus. "Good. Now, where's that brother of mine?"

For the next hour or so, Llewellyn and two of his warriors did a sweep over the entire office. When they were done, they had found no listening devices or hidden cameras.

"This makes it even more suspicious," Llewellyn said, taking a seat opposite Lairgnen after dismissing his men.

"I agree, but with no concrete evidence of being spied on, we can't do anything." Lairgnen glanced at the time. Gen had yet to arrive. "However, I asked Eryn to write up a report about the overdraft and am officially asking your office for help in the investigation."

"That's the most we can do for now," Llewellyn said.

Llewellyn had stopped speaking but continued to stare at him intently, which made him glare at his brother suspiciously.

"Why are you looking at me like that?"

"I don't know—there's something different about you." Llewellyn shrugged. "By the way, I got an interesting call from the university earlier."

Lairgnen raised a brow. "Oh, what did they want?"

"They wanted to confirm your status as a married man." Llewellyn winked.

"For Goddess' sake," Lairgnen said. He stood up and began to pace. "Do you know that they want me to sign a Guardian Approval Certificate before they would consider Gen properly registered as a student there? When did all that crap start?"

"That's the strange thing," Llewellyn said.

Lairgnen gazed suspiciously at his brother and saw the glint in his eyes. "What are you talking about?"

"After I confirmed both of your statuses, I called Uncle Fiacre and asked him about the certificate. In case you forgot, he's a member of the board of that university."

"I did forget but go on. What did he say? Is that certificate necessary?"

"No. He said that wasn't a part of the process, and he suspected that it was Martin's doing," Llewellyn said and winked knowingly at Lairgnen.

"That bastard almost ruined Gen's life and is not done trying to ruin it, is he?"

"Remember that although only a priest, he was considered a member of the royal family by marriage and had gained connections because of it. Even though his name has been revoked from the register, he still has some clout at the university as well as friends. On that point, the university is basically run by the cleric. In a roundabout way, you may be right to suspect he's still doing his best to ruin Gen's life. And I still don't know why he's doing it." Llewellyn frowned down at his hands, opening and closing them.

It was a habit Lairgnen recognized, one Llewellyn displayed when he was particularly bothered by the conclusions he was reaching inside his mind. Lairgnen sat back down on his chair and studied his brother, who appeared to contemplate his fingers when, in fact, Lairgnen knew Llewellyn was still lost in his thoughts.

"Remind me again about what this giant, Caitriona, said about her father?" Llewellyn finally said.

"Her fafa was the oenologist of the Toullec Vineyards. He worked for Frigga. Being long-lived creatures, her fafa must have worked for the Toullecs for several generations.

"And he died with her on the transporter, you said?"

"Yes," Lairgnen said. He didn't know where Llewellyn was going with his questions, but he was already intrigued.

"I'm going to have to dig deeper into the records about Toullec ties with the giants. Their ancestors fought on our side and decided to accompany us on the Great Passage. They're very loyal to the sprite, but they are not known for their deep friendships with us men."

"Well, see, that's the curious part, Llewellyn. Gen and Caitriona basically grew up together and have maintained their relationship."

"True, and there's this loyalty with the Toullecs." Llewellyn scratched his eyebrow and peered at him. "I'm going to have to go to Farholde myself and make an appointment to talk with the mayor there."

Lairgnen nodded. "Gentry. He's a shepherd. He's also Caitriona's husband and the mayor there."

"Interesting. And you said that Gen is quite familiar with this Gentry fellow?"

"Yes, and quite wary of him. There's also the situation with the *bakare* herd that watches over him and his kind."

"I'll take that into consideration, and I'll ask Gen about how to deal with him when he gets here. Where is he, do you know? Can you reach him?" Llewellyn stood up and went over to a buffet table, where Eryn had laid snacks for them just after Llewellyn and his men had first arrived.

Lairgnen didn't respond but closed his eyes and reached out with his senses. A smile broke over his mouth when he felt Gen's presence near him.

"I think he's here," he said, opening his eyes and standing up.

He walked over to the door and opened it. A wide-eyed Eryn stood there with her hand raised to knock on the door. Behind her stood Gen, who looked tired but smiling.

"I've got this, Eryn. Thank you," Lairgnen said, moving around his secretary so he could get to Gen.

Gen opened his arms, and Lairgnen walked into them. He wrapped his arms around Gen and leaned in so he could kiss him on the neck.

"You look tired," he said. "Let's get inside where snacks are waiting. Eryn, can you please send in something fresh for Gen to drink?" Lairgnen paused and looked at Gen. "What drink would you like? There's fresh fruit juice or some hot tea, anything you like."

Gen chuckled but pressed closer to Lairgnen. He looked at Eryn and smiled. "Just some water, if you don't mind?"

"Of course, Your Highness. I'll get it right up," Eryn said before excusing herself.

Lairgnen led Gen into his office. Once inside, Gen greeted Llewellyn, who looked at him with a frown.

"You look different, too," Llewellyn said, looking from Gen to Lairgnen.

Gen's brows rose. "Different? How?"

"There's a confidence about you that hadn't been there before." Llewellyn peered at them before shrugging. "Oh well, whatever it is that's going on suits you."

Gen laughed and glanced at the food. "Do you mind? I haven't eaten anything since breakfast and only had a snack while processing my registration."

"Of course, let me help you." Without waiting for Gen's response, Lairgnen walked over to pick up a plate.

He began selecting food he thought Gen would like and

ignored those he thought Gen didn't care for. Only when the food was piled high on the plate did he go back to where Gen sat beside Llewellyn. They were talking about the registration process, but Lairgnen wasn't listening. He placed the plate in front of Gen, only to frown when the setting didn't please him.

"Thank you, Lair," Gen said.

Lairgnen frowned before he dropped a kiss on Gen's head and left his brother and husband to their conversation. He went out of the office and asked Eryn for placemats, table napkins, and clean cutlery. Eryn didn't bat an eye and quickly got up to get them.

Lairgnen went back inside his office to find Gen was already eating. Nodding in satisfaction, he sat beside Gen and set the table to his liking. Content everything was in order, he got up once again to get Gen his water. When he returned, Gen had finished eating. Only then did Lairgnen feel pleased and sat down beside him.

"Is he always like this," Llewellyn asked Gen. He was frowning and pointing at Lairgnen.

Gen tilted his head to one side. "Like what?"

"Like this," Llewellyn said, waving his hand in front of him.

"Oh, Lair likes to serve me my food. Always," Gen said.

Lairgnen wasn't surprised at Gen's response, but from the way Llewellyn's eyes bulged, he was definitely astounded.

Lairgnen played with Gen's hair and ignored his brother's reactions. Llewellyn might have been the one to recognize the signs of the Heart Call, but he didn't know what it felt like. Serving his husband had become a need that he actually liked. It also gave him the chance to know his husband's likes and dislikes better.

"I thought that would end after you got married. Obviously, I was wrong in my assumption," Llewellyn said. He stood and began collecting his things. "I've got to get going. Thank you, Gen, for providing me with the education about how to deal with giants. I didn't know they were so formal and would have made a fatal mistake."

"They're really quite easy to be around, once you get past their size. As I told Lair, Gentry is far older than any of us. He's considered an elder by giant standards, which is one of the reasons why he's the mayor of Farholde. I'll send Cait a message about your wanting to speak with him and include a letter of recommendation should you need one."

"My thanks, brother-in-law," Llewellyn said. "I've got your number and will definitely call for advice when I need it. Lair, I'll go check out what we talked about. Don't worry, I'll get to the bottom of this." With a final nod, he left the room.

Gen let out a long sigh. "I'm suddenly sleepy," he said, following his words with a yawn.

"I'm almost done here, but if you want, you can stay and lie down on the sofa while I finish up."

"That sounds good. Why do they have to make registration so hard? Other than that, and the certificate, I enjoyed myself today. It felt good to walk around without having to look over my shoulder. Thank you for assigning Elley to me today. He was actually quite useful."

"He's a good man, and he's been with me for years. I think Llewellyn assigned him to me my second year as Minister, and he's been with me ever since."

When Gen yawned again, this time covering his mouth with his hand, Lairgnen stood and walked over to an ornate cabinet standing between two windows that overlooked the courtyard. He took out a pillow and blanket, which Gen took from him. They worked together quickly, and after lying down, Gen was asleep in seconds.

Lairgnen smiled and covered his husband with the blanket,

then went back to his desk and finished up reading and writing notes in the remaining files. After a soft knock on the door, Eryn poked her head in. She looked at Gen's sleeping form before tiptoeing inside. "I thought he would be sleeping, so I didn't bother to ring up before coming in. He looked beat when he got here earlier. Is he all right?"

"Yes, he said he was just tired from his activities," Lairgnen said, glancing at Gen to reassure himself.

"Can you come outside with me for a minute? I need to tell you something, and I don't want to disturb Prince Guénaël's nap."

"It's easier if you call him Gen, and yes, let's talk outside. Softly now, he's really tired," Lairgnen cautioned. He followed Eryn out of the office and went into hers.

Once there, Eryn closed the door and faced him. "Remember that intern who brought in the message from the treasury? Well, turns out he's the brother of one of my undersecretaries. I asked her to find out about the intern, and she readily told me that he was her younger brother. She also casually told me about her instructions about letting the department know when you returned to work. She said the orders came directly from Traherne's office."

"I see," Lairgnen said. "What's this young woman's name again?"

"Cartimandera Murchadha. She hasn't been with us for long, only about six months," Eryn said.

"And Traherne came in around ten months ago. He didn't waste time planting his people, did he?" Lairgnen thought over his next move. "Eryn, find out if my brother's still in the building."

Eryn quickly went to her desk and pressed a button. When a male voice answered the call, Eryn asked for the whereabouts of Llewellyn.

"He's just about to exit the building," the man said.

"This is Prince Lairgnen. Stop Prince Llewellyn at once, and tell him to get back up to my office," Lairgnen said.

"Yes, Your Highness. At once, Your Highness," the voice said.

After a few seconds of endless waiting, Llewellyn came on the line. "I just left you, now I'm needed again?"

"Never mind that, come back up here. I forgot to tell you something."

"Can't it wait until tomorrow? I've got a date in about an hour."

"Congratulations on the date, but it'll have to wait."

"All right, I'll be right up. But you owe me for this one, Lair," Llewellyn said before ending the call.

"Eryn, kindly have the young lady brought here and ask her to wait."

"Of course, I'll bring her over myself. Do you want her brother to be brought in as well?"

"No. But find out where he is. Have a warrior tail him until Llewellyn takes over the investigation. In the meantime, my apologies to your husband. But I think we're going to be in here much longer."

"What about Prince Guénaël? Should I have the transporter ready so he can go on ahead?"

"Inform his detail to come up. Oh, and tell them to increase his detail by another two men."

"Yes, Your Highness," Eryn said, her lips set in a grim line.

Lairgnen left Eryn to take care of things on her end and went back inside his office. Looking at Gen's peaceful sleeping face, he didn't have the heart to wake him. Reaching a decision, he went to his desk and began gathering the files related to the treasury issue. He dimmed the lights and exited his office just in time to see Llewellyn walk into the corridor.

"Gen's asleep. Let's take this to the other room," Lairgnen said, tilting his head in the direction of the meeting room.

Behind Llewellyn, he spotted Elley and motioned for the warrior to come closer. "Make sure no one disturbs Prince Guénaël," he said. "I've already had Eryn send in the request, but talk to me tomorrow about increasing his detail. Also, increase security for our house in Merifael."

"Is there a problem I need to know about, Your Highness?"

"I'm not sure yet, but I'm taking precautions. It's best we are ready for the unexpected rather than to have it get the better of us."

"Ah, I'm glad that you remember some of the things I've talked with you about," Llewellyn said, leaning against a wall.

"It's this bond I share with Gen. I need him to be safe at all times. That's all."

"I hope I'm not being presumptuous, Your Highness, but I agree," Elley said.

Lairgnen whipped his head. "What do you mean?"

"While the prince was registering earlier, there was a man who was following him around. Prince Guénaël didn't notice him, but I did. I didn't like the way he was tailing us and had one of the men tell him off. He disappeared right after."

"Did you find out who it was?"

Elley shook his head. "Not yet, but we were able to get an image of him. We'll find out who he is eventually."

"Let me know as soon as you find out." Lairgnen pressed his lips in a hard line. It didn't sit well with him that his office security had been compromised, and at the same time, someone was stalking Gen. Was it coincidental, or a sordid plan to compromise his position as Minister of Finance?

"Understood, Your Highness." Elley gave a brief nod before motioning for another warrior to come over.

Lairgnen turned to Llewellyn and indicated they should enter the meeting room.

"We found out who the intern was and who snitched on

us," Lairgnen announced.

"Oh, do tell," Llewellyn said.

Lairgnen was not deceived by the casual tone. Llewellyn was a sly fox, and when he acted unconcerned, he was usually on top of the case. He could only hope that Gen would sleep until the impromptu investigation was over. At least Gen was close by, and that was more than enough for Lairgnen.

Chapter Twenty-three

Gen fought through the fog of sleep and reached out a hand to search for the one he knew would always be by his side. When he met nothing but air, he opened his eyes and remembered he was lying on the sofa in Lairgnen's office, and he was alone. Outside the window was nothing but darkness. Curiously, he could feel Lairgnen was somewhere nearby — near him and yet inaccessible.

He reached out with his senses and immediately found him in another room. It was adjacent to the one he was in, and his husband was furious. Without thought or consideration, he swept aside the blanket someone had placed over him and jumped off the sofa. The Call was strong, and he couldn't run out fast enough. He slammed the door open only to be stopped in his tracks when Elley stepped in his way.

"Where is he?" Gen demanded. He was having trouble keeping his emotions at bay with the way Lairgnen's emotions were heightened, making coherent thoughts impossible. His hands began to shake as he felt himself lose control.

"Easy, Your Highness. He's just in the other room, and he's safe," Elley said, putting up his hands in a placating manner. "He's with Prince Llewellyn in the meeting. There is no danger."

"Then why is he so angry?" Gen put down his hands, closed his eyes, and took in deep breaths. Once more, he reached out to Lairgnen, and this time, he was acknowledged.

Somewhere to his right, a door banged against a wall, and he turned in the direction it came from. Seconds later, he saw

Lairgnen running across the hall, his face looking grim. Following close behind him was Llewellyn and a warrior he didn't recognize.

"Lair," Gen called out and ran to meet Lairgnen. "What's wrong? Why are you so mad?"

"I'm sorry, Gen. There's a situation, and I wasn't able to control my emotions." Lairgnen wrapped his arms around him. "I'm so sorry."

"Are you crazy, Lair? You need to learn how to control yourself, brother," Llewellyn said as he came closer.

Gen looked at the way Llewellyn's lips were set in a tight line and the angry look he aimed at Lairgnen.

"What is happening?" Gen asked.

He was confused. Lairgnen was usually so calm and logical, but he could feel the turmoil in his thoughts. Lairgnen's feelings were all over the place, making it hard for Gen to grasp why his husband was so angry. Desperately, he raised his hands and cupped Lairgnen's face. "Look at me," Gen said firmly.

He didn't know what he was doing, but somehow, he knew it was right. As their gazes met, he took hold of Lairgnen's anger. It felt like a storm, with crashing thunder in the distance and a darkness that only revealed its contents with each flash of light. He brought the light inside him and gave it to Lairgnen, easing the darkness away until it grayed out and eventually became light.

With the mood lightened, Lairgnen met Gen's gaze, and his expression softened. "That was amazing."

"You're lucky Gen's got logic enough for the two of you," Llewellyn said. He crossed his arms across his chest and glared at his brother. "Gen, I suggest you take my brother away from here and keep doing whatever it is you're doing. I think your bond is too strong and too new for either of you to be around others right now. You both need to learn to control your emotions. Well, at least Lairgnen, because I think Gen's got the hang of it. Must be because he's young."

"Stop being sarcastic. It's not helping. For your information, I was controlling it. I just didn't consider that what I wasn't outwardly showing was affecting Gen," Lairgnen said.

"Unless you can control your emotions, I would recommend you stay out of the investigation from now on, Lair. This situation has escalated and is now also a security issue. Let me take care of my end. You've already done your part," Llewellyn said. "As it is, the woman's scared of you, and we can't afford your instability to be public knowledge."

Gen leaned back from Lairgnen's embrace. "What happened? How did you scare the woman? What woman?"

Lairgnen let out a long sigh. "There's been a security breach, and one of my department's undersecretaries is involved."

"And how did you scare her?"

"He didn't do anything to her, Gen. He just sort of looked really terrifying with the way he was glaring at her. You should have seen him. I thought his eyes were going to shoot lightning, or worse." Llewellyn moved his hand in front of him to emphasize his words.

Gen had to smother a laugh at Lairgnen's embarrassed expression. Even in times of seriousness, Llewellyn's comic personality still managed to shine through.

"You're exaggerating, Llew. My eyes don't shoot lightning. I'm not Anwyll," Lairgnen said. "But you're right, I should stay off this investigation. As this has turned to involve independent parties, this case rightfully belongs in your department."

Llewellyn simply shook his head before facing Gen. "Go ahead and go home, both of you. It's getting late, and nothing's going to change unless that woman decides to talk some more."

Lairgnen nodded. "All right."

"Good boy," Llewellyn said, the sarcasm seeping into his tone again. "Gen, be the man and take my brother home and tell him to rest. You should also know that he owes me big time for this. I had to cancel my date, and I'd been planning that for a few weeks."

With a final glare in Lairgnen's direction, Llewellyn turned and walked back where he came from.

Gen pursed his lips and nudged Lairgnen's shoulder. "I think we should go. If Llew finds us still here when he gets out again, he's going to burst a vein."

"Wouldn't that be amazing to watch," Lairgnen said, glaring at the empty hallway.

"Now look who's acting the child," Gen admonished. "Come on, let' go home."

To Gen's surprise, Lairgnen didn't say a word but simply followed him back to the office, where they gathered their things and left the office together.

They were in the transporter flying back to their house when Gen remembered a conversation they'd had while still in the south.

"Lair, do you think I can have that test we were talking about a week ago?"

Lairgnen frowned in thought for a moment before answering. "The test to find out if you're Martin's son or not?"

Gen nodded. "Yes. I just remembered it. I was thinking about how I have to get your signature on a certificate to register at university."

"Yes, about that," Lairgnen said, shifting in his seat to look at Gen face to face. "Llewellyn talked to Uncle Fiacre about it."

Lairgnen then proceeded to narrate the conversation, and the more Gen listened, the more determined he became about taking the test.

"He's really doing everything he can to take control of me and the family properties, isn't he?"

"That's what I was thinking. That, and the fact that I discovered a spy in my office who's been reporting to someone who may be involved in the theft of royal and public funds had me stressed out. I'm sorry, Gen. I didn't mean to worry you." Lairgnen took Gen's hand in his and stared down at it.

Gen considered the downcast look on Lairgnen's face and marveled at how their relationship had grown. No longer was he the young naïve husband to an older, sophisticated prince. They had become partners in every way—supporting each other in their time of need, loving each other in a way he had never imagined loving someone before.

They reached their home and went inside. Lairgnen led the way up the stairs to their living quarters. As they walked shoulder to shoulder toward their bedroom, Gen turned to Lairgnen and saw how tired he looked.

"I love you," Gen said.

Lairgnen's grip on his hand tightened, and Gen met his astonished gaze.

"You shouldn't startle me with confessions like that," Lairgnen said, but his broadening smile revealed his pleasure. "Are you trying to give me a heart attack?"

"No, I'm just saying that I love you. I'll keep saying it whenever I feel like it. You should do the same thing." From what he had seen, Lairgnen's first day back at the office had been tough, and he wanted to lighten his mood.

"Why should I?"

"Hmm, I don't know. Why should you tell me you love me?"

"You're really pushing for it, aren't you?"

Gen gazed at Lairgnen lovingly before leaning forward to give him a kiss.

It was amazing. The more he kissed Lairgnen, the more he craved his taste. Lairgnen was like an addictive love potion that so many tales spoke about. There were times when his immense love for Lairgnen got the better of him, for it was all-consuming. He knew, through their connection, that Lairgnen felt the same way. But where his feelings leaned more toward seeking Lairgnen's approval and protection, Lairgnen's were the exact opposite.

"I love you," Gen whispered against Lairgnen's mouth.

"I love you, too," Lairgnen said.

Gen felt his desire mounting as Lairgnen used his body to guide him backward. They kept moving, their mouths never parting until Gen felt something hard against his back. He twisted to find he was backed up against a wall.

"Can't wait for the bed, *amaer*?" Gen teased.

Lairgnen shook his head, his hands fumbling to unlace first Gen's trousers and then his. When they were both free, Lairgnen took both their shafts into his hand and pumped in long strokes, making Gen's breath lock in his throat. He wanted to help, but Lairgnen swatted his hand away, making him laugh.

"Place your legs around me," Lairgnen said.

Gen didn't think twice. He jumped and wrapped his legs around Lairgnen's waist. Lairgnen cupped his ass cheeks and pressed his back against the wall, bracing him there so he wouldn't fall. His breath grew ragged, anticipation building inside him until Lairgnen slid into him. He didn't know what Lairgnen used to ease his way, but it didn't feel like oil.

Lairgnen moaned and held Gen closer, urging him to move with him. As they began to move faster and faster, getting more urgent, he clamped his muscles around Lairgnen's shaft, his body feeling alive with the pleasure. His need built higher and higher as Lairgnen brought them to the precipice. The blissful heat rose to fevered levels, and a moan escaped his lips. His mind filled with Lairgnen's passion, communicating all of his need and love for him.

Lairgnen pounded into him, grasping at Gen's body fran-
tically, and Gen relished the sensations. He arched against
Lairgnen as the same need, wild and violent, overtook his
senses. He wanted all of Lairgnen inside him. The harder Lairgnen drove into him, the more uncontrollable his body felt,
their intertwined minds making love just like their bodies
were.

Gen didn't know how long they were like that, but suddenly his body exploded, and a blur of pleasure swept over
him. A final, hard thrust, and Lairgnen released inside of him.
Gen held on until their violent shudders gentled. Although he
didn't want things to end, he knew that they had to.

When logic finally rose to the surface, Gen opened his eyes
and saw they were still just outside their bedroom. He felt
Lairgnen's shaft shrivel inside him and eventually pop out.
Gen closed his eyes, and exhaustion almost overtook him. He
would have fallen to the floor, but Lairgnen supported him
against the wall. They stood there for long minutes until he
finally found his balance once more.

"I think it's time we got inside our bedroom," Gen said, a
smile curling on his lips. He felt so free and relaxed.

Lairgnen nodded but didn't say anything. Instead, he bent
and pulled their trousers back on. He reached behind Gen and
turned the knob.

Two weeks passed, and it was the morning of the first day
of class. Gen woke earlier than Lairgnen, so he spent some
time preparing the things he would need for school. When he
was done, Lairgnen was still asleep, so he decided to take a
shower. By the time he got out of the bathing room, he found
Lairgnen sitting up in bed, sipping his morning tea.

"Good morning," Gen greeted.

He walked over to the bed and sat on the edge. Lairgnen

reached out to cup a hand on his nape and drew him closer until their lips met.

Gen sighed into the kiss. He loved mornings like this, where Lair's thoughts were calm, clear of the worries of running the finances of Kizerain. He'd had no idea about the heavy stress Lairgnen had been carrying on a daily basis. Now, as his Chosen, Gen saw and felt everything that Lairgnen did and was happy to be a stabilizing element. It made him thankful that the Goddess had gifted them with the Heart Call, for no one should go through pressure like Lairgnen did.

He wondered how it had been for former King Eljin, who had been king without a Chosen for decades before Anwyll found Pedr and took over the throne. At least for Anwyll, he'd never had to carry the heavy load of both the spiritual and magical well-being of the people. In Gen's eyes, it made Eljin a great king.

"You're up early. What time's your class starting?" Lairgnen said after pulling away from their kiss.

Gen stood and pulled on his shirt cuffs before walking over to the closet to take out his coat and shrugging into it. "Very early, but I still have time to join you for breakfast before I need to get there."

Lairgnen nodded and took another sip from his tea. "I can drop you off on the way to the office, but I'll have you picked up later, if that's all right with you? I've got several meetings scheduled today, so we might not be able to see each other until later tonight."

Gen looked down as he tied a bright blue sash around his waist. "That's all right, I guess. Can I call you today, or are you not accepting any?"

"If it's you who's calling, I'll answer. I would, however, urge you to do so only when it's a real emergency. The people I'm meeting today are not very pleasant, and I want to be able to focus all my energies on them."

"I won't disturb you then, promise." Gen smiled.

Lairgnen finished his tea and stood. "How do you feel now that you're back in school?"

Gen's gaze fell on Lairgnen's naked form. Almost immediately, his thoughts went back to the night before. Getting schooled in bed was something he enjoyed. But he'd never imagined a position like Lairgnen had managed while still pounding into him like he had. Shaking the mental images off, he sat down and started putting on his shoes.

"I'm a little nervous, I guess. It's so very different here. The university's larger than I ever imagined, and there are so many students. Back in Merifael, I knew everyone who attended. Here, I only know the warriors following me around."

"That'll soon change, I'm sure, but I must caution you. Although people here tend to be more sophisticated, they're still people, and can be just as intolerant and quick to judgment."

"I realize that," Gen said, jerking his shoelaces almost too tightly. "Don't worry, I left my naïveté at the auction."

Lairgnen didn't respond, but Gen felt his soothing caress and almost immediately. Whatever bitterness he felt about his former helplessness eased.

"I'm sorry, Lair," Gen said, not raising his eyes. He hadn't meant for Lair to see his anger.

"There's no need to hide, Gen. I've been inside your head and touched your emotions. I know how you feel."

Gen closed his eyes before looking up to meet Lairgnen's gaze. "I love you."

Lairgnen blinked at the sudden announcement. "You know, you really shouldn't tell me things like that when there's absolutely nothing I can do, *amaer*. I love you, too."

Gen chuckled as Lairgnen turned around to go to the bathing room. Lairgnen didn't look affected by his announcement, but his thoughts betrayed him, and Gen had to smother his laughter.

An hour later, Gen watched as Lairgnen's transporter rose slowly over the top of the trees and sped away. Elley stood behind him with three other warriors who had introduced themselves earlier as the twins Elwyn and Kerwin Moses, and Rhobat Griffin. Gen had immediately recognized the three men as full-blooded warriors, just like Elley was. The only difference was that all three looked just as young as he was and were dressed similar to him. Gen turned to Elley and made a face.

"Do I really need four men to follow me around, Elley?"

"I will be the only one following you around, as you put it, Your Highness. Elwyn, Kerwin, and Rhobat are experts in blending in with the crowd, so you won't see much of them unless absolutely necessary. As you can see, Elwyn and Kerwin are twins and come from a family of respected warriors. Rhobat may look like a warrior, but he is quite unique. He does not come from a warrior family, but he has trained hard and is very good at his craft, which is the reason why he has been assigned in your detail. As it is, the three of them have been registered as students in the university. Don't pay them any mind. They're here because of Prince Llewellyn's orders."

"Llewellyn? Not Lair?" Gen frowned and looked at the three warriors again. "Why would Llewellyn increase my security detail? Is there something going on I don't know anything about?"

"We're only told to guard you, Your Highness. Should there be another reason, please ask Prince Llewellyn or Prince Lairgnen. They arranged for your detail two weeks ago."

All Gen could do was nod his understanding, but he didn't like the additional warriors. He had nothing against them personally, but an increase could only mean one thing—he or Lair, or both of them, were in some kind of danger.

Gen decided to let the matter rest, at least for the moment. He would talk to Lairgnen or Llewellyn when the time was right. Just then, a gong resounded across the campus, and it was time for him to go to his first of many classes.

Time passed quickly, much to Gen's surprise. He had thought he would be bored on his first day, but unlike the school he'd attended in Merifael, the university ran on a very different system. There was no time for loitering around. Although it was only the first day, the instructors started with their lectures. Already, he'd penned in deadlines for papers, essays, and projects. He imagined his future as a student was going to put a lot of strain on him mentally as well as physically, but he was actually looking forward to it. In fact, he found it exciting.

The day went on, and Gen was having fun. It was unfortunate that other than Elley and occasional glimpses of the other warriors, he still didn't recognize anyone.

There was another hour before Gen's next class, and he decided he was hungry. As he walked toward the food court, the temptation to give Lair a call was hard to resist, but when he reached out with his senses, he found that Lair was deep in conversation with someone. He quickly backed away, but not before leaving a mental kiss on Lair's mouth. The spontaneous display startled Lair, who then responded with a mental caress before backing away and refocusing on the man he had been speaking with.

Gen sighed and went up the stone staircase that led to the food court. At the landing, he checked for a vacant table. The court was crowded, and he almost left to find another place to eat when he spotted an empty table on an upper level. He glanced around and saw the only way up there was via a staircase on the far side of the courtyard. He turned and hurried toward it when he bumped into someone.

"My apologies," Gen said automatically without looking at

the person. He was halfway up when he heard someone call out his name.

"Guénaël?"

Gen's initial reaction was a welcoming smile, but when he turned around and looked down to see who had called him by name, he froze. Looking up at him from the ground floor was Maccus. Gen's insides roiled, and his smile faded. Anger welled inside him, and not wanting to cause a scene, he decided to ignore his former friend.

"Guénaël, wait. Hold on a second," Maccus called out again, this time loud enough for people to glance their way.

Gen refused to respond and continued his way up the stairs. At the top, his way was barred by a group of students on their way down. He looked around them to see that more tables had been vacated. Knowing he had somewhere to sit in the crowded court, he chose the nearest vacant table, sat down, and started to search for Elley and his other guards. He didn't like eating alone, and he liked Elley, so he looked forward to sharing a meal. He pulled out his communicator and sent a quick message to Elley. From out of nowhere, a hand grabbed his elbow, startling him to lose his hold and drop his communicator. He quickly stood up, pulling his arm away, only to come face to face with Maccus.

"What do you want?" Gen asked, not bothering to hide his irritation at Maccus's presumptuous behavior. At that moment, he discovered something he never knew about himself. Seeing his former friend brought out the worst in him. "What the hell is wrong with you? Haven't you ruined my life enough? Who do you think you are? The last time we spoke, I told you I never wanted to see your face or hear from you ever again."

"Look, give me a chance to explain, Guénaël, please." Maccus leaned in and even held a palm to his chest.

The move disgusted Gen. How could Maccus stand there

and pretend they had anything else to say to each other? Especially after the *ius auction*. In Gen's mind, Maccus might have been indirectly responsible for what had happened after taking him to Cricirus' house that horrible night. But he was entirely at fault for Gen's being seen in an area Martin had forbidden him to go to.

"I would advise you to leave, Maccus," Gen said before taking his seat once more. He bent to pick up his communicator and saw Elley had responded, saying he had seen the commotion and was already on his way up the stairs.

"Look, you can call me all the names you want. I can take it, and I'll accept it. I know you're still mad at me," Maccus said.

When Gen continued to ignore him, he walked around the table and took the chair opposite his.

"You're not welcome to sit with me," Gen said, not bothering to lower his voice. Too many ears had already overheard their exchange, and just as many strange eyes were directed their way. He was too angry and upset to care about his background being outed publicly.

"Ah, come on, Gen, we've been friends too long for you to ignore me," Maccus said, smiling broadly.

Gen shook his head in disbelief. "Please take yourself somewhere else, Maccus."

"Why? What did I do?" Maccus spread his arms wide and looked around, smiling at those who met his gaze. When he turned back to face Gen, however, Gen met him with a look of contempt.

"You did enough. Because of you, my reputation was ruined for no just cause. I had to go through a humiliating *ius auction*. You ruined my life, and you're a coward. After what had happened, and after what everyone was saying about me, where did you go?"

Maccus opened his mouth to respond, but Gen pushed on.

"Did you come to defend my name or my honor? No, you disappeared. You left me alone. No one would listen to my side of the story. Why? Because they wanted to know your role in it, and because you never defended me, they assumed the worst. My father assumed the worst. You know, small minds and all."

Maccus reached out to take Gen's hand, but Gen pushed him away, causing the legs of the chair to grate noisily on the wooden floors.

Still, Maccus persisted. "Gen, look, I admit I am a coward, and I got scared. I panicked and ran. I didn't want people to know that it was I who took you there against your will. I didn't want to get arrested and have to speak to the clerics. I didn't want them to accuse me of . . . of . . . something. I don't know. And in any case, your father would never have believed me anyway. So I left, and I came here. I decided to transfer to school here."

Gen stood up and began to gather his things when something Maccus said caught his attention. He sat back down on the chair, and Maccus beamed down at him. If Maccus thought he had succeeded in getting Gen to eat again, he was wrong.

"It's not easy to get into this university without a sponsor. Who recommended your immediate transfer, Maccus? By any chance, was it my father?"

Gen stared at Maccus and studied his expression. When Maccus's smile wavered, Gen's suspicions were confirmed.

"I don't know." Maccus shrugged, as if to dismiss Gen's suspicions. "I just know that when I got here and registered, they immediately admitted me. Even I was surprised about how fast I got accepted. My grades are not at all that great."

Maccus laughed, but to Gen's ears, he sounded nervous. What was Maccus hiding?

"Are you even listening to yourself, Maccus?" Gen shook

his head but kept his gaze on Maccus. "How do you expect me to believe you when you're so bad at lying?"

Maccus smiled again, but this time, his lips were trembling. "Guénaël, please. I love you," he pleaded.

Gen had enough and decided it was time to walk away. Grabbing his things close, he stood up.

"You're crazy," Gen said and turned around, catching many faces quickly looking away.

"Please, Guénaël, I need for you to forgive me," Maccus called out.

Gen continued to walk away.

"I've accepted my shortcomings. I want to apologize to you, and I need you to accept my apology. If you want, I'll even kneel at your feet."

Gen stopped in his tracks and slowly turned around. "It's useless to continue this way, Maccus. In fact, you're an embarrassment. Why would you even think that I would accept your apology?"

Maccus ran over and reached out to touch Gen's sleeve, but Gen twisted away.

"Look, I know you love me. Deep inside, I know you care."

Gen's mouth dropped, but he had the sense to step away from Maccus. The desperation Maccus displayed was becoming alarming.

"What fantasy are you living in, Maccus?"

"We're still friends, right? We've known each other for a long time," Maccus said, stepping closer.

Gen took another step backward. "What has that got to do with it? And in case you've already forgotten, you destroyed that friendship."

"Come on, Guénaël, let's forget about what happened. We're still young. We can start anew."

At such a blatant attempt at flirting, words failed Gen. His anger eased only to be replaced with pity for a former friend.

"Maccus, you have got to drop the act. Also, for your information, I've already got a husband," Gen finally said.

Audible gasps of surprise rose from around them, which made Gen find the whole situation funny. He finally understood what Lairgnen had spoken to him about that morning. These were city folk, and yet they were cut from the same oak tree. Gossips. They were all gossips.

Maccus blinked several times, and his smile began to fade. Then he shook his head once, and his smile broadened once more. "I don't believe you."

From the hushed voices and relative silence around them, Gen knew they had everyone's attention. He was tempted to shout at the crowd to leave him alone, but then maybe he could use this to his advantage. Perhaps the time had come when he could clear his name. It might not be Merifael, but the university was populated with students from all over, and word about this conversation was sure to spread like wildfire. Gen straightened his shoulders and squarely faced Maccus.

"I'm not joking around, Maccus." Gen pitched his voice loud enough to ensure he could be heard by all without necessarily shouting. "In fact, I'm quite serious. Stop hounding me like a desperate *canes* begging for scraps. You can never have me. I will never want or even think of being in love with you. I never did in the first place, so I don't see how you were delusional enough to think that. I'm married to Prince Lairgnen, Finance Minister, and Chosen Counselor to King Anwyll. From now on, you don't come near me, you don't attempt to talk to me or contact me." He pointed to where Elley and the three warriors were standing. He almost smiled when Maccus looked over his shoulder and visibly paled. "You see those men there? They're my warriors and really quite lethal unarmed. Imagine how dangerous they are. They're here to protect me from slime like you. So I'm asking you, Maccus. Please. Don't approach me ever again."

Maccus turned around and gazed at Gen. "And what if I don't listen to you? What happens then?"

Gen chuckled—Marcus was so obtuse. "Then I won't stop my warriors from acting on my behalf."

Maccus opened his mouth to say something, but Gen had had enough. He turned around to leave, but another thought entered his head, and he faced Maccus once more.

"If I hear anything about you talking about me or of our past friendship, you'll find out that I'm no longer the Guénaël that you once knew. On a final word, thank you, Maccus, for opening my eyes and making me see who my real friends and family are."

A tiny voice in his mind tempted him to allow his anger to rise to the surface. To show how he felt—his anger, his fears, his terror—about having had to go through an unfair ritual. He gazed at Maccus for a moment, and without another word or glance at his former friend, he walked away. In his mind, it was a symbolic gesture, similar to how Maccus and many of his friends had turned their backs on him in his time of great need. He'd read that one learns who his true friends and family are in times of great need.

Well, Gen now knew that his father and Maccus no longer belonged in his life. He couldn't wait for the genetic sampling results to come back. He was ready to place the two among those who shouldn't matter to him. The hurt was gone, and the time had come for him to sever himself completely from those who'd hurt him most.

Choosing the higher road was the hardest and yet most freeing decision he'd ever made, and it felt good. That he had been given a chance to face Maccus and confront him for his abuse gave him newfound confidence in who and what he was. Maccus, whom he'd thought of as a friend, had used their friendship just so he could gain access into a society he'd long dreamed of being part of. Further thinking about it, Gen realized Maccus was not that much different from Martin, and with the realization, his mind gained an understanding of his father's motives. Now, if he could find the courage to face his father without fear, that would be a blessing indeed.

"Your highness, you must be hungry. As it is, you've less than an hour to eat before your next class begins," Elley said.

Gen stumbled over his own feet before hurriedly correcting himself. He'd been lost in his own thoughts and hadn't noticed Elley step up beside him. Elley held on to his arm and helped him regain his balance.

"Are you all right, Your Highness?" Elley asked, his brows furrowing in concern.

Gen cleared his throat and shook his head. "I'm fine, thank you, Elley. Come, let's find a table big enough for the five of us. I'm sure I'm not the only one who's developed an appetite after this embarrassing debacle."

A loving, inquiring mind touched his, and his heart called out to Lairgnen. It wasn't so much desperation as it was a need to have his love confirmed. The response was instantaneous, and Lairgnen's love flooded his mind and body. Gen held onto it and smiled, but he couldn't stop the tears of happiness from falling down his cheeks. It was the most perfect feeling, and he didn't even bother to wipe them away. Elley moved closer, but Gen shook his head and continued to walk.

"Everything's all right, Elley. Everything's going to be all right."

CHAPTER TWENTY-FOUR

Lairgnen opened the file Llewellyn handed to him and began to read. After dropping Gen off at the university that morning, it had been nonstop meetings for him. He had been looking forward to a quiet lunch with Anwyll and Llewellyn when said brother walked into his office carrying the report in his hand. Llewellyn's face was set in a grim mask, which made him suspect whatever news his brother had was not going to be good.

"I thought you should be the first to see it," Llewellyn said.

Lairgnen's curiosity grew when Llewellyn's expression flitted from worry to agitation and back again.

"Has Anwyll seen this?" Lairgnen continued to read but started tapping his index finger against the edge of the file.

"Not yet. I was thinking the two of us should present it to him," Llewellyn said.

Lairgnen finally finished reading. He closed his eyes and leaned back into his chair. "We're supposed to have lunch with him and Pedr in a few minutes. He mentioned in passing he wanted to catch up." He let out a heavy sigh.

"Yes, I know. He mentioned the same to me when we spoke," Llewellyn said.

Lairgnen steepled his fingers and stared at Llewellyn, sitting across the desk from him. His brother stared back, stoic as always.

"This whole thing is going to cause a scandal," he said in a grim tone. Scandals were nothing new with the royal family, but when it involved money, things always turned nasty.

"Of course it is," Llewellyn agreed. "When a minister is found to have embezzled public funds for the past decade, or even more, it's going to cause a furor. As it is, Anwyll has been itching to discover who's been working against him."

"Traherne's a fool. He never should have allowed himself to get involved in this."

"And yet he has—all for the sake of covering up his many affairs. Who would have guessed that little undersecretary of yours and her brother were his lovers? Not to mention the three others he's also seeing."

Lairgnen muffled a derisive laugh. "He's over eighty years old. Where did he find the energy?"

Llewellyn shook his head. "Goddess if I know."

"I never thought he was the type," Lairgnen said. "He'd always come across as a conservative, full of pomp and circumstance." The more he thought about the situation, the more he wanted to laugh and cry at the same time.

"Well, we've got less than an hour to join Anwyll and Pedr for lunch. He's got half an hour left with the weekly public hearings. I think we should get going and talk to him in private about this before word gets out," Llewellyn said.

Lairgnen nodded and stood up. "All right. Let's get this over with."

Llewellyn muttered a curse under his breath but also stood up to follow Lairgnen out of the office.

"There's no question, Traherne's going to have to be replaced," Llewellyn said as they boarded the transporter.

Lairgnen sat in the back seat with him, the front being occupied by their guard and driver. Another transporter that carried four more of their detail hovered behind them.

"Let's leave that for Anwyll to decide. We did our job. Now it's his turn to assign somebody else to hunt for someone to take over the vacancy. Hopefully, they manage vetting the applicant properly and don't get fooled by appearances,"

Lairgnen said. After a while, he tapped Llewellyn's arm. "When do you think Gen's test results are going to come out?"

Llewellyn shrugged. "It shouldn't be long, but it's only been two weeks since he took it. I'll remind the physician about it once I get back to my office this afternoon."

"It shouldn't take long, then. From what I understand, it takes about three weeks to get the final results. What do you think of Gen's suspicions about his parentage?"

"I can't say I blame him for his doubts. Martin never treated Gen right, from what I gathered from him, and Gen's the type to cut clean."

"Do you think that's the reason why Frigga married Martin? Because she was having another man's child and couldn't marry him?"

"I refuse to speculate about that, and with Frigga dead, Gen's only chance of finding out the truth, or at least part of it, is through that test."

They both fell silent, but after a moment, Lairgnen spoke up again.

"You know, if Martin isn't Gen's father, that means whatever chances he still had of gaining control of the properties would be gone forever."

"Laoghaire is most definitely his daughter, though."

"Yes, but even then, he still loses any chance of controlling her share of the property, since Gen has full guardianship over her."

"Ah, I'd forgotten that little detail," Llewellyn said. His communicator vibrated just then. "Hold on, I have to take this."

"Go ahead," Lairgnen said.

Llewellyn nodded before turning his attention to the call. Llewellyn's face gradually began to tighten as he listened to whatever the caller was telling him. The transporter started to descend as Llewellyn ended the call.

"That was the palace security. They said there's a crowd gathered outside the throne room."

Lairgnen grew alarmed. "Are Anwyll and Pedr safe?"

"Chief Caddel assured me there's nothing to worry about, but he's added more warriors to keep the place secure just in case. Come, let's hurry inside. I don't like surprises, especially when it involves Anwyll," Llewellyn said as he led the way to the wing where the offices were.

It didn't take long for them to arrive near their destination. However, once they reached the outer corridors they couldn't proceed, because a crowd of courtiers prevented their entry into the throne room.

Llewellyn motioned to one of the palace warriors. "Is the king secure?"

"Yes, Your Highness," the warrior said, bowing his head, first to Llewellyn and then to Lairgnen.

It looked like Caddel had everything under control.

"I don't recognize any of these people," Lairgnen said, craning his neck to look over the crowd in search of Anwyll.

A mature-looking palace warrior dressed in the gold officer's uniform glanced their way. He excused himself from the warrior he was speaking with and made his way through the throng. Lairgnen immediately recognized the Chief of palace warriors, Caddel Beddow, as he pushed his way through the crowd, which automatically parted to give way to him.

"Prince Lairgnen, Prince Llewellyn, please come with me. The king is expecting you," Caddel said after a brief bow.

"Is the king secure?" Llewellyn asked again. The frown between his brows deepened. "Why were these people allowed to come here? Who approved their passes?"

"Word got out that Lord Traherne had embezzled public funds, and these are some of his relatives who accompanied him and are claiming his innocence."

Llewellyn stopped walking and let out a curse as he looked

around him. "Who leaked the news? I gave strict instructions that no one was to speak of this until I'd spoken to his majesty. Traherne shouldn't have found out before the king did."

"From what I know, Your Highness, it was Lord Traherne who volunteered to come and confess his involvement before results of the investigation are made public."

"What?"

"That's all I know, Your Highness," Caddel said.

"Come on, let's hurry," Lairgnen said, cursing under his breath.

The day had quickly taken a downturn, and Lairgnen didn't know how long he was going to be held up in the palace.

Fifteen minutes later, Lairgnen found himself counting in his head as he struggled to keep his rising anger under control. He stood beside Llewellyn and several other ministers, listening to Lord Traherne narrate his involvement in embezzlement. Anwyll looked grim as he sat on his throne, while Pedr stood behind him with his hand on Anwyll's shoulder. Pedr's role as Consort to the king did not just involve being his lover and husband. He was also there to serve as the impartial support who would give logical advice to Anwyll.

At that moment, Lairgnen felt Gen's mind touch his, and he welcomed his husband's presence. Unfortunately, Traherne chose that moment to describe a salacious act, and Lairgnen involuntarily winced in disgust before sending Gen a soothing thought and breaking off the communication. Traherne's lack of wisdom was astounding, and hearing more than he expected gave him a bad taste in the mouth.

Lairgnen breathed a sigh of relief when Lord Traherne finally reached the end of his narrative and bowed his head.

"I am your loyal subject, your majesty, and accept your judgment."

As king, Anwyll's role was like a double-edged sword. He

was both the spiritual and magical representative of the people of Kizerain. Anwyll would need Pedr's logical background to balance his temperament, as magic had a tendency to react violently when it encountered a crime.

Anwyll's face grew stern, and the glow in his eyes brightened to the point that Lairgnen had to look away. He had seen Anwyll's magical persona before but continued to be awed every time Anwyll displayed his power.

"Lord Traherne, when you took over as Lord Chamberlain, you swore an oath to protect the funds in the name of the royal family and the people of Kizerain. The same money you stole to buy lavish gifts for your lovers came from my people's hard-earned labor. Those particular funds were meant in part to pay for medical and magical services for those in need or couldn't afford it."

Traherne nodded but didn't look up or say a word.

Beside Lairgnen, Llewellyn raised a hand to partially cover his eyes but continued to observe the proceedings. Pedr moved one step closer to Anwyll, and almost immediately, the light dimmed a little, and Lairgnen could see better again.

"Before I pass judgment, may I ask if you have enough funds to pay back the money you stole?" Anwyll asked.

Traherne cleared his throat and shook his head. "I don't, Your Majesty."

Anwyll stared at Traherne, but his expression didn't change. After a moment, he turned his head and examined the crowd that had gathered behind Traherne. He looked searchingly at each of the faces before he turned and motioned for Llewellyn.

Llewellyn quickly moved from Lairgnen's side to stand in front of Anwyll. He had to look up, since the throne was set high on a pedestal.

"Prince Llewellyn, as my Chosen Protector, and in the name of the people of Kizerain, I instruct you to arrest

Claudius Traherne and all of his family, Cartimandera and Camulos Murchadha, and their families. As well as all others involved in this crime. The laws provided by our ancestors are very clear regarding the embezzlement of public funds. Therefore, all properties and holdings belonging to the Traherne and Murchadha families are to be confiscated by the crown and used to pay for their theft. Above all else, the people of Kizerain are not to be abused by those who think they are above them. Such is my judgment. Such is my will."

Cries of despair rose at the back of the room, but no voices were raised in protest, as everyone knew Anwyll was far from done.

"Claudius Traherne, your name and all who bear the Traherne name shall be stricken from the roster. Those of your family who are found innocent shall not suffer the shame you have brought upon them. All their properties and wealth shall be restored unto them. The same goes for the others involved in this scandalous affair. Such is my judgment. Such is my will."

Llewellyn bowed low to Anwyll. "By your will, Your Majesty."

Anwyll sat back on his throne and took Pedr's hand. "Prince Lairgnen, Chosen Counselor, please step forward."

Lairgnen felt Anwyll's touch in his mind as he moved forward until he stood beside Llewellyn and bowed before his king.

"Sire," he said.

"You are tasked to guarantee that everything stolen from my people is to be repaid at ten times its value. In addition . . . As compensation for the blatant disrespect by Traherne to my people, you are to set aside these funds. You are obliged by your king and people to use said amount to establish a foundation aimed at helping those who are in need of medical and magical services. Such is my judgment. Such is my will."

Lairgnen bowed from his waist. "By your will, Your Majesty."

He would obey his king, but in his mind, he worried about not being able to go home early in the next months. Because of Traherne and his lovers, he now had more work ahead of him. Anwyll's mind touched his and reassured him. Immediately, Lairgnen felt the calm wash over him. Although he wasn't fooled by Anwyll's trick, he appreciated it. He straightened up just in time to see Anwyll take to his feet and step to the edge of the pedestal. He motioned for Caddel, who hurried to stand between Lairgnen and Llewellyn.

"I am done for the day, Chief Caddel. I need some quiet time with my Consort," Anwyll said. "Kindly clear the palace of all visitors."

Caddel bowed his head before turning to motion for his men to arrest Traherne. It didn't take long for the palace guards to clear the room. Anwyll turned to Llewellyn and Lairgnen and tilted his head toward the exit.

"I hope you're as hungry as Pedr and I are," Anwyll said in a voice low enough so only those nearest him could hear.

Lairgnen and Llewellyn followed Anwyll and Pedr out of the throne room. Once they exited, Anwyll groaned out loud.

"I don't know why these things can never wait until after I've had something to eat."

"At least Traherne wasn't stupid enough to escalate the situation or cause more embarrassment to everyone concerned," Pedr said.

"I read his mind, and that was exactly how he thought about it. He knew he had been found out and wanted to spare his family of a public trial."

"They're still going to suffer through his crime, though," Pedr said grimly.

"That can never be avoided. He knew it. Everyone knows it," Anwyll said, shaking his head. "Pedr, it is now your duty to make sure the innocents are spared the repercussions. Llewellyn can give you their names once he's done with the investigation. Lairgnen, there should be more than enough funds to satisfy the law. Please provide them enough to have a fresh start. Pedr can decide on the details. The law can be vicious, but it doesn't mean we can't soften the blow."

Pedr's face tightened, but he didn't respond, only nodded his agreement. Lairgnen knew Anwyll was in the right and was glad he had a good heart and would never allow innocents to suffer needlessly. Losing name and status was already enough of a burden nobody deserved. Without Anwyll's spiritual and magical interference, Kizerain laws were clear, to the point, and ruthless. It made Anwyll's position even more important as he alone had the will, power, and capability of balancing lawful, spiritual, and magical orders.

Through the thousand years since the Great Passage, there were not that many who had dared break the laws. Lairgnen didn't understand why Traherne had done what he had. How could he have risked his family's name for the sake of sexual affairs? Maybe Lairgnen was naïve in the sense that he doubted he could ever look at another man. Gen was everything for him, and he knew Gen felt the same way.

Their group turned the corner of the narrow passageway and entered Anwyll's private office. Lairgnen entered the room after Llewellyn and sniffed appreciatively at the wonderful aroma. Trays of food had been laid out on one of the buffet tables set against a wall. A smaller table was set with pitchers of drinks while a third bore stacks of plates and cutlery.

"No need for ceremony here. I'm quite aware we're all hungry," Anwyll said, waving a hand in the direction of the tables.

Lairgnen didn't have to be told twice, since his stomach felt like it was being squeezed tight from the lack of food. A knot had formed in his belly, and he wondered at the sensation. Shaking his head and thinking it was just the hunger making itself known, he went ahead and took up a bowl and filled it with soup before taking his seat. He was halfway done with it when he felt Gen's gentle touch and quickly excused himself to call Gen.

"You didn't have to call," Gen said as soon as he picked up the call. "Am I disturbing you? You were busy earlier."

"I was busy, and no, you're not disturbing me at all. In fact, I was just having soup. What's going on?"

"I'm actually on my way to the palace. Some officer called one of my guards, Rhobat, and instructed him to take me there as soon as my classes were over. Do you know what this is all about?"

Lairgnen stiffened. "Hold on, let me find out." He looked over his shoulder and motioned for Llewellyn, who didn't look like he appreciated being interrupted.

"What is it?" Llewellyn said as soon as he neared.

"Did you organize someone to have Gen brought here to the palace?"

Llewellyn blinked. "No. Let's ask Caddel." He quickly turned on his heel and walked back inside the office.

Lairgnen brought the communicator back to his ear. "Gen, where are you right now, and who's with you?" He looked up when Llewellyn returned with Caddel following right behind him.

"We're flying over our house as we speak and going in the direction of the palace. I can actually see the king's office in the distance. Elley's sitting beside me. In front, Rhobat is driving," Gen said.

"Caddel, did you order someone to bring Prince Guénaël here?" Llewellyn asked.

At the same moment, Gen spoke again. "If you want, I can show you."

Lairgnen immediately felt Gen touching his mind, followed briefly by a sense of displacement. Suddenly, he was looking through Gen's eyes.

"Keep it up, *amaer*, but don't be obvious about what you're doing. Talk to me as normally as you can," Lairgnen said.

"There's a lovely view of the forest beyond the palace. I never realized how gorgeous their flowers are this time of the year," Gen said.

Lairgnen closed his eyes and sent a prayer of thanks that Gen was sharp enough to follow his lead.

"I wonder what Anwyll wants to speak to me about. The last time I talked to him, he and Pedr were teasing me about our sex life," Gen said.

Lairgnen gritted his teeth when he saw the driver turn his head slightly to look at Gen.

Gen turned his head again, and Lairgnen watched as Elley motioned for Gen to continue talking while his other hand reached down. Lairgnen was aware of how Elley habitually armed himself with more than the prescribed regulations, so he was not surprised when Elley removed a weapon strapped to his ankle. Slowly, Elley straightened and sat still, but then he turned his head and gazed at Gen. Lairgnen frowned. Elley's pupils were dilated as though he'd been drugged.

"You should know, Your Highness, the petals of the flowers of the *cachia* tree are edible?" Elley said in a monotone voice.

"Are they? I didn't know that. Do you know much about plants, Elley?" Gen asked.

Lairgnen could feel his husband's confusion through their connection.

"Gen, keep up the conversation but stay mentally connected with me," Lairgnen instructed.

Gen gave a slight mental push to indicate he understood.

"Gen's name is not on the roster for those expected to come

to the palace today," Llewellyn said.

"I talked to my officers, and none of them gave Elley a call," Caddel said. The furrows between his brows deepened.

Lairgnen's grip on the communicator tightened. "Gen, I want you to look at the guard who spoke to the palace officer," he said.

Llewellyn crossed his arms over his chest. "Is Gen connected to you in some way?"

"Yes, we can communicate this way. We can exchange images of what we can see or think about, but we can't talk to each other," Lairgnen said to Llewellyn just as Gen moved his head and looked at the driver of the transporter.

"He's showing me the driver. I think his name's Rhobat," Lairgnen said.

Caddel raised an arm and began tapping on the device strapped to his wrist. After a moment, Llewellyn looked up and met Lairgnen's gaze.

"I was the one who recruited Rhobat. He doesn't come from a warrior family, but his skills in combat are impressive," Caddel said. "I assigned him to Prince Guénaël's detail because he's perfect for the job of blending in a young crowd while the prince attends school."

"Gen's looking at him," Lairgnen reiterated.

"What does he look like?" Caddel asked.

"If you have a picture, it would be faster to identify him," Llewellyn said.

Caddel typed on his device once more. He raised his hand to show the screen monitor. "Is this him?"

Lairgnen peered at the small screen and nodded. "Yes, that's him."

"Who else is with Gen?" Llewellyn asked.

"Elley's with him."

"Where are the other two?" Llewellyn's gaze became more intense.

Lairgnen shook his head. "I'm not sure, but I'm assuming they're shadowing from the other vehicle."

"If Elley's with him, why isn't he doing anything to stop Rhobat?"

"I suppose because Gen doesn't seem alarmed. Nothing extraordinary is happening other than what we know," Lairgnen said, shaking his head. He didn't know what Llewellyn was getting at.

"Didn't Elley ask for details?" Llewellyn shook his head, his frown deepening. "Something's not right. As the senior guard, Elley should have confirmed with the palace about the change of plans. As it is, he's accepting without raising any questions."

"Are you saying Elley is the one we should be watching and not this Rhobat?" Lairgnen asked.

"I'm saying exactly that," Llewellyn said. "I've trained enough palace guards on the basics of personal security to know when someone makes a stupid mistake. Elley is too experienced to make a mistake like this."

"If I may interrupt, Your Highness," Caddel said. "I think we need to raise an alarm and request assistance from the Protector's people."

"Why would you want to do that?" Lairgnen asked, but as soon as he said the words, he knew why, and Llewellyn was already nodding his agreement.

"You have it," Llewellyn said, his face set in a grim mask. He tapped on his communicator and began to relay instructions to whoever was on the other side.

"I'm sorry, Your Highness, but there's a clear possibility that Prince Guénaël has been kidnapped," Caddel said before turning on his heels and leaving Lairgnen to gape after him.

CHAPTER TWENTY-FIVE

Gen fought his alarm down. He'd felt the lurch in Lair-gnen's mood, as though he'd been trapped and was on the verge of a panic attack. Gen also caught his worry about how he didn't want Gen to know that he was in danger and that the driver, Rhobat, might have betrayed him. He turned to Elley and saw how oddly still he sat on the seat.

He didn't know what to do other than continue his inane conversation. Talking about the birds and the bees had always been interesting, especially when viticulture was the topic. But he'd never thought he would be doing it to distract kidnappers from finding out what he was really doing.

He thanked the Goddess for the millionth time for giving him the gift of the Heart Call and the ability to communicate with Lairgnen through their bond. As it was, he could feel Lairgnen's heart beating fast, among other things he could sense. Predominant was Lairgnen's anger that simmered in the background.

Gen could also sense that Llewellyn was with Lairgnen. He'd learned to recognize Lairgnen's feelings and thoughts about his brother. It was like a specific type of signature that was both reassured and irritated at the same time. Right that minute, it felt reassuring, so Gen interpreted that Lairgnen was thankful his brother was there. Llewellyn was not just famous for his looks. His skills with the sword and tactical thinking were just two of the reasons why he was the Chosen Protector to the king.

A sudden change in Lairgnen's mood snapped him out of

his thoughts, and he suddenly found himself seeing through Lairgnen's eyes.

Lairgnen appeared to be standing on a balcony. A few steps to his side was Llewellyn, who was moving his hands and speaking to an older palace security guard. In the distance, Gen could see that Anwyll and Pedr were also there. Both royals looked concerned, but they didn't appear to be speaking. Knowing what he and Lairgnen now shared through their bond, he recognized the signs of the two bonded men communicating on a different level.

A momentary hope flared inside Gen that there would be a point in their bond that he and Lairgnen would be able to achieve full mental communication. The ability would be extremely helpful for a situation like this one.

Lairgnen shifted his gaze, and Gen saw three transporters hovering beside the balcony. One opened a door, and its ramp was lowered onto the balcony. Lairgnen turned to Llewellyn, who was saying something and pointing toward the transporter. Lairgnen went inside, and Llewellyn followed from behind and sat beside him. They were joined by two warriors, who dwarfed Llewellyn in both size and height.

Both wore black tight-fitting leather uniforms and knee-high boots with inch-high soles, which added height to the warriors. Gen couldn't tell what their gender was because of the helmets and lowered visors that covered their faces.

Strapped to their waists were mean-looking weapons that looked like they belonged in the hands of a butcher. Each wore decorative armbands, which Gen knew were actually ingenious devices that allowed a force shield to surround the warrior's body as added protection.

Gen made an involuntary shiver. He recognized the type of warriors accompanying Lairgnen and Llewellyn. Who wouldn't? Seeing a pair equipped like they were usually meant they were members of the highly skilled clan of warriors called the Hummingguard. They were perceived to fear no weapons or enemies but had sworn allegiance to the king.

From the insignia on their shoulder pads, they were trained in the use of specialized techniques for hand-to-hand combat as well as technical weapons. That Llewellyn had brought in the precision killers meant Gen was in more danger than he'd originally thought.

The doors shut, and through his connection with Lairgnen, he felt the lurch as the transporter took off. At that moment, his connection with Lairgnen faded, and he was once more inside his own transport. Beside him, Elley looked tense but sat unmoving. Rhobat was just as still and silent.

Gen worried about what was going on. Who was the mastermind of his abduction, and why wasn't Elley doing anything to stop Rhobat? Something didn't add up, and he wracked his mind to find what piece didn't fit. He looked out the window and saw they had passed the palace and were flying low over hills. In the distance, he could see they were nearing the edge of the plateau.

"Where are we going?" Gen asked, looking at Elley.

"We're going to take a detour, Your Highness," Elley said but didn't look in Gen's direction.

Gen's heart sank, and he suspected he had probably misunderstood Elley's actions when he took out the weapon strapped to his leg. He'd thought it was for his protection.

"Why are you doing this, Elley? Can you at least tell me that?"

In Gen's periphery, he saw Rhobat jerk as though he were startled. He looked over his shoulder, but Elley raised the arm that held his weapon and pointed it at the guard.

"Keep your eyes to the front, and don't make any sudden moves," Elley said before turning to Gen. His eyes twitched as though there was something in them. When he moved his arm, his movements looked stiff, as though he were fighting himself. "I would suggest, Your Highness, that you keep quiet. All will be revealed once we get you to your father." Again, Elley's eyes twitched.

Gen froze at the mention of Martin. "My father? What has he got to do with this?"

"He wants to speak with you," Elley said.

The way Elley was speaking—like everything was normal—began to irritate Gen. Then Elley's hand holding the stunner jerked, and immediately, his other hand grabbed it and held it down.

"If he wanted to do that, why go through all this secrecy? All he needed to do was to contact me, and I could have arranged a time and place," Gen said, but his thoughts were going a mile a minute. Was he crazy thinking that Elley was not in full control of himself?

Elley shrugged, but even that looked forced to Gen.

"I cannot answer that, Your Highness. I'm just doing my job," Elley said. His mouth clamped shut, which made his whole body jerk again.

"Your job is to protect me, not kidnap me." Gen was rapidly getting angry, but he couldn't take his gaze off Elley.

"I am not kidnapping you, Your Highness," Elley hissed out. His face twisted as though he were in pain, then like a switch, it relaxed, and his expression blanked out.

There was no longer any doubt that something, or someone, was controlling Elley.

"Then kindly explain to me what it is you are doing," Gen challenged. Maybe if he provoked Elley, he could snap him out of whatever was controlling him.

"I don't need to explain anything," Elley said before turning away to face the front.

"Oh, for Goddess' sake," Gen said under his breath. What did he have to do to get some answers?

Elley jerked in his seat and grabbed at Gen's arm. "Don't take the Goddess' name in vain, Your Highness. It is derogatory and speaks of a lack of respect."

Gen pulled his arm free and readied to defend himself, but Elley let him go and sat rigid in his seat again.

"Are you for real? Where did this sudden spirituality come from?" Gen looked away, feeling too impatient to continue looking at Elley.

He'd been a fool thinking that Elley was his friend. He really should improve on his skills at spotting fake friends from real ones. He just had to figure out what was going on and call Lairgnen. Maybe he could reach out again and write something so they could communicate.

He suddenly realized there was something about what Elley said that sounded familiar. The words were just what his father used to say. Elley had never said such things before.

He was still trying to figure out how to communicate better with Lairgnen without causing Elley or Rhobat to react when another transporter came into view beside them. His heart leapt when he recognized the palace crest painted on its sides.

"Oh, look, we have company," Gen said. He hoped his faked excitement would get Elley to reveal his true motives.

Elley moved closer to look through the portal. "Ah, it's Prince Lairgnen," he said before moving back to his seat.

"Is that all you're going to say?" Gen asked, surprised.

But Elley didn't respond. He just stared blankly into space. What was wrong with the man?

And then it hit him. Only a spell could have that effect on someone. From the trancelike behavior of Elley and Rhobat, it meant that they were under some form of enchantment, one that took control of the minds of those targeted by the spell caster. Elley had mentioned Martin's involvement, so Gen had no doubt of the high possibility Martin was behind the unlawful curse. Especially after what Elley had said.

"Do you mind if I call my husband again, Elley? He must be wondering where I'm at," Gen said, striving to make sure his tone sounded calm and unaware he was in danger.

Elley nodded, but his gaze didn't move from where he stared in front of him. Thankfully, he'd lowered his arm that still held the weapon.

Gen shook his head and took out his communicator again. At the first beep that signaled his call had gone through, Lairgnen answered.

"Are you all right?"

"I actually am, which is very surprising. Also, I'm sure someone's placed some sort of charm on Elley. He looks confused and unemotional."

"So he's not behind your abduction?"

"At first, I thought he was, but then I recognized the signs. He also mentioned my father wanted to speak to me. So I think, and I'm just speculating here, that he's the one who placed some sort of spell on Elley to take me somewhere. But I believe the spell's not working properly, because Elley isn't even stopping me from talking to you."

"Where is he taking you?"

"I didn't get to that part yet, hold on." Gen turned to Elley. "Do you know where my father wants you to take me?"

"To the Common Grounds. At the port." Elley spoke woodenly, but the muscles on his cheeks twitched.

"He says at the port in the Common Grounds, I'm just not sure which one. Lair, I think the spell's wearing thin. Elley's showing signs of rejection." Gen kept his gaze on Elley, who sat frozen once more, except for the muscle on his cheek. It kept twitching.

"Do you think Rhobat has been cursed as well?"

Gen leaned over to check, but the guard kept his back to him. He shook his head. "I can't see, but he's also unresponsive, so yes, I think he is, too."

"As a priest, your father would know this type of spell," Lairgnen said.

"He should, but I'm not sure why he's cast it. Even I know the spell's unlawful."

"Desperate perhaps?"

"I'm the one who's desperate if we're talking desperation here." Gen immediately regretted his tone. "I'm sorry, Lair, I'm nervous and . . . Well, I'm sorry."

"Don't apologize. I know sarcasm when I hear it. Coming from you, and knowing your situation, I'm surprised you're not panicking," Lairgnen said.

Gen looked out the window and saw Lairgnen gazing back at him. He could also see Llewellyn and the two Hummingguards.

"I'm glad you're here, Lair," Gen said.

"I'm fairly certain Martin isn't going to hurt you. He just wanted to see you. Anwyll prohibited him from contacting you, so he might have thought this was the best way to do it."

"If he's desperate enough to do something unlawful, then I think I should be wary of him. He's never hit me, but he can do other things that may harm me."

"He will never get the chance to touch you, though I'm worried about the magic he'll use against you,"

"No, don't be," Gen said. "Mother took care of that."

"What do you mean?"

"Well, remember Cait's fafa? Mother asked him to place a protection spell over me to make me immune to harmful magic. It was against Father's wishes, but there was nothing he could do about it."

"I didn't even know giants knew magic," Lairgnen said.

"Well, they are creatures of the Goddess, so yes, they do have magical abilities. It's different from ours, but also similar. Does that make sense?"

"I'm not sure what you're talking about, but it leads me to

believe that Martin may do something drastic. Maybe that is why he turned to *ius auction,* because he couldn't control you any other way. The bastard," Lairgnen said.

"I'm not aware my father is illegitimate, or myself for that matter, which is why I can't wait for the results of the blood test to arrive," Gen said.

"I'm not talking about your birth, Gen," Lairgnen said.

"I know," Gen said, rolling his eyes.

"Then why did you say that?"

"So I can vent my anger without revealing it to Elley or Rhobat here. Who knows the extent of this spell? Father may even be listening in as we speak," Gen said.

"True. I see you've changed direction. Hold on, let me check which port you're headed to," Lairgnen said.

"The problem is, I believe Martin is my father. Because I can't see Mother being with another man. Then again, I wouldn't know about that, but she never hinted I may not be his son,"

"If that's the case, then Martin shouldn't have done what he did, but he did it anyway, which leads me to believe that Martin has other plans concerning you."

"Oh, I'm pretty sure he has other plans, like maybe kidnapping me, and probably trying something that would change my mind or yours, so he regains control over me."

"But then again, you've had your twenty-first birthday, so whatever happens today, he's already lost his opportunity."

"He's not dumb—" Gen's words cut off when the transporter lurched suddenly. Quick thinking had him bracing on his hand to avoid going face down on the floor. The transporter lurched several more times, and Gen thought he was going to spill his guts. As suddenly as it started, the transporter righted itself.

Elley held out his hand and helped Gen back to his seat.

"Gen? Gen? Are you all right?" Lairgnen shouted into the

earpiece.

"Your Highness, are you all right?" Elley asked, his face a mask of concern.

"I don't know what's happening, but I'm all right," Gen said, speaking to both Lairgnen and Elley.

He examined Elley's face and thought he saw some clarity in his gaze.

"If you don't mind, Your Highness, I'm going up front to help Rhobat find out what's going on." Elley quickly unbuckled himself and placed his weapon back in his ankle holster.

"I believe Elley's shaken off the curse, Lair. He sounds more like himself," Gen said.

Rhobat's face came into view as he turned around and glared at Elley.

"What the hell happened? I don't know how we got here," Rhobat said.

"Rhobat, too," Gen reported.

"Good. Tell him to land at once," Lairgnen snapped the order.

Gen barely stopped himself from saluting his husband. "Yes, sir, Your Highness," he said instead.

"I'll talk to you later, Gen. And stop calling me sir. You know how that affects me," Lairgnen grumbled.

Gen couldn't stop grinning. He didn't know if it was because the transporter was landing or that Lairgnen had threatened — promised — to do something to him later that night.

The transporter doors opened, and Elley helped him out. The ground felt good under his feet, and he breathed in deep. The fragrance of the forest smelled of wood and flowers, one of his favorite odors in the world. Just ahead of him, four transporters lowered. He recognized the one with the twins and the other three that had accompanied Lairgnen. From the one in the middle, two of the biggest men that Gen had ever seen came out. But it was the shorter man that followed them who wore the deepest scowl and worried look on his face that drew Gen the most. Without a thought, he answered the Heart Call, which seemed to shout over the canopy above. Before he knew it, he was in Lairgnen's arms, and he was safe once again.

"Are you sure you're all right?"

"Very sure, now that you're here," Gen said.

"You two, get inside the transporter," Llewellyn snapped. "I've ordered the Hummingguards to get you back home while I sort out what happened to your guards. I've deployed two units to intercept Martin."

"Thank you, Llewellyn, but please, don't be too harsh on Elley and Rhobat. They were not in control," Gen said.

"Don't worry, I was listening in on your conversation with Lair. Thank the Goddess, the spell was clumsily cast, and they were not fully under Martin's control. Now, do as I say, go home and stay there. I'll join you tonight or as soon as I'm done here and update you."

Gen walked with Lairgnen to the transporter, ever conscious of the two quiet men following them. "Who are they?"

"I'll tell you all about it later, Gen. Let's go home where I can make certain you're all right."

CHAPTER TWENTY-SIX

L airgnen looked out the window of his office and smiled when he saw a couple of birds flitting and tumbling in the air. Another two months, and it would be that time of the year all of Kizerain looked forward to. The year-end break, when all work stopped, and families could come together in honor of the Goddess. He couldn't wait to get away from the city and relax. Gen was just as excited, but because of last-minute assignments, he had to cram many hours in very few days to get through them.

The days following Gen's attempted kidnapping hadn't been happy ones. No one would have imagined that Martin's trial would reveal a sordid tale of greed and murder. Thinking about it now turned Lairgnen's stomach.

Llewellyn had successfully intercepted Martin and had him brought to the Ministry of Security for interrogation. Because of Martin's status as a priest, a cleric had to be brought in to witness the questioning. To everyone's surprise, it was Anwyll himself who had come. According to Llewellyn, once Martin saw who he was going to face, he lost all confidence and surrendered himself to Anwyll's justice.

When Gen had first heard about his father's apprehension, he had looked angry and then exultant.

Then Laoghaire called.

Gen had spent about an hour talking to his sister, and when he returned to their bedroom, he looked thoughtful. He announced that he no longer wanted to hear Martin's confession and was only interested in Anwyll's judgment. Gen's dejection had alarmed him, and he couldn't help feeling frustrated.

"Where is this attitude coming from?"

Gen sat beside him on the bed and took his hand. "Laoghaire was crying and said something that made me think about Father's deeds. She said she knew why, but when I asked her about it, she said I didn't want to know. I continued to press her, but she was adamant. She then told me that Anwyll would find out about Father but that he wouldn't be able to do anything about it. I asked her how that was, but she refused to answer me."

"The way you're talking, it's as if you're making it sound like Laoghaire's some kind of a seer," Lairgnen said softly, his forehead furrowed.

"I was surprised myself, and that thought did cross my mind, but I'm not sure what she is. She's changed. I first noticed it when I spoke to her after Llewellyn got her back from the convent. She's not sad, quite the contrary. It's like something inside her woke up, and I can't figure out what it is, only that she's changed." Gen shook his head. He spread his fingers and wove them with Lairgnen's. "Maybe Father knew about her talent, and that's why he took her to the Sisterhood of Gallizenae. I don't know. What I am sure of is that Laoghaire has convinced me not to go to the trial or listen firsthand to whatever it is Father has to confess."

Frustration welled inside Lairgnen. After all that Martin had done to Frigga and Gen, he thought it was only right that justice was served.

"I can feel your emotions, Lair, and I understand. Truly I do. But I feel that I must heed Laoghaire's caution. She startled me earlier, and I didn't know how to react. But deep in my heart, I know she has a talent that needs to be assessed by the *cleric*, so she can be trained properly. In fact, when I hinted that possibility, she was very excited and started talking about her time with the nuns."

Lairgnen tightened his grip on Gen's hand. "What can I do?"

"I won't go, but I won't stop you from going in my stead. Promise me that you won't tell me the details, only what Anwyll's justice will be."

Lairgnen had felt he had no choice and agreed to Gen's request.

When Llewellyn's call had come the following day, Lairgnen went to the palace to stand as witness in Gen's place, not as Minister of Finance or as Chosen Adviser, but in his capacity as Gen's husband. Llewellyn didn't mention Gen's absence, but Lairgnen could see he was curious about the reason behind the decision.

Martin stood in the very place where Traherne had stood only three days past, but where Traherne had the support of his family crowding the throne room, Martin stood alone. It was a telling picture of a priest, a man who had burned his bridges among friends and family.

Anwyll sat on his throne, looking down on Martin, his face devoid of any expression. His golden glow was muted, yet it was clear that Anwyll was anxious to hear what Martin had to say. Pedr sat on the throne beside Anwyll, his face as blank as his husband's.

"Martin Leafbow, once priest and husband to Frigga, Princess of the Royal House of Toullec, I urge you to speak the truth in my presence today. What say you?"

"As your will, Your Majesty," Martin said and bowed his head.

The obeisance startled Lairgnen, for Martin was not one to show fealty to anyone. Maybe he was wrong, but the man truly rubbed him the wrong way, and he was biased, after all. A throat cleared, and he looked up to see Anwyll gazing at him. His face burned, having been caught by his king. How could he have forgotten that when Anwyll was sitting on the throne all glowing in the golden light of magic, he could read the minds of all his people? Anwyll's mouth twitched as though he were biting back his amusement before facing Martin once more.

Anwyll's expression sobered and turned grim. "Martin Leafbow, I will keep this questioning short and to the point. Answer my questions briefly, and bear in mind, I can read your thoughts. Remember, if I suspect you are lying, I will invade your mind to extract the truth. I don't want to hurt you. Do you understand me?"

"I do, Your Majesty. And I will," Martin said, but he didn't look up.

Anwyll looked at his ministers and studied their faces. Lairgnen felt a gentle probing and knew the same was happening with the rest from the way his colleagues were shifting on their feet. When no one made a comment, Anwyll pulled back his probing and turned to look at Martin.

"Did you cast a spell of manipulation over Guénaël, Prince of the Royal House of Kizerain?"

"No, sire. In truth, my wife, Princess Frigga, had a giant cast a spell on my son to make any attempts on him ineffective."

"What kind of spell?" Anwyll looked thoughtful as he played with the signet ring on his finger.

"A spell of protection. It's a spell no man, priest, or cleric knows. Only the giants have the strength and ability to do it."

"Is it a dangerous spell?"

"As far as my research has revealed, not if it is done correctly." Martin shrugged.

Lairgnen closed his eyes and counted. Martin's attitude wasn't helping his cause. Beside him, the other ministers muttered among themselves, but a glance from Anwyll quieted them.

"Who cast the spell for my cousin, Frigga?"

"The giant, Crannog. He was oenologist for Toullec Vineyards during my wife's time." Martin's lips briefly twisted into a smirk.

But Lairgnen saw it. From Pedr's raised brow, he caught the look as well.

"Is he still around?" Anwyll looked relaxed enough, having lowered his arms over the arms of his chair.

Lairgnen was not fooled, however.

"No, Your Majesty," Martin said, placing his hands behind him and rolling on his heels. "He died with my wife when the transporter they were in crashed into the hills as they were flying to the capital."

"I see. We'll go back to the subject of that crash later. I want to proceed with the next question. I ask you frankly, Martin. Is Guénaël your biological son?"

"He is, Your Majesty."

"And how are you so certain about that? My brother does not look like you, but I must admit my sister Laoghaire does resemble you. Explain the relationship, if you don't mind."

"Indeed, my son Guénaël does not resemble me. As I had noted once to my wife, he is a Toullec through and through. Many say he resembles my father-in-law, but in fact, he is almost identical to one of his grandfather's brothers, now dead for over sixty years."

Anwyll's brows furrowed. "Are you speaking of Prince Maik, Martin?"

"No, sire. Prince Maik was my father-in-law. His younger brother, Garan, died when he was only a young boy. I never met him, neither had my wife, Frigga."

"Your certainty of Guénaël's parentage is astounding, Martin. I say this because your treatment of my brother was questionable."

Martin blinked and didn't respond as quickly as before. He shifted on his feet before answering. "I am quite certain he is my son, Your Majesty. Frigga was a virgin when I first lay with her."

Lairgnen blinked at the confession. He couldn't believe Martin actually said what he'd just said.

"A virgin, you say?" Anwyll asked, his voice deceptively calm.

"Yes, Your Majesty."

Anwyll turned to look at Pedr. "I remember the day Frigga married Martin. She looked very beautiful, but she always had been." Anwyll frowned as he turned back to Martin. "I don't recall Frigga looking virginal at all. In fact, I would say she was nearing her time to give birth."

Lairgnen's eyes widened. Beside him, the other ministers started to murmur among themselves, but Lairgnen ignored them. That Frigga had been pregnant upon her marriage was one detail he never knew about. Did Gen know he had been born only a few months, if not weeks after Frigga married Martin?

"Frigga and I married just two weeks before Guénaël was born."

Lairgnen closed his eyes and said a prayer to the Goddess. What was Martin trying to do? He was being tried for his deeds, not to bring shame on a dead woman who had no chance of defending herself. Anwyll cleared his throat, and the muttering died.

"I also recall Frigga's type in men, so I was surprised when she married you. You neither have the looks nor the temperament that would have attracted her. Tell me the truth, Martin. Why did my cousin marry you so suddenly and already pregnant?"

Martin wavered, and instantly, the muted golden light brightened, and Anwyll climbed to his feet. He approached the edge of the dais and frowned down at Martin.

"Speak the truth now, Martin."

Lairgnen had no doubt Anwyll was probing Martin's mind, and his suspicions were confirmed when Martin grimaced. He opened and closed his mouth as though he was fighting something invisible but lost under its pressure.

"I cast a spell of manipulation on her, Your Majesty," Martin said in a rush. "I raped her, and when she was pregnant, I cast another spell so she would keep the child. I cast a third one so she would agree to proceed with the marriage." Martin visibly slumped when the words were wrought from his mind. He gasped for air and glared up at Anwyll.

Bile rose in Lairgnen's throat. He couldn't bear to listen any longer and took a step to leave the throne room, but Llewellyn grabbed his arm and hissed a warning in his ear.

"You're going to stay and listen, brother. With Gen being absent, you are his representative. We need you here so Martin's trial is legal and binding. Stay strong. Please Lair. Think of Gen."

Lairgnen swallowed down his anger and nodded jerkily at Llewellyn. His brother was right. Should he leave now, Martin could claim that Gen had no interest in the trial, and any crime against him by Martin could be nullified.

"At last we're getting somewhere, Martin." Anwyll folded his arms in front of him. "Now, shall we go back to Frigga and talk about how she died? Did you cast a spell on her a fourth time?"

"It was more than the fourth, Your Majesty. Frigga was easy to manipulate, for she was weakened by our children and her need to protect them. I blame that creature, that giant, Crannog. He was the one who convinced her to seek a divorce."

Anwyll waved a negligent hand in front of him. "Forget about Crannog for now. Let's go back to your spell. It was the

261

same one you cast on my brother's warriors, wasn't it?"

Martin closed his eyes and nodded. Even from where Lairgnen stood, he could see the sweat bead on Martin's temple. "Yes, yes, but they were too strong. Warriors have a mindset I find difficult to control. They fought me every which way."

Anwyll nodded. "Yes, the warriors are strong. But Frigga wasn't, was she? She was the one who was driving that transporter. You were able to control her mind, but in the end, you caused the transporter to crash."

Martin shook his head vehemently, tears coursing down his cheeks. "No, no, it was an accident. Crannog, I felt his influence on her. Frigga fought off the spell, and as I struggled with her mind, she veered the transporter in the wrong direction. I tried to control the transporter through her. I didn't want her to die. I loved her, but Crannog's influence on her had been too strong. I didn't mean for her to die. I just wanted her to turn around and come back to me. To us."

Anwyll stared angrily at Martin. "Frigga died because of your manipulation. Because of your greed."

"No." Martin tugged at his hair. "It was never greed. You have to believe me, Your Majesty. It was because of that Crannog."

"You keep going back to him. Why is that? Was it because Frigga had him cast a protection spell over her?"

"No. It was because he loved her. How dare he! He's a monster. How could Frigga have loved him over me?"

"Mother did love Crannog, but as one would love a brother." The soft young voice came from the entrance.

Lairgnen's heart stopped. He recognized that voice.

"Mother loved Crannog because he had been her friend since they were young."

Martin looked over his shoulder and visibly trembled. "Laoghaire," he whispered.

Laoghaire walked into the throne room, and despite her

serious expression, Lairgnen gasped at her beauty. It was the first time he had seen her without the nannies Pedr had assigned to her. Today, she was dressed in a pretty pink gown with flowers in her hair. Lairgnen thought she looked like a little fairy in her getup and wondered who had dressed her that way.

"On the day Mother died, I remember how pretty she looked, how fragrant. She was going to see the king, she said. And she made me a promise that all would be well, and we'd be finally safe when she got back. But she never came back."

"You're too young to remember that," Martin said.

"I remember, Father." Laoghaire's voice was gentle, but the look of pity on her face was a surprise. It was such a mature expression for someone her age.

Lairgnen had to agree with Gen that his sister was truly gifted in some magical way.

"Laoghaire, come to me." Anwyll extended his arm toward her.

Laoghaire looked up at Anwyll. She gave him a bright, toothy smile before running up the dais. Anwyll took her in his arms, and they gazed into each other's eyes.

"I thought I told you not to come here," Anwyll said.

"I know," Laoghaire said. "I'm sorry."

Anwyll shook his head. "No need to be sorry. It is your right to be here, no matter that you're too young."

"I wanted to be here."

"As I said, your choice. Now, why don't you go sit with Pedr and allow me to continue my questioning. Is that all right with you?"

Pedr took Laoghaire from Anwyll. He brought her to his throne, where he set her on his lap, and they looked up and faced the assembly once more.

Anwyll smiled fondly at Laoghaire before turning around.

"I have one last question to ask you, Martin."

Martin nodded, but his gaze stayed locked on Laoghaire.

"Prince Maik." Martin's voice was so low it could hardly be heard. "He found out about what I'd done and threatened to have our marriage annulled. I had to protect my family."

"I see now." Anwyll bowed his head and took a deep breath.

Lairgnen closed his eyes and prayed to the Goddess. He now understood why Laoghaire had cautioned Gen from attending the trial. She wanted to spare him the pain of hearing Martin's confession. He glanced at where Laoghaire sat, expecting her to have hidden her face in Pedr's shoulder as a child would do, but she was sitting straight and looking directly at her father. The look of seriousness on her face disconcerted Lairgnen, and he had to admit, he found his sister-in-law strange.

Anwyll stood with his head bowed for a long moment, appearing to be thinking about his options. But Lairgnen already knew where this was going. There was only one punishment for murder, and that was death. Anwyll raised his head and opened his eyes. Where once they were blue, they now gleamed with golden light. His whole body began to glow until Lairgnen had to cover his eyes.

"Martin Leafbow, once married to Frigga, Princess of the Royal House of Toullec, hear my judgment. On the grounds of attempted kidnapping of your son, my brother, Prince Guénaël, I find you guilty. On the grounds of casting an illegal spell of mind manipulation, I find you guilty. On the murders of Prince Maik and Princess Frigga, both of the Royal House of Toullec, I find you guilty. Finally, on the grounds of the murder of the giant, Crannog, I find you guilty."

Martin groaned and fell to his knees. He started sobbing, but Lairgnen couldn't find it in his heart to feel sorry for the man. Anwyll stepped closer to Martin and crouched down before him.

"You attempted to steal royal lands from my brother, and because you couldn't do it legally, you called for an *ius auction*." Anwyll's voice was low and grave, his face a mask of self-control. "It wasn't to save the name of Toullec. It was so you could take control of your son through his bidder. Martin, the auction ritual did not come to be for the abuser to further their greed and personal agendas. It was created to help keep the innocent safe from their abusers. You twisted an archaic but justifiable practice to fit your own agenda and made it into something cruel and unjust. For that, you are found guilty."

Anwyll shook his head and took to his feet. "Unfortunately, I cannot pass your sentence."

Lairgnen's eyes widened, and he felt his heart stop. He couldn't believe what he was hearing. Why was he letting Martin go?

Martin's sobbing stopped. He stared up at Anwyll, looking as though he had been given a lifeline. But when Martin started to smile and open his mouth to speak, Anwyll raised a hand to stop him.

"As king, I am Kizerain's spiritual leader, but I am also a man of magic. It is a gift the Goddess gave me. At the time of the Great Passage, certain pacts were made between man and sprite. One of them was that the sprite would help us through the dimensional barrier in exchange for our protection. That protection extends to their closest allies. The giants sacrificed their people to guarantee that the sprite succeeded in their mission. For their service, we, the kings of Kizerain, made a promise never to harm the giants, for they are not for us to use or abuse. They are the sprite's most loyal subjects and are beyond man's control. Therefore, the responsibility for your punishment no longer falls on me. If you had kept your killing to man only, you would be sentenced to death. But because you killed Crannog, I have no choice but to step aside for the sprite."

Thunder rattled the windows, followed by a storm of humming the likes of which Lairgnen had never heard before. Winds lashed through the throne room as though the elements would tear down the walls of the palace. As suddenly as it happened, it stopped, leaving a deafening silence. For a moment, Lairgnen thought the unusual event was over. Then the sound of thousands of wings broke through the silence, and the purring, chattering, trilling sounds began. It started out low, steadily increasing in volume until it became screaming. Lairgnen had never seen or heard the sprite that angry in his life. He didn't know what to think . . . or where to look. Sprite were everywhere. Hundreds, probably thousands of the tiny creatures were flying and swooping in intricately coordinated patterns close to the high ceiling.

Llewellyn stayed firm where he stood beside Lairgnen, but the shock on his face reflected what Lairgnen felt. In truth, he wanted to run. Looking around him, he saw that the other ministers were just as frightened, but no one was budging from their positions. The warriors stood unmoving at their posts, and Lairgnen realized Anwyll had expected the sprite's reactions.

Lairgnen looked to the dais. Anwyll stood bathed in golden light. He was craning his neck, watching the sprite express their anger over the death of one of their own. Anwyll closed his eyes and turned his back to the room. Martin started to stand up, only to fling his arms over his head and fall to the ground. Like a dark cloud, the sprite screamed as one and dived, engulfing Martin with their tiny bodies. For a brief moment, Lairgnen could hear him screaming in fear. In a flash of lightning, the sprite disappeared, taking Martin with them.

"Such is the will of the sprite. Such is their justice," Anwyll said.

The weeks and months had gone by quickly, and before Lairgnen knew it, the university was one week away from the regular end of the year break. Gen still had another half-day of classes to attend, then they would both be free for a month.

There was no Yula that year, nor would there be until time to crown the next queen or king. They would have to wait. Nevertheless, it was still a holiday and a time celebrated with much anticipation. Lairgnen knew he was expected to attend Anwyll and Pedr's anniversary, but he wasn't feeling it. What he really wanted was to go back to Merifael and spend some alone time with Gen.

"What's got your mood down, Lair? I swear, your emotions were yelling at me to help you make a decision, yet I'm lost as to what you're trying to convey. Want to talk about it?"

Lairgnen jumped at the sound of Gen's voice behind him. Grimacing for having been caught out, he slowly turned around to face his husband.

"I was actually thinking about us going to Merifael and spend the holidays there," he said.

Gen's brows rose as he seemed to think about it. "What you're saying is you're tired of the city and want to smell the fresh air and sleep all day when you want to without anyone calling you in for whatever matters of the planet." He grinned broadly.

The way Gen managed to summarize all of his thoughts and feelings in one sentence brought a bright smile to his face. "I knew you'd understand." Lairgnen perked up happily.

"Of course, I do. When do you want to go?"

"I have one final meeting to attend tomorrow morning, you have your half-day of classes, so I think we can go in the afternoon?"

Gen gave a brief nod without meeting Lairgnen's gaze. He appeared to think for a moment, biting his lower lip as was his habit, before nodding one more time and meeting

Lairgnen's gaze.

"Which house are we staying in?"

Lairgnen thought about it and settled on the Bolton manor. "We still haven't had a chance to find out what's in that hidden room."

Gen dropped his hands to his sides. "I'll call ahead and arrange for our trip. Now get back to whatever you are doing and concentrate. I was finishing up an essay I need to submit tomorrow when you distracted me with all sorts of worries." Gen gave him a mock glare and quickly followed it up with an air kiss before turning around and walking away.

"Sorry," Lairgnen called out after Gen.

Although he couldn't see him, he got the impression of Gen waving a hand over his head to dismiss Lairgnen's apology. But the kiss on the cheek was the perfect bonus.

Lairgnen went back to the file he had been reading before he'd lost himself in his desire to get a break from the city. It didn't take long to get himself lost in the alluring world of numbers and balance sheets.

By the time he reached the bottom of the pile, he was ready for another break. Standing up, he stretched his arms to the ceiling, twisting his torso side to side before going out of his office to search for Gen. His communicator vibrated inside his pocket, and he reached for it automatically. A quick glance told him the call came from Anwyll himself.

"Lair, we're eating out," Anwyll said as soon as he answered the call.

"All right," Lairgnen said, resigned that once more, he had to forego dining with Gen because of royal affairs.

"Stop moaning. This is purely for enjoyment. I'm taking Pedr down to the Common Grounds. Bring Gen with you."

Lairgnen blinked in surprise. "Oh, thank you. I'll let Gen know."

"You two get over here in about an hour."

Lairgnen frowned at the wall. "Where are we going?"

"It's a place Pedr took me to on our first date, although at that time, it wasn't technically a date."

"Good to know." Lairgnen chuckled. He could still remember how the two had met and reacted with each other.

"See you in an hour," Anwyll said before ending the call.

Lairgnen sought Gen out and sensed his focus on reading a case study about embezzlement. He didn't want to distract Gen from his studies. They had time. From what he could tell, Gen would be done soon. Changing directions, he went out into the balcony overlooking the gardens.

Not for the first time, he was glad he'd bought the house. It wasn't as large as the Bolton manor, but it served its purpose when they stayed in the city. It only had room enough to house his three staff as well as Gen and himself. A third bedroom could serve as a guest room should anyone choose to stay with them. By royal standards, the house was minimal, but he knew that many had lauded his decision to buy it. Not only was it placed on one of the more expensive lots in the capital, but it also came with security. That had been his priority when he'd first looked over the place, because it satisfied his need to keep Gen safe at all times.

Thinking about his young husband, Lairgnen still found it hard to believe that they'd found each other. The Heart Call ensured their compatibility, but the love they had for each other was independent of it. With or without it, he knew their love was the forever kind. He was lucky. Very lucky.

Lairgnen didn't know how long he stood there, staring down at the gardens below, when he felt Gen's touch in his mind. Without hesitation, he returned the caress with one of his own. Through the months they had been living together and getting to know each other, it was startling that it was Gen who had the stronger connection with him. According to Anwyll, it was the same between him and Pedr. Anwyll's

connection was stronger, while Pedr's tended to be more passive. For Lairgnen, he wasn't passive at all, far from it, but
Gen was just more intense.

Maybe it was his youth or the way his mind worked, but
Gen could, should he wish to, get inside Lairgnen's mind and
see through his eyes what he was doing in real time. The best
thing about Gen was he always asked permission before he
went all in. Most times, Lairgnen allowed him inside, which
made making love to him all the more enjoyable.

"Lair, stop it with those thoughts. You're distracting me,"
Gen said as soon as Lairgnen entered his office.

While Lairgnen's office was on the second floor, Gen had
chosen what used to be the morning room on the first floor.
His reasoning had been that there were times when his fellow
students needed to join him when they had to work on projects together, and he didn't want them to disturb Lairgnen's
time. It worked well for both of them, but now, all Lairgnen
wanted to do was tell Gen about the invitation.

"Where are you planning on taking us?" Gen asked, looking up from his books.

Gen looked so handsome that it took a moment for Lairgnen to respond. He felt his face heat up, but he pasted a smile
on anyway, to hide the sudden lust that hit him.

"Anwyll called and invited us to join him and Pedr for dinner. We're going to this place Pedr had told me about before
but never had the chance to visit. It's at the Common
Grounds. It's nothing fancy, but the food's great. Anwyll said
to meet them at the palace in an hour."

"Thank the Goddess." Gen quickly closed the book he had
been reading and set it aside on top of a pile of other books.
"I thought my eyes were about to cross from reading."

"Oh? I thought you were caught up in your studies, so I
gave you enough time to finish."

Gen squinted at him. "Once we get to Merifael, we have

got to work on our connection."

Lairgnen raised his brows. "Should I apologize?"

"No, in fact, I want to thank you for the interruption, but working on your connection with me is still a must. I was actually finished, but I want to stay ahead of the lectures. It's the only way to get good grades. I don't want to work this hard only to give up because I couldn't stay on top of my game."

"Are you happy, Gen? About studying law?"

"Yes, I'm not regretting my choice." Gen's smile lit up the already bright room.

Lairgnen cleared his throat. His love and desire for Gen had only gotten stronger over the months they'd been married.

"Good. Why don't we go upstairs and freshen up? We have less than an hour to get to the palace."

A half-hour later, they were on their way to the palace. Lairgnen decided to fly the transporter himself, wanting some time alone with Gen. They had both been busy with their own schedules and only found time at night. Elley and Rhobat were shadowing their movements from the transporter hovering above them.

"I'm looking forward to our time in Merifael," Lairgnen said, looking at the coordinates. Everything looked normal.

"Let's get through tonight first, then we talk about Merifael," Gen said.

Lairgnen looked at Gen curiously. "What's going on in that head of yours?"

Gen shrugged. "Nothing. Well, it's not *nothing*, it's just that . . . We haven't spoken or seen the king or Pedr for several weeks now, and I was wondering why this sudden invitation."

"Well, maybe you haven't seen them, but I have. In fact, I spoke to Anwyll yesterday."

"I don't know, but I've got this feeling that it's not all going to be a simple dinner tonight." Gen shrugged again.

"Well, we're going to find out soon enough, I suppose," Lairgnen said.

They kept quiet throughout the short flight to the palace, Lairgnen thinking about Gen's words while Gen looked out the window and saying nothing.

Lairgnen figured Gen might not be far off the mark. It was true, he'd seen and spoken to Anwyll on an almost daily basis, but whenever they spoke, it had mostly been conversations limited to the running of Kizerain. Whenever personal topics came up, they were usually more commentary than an actual discussion.

Gen was probably correct in thinking Anwyll had another purpose in mind inviting them out to dinner. That the place they were going was far from the palace was another telling clue. Lairgnen only hoped whatever it was wouldn't mean having to stay in the capital for the holidays.

They landed at the palace side entrance, where to Lairgnen's surprise, Anwyll and Pedr were waiting for them. By their feet stood two bulging bags. Absent were the many guards that usually surrounded the royal pair. He looked past Anwyll's shoulder, expecting to see Llewellyn or Caddel, but to his surprise, neither man was around.

"If you're looking for the usual retinue, think again," Pedr said, a self-satisfied smile curling his lips.

"Is there something I should know about?" Lairgnen asked, looking at Pedr, then Anwyll, and back again.

Pedr chuckled while Anwyll grinned broadly. Lairgnen looked at Gen, who appeared just as confused as he was.

Lairgnen turned to Anwyll. "Cousin? What's going on?"

"I must apologize, Lair, but Pedr didn't want the usual gaggle of followers. He said he wanted some time alone with me, and I didn't know how else to go about this without raising suspicions from the warriors." Anwyll gave Pedr a glance, leaned closer, and spoke in a very serious voice. "We're running away. Would you and Gen mind taking us to Merifael? Llewellyn was kind enough to lend us his house there, so we thought, why not have you and Gen take us there."

"What? Now?" Lairgnen stared at the two royal men in disbelief before letting out a loud groan.

"Uhm, Your Majesty —" Gen began.

Pedr immediately held up his palm. "Please, stop. I beg of you, no titles. Just call me Pedr and this guy here, Anwyll." Pedr chucked his thumb in Anwyll's direction. "We understand each other? Good. Now, just take us to Merifael, I'm begging you."

Lairgnen turned to Gen and met his gaze. Outwardly, Gen didn't react but sent him a mental shrug that suggested he was on with the plan.

He turned back to Anwyll. "I guess we can take you there, but we'll have to come back here immediately. I've got a meeting to attend tomorrow morning, and Gen still has a class to attend, among other things, and we don't have any clothes packed."

Anwyll rocked on his heels and grinned mischievously. "Don't worry about those things. All that's taken care of."

"How?" Gen stepped closer to Anwyll.

"Well, I had a feeling that you two didn't want to stay on for the holidays, and when I told Pedr about it, he pounced on the idea and confessed he wanted to stay out of the capital this year."

"But what about the celebrations?"

Anwyll shrugged. "It's not an ascension year, not like last year when I became king. Also, my presence is not really needed here, and I can work from Merifael without anyone knowing where I am."

Lairgnen glanced at Gen. "What do you think?"

Gen bit on his lower lip as he thought about it briefly and then his stomach rumbled. "I can't make a decision until I've eaten. I'm sorry, Pedr, but I'm too hungry to think." He looked sheepishly at Pedr, who barked out a laugh.

"I can't think, either. I've been hungry for about two hours, and Anwyll doesn't seem to understand my cravings for regular food. The palace cooks are good, but there's only so much rich food I can take. How about we go find somewhere to eat and make plans while we're at it?" Pedr picked up his bag and looked expectantly at Gen and Lairgnen.

Before Lairgnen or Anwyll could say anything, Gen nodded and picked up the bag by Anwyll's feet.

"Yes, let's, please. I miss regular, home-cooked meals. Lair mentioned a place you and Anwyll went to on your first date."

"He did?" Pedr gave Anwyll a side glance before grinning. "I'll provide Lair with the coordinates."

They didn't waste any more time speaking, and the four of them boarded Lairgnen's transporter. Gen and Pedr sat in the back while Anwyll sat in front with him. Pedr gave out the coordinates, and they were on their way.

"Are you sure about this, sire?" Gen asked when they neared the Common Grounds. "What about your head of security and court magician? What did they have to say about this?"

"Don't worry, I took care of them both."

"May I ask how, sire?" Gen asked.

Lairgnen touched Gen's mind and cautioned him against questioning Anwyll's will.

"I told them, of course," Anwyll said, grinning broadly over his shoulder. "Don't worry, Gen. My head of security is not as gullible as you think he is. He's been with me since my birth and knows what I'm planning before I even managed to do it. He's on top of everything I do. He allows me these little jaunts of mine, making me think I can escape their monitoring."

"Where is the old man, anyway?" Lairgnen asked. "Caddel's not the type to just let you go off on your own without making sure you're safe."

"Well, of course not. As I said, he's on top of everything. In fact, he should be right above us as we speak."

"What?" Lairgnen stared at Anwyll for a brief moment before he checked the control panel. Nothing showed up.

He glanced at Anwyll when the king tapped his shoulder. Anwyll pointed outside the windows, and Lairgnen looked out. To his surprise, Anwyll had been telling the truth. There was another transporter flying just above them, and his vehicle sensors hadn't even picked up their presence.

"How is that possible?"

Anwyll chuckled. "You can thank Llewellyn for that piece of magic. He convinced the court magician to create this spell that would prevent detection. Oh, and I forgot to tell you earlier. While we were talking, the same spell was cast over this vehicle. So, you see? We're quite safe." Anwyll grinned broadly.

Lairgnen stared at him in disbelief. "The least you could have done was tell me about it," he grumbled under his breath.

"And where's the fun in that?"

"Never mind," Lairgnen said.

"Stop teasing Lair, Anwyll. You know how he is," Pedr said.

"How is he?" Gen asked.

Pedr's mouth dropped, and his cheeks reddened. "Well, Lair's kind of by the book, if you know what I mean."

"He is?" Gen's brows rose high with his surprise.

Lairgnen controlled his urge to laugh at the discomfort on

the Consort's face.

"Well, there you go, Pedr. I told you Gen can take care of himself." Anwyll chuckled.

"Yes, I see what you mean now," Pedr said. "He's quite the strong character, isn't he? Not the quiet mouse he was before he married Lair."

Gen shrugged and relaxed into his seat. "Lair's good for me. He's taught me how to stand on my own and is very supportive."

Lairgnen felt his face heat up when Anwyll and Pedr gazed at each other in silent communication before laughing as if they knew something he didn't. He felt a little embarrassed at first, but then, he felt Gen's mental caress and held on to it. Gen read his mind and gave him a mental kiss. Love washed over him until Lairgnen relaxed in his chair.

When had their roles reversed? When had Gen become his savior instead of the other way around? A chuckle escaped his lips.

It didn't matter who was older or younger. Lairgnen and Gen had both grown into their relationship. They were now at the point in their lives where their ages had become irrelevant numbers. For someone like him, who had been conscious about their age gap and how people would perceive them at the beginning of their relations, that epiphany was an accomplishment by itself.

CHAPTER TWENTY-SEVEN

Gen pulled a dark, woven cloak out of one of the armoires and was immediately engulfed in a cloud of dust. He let out a loud sneeze. Almost instantaneously, he was consumed in a fit of sneezing. When he was finally done, his eyes were watering, and his nose was itching up a storm.

"Are you all right, Gen?" Lairgnen said, looking over his shoulder. He was on the other side of the secret room and was pouring over a collection of scrolls he'd pulled out from a chest.

"It's nothing, just dust." His voice sounded nasal even to his own ears, but the itching was subsiding. Not much, but he was able to stop the next sneeze by pushing the tip of his tongue over his upper palate.

He looked over the cloak and wondered how old it was. There was a brooch pinned on it, and its collar was lined with tiny jet beads.

"How old do you think this is?" Gen turned around to show Lairgnen the cloak.

Lairgnen slowly shook his head. "I have no idea, but from those beads on the collar, it must be at least two, maybe three hundred years. There's a similar beading design on display at the museum back at the capital, but the cloak didn't look as good as that one does."

"Interesting." He placed the cloak carefully over a chair and turned back to the armoire. There was an intricately carved chest set in a back corner, and he pulled it out. The heaviness was a surprise, for it looked too delicate to hold such weight. After setting it down on the seat of the chair he'd placed the cloak on, he carefully opened the domed lid. Expecting to see jewelry, he was surprised that it wasn't what was in it.

"Lair," Gen called over his shoulder. "Come here. I need to show you something."

"What is it?"

A scrape on the floor was followed by Lairgnen looking over his shoulder.

"Oh, what is this?" Lairgnen said, his voice filled with wonder.

Gen nodded. "If I'm not mistaken, this might have once belonged to a magician."

"What kind of magician, though? Because I recognize two or three surgical instruments here," Lairgnen said. He pushed the tools aside to reveal more at the bottom of the chest. There were hooks, needles, a rusted pair of forceps, and a strainer.

"Maybe the owner was a collector?" Gen shrugged, losing interest in the chest. He stood up and went back to the armoire.

"You know, we've been at this for a few days now, and I still haven't seen anything that explains why this place was walled up." Gen pushed on layers of scrolls that turned to dust at his touch. He reached inside and felt around when his fingers encountered something metal and pulled it out.

"Oh, I think I've found something else. I hope it not another—" Gen's mouth dropped open.

In his hand was one of the most mysterious and beautiful things he'd ever seen.

"What is it?" Lairgnen said. His back was still turned as he continued to poke around in the chest.

"It's a crown," Gen said. "It's an actual crown."

"What?" Lairgnen whirled around and quickly came to his side.

Gen raised his head and met Lairgnen's gaze.

"I think we need to show this to Anwyll," Gen said.

Lairgnen nodded. "I agree."

They were at Llewellyn's manor in less than an hour. The butler showed Gen and Lairgnen inside and led them to the salon where the two royals were lounging on a sofa. Anwyll had his eyes closed and appeared to be sleeping, while Pedr was pouring over a book. Pedr looked up and welcomed them with a smile.

"Hey, what brings you two here?" Pedr said.

Lairgnen stepped forward and bowed. "Gen and I have found something at the Bolton manor and thought we should show it to Anwyll."

"I'm not sleeping," Anwyll said without opening his eyes.

"Sire, I—"

"No titles, please. Not here," Anwyll said. He finally opened his eyes and peered at Gen and Lairgnen. "You know, for two men who said they wanted to be alone for the holidays, you seem to be coming here often."

Gen bit back a grin. What Anwyll said was true. He and Lairgnen often came to Llewellyn's manor to visit. Spending some quality time together had been the main reason why they both came to Merifael, but that didn't mean they couldn't socialize.

Although it wasn't the season for harvesting grapes, Gen also found reasons to visit all their properties and talk with the managers and supervisors. Caitriona had prepared a whole list of things to be done before the harvest season, which needed Lairgnen's attention. Their trip to Merifael was not spent lounging in the salon like the two royals, but Gen kept the thought to himself.

"There's a good reason this time," Gen said. "We have something to show you."

He didn't wait for Anwyll's response and took a seat on one of the chairs closest to Pedr, then placed the wrapped crown on the table and peeled away the cloth. The crown was made of beaten gold and fashioned as an encircling headband with two bands crossing at the apex. There were no gemstones decorating it, but the etchings on the metal could only have been from an artist's hand. The two bands were shaped to depict oak branches and at the apex was an engraving of the sacred oak tree back on the homeworld.

Pedr leaned forward and stared at the crown. "That's beautiful," he whispered. "Where did you find it?"

"There's this hidden room right next to our bedroom. Lair and I have been poking around its contents. So far, we've found several scrolls that haven't disintegrated when we touch them, a cloak, a chest with some items in it, and this."

Anwyll raised himself on his elbow and his gaze locked on the crown. After a moment, he got to his feet and knelt on the floor for a closer look.

"After all this time, you find this treasure," Anwyll whispered.

"Is it what I think it is?" Lairgnen asked.

Anwyll nodded. "I'm not a hundred percent sure, and we'll need to get this analyzed and confirmed, but I think you've found something that belonged to one of the first queens of Kizerain." Anwyll looked up to gaze at Gen and Lairgnen. "You mentioned scrolls. Were you able to decipher what was written on them?"

Lairgnen shook his head. "No. They were too old and frail, and I must admit, I destroyed some when I touched them. They collapsed and disintegrated right before my eyes. However, I know there are more of them in the crates."

Anwyll nodded. "I hope you don't mind, but I think you've stumbled onto something that may hold the answers to some of our forgotten lore. We'll need to bring in experts who know how to handle such delicate items."

Lairgnen sighed. "Gen and I were naïve in thinking we could keep this between us, but when Gen discovered the crown, we knew we were in over our head. Go ahead and call in the experts. However, I would like to ask that they come after we get back to the capital."

"Of course, I meant after the holidays. As it is, should I ask them to come now to examine this treasure? They will come, but with much grumbling. They want to spend their time with their loved ones as much as we do."

Gen leaned his arms over his thighs and stared down at the crown. "If you don't mind, can you keep the crown here with you? This manor has better security and it would be in safer hands."

"I agree," Anwyll said as he climbed to his feet. He dusted his hands and placed them on his hips. "I'm tempted to wear it, but I don't want to risk any magical protection around it. It's different when it's being handled than when it is worn. If I remember correctly, Llewellyn has a safe somewhere in his room."

Lairgnen rose to his feet. "I'll give him a call so the two of you can talk. I don't want to know where you're keeping the crown just to be on the safe side."

Pedr frowned. "Is the crown really that important?"

Anwyll smiled. "I have heard tales that the wearer of the crown was the most powerful magical queen of all history. I am not risking anyone finding out about its existence."

Gen's heart stuttered. "It never occurred to me it was that great of a deal. I mean, I knew it was old and valuable, but . . . the Queen's crown?" He shook his head and wondered. "Why was it hidden in the Bolton manor?"

Lairgnen came back into the room. "Llewellyn said he's flying in and will be arriving within the hour. Said he got lonely at the capital and decided to join us. However, he said that if Gen didn't mind, he would stay in either the Toullec manor or at Thréinfhir. Whichever was convenient."

"We could move to Toullec," Pedr said. "I've always wanted to know what it was like to be surrounded by a vineyard of that capacity."

Gen laughed. "I'll send somebody over to get the place ready for you. My old butler, Horst, stayed around and will be more than honored to serve you there."

The four of them spent the rest of their time talking and just enjoying each other's company, but when it came time for dinner, Lairgnen begged off, much to Gen's relief. On their way back to Bolton manor, Gen reached for Lairgnen's hand and gave it a squeeze.

"I enjoyed myself today," he said.

"I'm glad that you did. I enjoyed myself, as well." Lairgnen leaned over to give Gen's mouth a kiss. When they parted, he studied Gen's face.

"How are you really feeling, Gen? Ever since Martin's trial, you haven't spoken a single word about him."

Gen looked away. "I haven't thought about him, actually. Or at least, I try not to."

"Why? I'm asking because I have a feeling that his disappearance has affected you more than you're letting on."

Gen shook his head and smiled. "You know, for someone who is not so great at communicating his emotions, you sure are well versed in interpreting mine."

"Should I apologize?"

"No, I didn't mean it like you think. It's just that you know me more than I find comfortable at times, but I don't resent it. Or you."

"You're hiding behind your charm and smiles, but I see the deep hurt inside you. I can sometimes feel it when you're asleep."

"As I said, I try not to think about Father. He never loved me, and I never found peace until the sprite took him away."

"Do you ever wonder where they took him?"

"To hell, I hope. If such a place exists."

"I'm so sorry, Gen. I shouldn't have asked."

"If you didn't ask, I would have been worried. So no, don't ever apologize for worrying about me. I know you love me as much as I love you."

"I do love you. That's why I'm worried."

"Don't be. Remember, I was ready to accept he wasn't my father. In fact, I'd hoped he wasn't. At least that way, I had a reason why he hated me. The truth, as it turned out, hurt even more. After you told me about what happened, I prayed to the Goddess to help me get over my hurt from what my father had done to us. It still hurts, but the more I pray to her, the more I think she hears me, because the hurt is easing. Also, talking to Laoghaire helps. She's such a darling, and yet she went and witnessed his downfall."

"I was surprised Anwyll allowed her to stay, but once I saw her there and saw how she was, I have come to think she's more special than any of us are thinking."

"She's with the cleric now. She's happier there, and she does sound like she's enjoying herself. Don't tell Pedr, but she said she was getting tired of the pretty dresses and mundane days spent in embroidery. She much prefers learning about her abilities."

The transporter slowed down to a hover before it gradually landed in front of Bolton manor.

"You know, I was thinking," Gen said once he and Lairgnen entered their bedroom.

"What about?" Lairgnen asked as he started taking off his clothes.

"We always refer to this house as Bolton manor."

Lairgnen paused and looked back at Gen. "I see what you

mean."

"Don't you think it's about time to call this something else other than its previous owner's name?"

Lairgnen sat on the edge of the bed and took off his shoes. "Like what?"

Gen shrugged. "I don't know. I was just thinking out loud."

Lairgnen stared into space for a long moment before blinking up at Gen. "I don't have a last name, so I was thinking . . . How about, Toullec Cottage."

Gen's eyes grew large. "Cottage? This is not a cottage."

"Well, I was thinking, there's Toullec manor and the Thréinfhir house, so why not call this Toullec Cottage, because it's smaller than the manor."

Gen thought about it. The name did have a ring to it except for one thing. "But I'm married to you and been adopted into Anwyll's family, which is the same as yours, so that means we can't call it Toullec because both of us don't have a last name."

"You're overthinking this, Gen."

"What I'm saying is, why not just call this place *The Cottage*, my old home *The Manor*, and Thréinfhir . . . What do you suggest?"

"The Guesthouse?"

Gen chuckled. Their conversation was becoming muddled, and he was loving it. "I guess that works?"

"Are you asking me?"

"No, are you?"

Lairgnen shook his head. "I think we're both tired and hungry. Let's take a bath and then go downstairs to eat. We're not making sense."

They were headed down the hall, and the smell of food wafting from the kitchens made Gen's stomach rumble in hunger. When they entered the dining room, two servants were scurrying about, pouring water into the goblets.

When they had first arrived at the manor, Lairgnen had insisted their food be plated in serving dishes and set in front of their place settings. At first, the servants had looked scandalized, but when he explained that he wanted to relax while in Merifael, they had smiled their understanding and had since set the table that way.

He and Lairgnen didn't talk much as they ate, but when they did, it was centered on what to call the houses. Eventually, they decided to drop naming any of them altogether and settled with keeping the original names.

"Really, I can't be bothered. And I was thinking, it's a form of homage to the great families that had settled here in Merifael after the Great Passage."

"I don't know why we even bothered in the first place," Lairgnen said as he cut the meat on his plate.

Gen placed his knife and fork on the plate and leaned his elbows on the table. He studied Lairgnen while he cut the meat on his plate and ate it. Outside, the insects were chirping, and a cool breeze wafted through the windows. It was an ideal setting for a perfect day, in his opinion. He loved the coziness and security Bolton manor provided them. It was warm and homey despite its size. The contrast between this house and the one they had in the capital was striking. Even though they made their home in the city, for now, he knew they both really preferred the quiet of Merifael.

A seductive smile curved his mouth, and he grinned broadly when Lairgnen looked up and caught him watching him.

Lairgnen's brow rose questioningly. "What?"

Gen shook his head. "Nothing. I was just wondering when you'd finish eating. That's all."

Lairgnen lowered his knife and fork and gazed at him intently. "Can I at least finish my dinner?"

A laugh escaped Gen's lips. "I wasn't rushing you."

Lairgnen raised a brow. "Really?"

"Well, if you really want to know . . ." Gen let his voice drift questioningly and seductively.

Almost immediately, Lairgnen reacted to his unspoken suggestion.

Gen grinned happily. "I'll wait for you upstairs." He didn't wait for a response. He stood up and dropped a kiss on Lairgnen's startled mouth. "I love you."

Without another word, Gen walked out of the dining room. Behind him, a chair scraped across the floor, and he lengthened his steps. He'd just turned the corner when he heard Lairgnen's rapid footsteps. Laughing happily, he raced across the hall and up the stairs, but when he reached the door to their bedroom, Lairgnen had caught up to him.

"For an old man, you sure are a fast runner," Gen said, trying to catch his breath. He chuckled when Lairgnen pressed him against the wall and kissed him.

The kiss sizzled through his body, making his legs crumble beneath his weight. He wrapped his arms around Lairgnen's neck and pressed against him. Lairgnen groaned as he pulled Gen closer, deepening their kiss, the evidence of his need pressed firmly between them. Gen moaned and eagerly responded to the kiss. Lairgnen pulled away, dragging his mouth down the side of Gen's neck.

"Let's get inside, Lair," Gen gasped.

Lairgnen's only response was a grunt as he opened the door behind Gen. He walked backward until the back of his legs hit what he knew to be the edge of their bed. Behind Lairgnen, he spotted the door was still wide open. All thoughts of doing something about it disappeared when Lairgnen divested them both of their clothes. Gen lost track of time, and before he knew it, he was lying on top of their bed.

A hand slipped between his legs, the tip of a finger grazed

across his opening, and his hips rocked into Lairgnen's touch. A smile curled on his lips when he reached out tentatively and found Lairgnen lost in the haze of lust. Lairgnen gripped his cock in a firm hold and stroked it up and down.

"Harder," Gen said.

"You're getting greedy, *amaer*," Lairgnen said with a soft chuckle, but he did as requested.

The sensation intensified, and Gen couldn't help raising his hips to meet Lairgnen's strokes. The pleasure grew hot and strong very quickly, and he wanted to come very badly. He strained against Lairgnen, lost in the sheer joy of loving each other.

"I need to be inside you." Lairgnen slid his hands up Gen's thighs then stroked a hand over Gen's stomach while a finger played with Gen's slit.

Gen's eyes rolled upward, a groan escaping him. He pushed against Lairgnen's hand until he felt a finger enter his hole.

Lairgnen moved away, and when Gen took a peek, Lairgnen was opening the jar of oil on the nightstand. Oil dribbled down Gen's cock and slid down his backside. Lairgnen pushed a finger inside at the same time as setting the jar back on the table. He slipped his finger inside, quickly following it with a second and a third. And then Lairgnen was gripping his hips and dragging him to the side of the bed. He pushed Gen's knees up and apart. The hungry look on Lairgnen's face as he gazed down should have made Gen feel embarrassed, but it didn't. Instead, it only made him feel wanted.

Lairgnen took his cock with one hand, pumped it once, and pressed the thick head against Gen's entrance. Gen panted as his need rose higher inside him. Lairgnen circled his cock head against his guardian muscle and pushed. It wasn't gentle, but it was exactly what he wanted. Lairgnen continued to push until he was completely inside. The pleasure-pain of being stretched sent tingles through Gen's body. He wound his legs around Lairgnen's waist.

"Don't hold back."

Lairgnen didn't hesitate. He began to move, pulling out and then thrusting hard. Faster and faster, harder and harder, he pounded into Gen, causing his head to thump on the bed. Gen didn't close his eyes. He watched Lairgnen as he lost himself to the pleasure. The look on his face was so intense it almost took his breath away.

Gen felt his orgasm build too fast, and before he knew it, his body took over as all feeling inside of him exploded. His hips jerked even as Lairgnen leaned over him. Their skin grew slick from their exertions, but neither of them paused their thrusting against each other. Even as Gen's orgasm continued its onslaught, Lairgnen didn't give him a chance to relax or calm down, until at last, Lairgnen's grip on his hips grew tighter and painful. With one final thrust, Lairgnen poured himself into Gen.

Lairgnen dropped on the bed beside Gen and pulled him into the curve of his body. Gen couldn't move even if he wanted to, so he stayed right where he was, his legs sprawled over the edge of the bed. They remained that way for a long moment until Gen remembered something.

"We forgot to close the door," Gen said.

Lairgnen's body began to shake. Gen looked up to see Lairgnen's eyes closed tightly but his face wearing a broad grin.

He leaned up and kissed Lairgnen's temple. "I love you, *amaer.*"

"I love you, too." Lairgnen tugged him closer and buried his face in the crook of his neck.

As sleep threatened to take over, Gen remembered when he and Lairgnen had first explored the Bolton estate. Never in his wildest dreams had he once thought that as miserable as he had been then, he was on his way to the happiest moments of his life. For him, all roads led to Lairgnen, and he wouldn't have it any other way.

Other Books by Jo Tannah

Compelled
Winter Roses
Grass Stains and Flip Flops
Around the Block (Divorced Divas Collection, 2019)
His Christmas Valentine
His Gentle Incubus (Scorched Souls Collection)
The Knockers (Love At Stake Anthology)
A Calling Bird (Twelve Days of Christmas Collection, 2019)
Calling Birds (Twelve Days of Christmas Collection, 2020)
It's Not That Complicated

Tales from the Archipelago:
    Kilig
    The Secrets He Keeps

Taboo Series:
    Taboo
    A Taboo Christmas
    Taboo Pleasures
    Christmas Unwrapped
    The Summer Knows

Hidden Series:
    Hidden Evils
    Hidden Dimensions
    Hidden Fates

Rise of the Symbionts:
  Royal Guardian
  Royal Consort
  Royal Symbionts
  Tarragon

CyNapse Security, Inc.:
  Objectified
  Kaleidoscope

The Adventures of Marcus Kildud:
  The Hunt

Chronicles of the Serai:
  Heart Held Hostage

The Phantom Hunters:
  Waylaid

With Ann Mickan:
  Lemonade Stand
  A Lemon Flavoured Christmas

With Lynn Michaels:
  Unchained (Love At Stake Anthology)

Free Stories:
  Sock It To Me
  Tell Him

You may also enjoy the following from eXtasy Books Inc:

Calling Birds
Jo Tannah

Excerpt

Later, as he lay dozing on top of Michael, listening to the silence outside, Cole's mind returned to what Michael had said about their children's—or fledglings'—development. If Cole were a weaker man, he would have gone crazy by now. Thanks to his love for the supernatural, he had, somehow, been ready to discover that myth was in fact real, and shifters existed in the real world.

"About the boys," Cole started.

"You're overthinking again, Cole." Michael ran his fingers down Cole's chest.

"I'm just confused, that's all. I mean, all my readings said shifters are born and raised as human children until they eventually learn how to shift. Instead, it's the complete opposite."

"What's so hard to understand?" Michael sat up and pushed Cole down until he was looking down at him. "I laid eggs, and the eggs hatched. Think about it. Be logical. What human, mammal, baby, can form inside an egg? It's completely and biologically impossible."

"So, all shifters start out as their animal form?" Cole

thought over the implications of the information. The more he thought about it, the more logical it sounded, but his mind kept screaming impossible.

"Yes," Michael said, nodding briefly before lying back down on the bed beside Cole.

Cole scrunched his forehead. "But . . . how?"

"How did it all begin, you mean?"

"Yes," Cole said. "You must have an idea how your kind first started out, right?"

"Well, let's see." Michael narrowed his eyes. "Our existence predates written history, but through the millennia, our kind took care to write down oral stories. Thousands of years ago, there was a tribe that developed a rapport among certain animals. Eventually, certain tribes with gifted individuals, maybe what we call witch doctors these days, developed the ability to invoke those animals that best serviced them as guardians or protectors in times of crisis. I forget what happened exactly, but there came a time when the tribes were almost decimated. I'm not sure if it was disease or war, but one powerful witchdoctor sacrificed his spirit to save his people. His spirit animal came to the rescue and entered his body. Thus the witchdoctor was able to save some of his people. The remaining tribesmen learned from the witchdoctor, and that was the beginning of when the totem animals became one with the survivors."

"There, you see. You just contradicted yourself."

Michael raised a brow. "No, I haven't. Listen to the whole story, okay?"

"Sorry, go ahead," Cole said. Michael was right, he should listen and learn.

"The human tribe disappeared, and the shifters were born."

Cole's eyes widened. "Oh."

A gentle smile curled over Michael's lips. He raised a hand and weaved his fingers through Cole's hair. The gentle caress was something Cole had gotten used to since his mating.

From his observation, the action was Michael's way of connecting with him on a physical level.

"Legend has it that in order to save themselves, the surviving tribe members hid from their enemies in their shifted forms," Michael continued. "Years passed until eventually, their existence was forgotten. Time passed, but something must have happened to make them break from their hiding. One by one, the shifters came out of the forest as full adults equipped with the innate ability to defend themselves in hand to hand combat. Nobody knew who they were or where they came from, but they were revered for their skills and knowledge. Shifters had lived quietly out of sight from the rest of the world, but they hadn't hidden in idleness. Through the millennia, they studied and learned. I read once about a shifter wolf pack where there was no mention of children at all. I now know that it wasn't true. They had found a way to survive. Shifting became a choice and only happened when the individual willed it."

Cole didn't respond immediately, taking some time to think over what Michael had just told him. "What you're saying is that it is the individual who decides when they are ready to shift into their human forms."

Michael nodded. "You asked me if I remember my fledgling days, and I told you that I didn't. There's some truth to that. However, what I didn't tell you is about the awareness that slowly came over me. I remember being hungry and surveying the land I was flying over. Usually, I would spot prey and swoop in for the kill. But that day was different. I began to think. It didn't last long, so I acted on instinct and forgot about it."

"What changed?"

Michael took in a deep breath and stretched his limbs. "Hm, I remember opening my eyes one day, and I saw my mother and thought, wow. I really, really loved her. The next thing I knew, I was standing on my two feet and was reaching up to her. She began to cry, and it upset me, but she bent and picked me up. The second thought or realization I remember was thinking that I itched, and I wanted a bath. That's another story, but what I'm saying is, let the children be. Give them time to learn how to perfect their skills in flying and hunting. They know we are their parents. Last night, when you got mad because they were making a mess in the aerie, they immediately settled down and placed their heads under their wings to sleep. Remember?"

"Yes, they did do that, didn't they?" Cole chuckled. He remembered how he had let out a frustrated growl and told the boys how disappointed he was in them. The wing flapping and cawing stopped immediately before the boys waddled up to their perches to sleep.

"They understand us. Given time, they will understand the duality of their nature and will shift."

"I just want to see what they look like." Cole couldn't help feeling disappointed. Instead of changing diapers, he was cleaning out a nest of twigs and leaves on a daily basis. Not exactly how he imagined raising children would be.

"They're our children, who do you think they will take after?" Michael wondered.

"Well, I was hoping they'd look like you, actually." Cole meant what he said. Michael was a beautiful, intelligent man and everything he'd always wanted in his partner.

"Why, thank you." Michael's smile was brilliant.

Cole couldn't help pressing a kiss on his lips. When the kiss ended, he asked, "What about you? What do you think they'll look like?"

"I was hoping like you," Michael said, a blush creeping up his cheeks.

Cole chuckled. "Me? Why me? I'm regular. I'd much rather they look like you."

"I'm boring, though," Michael grimaced. "I'm such a cliché."

"No you're not. Wherever did that thought come from?"

"Someone once said that to me a long time ago. I can never

forget feeling inadequate after that, and I couldn't shake my reaction. It was because of that incident that I studied harder and made sure I didn't end up that particular cliché of a man."

"And what is that exactly? Which cliché are you talking about?"

Michael let out a long sigh. "A rich, entitled, white man who has all the power and influence to back him up because of his name and the size of his fortune. I wanted to make a difference in the world. To be different."

Cole's heart overflowed. There was the man he had fallen in love with.

"That's exactly why I want our boys to be like you. Because you are different. In spite of your wealth, power, and status, you continue to surprise everyone. You're not exactly predictable, my love."

"Aw, admit it, Cole. You're biased." Michael's lips quivered as he appeared to fight off the broad grin forming over them.

"I am biased." Cole huffed.

"That's because you love me."

A smile tugged at Cole's lips. Through their brief time together, he had learned one thing about his mate. Michael was quite vocal about his feelings. Although Cole usually kept things close to himself, he couldn't deny that hearing the words of affirmation warmed his heart. Never one to disappoint Michael, Cole closed his arms around him, pulled him closer until there was nothing between them. Not even air. Michael's eyes glistened as their gazes locked. Together, in perfect synchrony, they leaned into each other until their foreheads touched. Cole closed his eyes and breathed deeply, taking in his lover's scent into his lungs. Memorizing the subtle tones, vowing to never forget them.

Softly, so as not to betray the depth of his feelings, he said, "Because I love you."

Michael didn't respond, but his arms tightened around Cole. Only then did he breathe out.

ABOUT THE AUTHOR

I grew up listening to folk tales my father and nannies told either to entertain us children or to send home a message. These narratives I kept with me, and finally, I wrote them down in a journal way back when I kept one. Going through junk led to a long-forgotten box, and in it was the journal. Reading the stories of romance, science fiction and horror I had taken the time to put to paper brought to light that these were tales I had never met in my readings.

The tales I write are fictional, but all of them are based on what I grew up with and still dream about. That they have an M/M twist is simply for my pleasure. And I hope, yours as well.

Twitter: @JoTannah
Instagram: https://www.instagram.com/jo_tannah/
Facebook: https://www.facebook.com/pro-file.php?id=100012354600386
Website: http://jotannah.com
Email: jotannah1@gmail.com